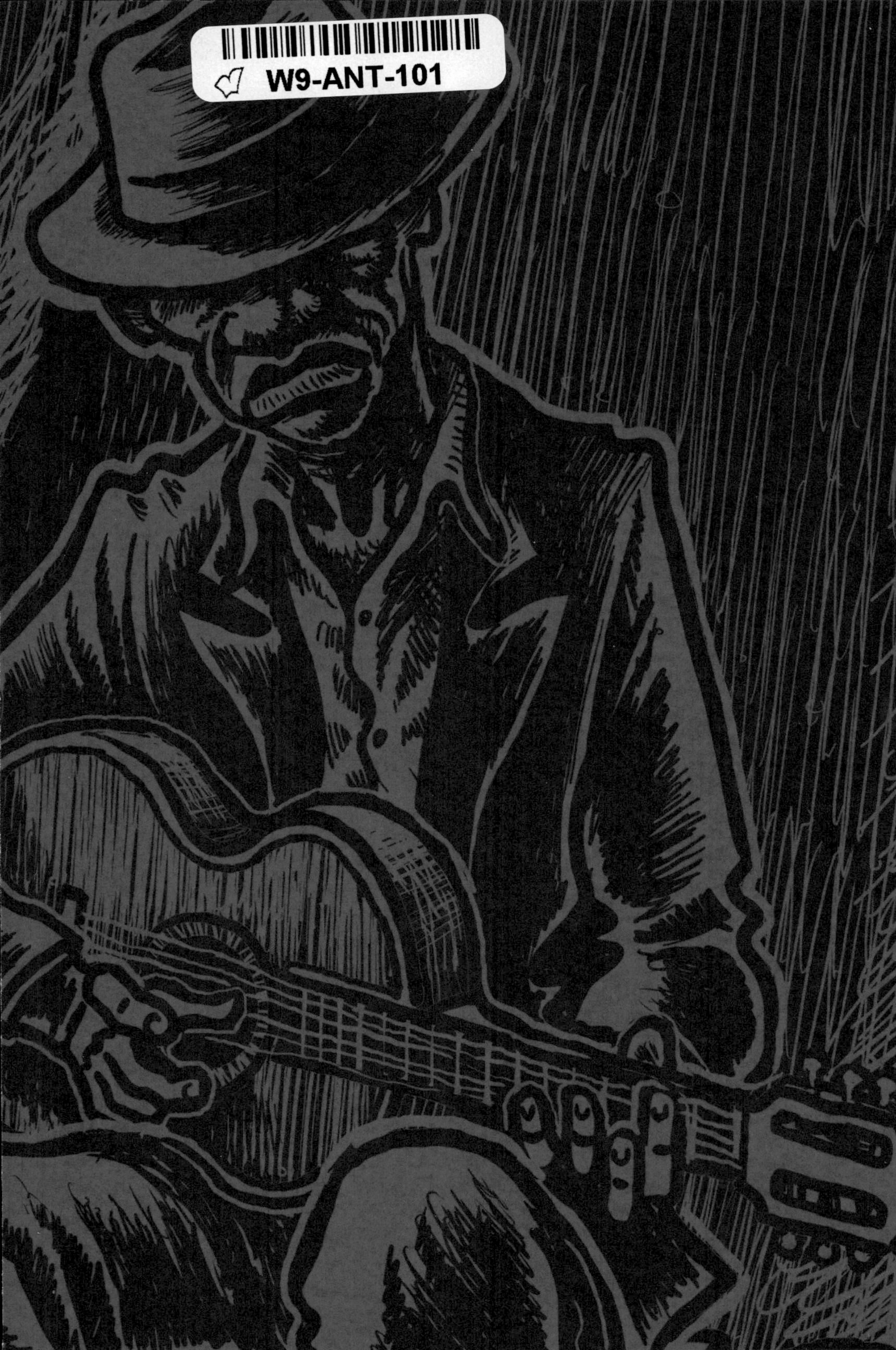

BLUESMAN

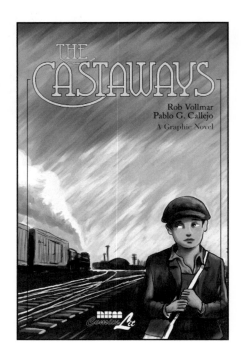

Also by the authors:
The Castaways, $17.95

P&H: $4 1st item, $1 each addt'l.

We have over 200 titles,
write for our color catalog:
NBM
40 Exchange Pl., Ste. 1308
New York, NY 10005
See our website at
www.nbmpublishing.com

BLUESMAN

A twelve-bar graphic novel
by Rob Vollmar and Pablo G. Callejo

ISBN 10: 1-56163-532-4
ISBN 13: 978-1-56163-532-0
© 2006 Rob Vollmar & Pablo G. Callejo
Printed in China
3 2 1

ComicsLit is an imprint
and trademark of

NANTIER ○ BEALL ○ MINOUSTCHINE

Publishing inc.
new york

1

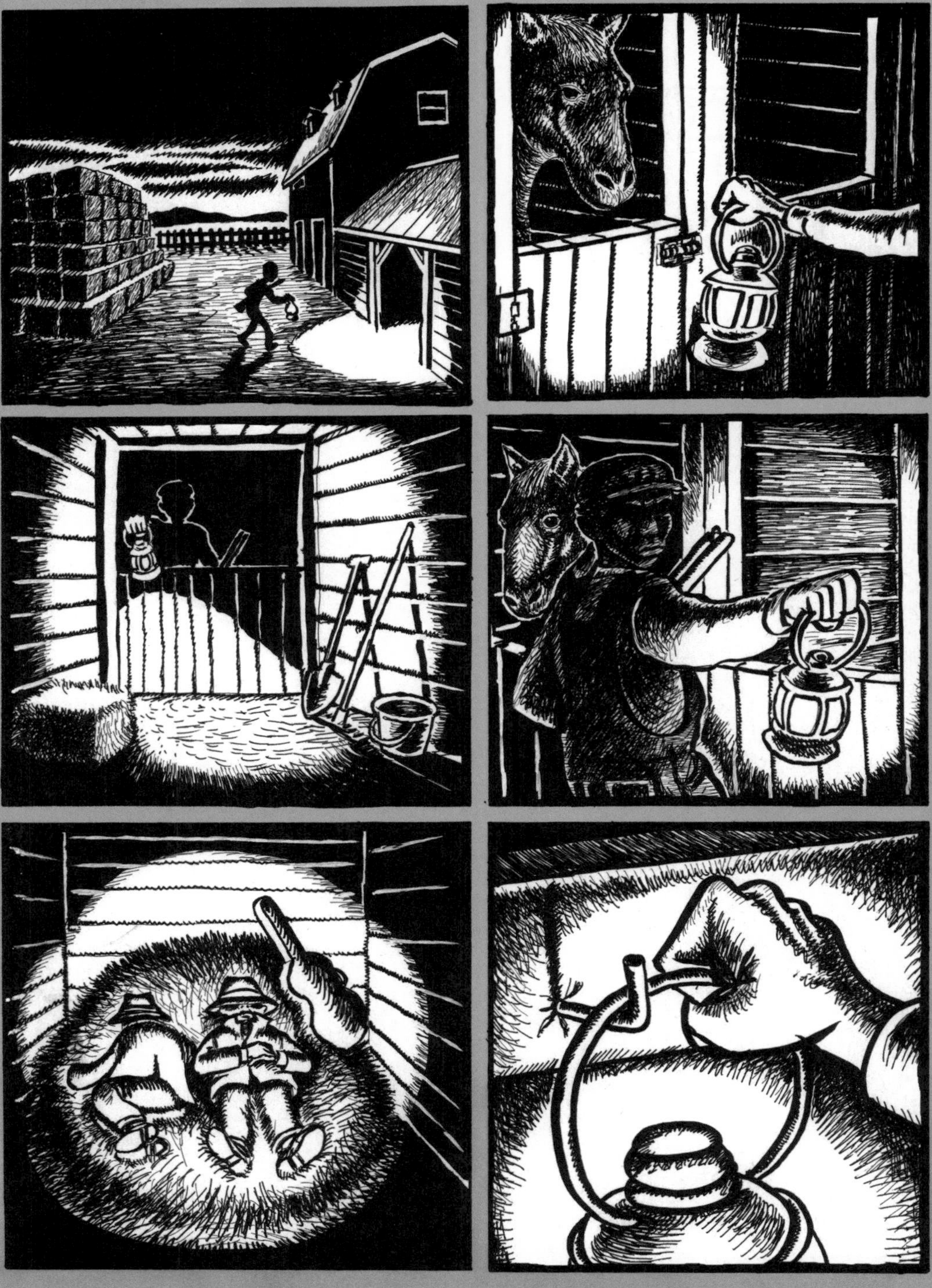

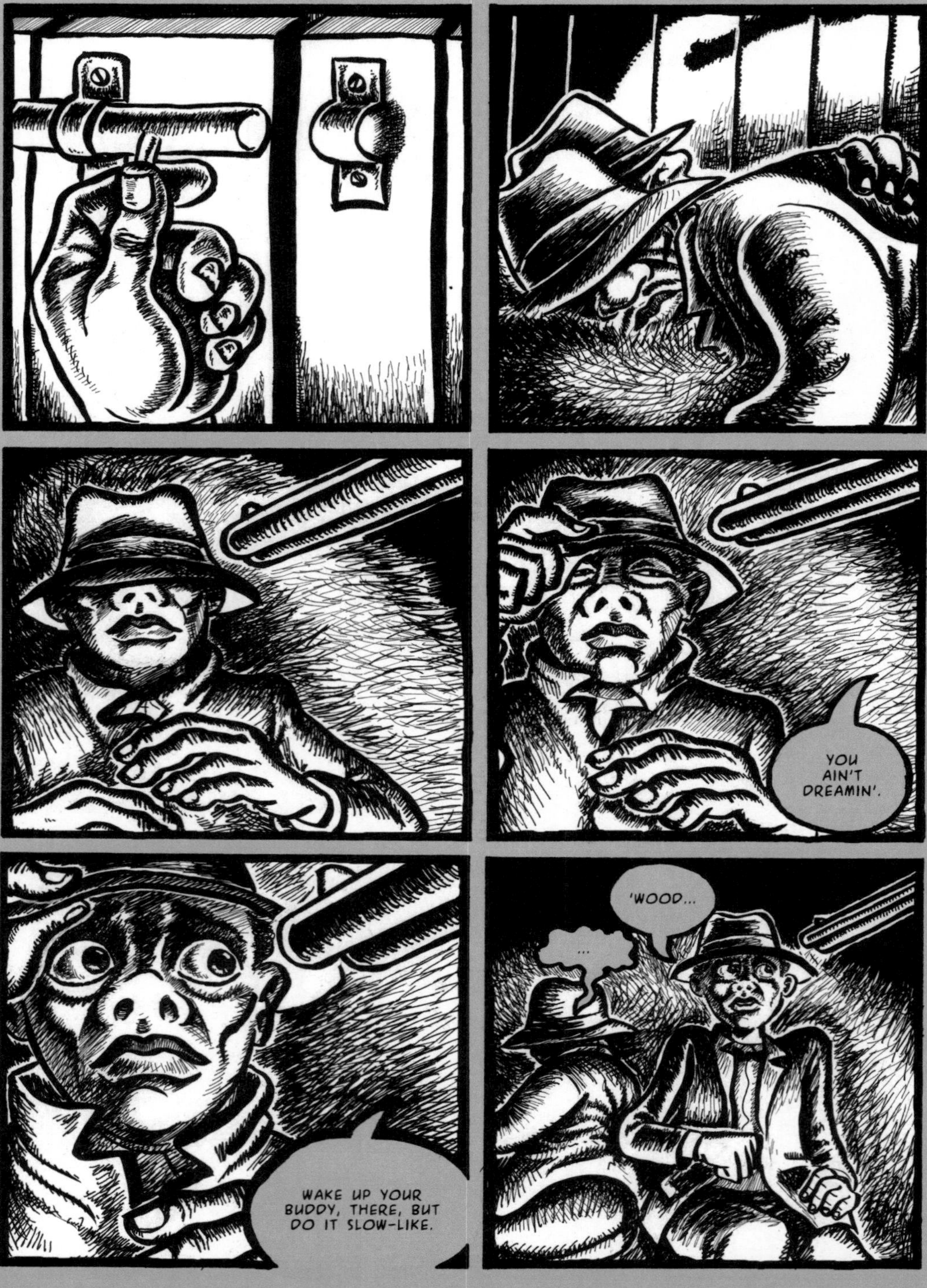
YOU AIN'T DREAMIN'.
WAKE UP YOUR BUDDY, THERE, BUT DO IT SLOW-LIKE.
'WOOD...
...

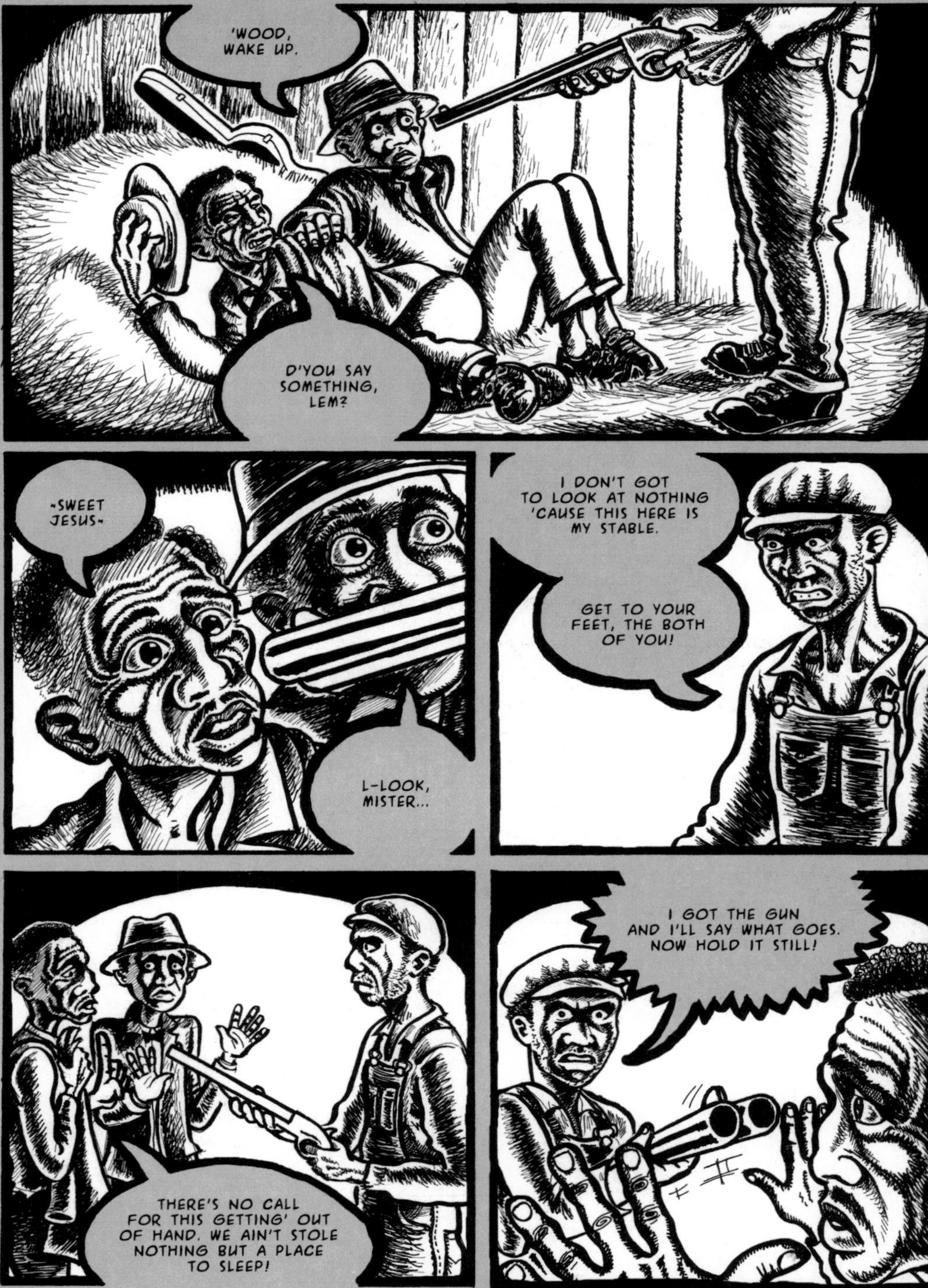
'WOOD, WAKE UP.
D'YOU SAY SOMETHING, LEM?
~SWEET JESUS~
L-LOOK, MISTER...
I DON'T GOT TO LOOK AT NOTHING 'CAUSE THIS HERE IS MY STABLE.
GET TO YOUR FEET, THE BOTH OF YOU!
THERE'S NO CALL FOR THIS GETTING' OUT OF HAND. WE AIN'T STOLE NOTHING BUT A PLACE TO SLEEP!
I GOT THE GUN AND I'LL SAY WHAT GOES. NOW HOLD IT STILL!

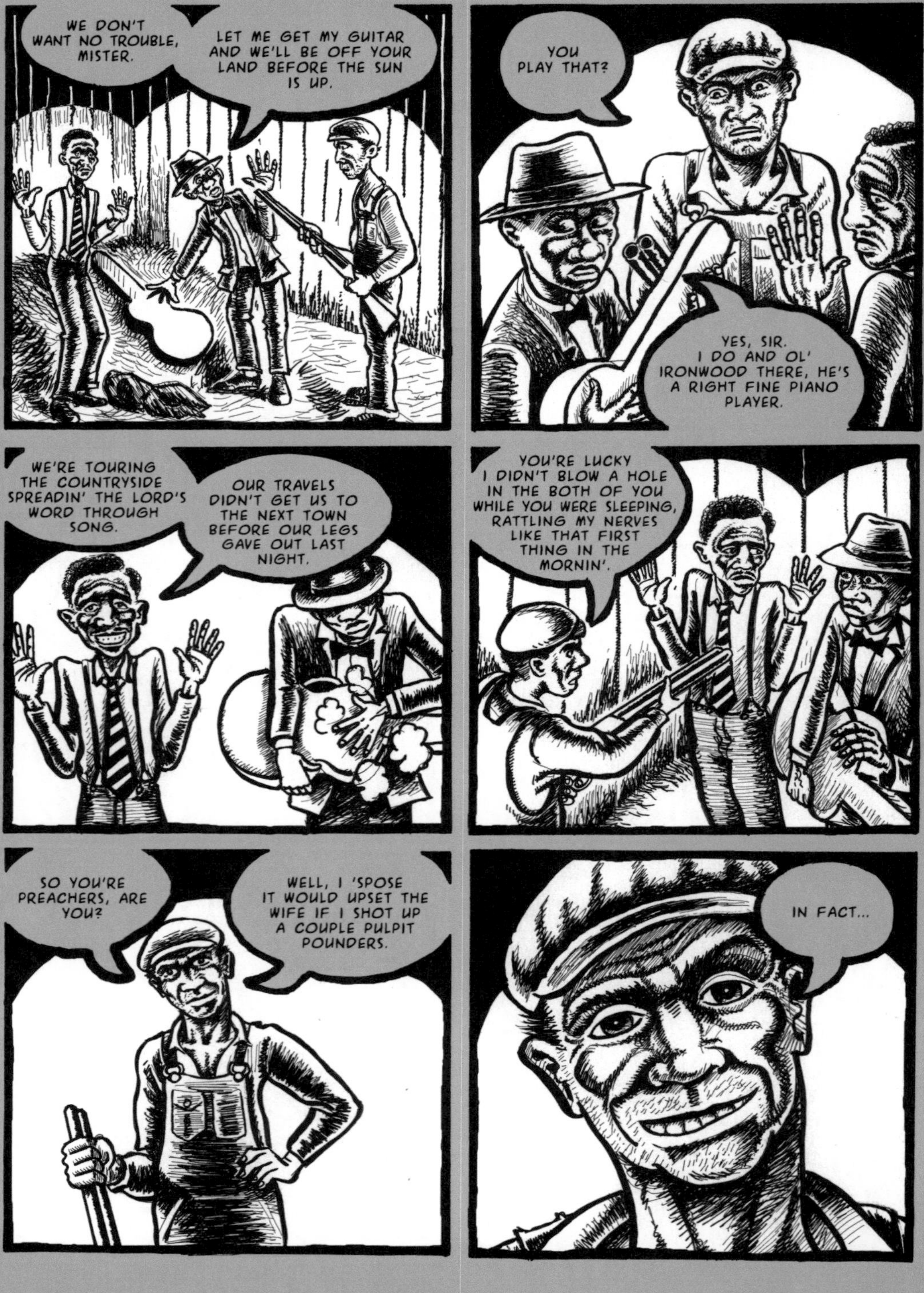
WE DON'T WANT NO TROUBLE, MISTER.
LET ME GET MY GUITAR AND WE'LL BE OFF YOUR LAND BEFORE THE SUN IS UP.
YOU PLAY THAT?
YES, SIR. I DO AND OL' IRONWOOD THERE, HE'S A RIGHT FINE PIANO PLAYER.
WE'RE TOURING THE COUNTRYSIDE SPREADIN' THE LORD'S WORD THROUGH SONG.
OUR TRAVELS DIDN'T GET US TO THE NEXT TOWN BEFORE OUR LEGS GAVE OUT LAST NIGHT.
YOU'RE LUCKY I DIDN'T BLOW A HOLE IN THE BOTH OF YOU WHILE YOU WERE SLEEPING, RATTLING MY NERVES LIKE THAT FIRST THING IN THE MORNIN'.
SO YOU'RE PREACHERS, ARE YOU?
WELL, I 'SPOSE IT WOULD UPSET THE WIFE IF I SHOT UP A COUPLE PULPIT POUNDERS.
IN FACT...

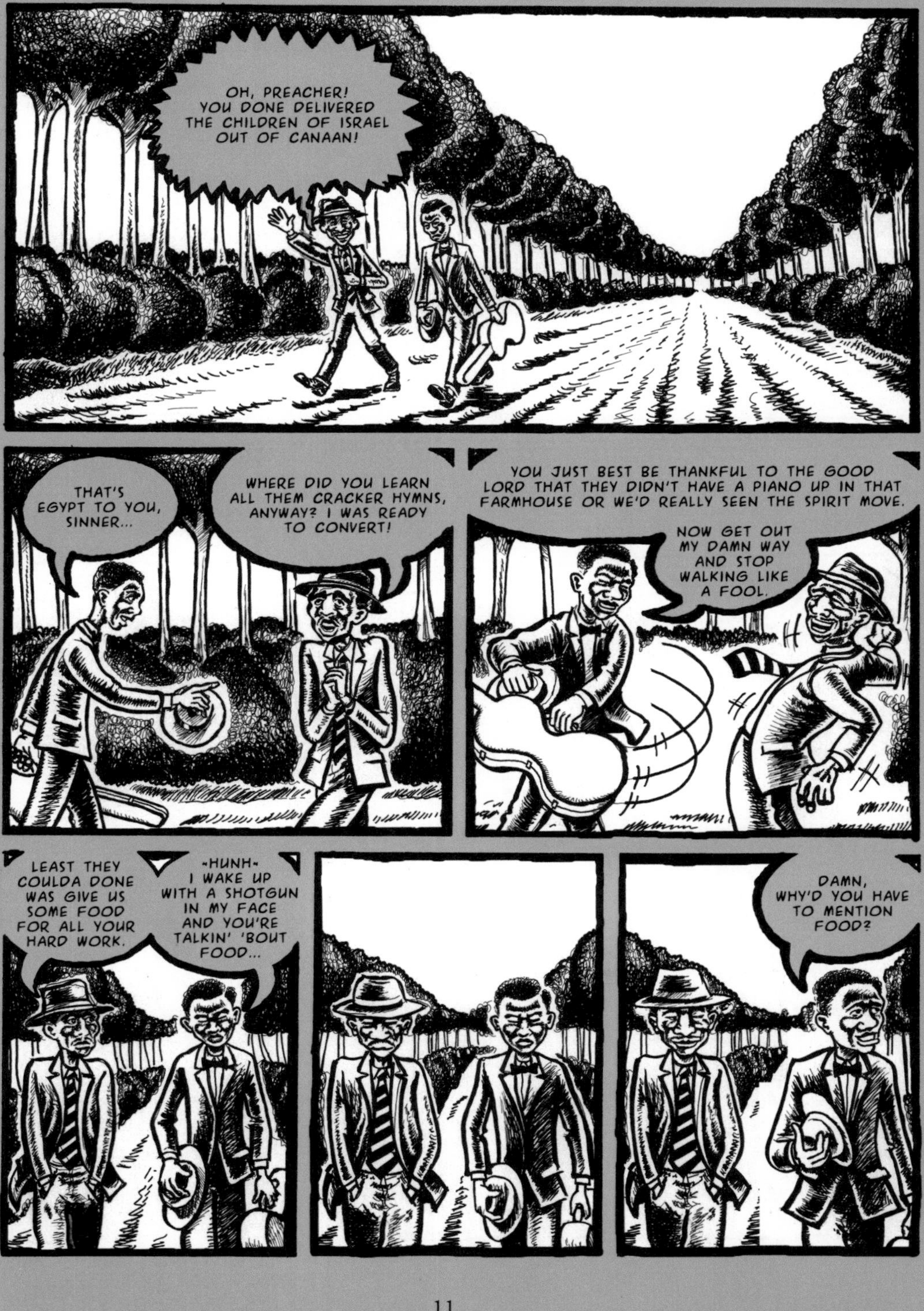
OH, PREACHER! YOU DONE DELIVERED THE CHILDREN OF ISRAEL OUT OF CANAAN!
THAT'S EGYPT TO YOU, SINNER...
WHERE DID YOU LEARN ALL THEM CRACKER HYMNS, ANYWAY? I WAS READY TO CONVERT!
YOU JUST BEST BE THANKFUL TO THE GOOD LORD THAT THEY DIDN'T HAVE A PIANO UP IN THAT FARMHOUSE OR WE'D REALLY SEEN THE SPIRIT MOVE.
NOW GET OUT MY DAMN WAY AND STOP WALKING LIKE A FOOL.
LEAST THEY COULDA DONE WAS GIVE US SOME FOOD FOR ALL YOUR HARD WORK.
~HUNH~ I WAKE UP WITH A SHOTGUN IN MY FACE AND YOU'RE TALKIN' 'BOUT FOOD...
DAMN, WHY'D YOU HAVE TO MENTION FOOD?

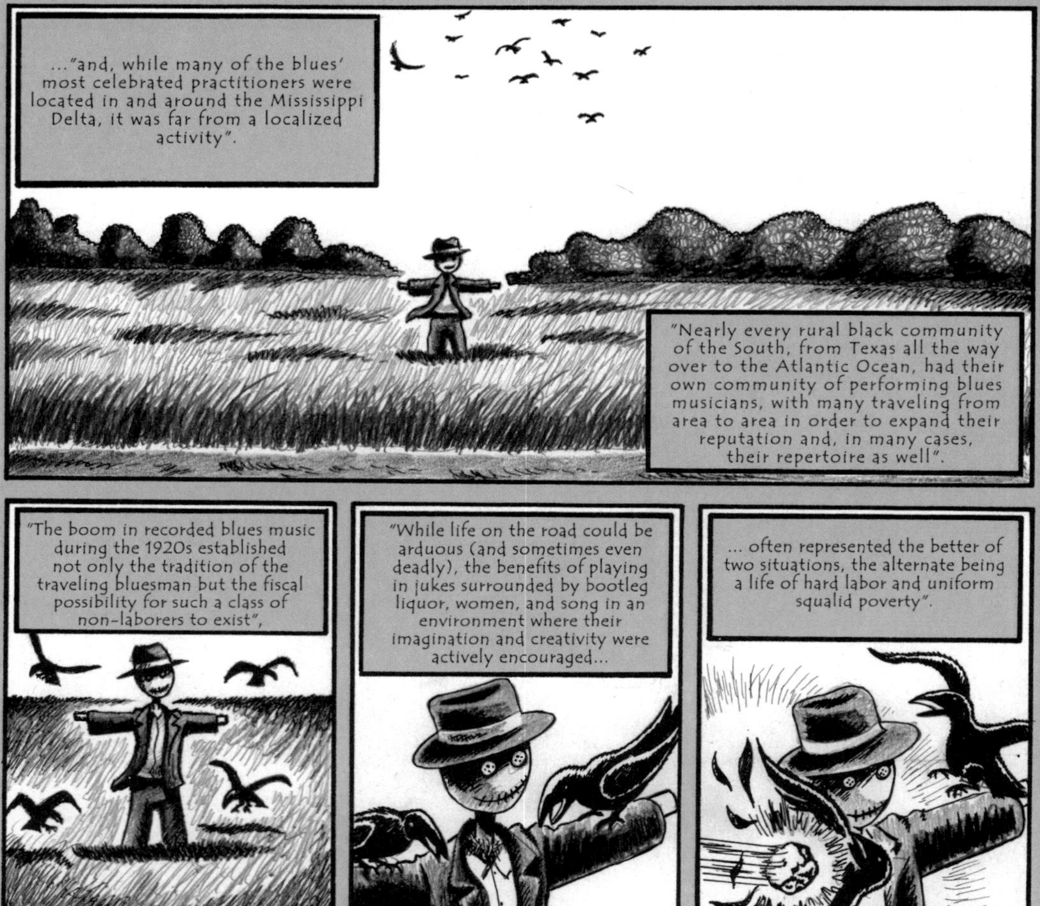
..."and, while many of the blues' most celebrated practitioners were located in and around the Mississippi Delta, it was far from a localized activity".
"Nearly every rural black community of the South, from Texas all the way over to the Atlantic Ocean, had their own community of performing blues musicians, with many traveling from area to area in order to expand their reputation and, in many cases, their repertoire as well".
"The boom in recorded blues music during the 1920s established not only the tradition of the traveling bluesman but the fiscal possibility for such a class of non-laborers to exist",
"While life on the road could be arduous (and sometimes even deadly), the benefits of playing in jukes surrounded by bootleg liquor, women, and song in an environment where their imagination and creativity were actively encouraged...
... often represented the better of two situations, the alternate being a life of hard labor and uniform squalid poverty".
"This privileged status, pocked as it was by chronically poor living conditions for these itinerant musicians, over time fostered a love-hate relationship with the communities they serviced".
"To the rural black society of this diverse region of the South, these bluesmen represented both an escape from their misery and an easy target on whom to pin the negative attributes uniformly assigned to all members of their race by the Anglo dominated society which surrounded them".
[Excerpted from Sheldon Doldoff's "America's Troubadors: Blues Musicians of the Deep South 1900-present", Real Folk Quarterly, March 1961]

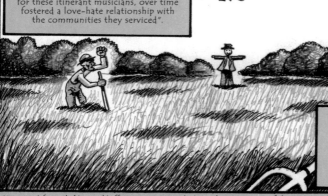

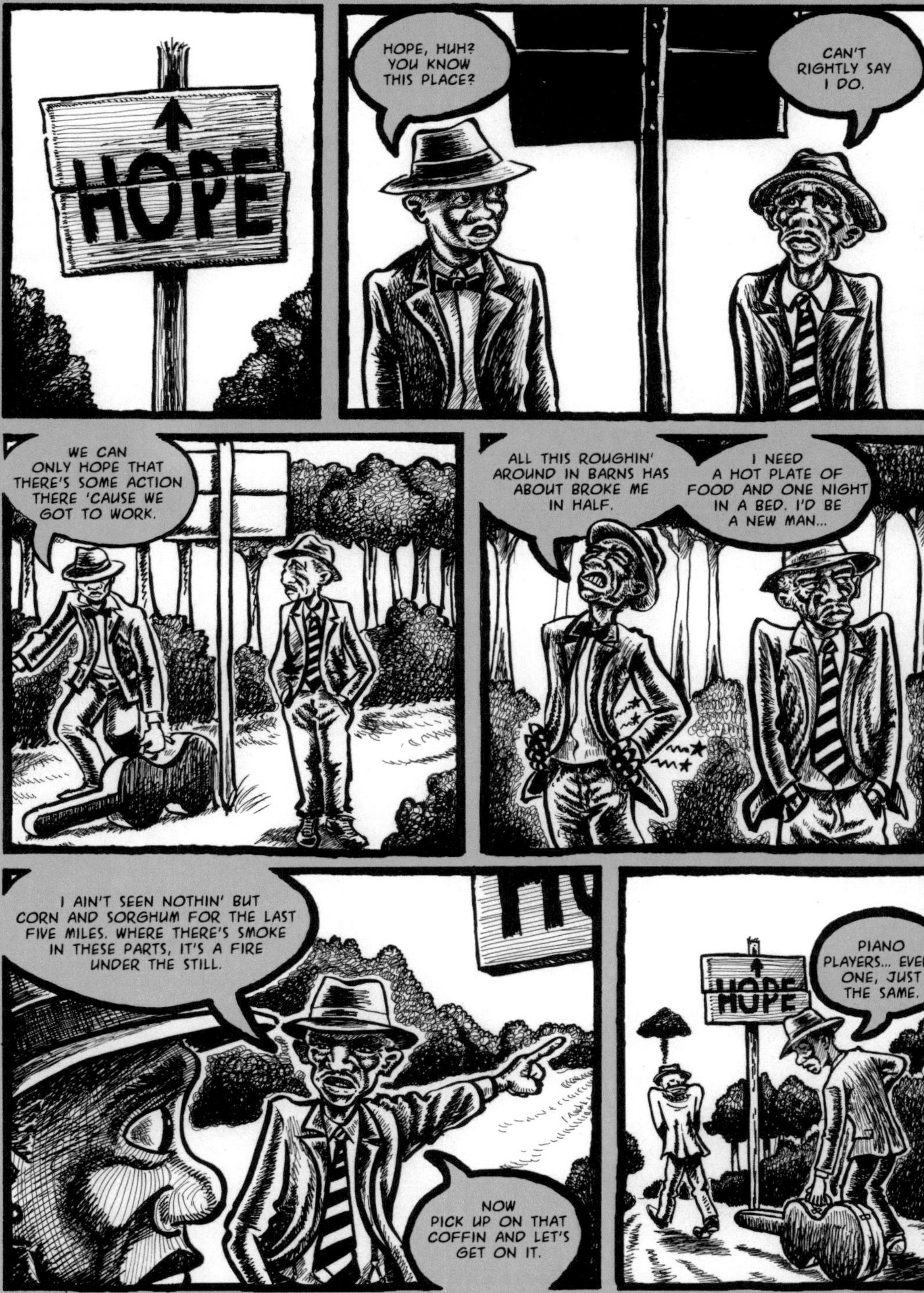
HOPE
HOPE, HUH? YOU KNOW THIS PLACE?
CAN'T RIGHTLY SAY I DO.
WE CAN ONLY HOPE THAT THERE'S SOME ACTION THERE 'CAUSE WE GOT TO WORK.
ALL THIS ROUGHIN' AROUND IN BARNS HAS ABOUT BROKE ME IN HALF.
I NEED A HOT PLATE OF FOOD AND ONE NIGHT IN A BED. I'D BE A NEW MAN...
I AIN'T SEEN NOTHIN' BUT CORN AND SORGHUM FOR THE LAST FIVE MILES. WHERE THERE'S SMOKE IN THESE PARTS, IT'S A FIRE UNDER THE STILL.
NOW PICK UP ON THAT COFFIN AND LET'S GET ON IT.
HOPE
PIANO PLAYERS... EVERY ONE, JUST THE SAME.

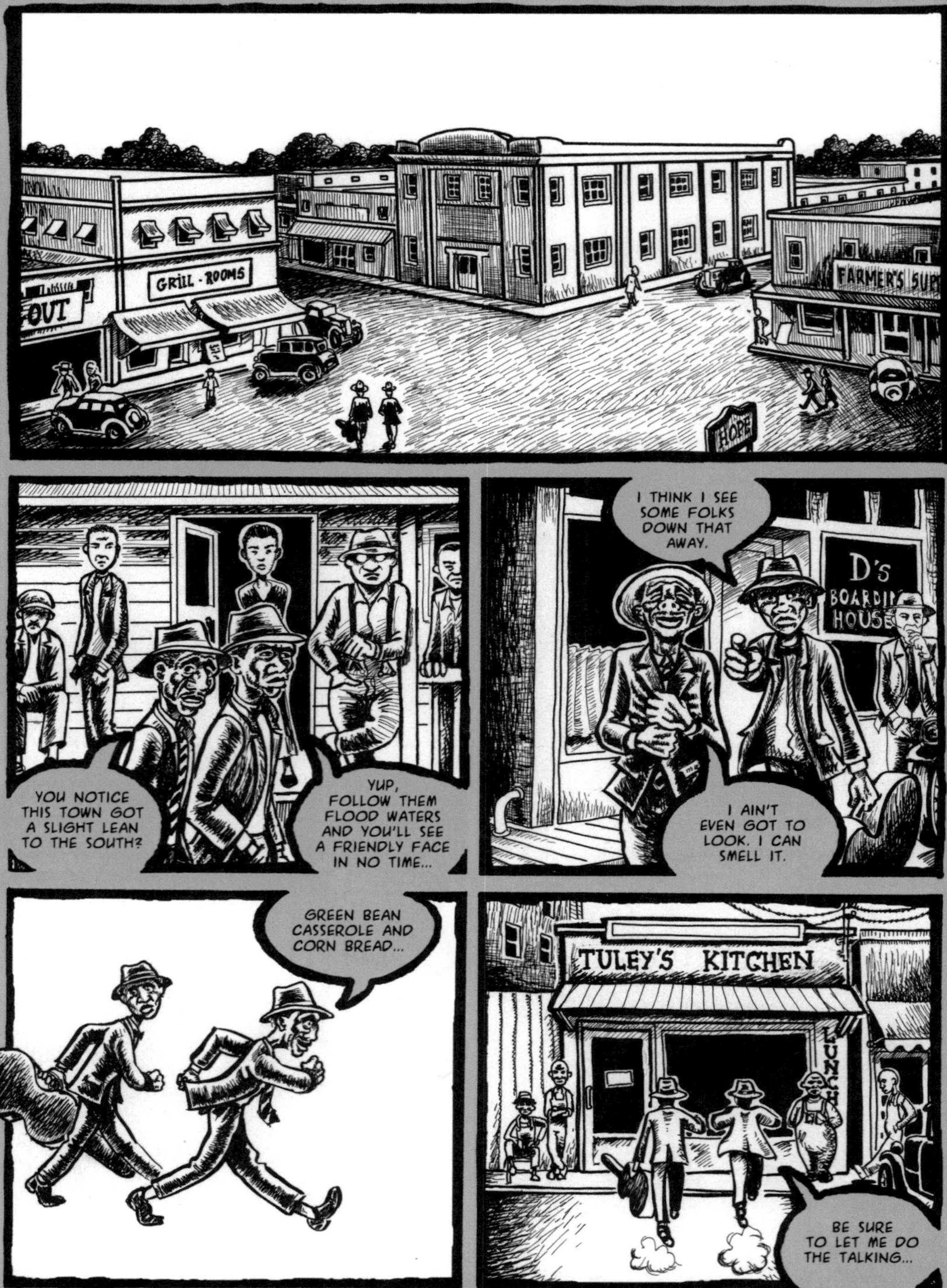
GRILL - ROOMS
OUT
FARMER'S SUP
HOPE
YOU NOTICE THIS TOWN GOT A SLIGHT LEAN TO THE SOUTH?
YUP, FOLLOW THEM FLOOD WATERS AND YOU'LL SEE A FRIENDLY FACE IN NO TIME...
I THINK I SEE SOME FOLKS DOWN THAT AWAY.
D's BOARDIN HOUSE
I AIN'T EVEN GOT TO LOOK. I CAN SMELL IT.
GREEN BEAN CASSEROLE AND CORN BREAD...
TULEY'S KITCHEN
LUNCH
BE SURE TO LET ME DO THE TALKING...

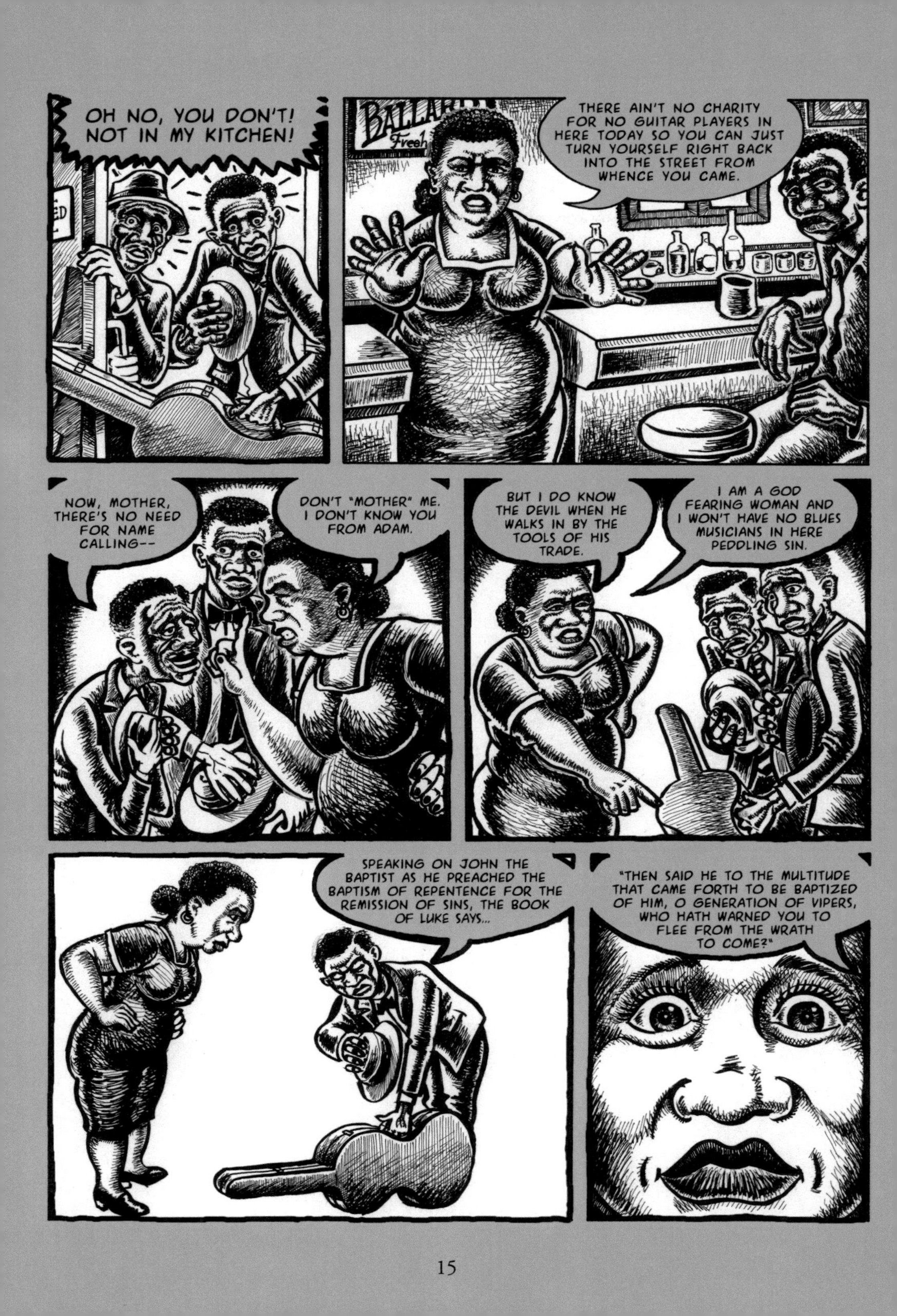
OH NO, YOU DON'T! NOT IN MY KITCHEN!
THERE AIN'T NO CHARITY FOR NO GUITAR PLAYERS IN HERE TODAY SO YOU CAN JUST TURN YOURSELF RIGHT BACK INTO THE STREET FROM WHENCE YOU CAME.
NOW, MOTHER, THERE'S NO NEED FOR NAME CALLING--
DON'T "MOTHER" ME. I DON'T KNOW YOU FROM ADAM.
BUT I DO KNOW THE DEVIL WHEN HE WALKS IN BY THE TOOLS OF HIS TRADE.
I AM A GOD FEARING WOMAN AND I WON'T HAVE NO BLUES MUSICIANS IN HERE PEDDLING SIN.
SPEAKING ON JOHN THE BAPTIST AS HE PREACHED THE BAPTISM OF REPENTENCE FOR THE REMISSION OF SINS, THE BOOK OF LUKE SAYS...
"THEN SAID HE TO THE MULTITUDE THAT CAME FORTH TO BE BAPTIZED OF HIM, O GENERATION OF VIPERS, WHO HATH WARNED YOU TO FLEE FROM THE WRATH TO COME?"

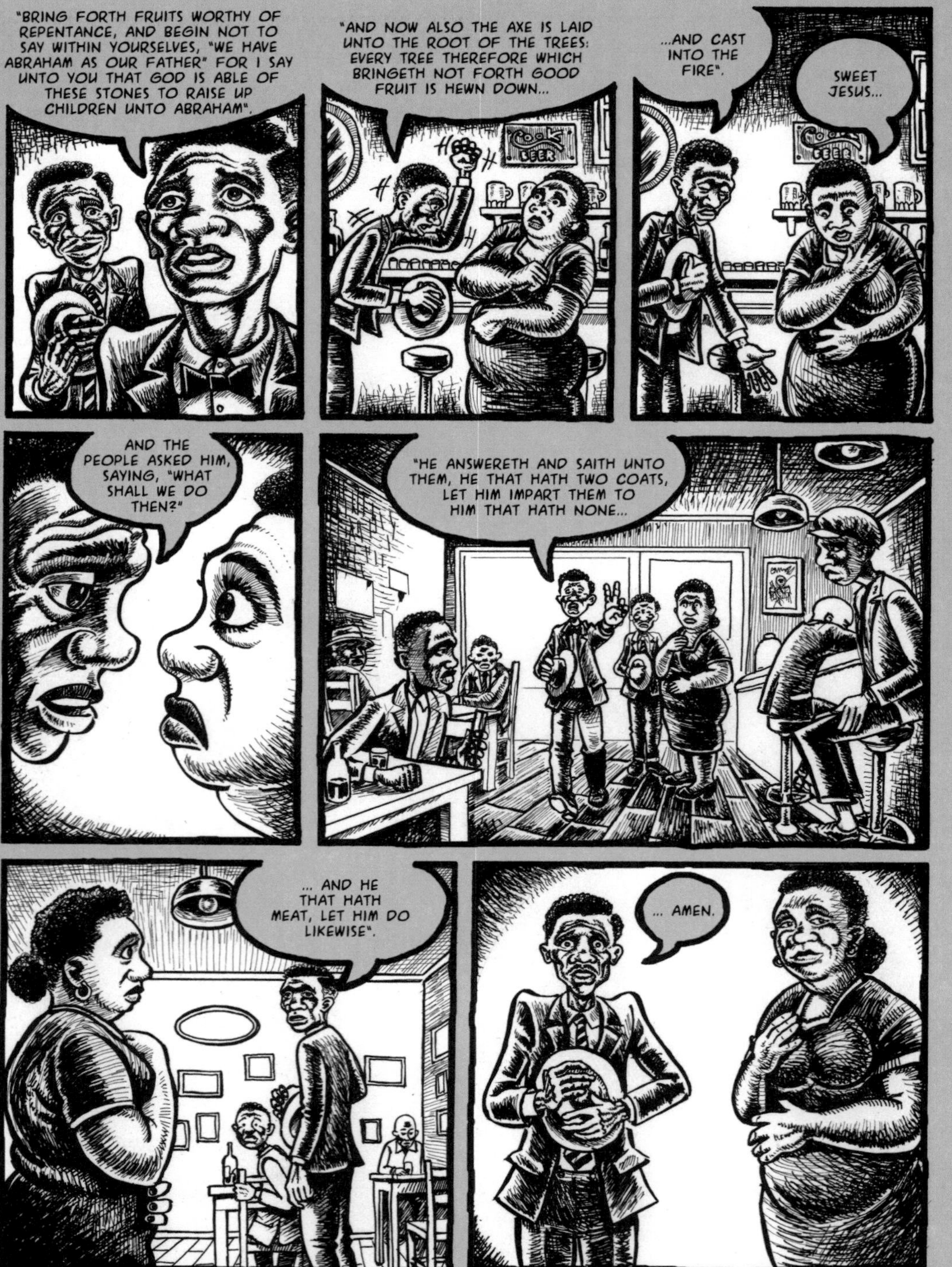
"BRING FORTH FRUITS WORTHY OF REPENTANCE, AND BEGIN NOT TO SAY WITHIN YOURSELVES, "WE HAVE ABRAHAM AS OUR FATHER" FOR I SAY UNTO YOU THAT GOD IS ABLE OF THESE STONES TO RAISE UP CHILDREN UNTO ABRAHAM".
"AND NOW ALSO THE AXE IS LAID UNTO THE ROOT OF THE TREES: EVERY TREE THEREFORE WHICH BRINGETH NOT FORTH GOOD FRUIT IS HEWN DOWN...
COOK'S BEER
...AND CAST INTO THE FIRE".
SWEET JESUS...
AND THE PEOPLE ASKED HIM, SAYING, "WHAT SHALL WE DO THEN?"
"HE ANSWERETH AND SAITH UNTO THEM, HE THAT HATH TWO COATS, LET HIM IMPART THEM TO HIM THAT HATH NONE...
... AND HE THAT HATH MEAT, LET HIM DO LIKEWISE".
... AMEN.

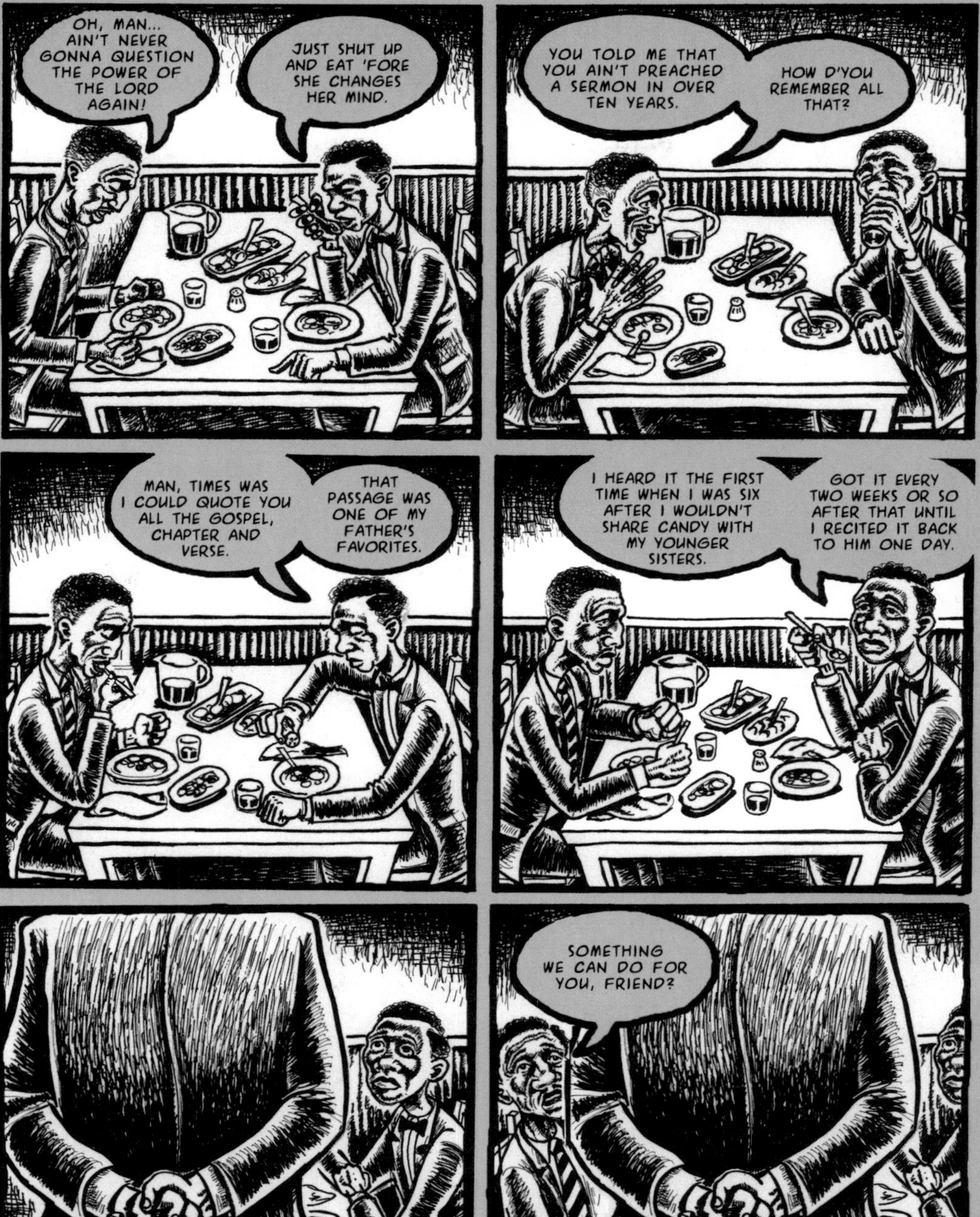
OH, MAN... AIN'T NEVER GONNA QUESTION THE POWER OF THE LORD AGAIN!
JUST SHUT UP AND EAT 'FORE SHE CHANGES HER MIND.
YOU TOLD ME THAT YOU AIN'T PREACHED A SERMON IN OVER TEN YEARS.
HOW D'YOU REMEMBER ALL THAT?
MAN, TIMES WAS I COULD QUOTE YOU ALL THE GOSPEL, CHAPTER AND VERSE.
THAT PASSAGE WAS ONE OF MY FATHER'S FAVORITES.
I HEARD IT THE FIRST TIME WHEN I WAS SIX AFTER I WOULDN'T SHARE CANDY WITH MY YOUNGER SISTERS.
GOT IT EVERY TWO WEEKS OR SO AFTER THAT UNTIL I RECITED IT BACK TO HIM ONE DAY.
SOMETHING WE CAN DO FOR YOU, FRIEND?

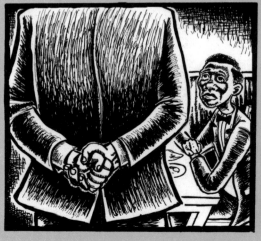

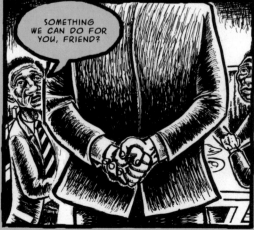

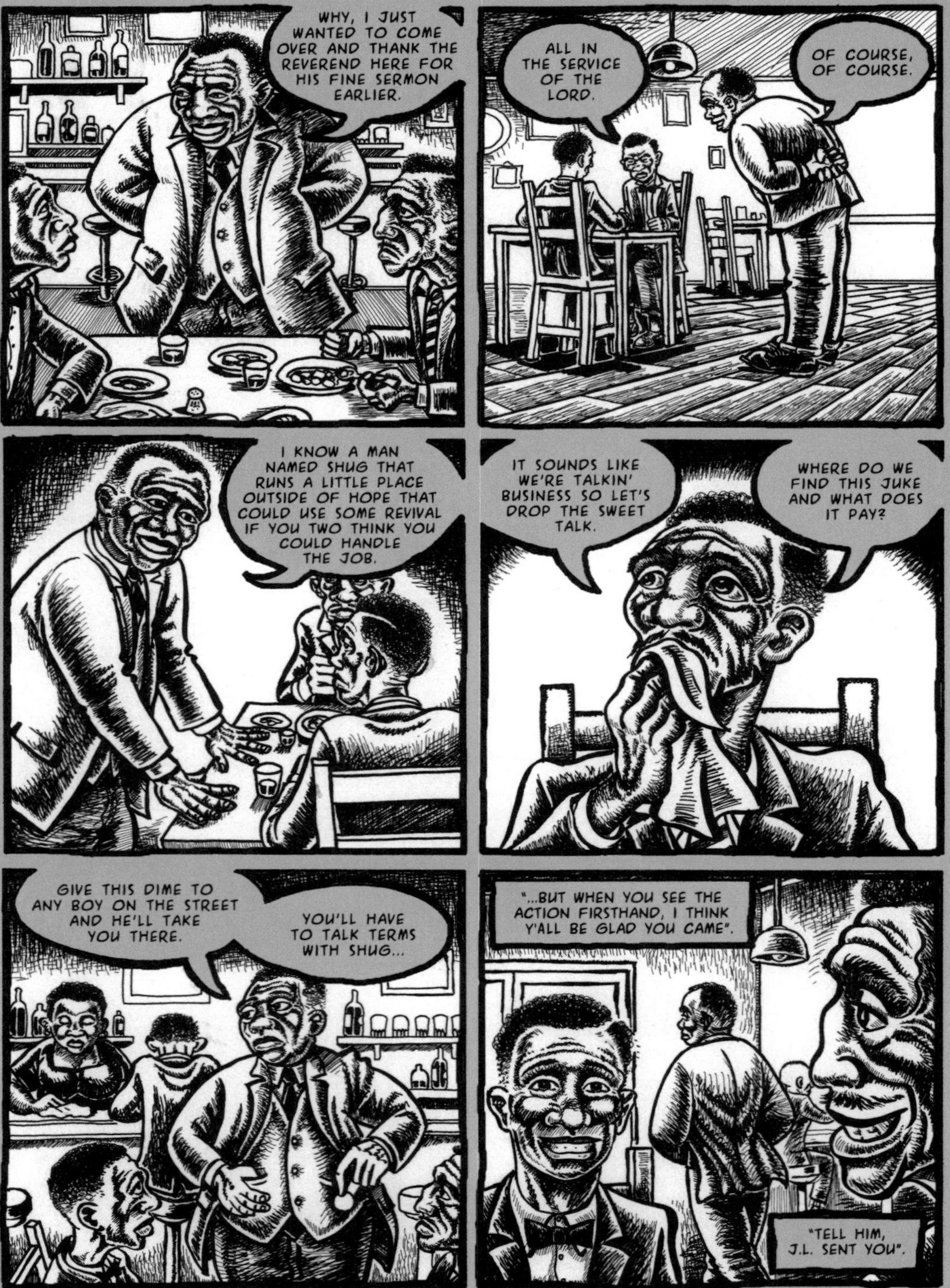
WHY, I JUST WANTED TO COME OVER AND THANK THE REVEREND HERE FOR HIS FINE SERMON EARLIER.
ALL IN THE SERVICE OF THE LORD.
OF COURSE, OF COURSE.
I KNOW A MAN NAMED SHUG THAT RUNS A LITTLE PLACE OUTSIDE OF HOPE THAT COULD USE SOME REVIVAL IF YOU TWO THINK YOU COULD HANDLE THE JOB.
IT SOUNDS LIKE WE'RE TALKIN' BUSINESS SO LET'S DROP THE SWEET TALK.
WHERE DO WE FIND THIS JUKE AND WHAT DOES IT PAY?
GIVE THIS DIME TO ANY BOY ON THE STREET AND HE'LL TAKE YOU THERE.
YOU'LL HAVE TO TALK TERMS WITH SHUG...
"...BUT WHEN YOU SEE THE ACTION FIRSTHAND, I THINK Y'ALL BE GLAD YOU CAME".
"TELL HIM, J.L. SENT YOU".

2

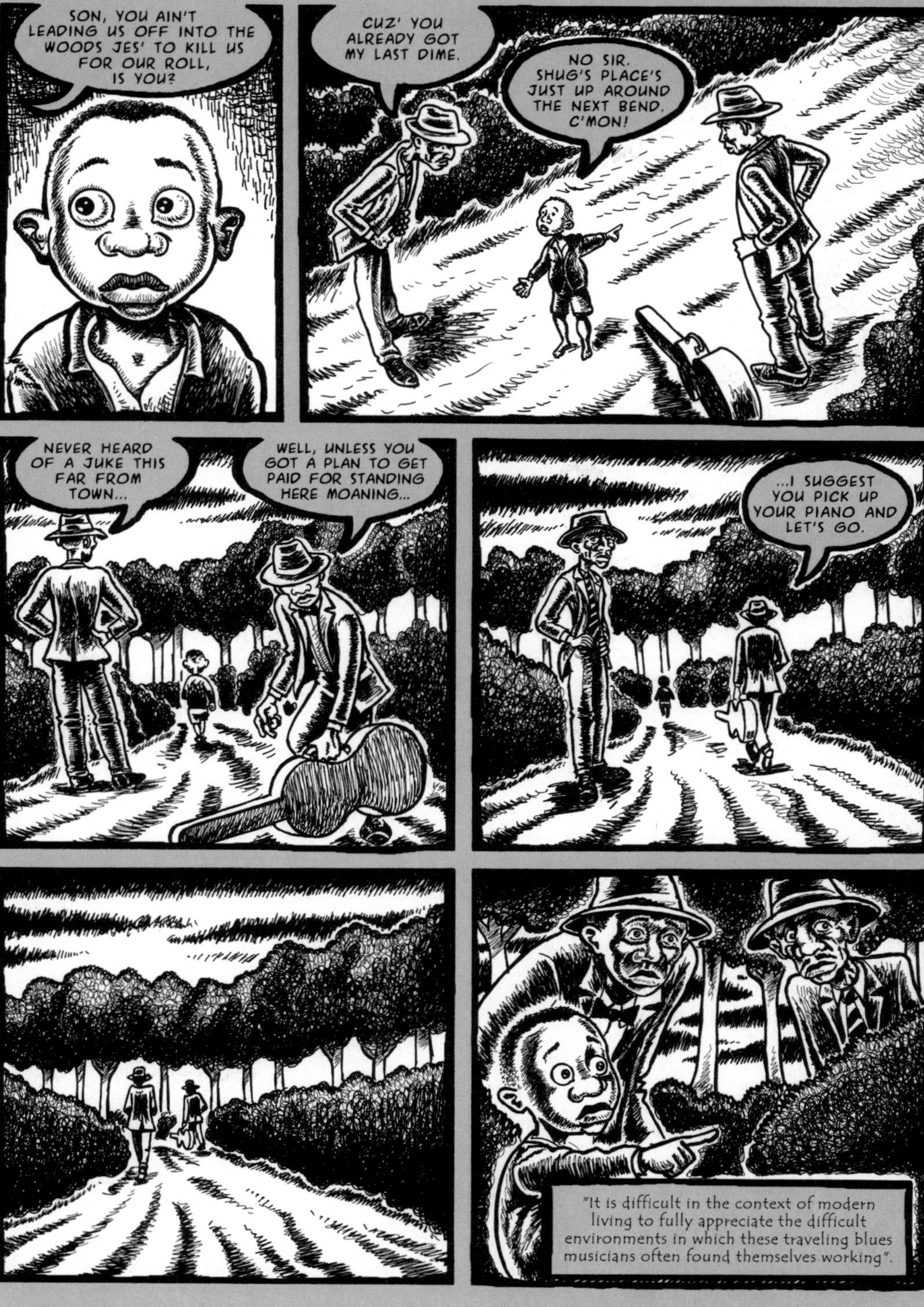
SON, YOU AIN'T LEADING US OFF INTO THE WOODS JES' TO KILL US FOR OUR ROLL, IS YOU?
CUZ' YOU ALREADY GOT MY LAST DIME.
NO SIR. SHUG'S PLACE'S JUST UP AROUND THE NEXT BEND. C'MON!
NEVER HEARD OF A JUKE THIS FAR FROM TOWN...
WELL, UNLESS YOU GOT A PLAN TO GET PAID FOR STANDING HERE MOANING...
...I SUGGEST YOU PICK UP YOUR PIANO AND LET'S GO.
"It is difficult in the context of modern living to fully appreciate the difficult environments in which these traveling blues musicians often found themselves working".

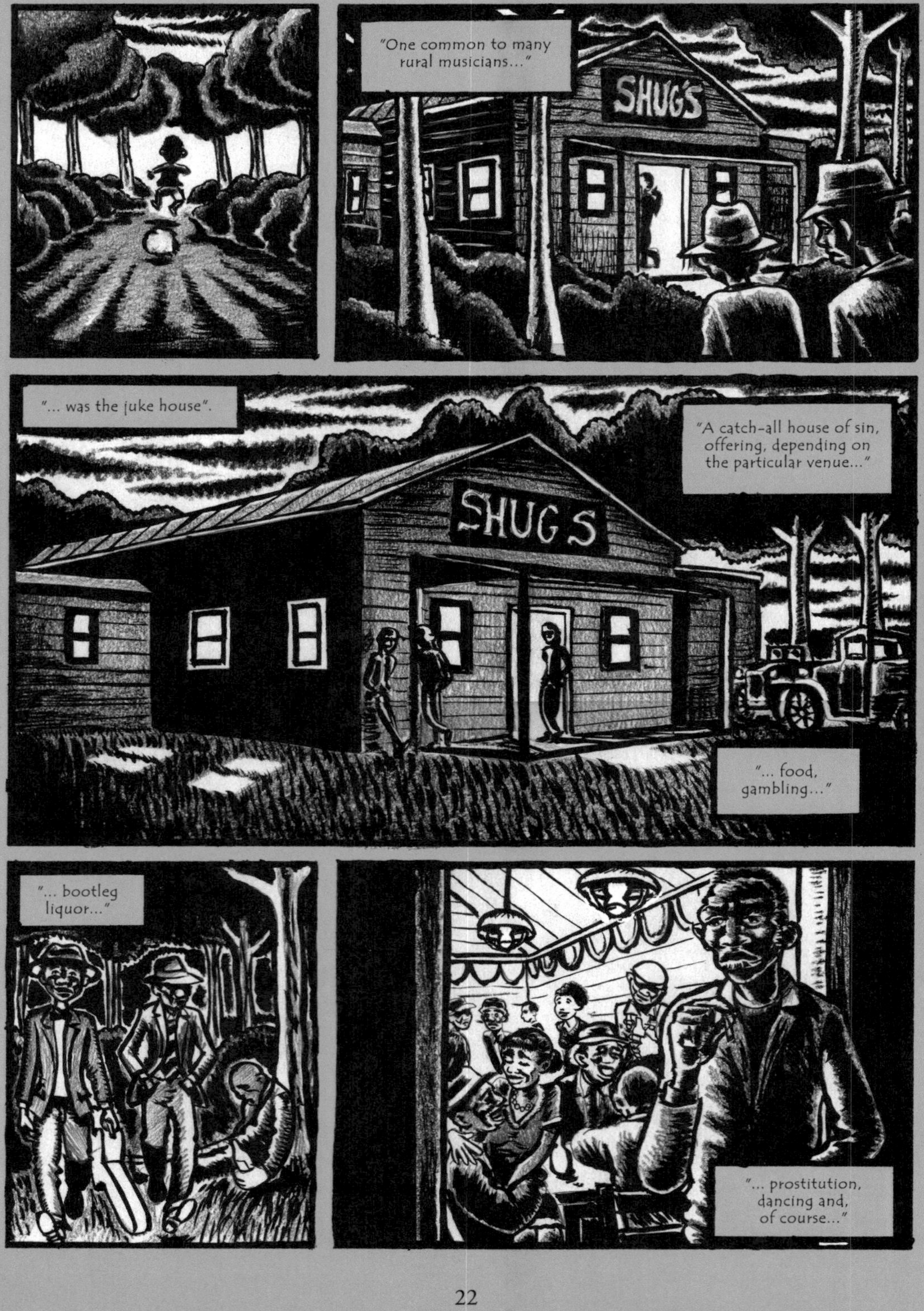

"One common to many rural musicians..."
SHUG'S
"... was the juke house".
"A catch-all house of sin, offering, depending on the particular venue..."
SHUG'S
"... food, gambling..."
"... bootleg liquor..."
"... prostitution, dancing and, of course..."

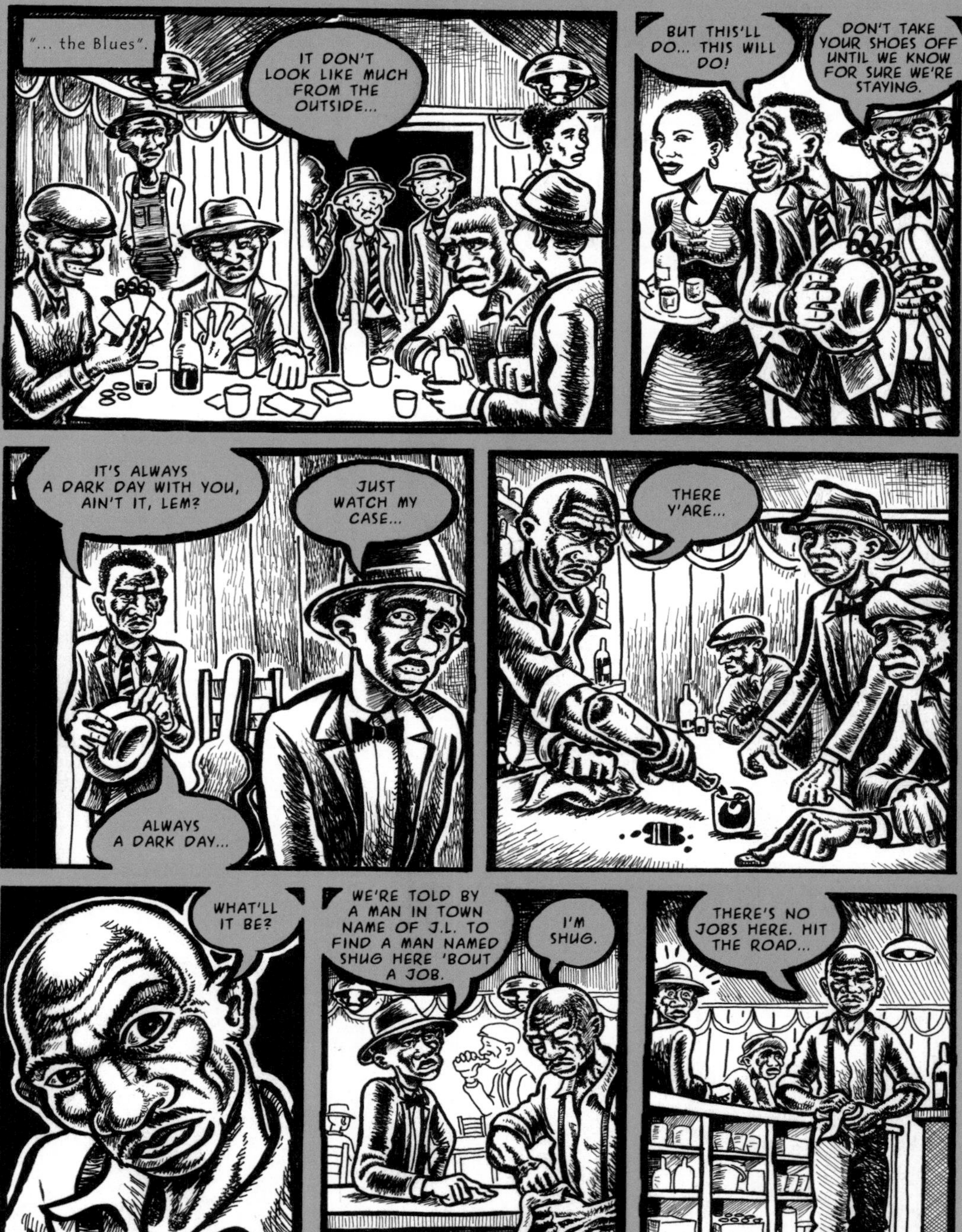

"... the Blues".
IT DON'T LOOK LIKE MUCH FROM THE OUTSIDE...
BUT THIS'LL DO... THIS WILL DO!
DON'T TAKE YOUR SHOES OFF UNTIL WE KNOW FOR SURE WE'RE STAYING.
IT'S ALWAYS A DARK DAY WITH YOU, AIN'T IT, LEM?
JUST WATCH MY CASE...
ALWAYS A DARK DAY...
THERE Y'ARE...
WHAT'LL IT BE?
WE'RE TOLD BY A MAN IN TOWN NAME OF J.L. TO FIND A MAN NAMED SHUG HERE 'BOUT A JOB.
I'M SHUG.
THERE'S NO JOBS HERE. HIT THE ROAD...

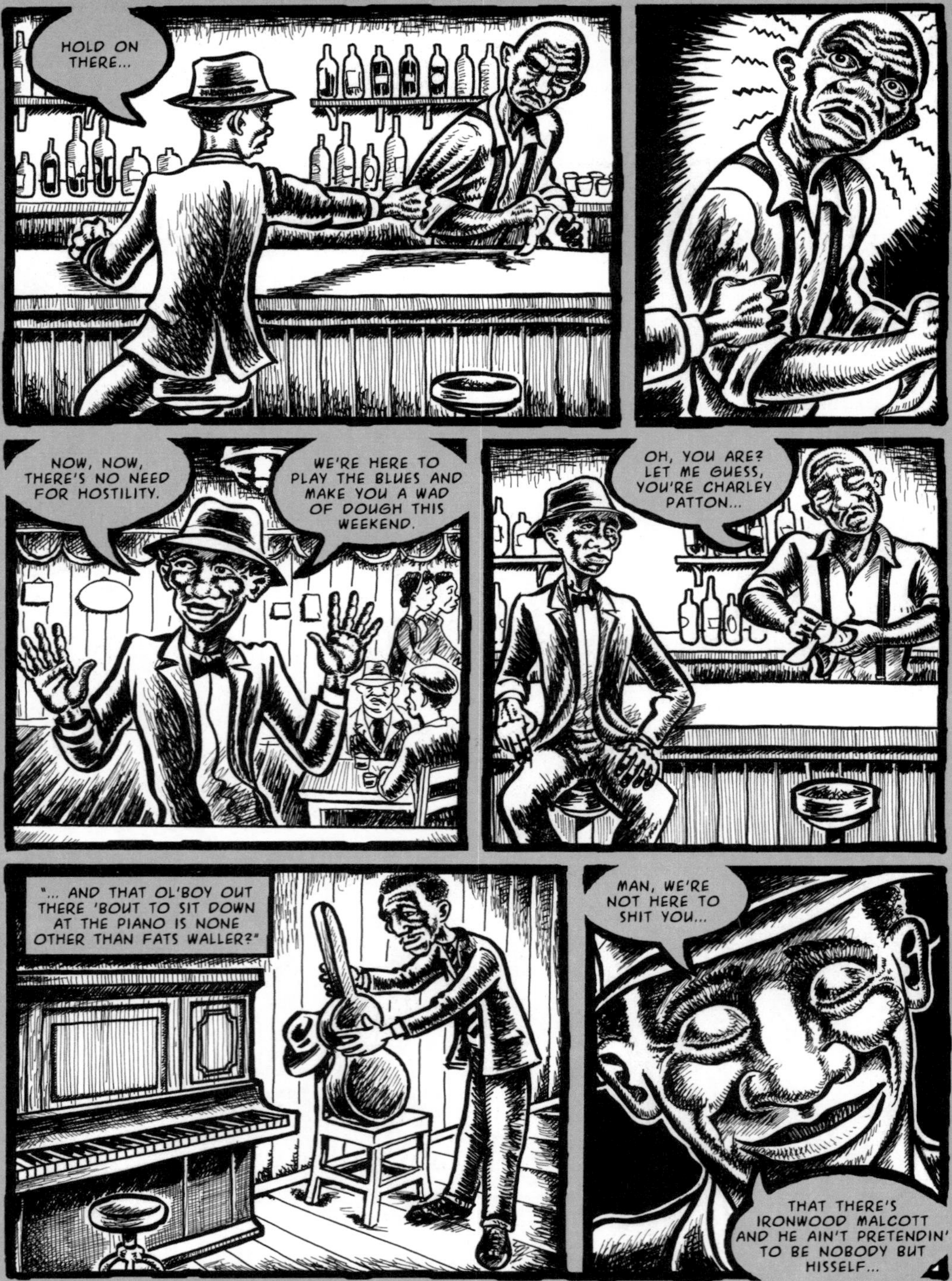

HOLD ON THERE...
NOW, NOW, THERE'S NO NEED FOR HOSTILITY.
WE'RE HERE TO PLAY THE BLUES AND MAKE YOU A WAD OF DOUGH THIS WEEKEND.
OH, YOU ARE? LET ME GUESS, YOU'RE CHARLEY PATTON...
"... AND THAT OL'BOY OUT THERE 'BOUT TO SIT DOWN AT THE PIANO IS NONE OTHER THAN FATS WALLER?"
MAN, WE'RE NOT HERE TO SHIT YOU...
THAT THERE'S IRONWOOD MALCOTT AND HE AIN'T PRETENDIN' TO BE NOBODY BUT HISSELF...

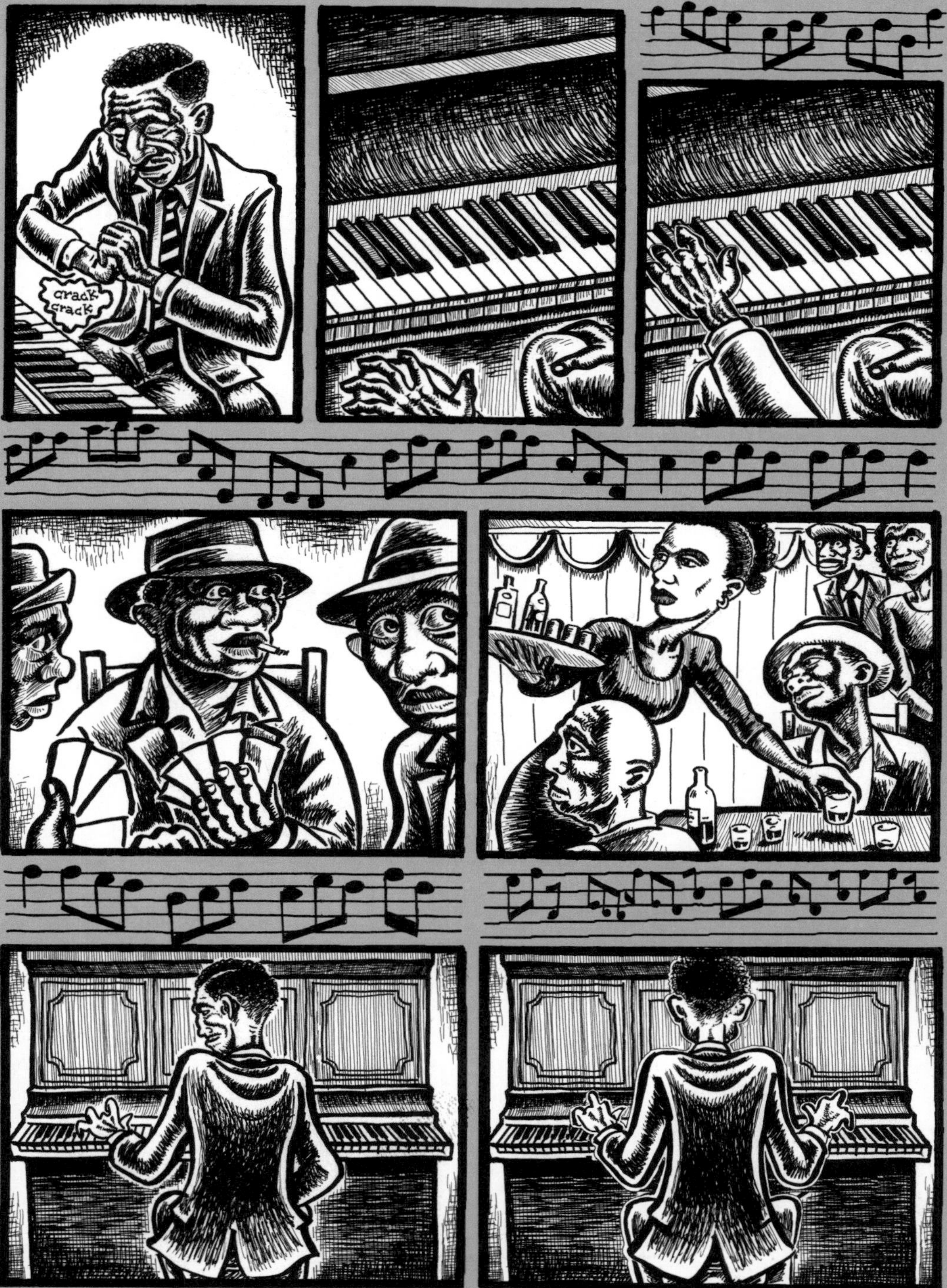
crack
crack

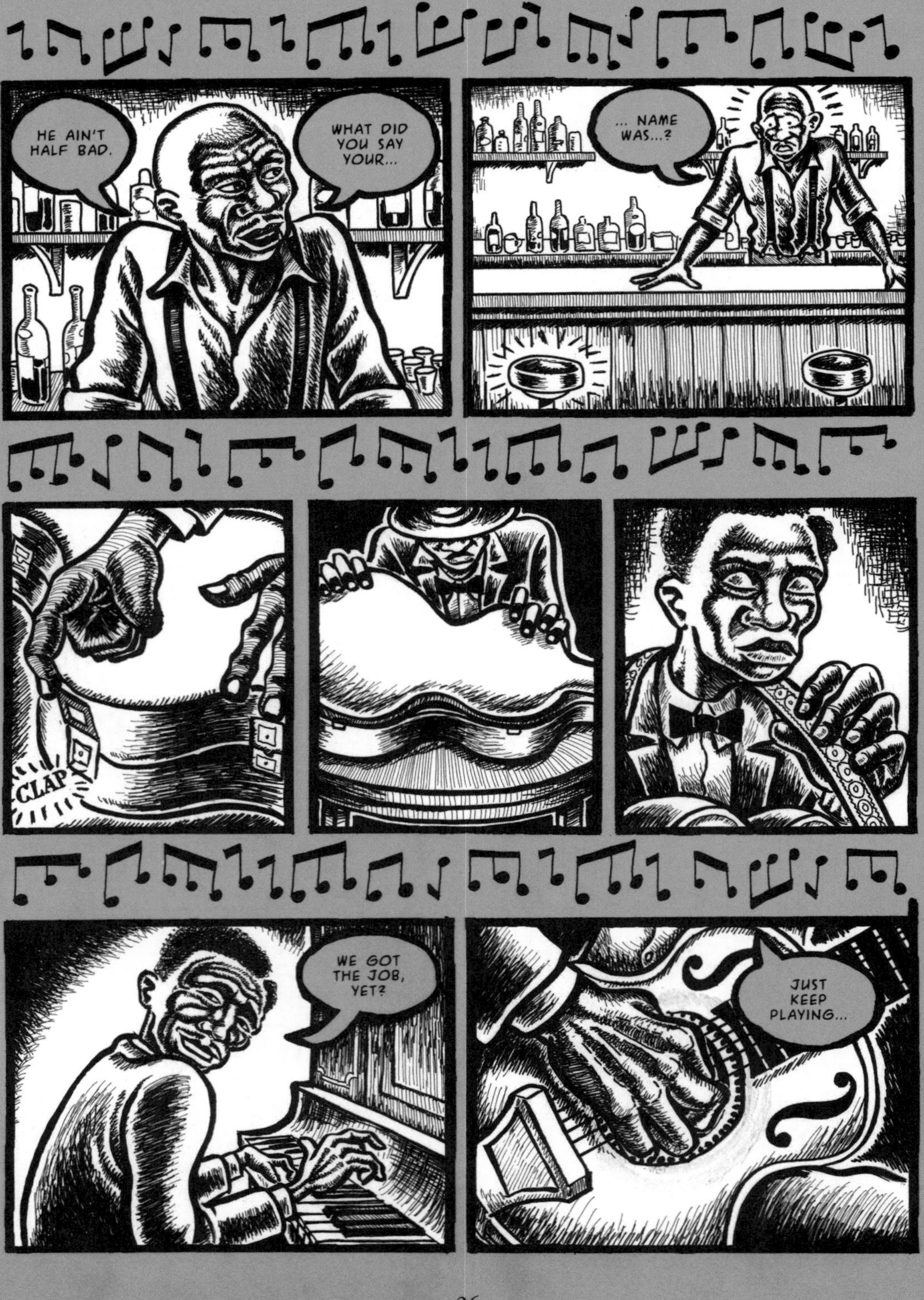
HE AIN'T HALF BAD.
WHAT DID YOU SAY YOUR...
... NAME WAS...?
CLAP
WE GOT THE JOB, YET?
JUST KEEP PLAYING...

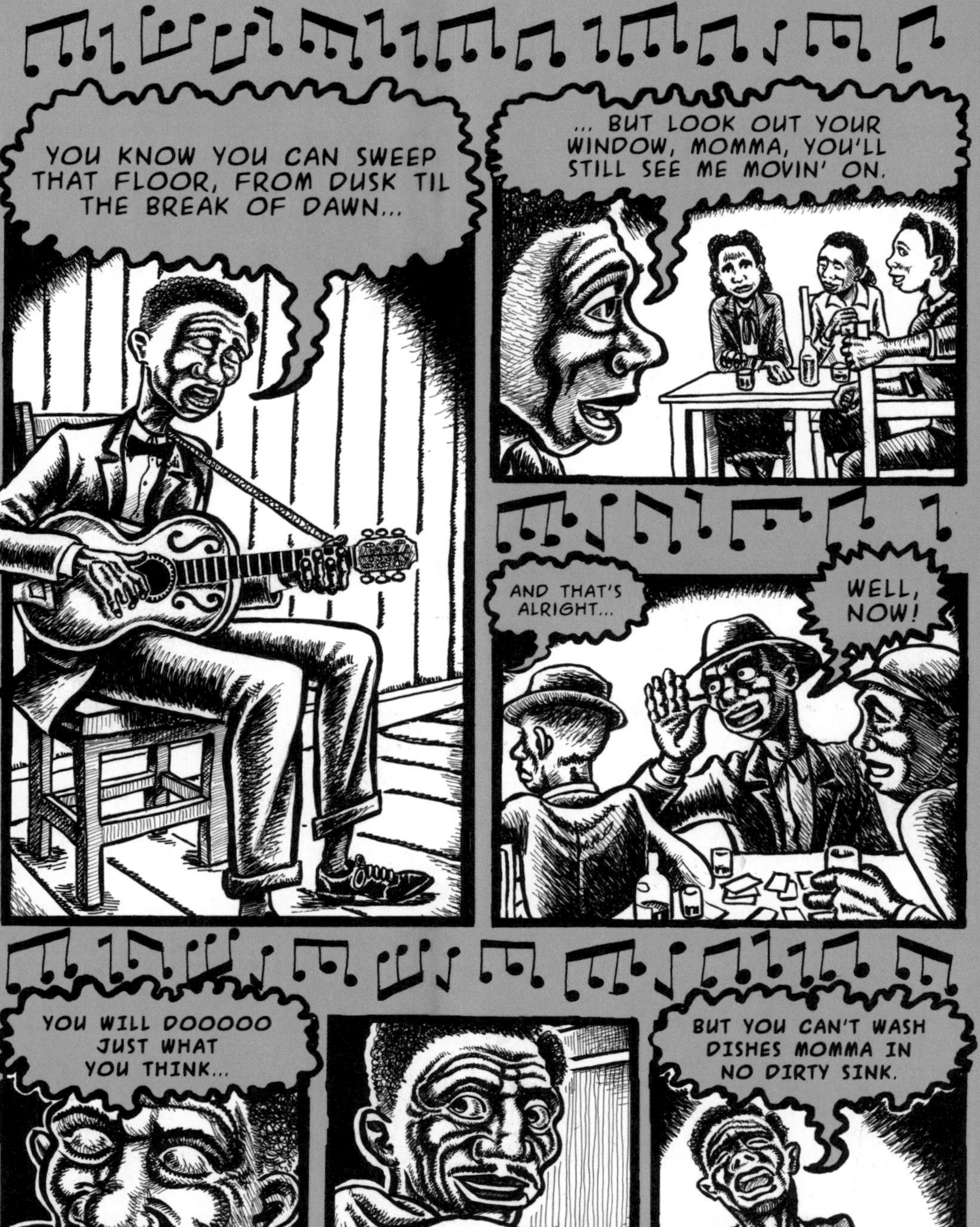
YOU KNOW YOU CAN SWEEP THAT FLOOR, FROM DUSK TIL THE BREAK OF DAWN...
... BUT LOOK OUT YOUR WINDOW, MOMMA, YOU'LL STILL SEE ME MOVIN' ON.
AND THAT'S ALRIGHT...
WELL, NOW!
YOU WILL DOOOOO JUST WHAT YOU THINK...
THAT'S RIGHT, THAT'S RIGHT...
BUT YOU CAN'T WASH DISHES MOMMA IN NO DIRTY SINK.

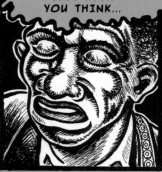

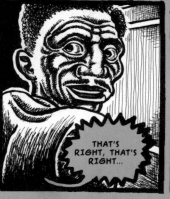

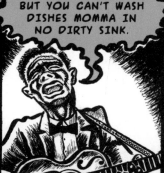

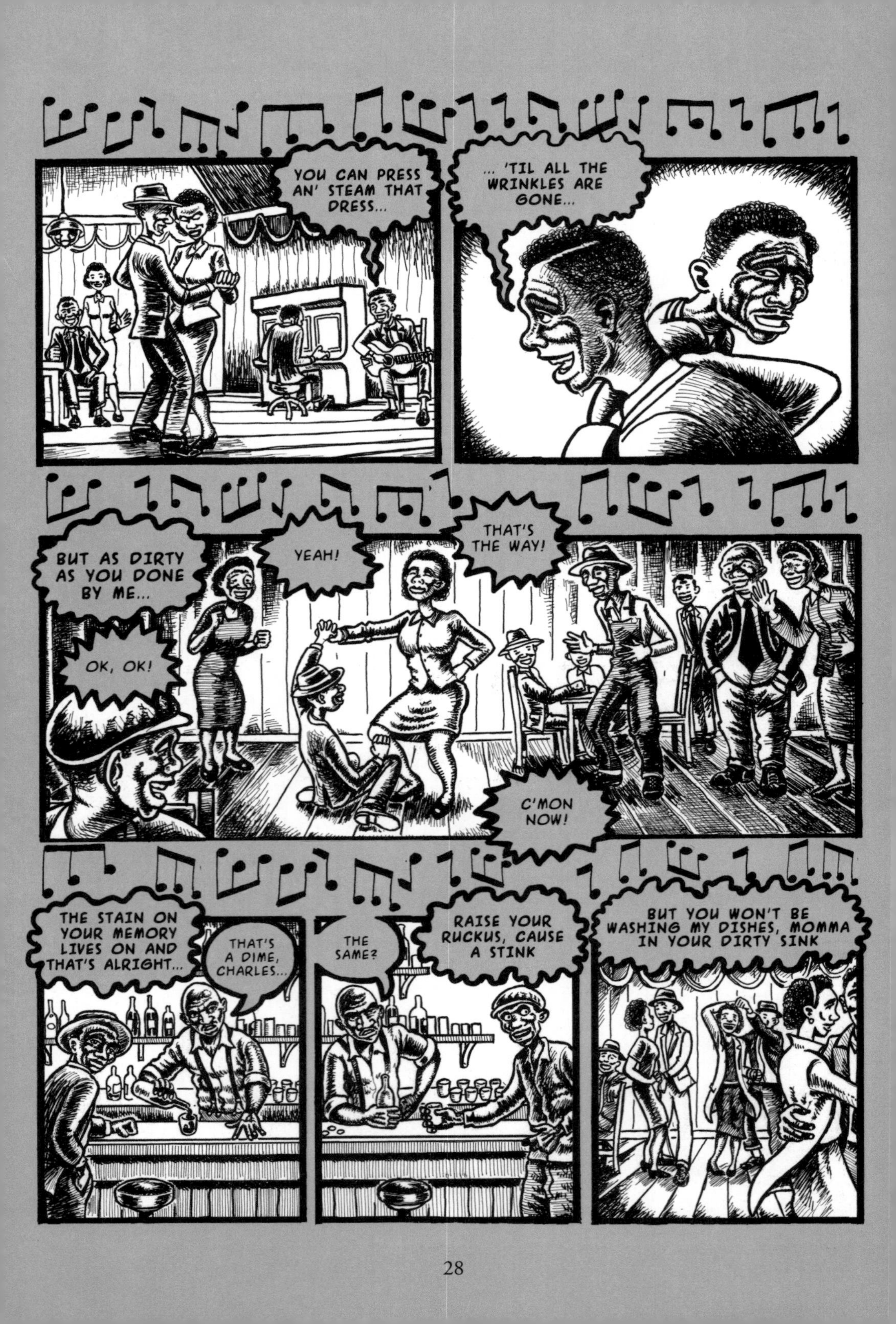

YOU CAN PRESS AN' STEAM THAT DRESS...
... 'TIL ALL THE WRINKLES ARE GONE...
BUT AS DIRTY AS YOU DONE BY ME...
YEAH!
THAT'S THE WAY!
OK, OK!
C'MON NOW!
THE STAIN ON YOUR MEMORY LIVES ON AND THAT'S ALRIGHT...
THAT'S A DIME, CHARLES...
THE SAME?
RAISE YOUR RUCKUS, CAUSE A STINK
BUT YOU WON'T BE WASHING MY DISHES, MOMMA IN YOUR DIRTY SINK

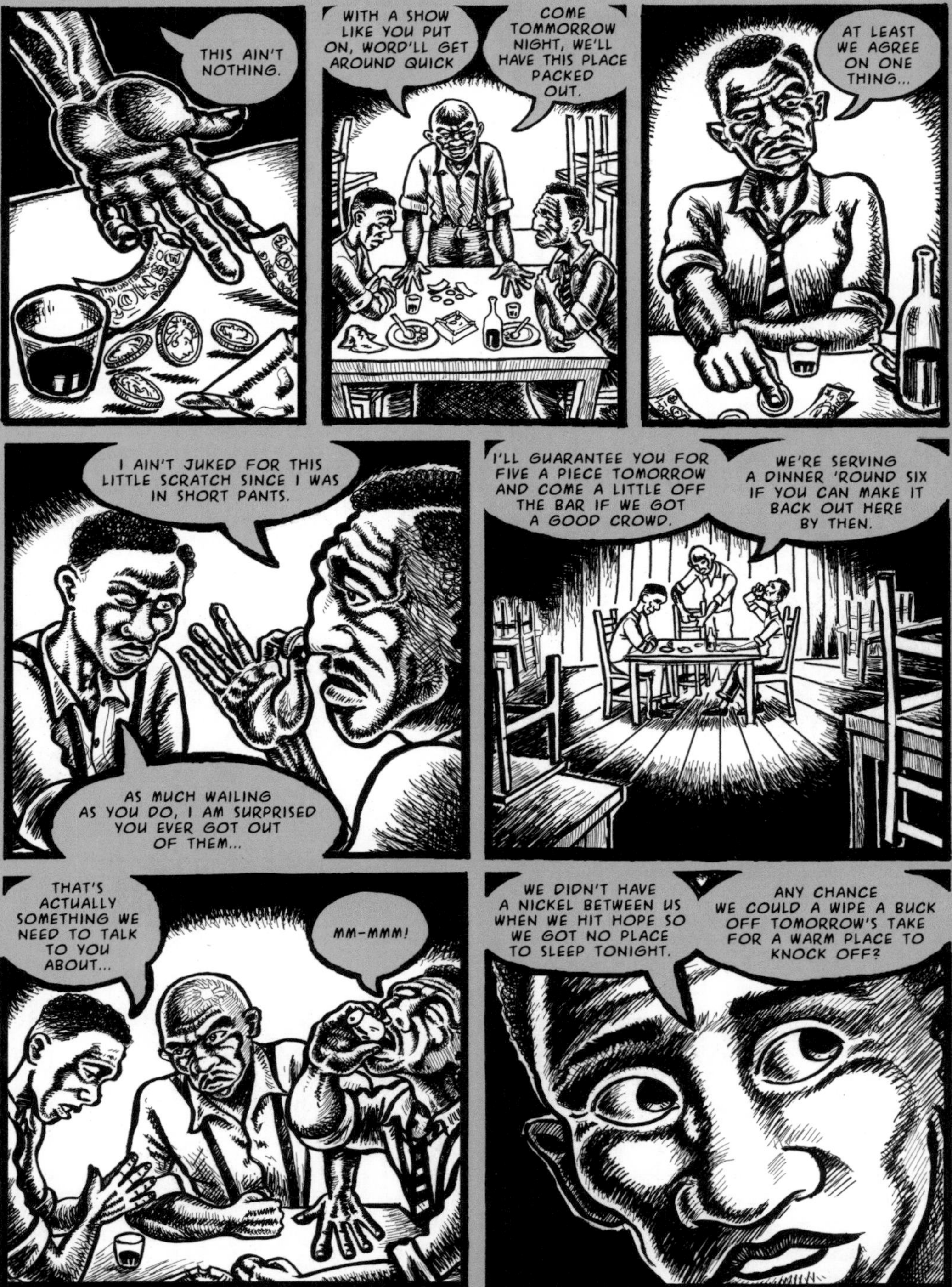
THIS AIN'T NOTHING.
WITH A SHOW LIKE YOU PUT ON, WORD'LL GET AROUND QUICK
COME TOMORROW NIGHT, WE'LL HAVE THIS PLACE PACKED OUT.
AT LEAST WE AGREE ON ONE THING...
I AIN'T JUKED FOR THIS LITTLE SCRATCH SINCE I WAS IN SHORT PANTS.
AS MUCH WAILING AS YOU DO, I AM SURPRISED YOU EVER GOT OUT OF THEM...
I'LL GUARANTEE YOU FOR FIVE A PIECE TOMORROW AND COME A LITTLE OFF THE BAR IF WE GOT A GOOD CROWD.
WE'RE SERVING A DINNER 'ROUND SIX IF YOU CAN MAKE IT BACK OUT HERE BY THEN.
THAT'S ACTUALLY SOMETHING WE NEED TO TALK TO YOU ABOUT...
MM-MMM!
WE DIDN'T HAVE A NICKEL BETWEEN US WHEN WE HIT HOPE SO WE GOT NO PLACE TO SLEEP TONIGHT.
ANY CHANCE WE COULD A WIPE A BUCK OFF TOMORROW'S TAKE FOR A WARM PLACE TO KNOCK OFF?

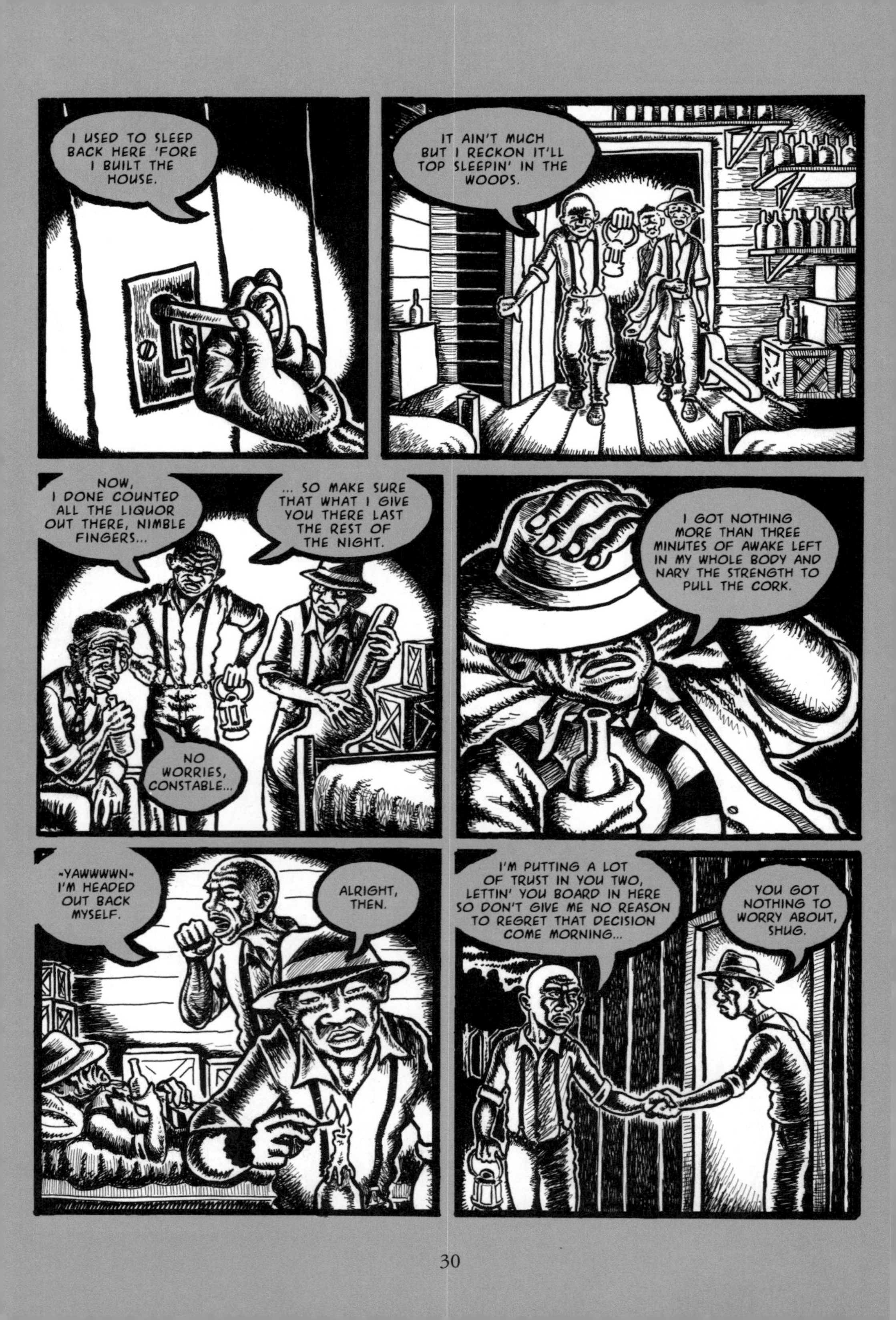
I USED TO SLEEP BACK HERE 'FORE I BUILT THE HOUSE.
IT AIN'T MUCH BUT I RECKON IT'LL TOP SLEEPIN' IN THE WOODS.
NOW, I DONE COUNTED ALL THE LIQUOR OUT THERE, NIMBLE FINGERS...
... SO MAKE SURE THAT WHAT I GIVE YOU THERE LAST THE REST OF THE NIGHT.
NO WORRIES, CONSTABLE...
I GOT NOTHING MORE THAN THREE MINUTES OF AWAKE LEFT IN MY WHOLE BODY AND NARY THE STRENGTH TO PULL THE CORK.
~YAWWWWN~ I'M HEADED OUT BACK MYSELF.
ALRIGHT, THEN.
I'M PUTTING A LOT OF TRUST IN YOU TWO, LETTIN' YOU BOARD IN HERE SO DON'T GIVE ME NO REASON TO REGRET THAT DECISION COME MORNING...
YOU GOT NOTHING TO WORRY ABOUT, SHUG.

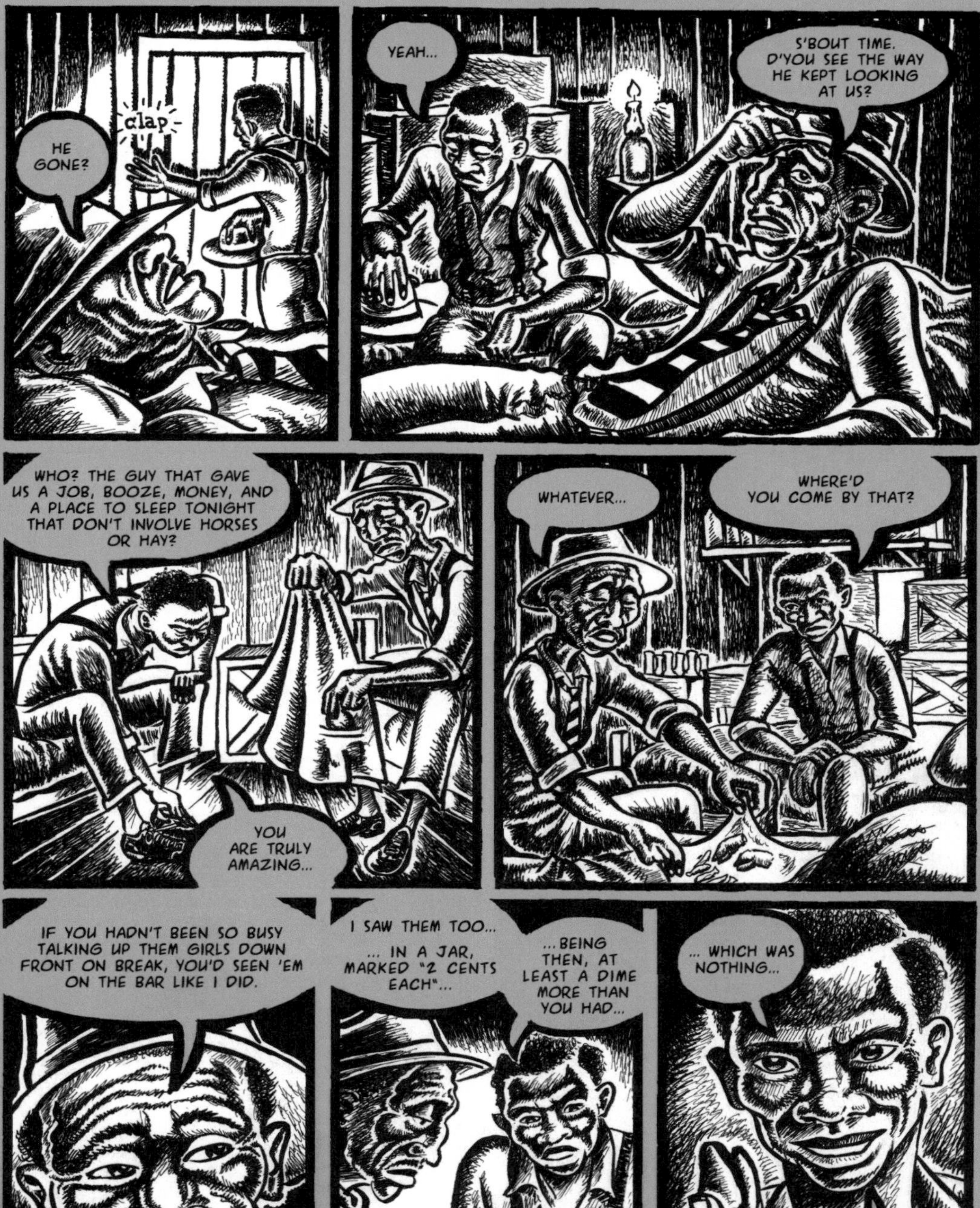
clap
HE GONE?
YEAH...
S'BOUT TIME. D'YOU SEE THE WAY HE KEPT LOOKING AT US?
WHO? THE GUY THAT GAVE US A JOB, BOOZE, MONEY, AND A PLACE TO SLEEP TONIGHT THAT DON'T INVOLVE HORSES OR HAY?
YOU ARE TRULY AMAZING...
WHATEVER...
WHERE'D YOU COME BY THAT?
IF YOU HADN'T BEEN SO BUSY TALKING UP THEM GIRLS DOWN FRONT ON BREAK, YOU'D SEEN 'EM ON THE BAR LIKE I DID.
I SAW THEM TOO...
... IN A JAR, MARKED "2 CENTS EACH"...
...BEING THEN, AT LEAST A DIME MORE THAN YOU HAD...
... WHICH WAS NOTHING...
A HOGSFOOT BUYS YOU MY SILENCE...

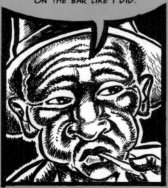

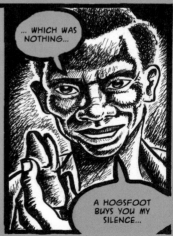

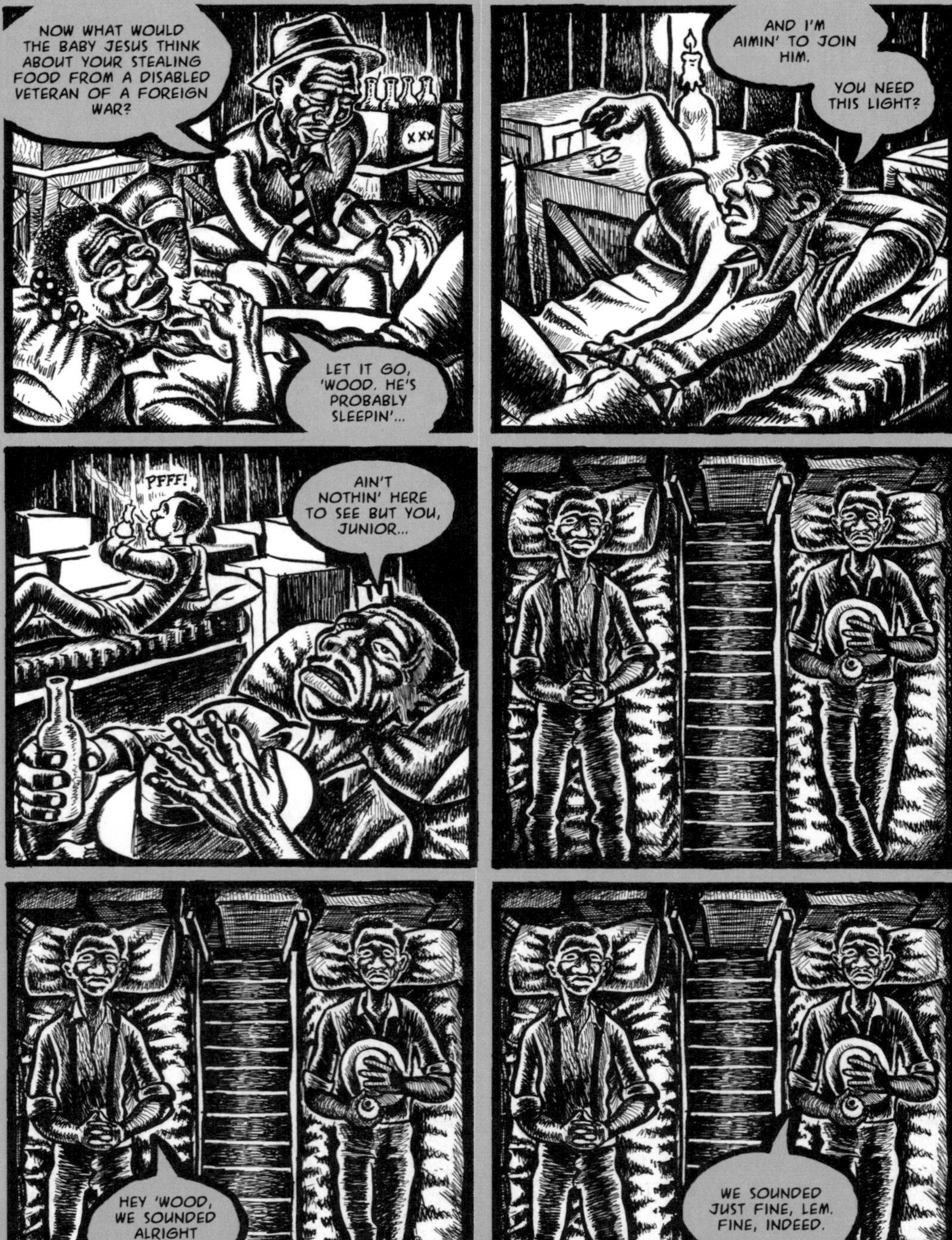
NOW WHAT WOULD THE BABY JESUS THINK ABOUT YOUR STEALING FOOD FROM A DISABLED VETERAN OF A FOREIGN WAR?
XXX
LET IT GO, 'WOOD. HE'S PROBABLY SLEEPIN'...
AND I'M AIMIN' TO JOIN HIM.
YOU NEED THIS LIGHT?
PFFF!
AIN'T NOTHIN' HERE TO SEE BUT YOU, JUNIOR...
HEY 'WOOD, WE SOUNDED ALRIGHT TONIGHT, HUH?
WE SOUNDED JUST FINE, LEM. FINE, INDEED.

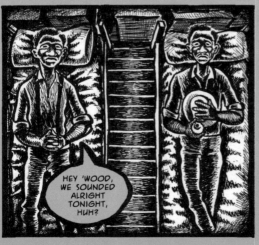

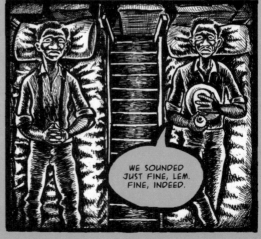

3

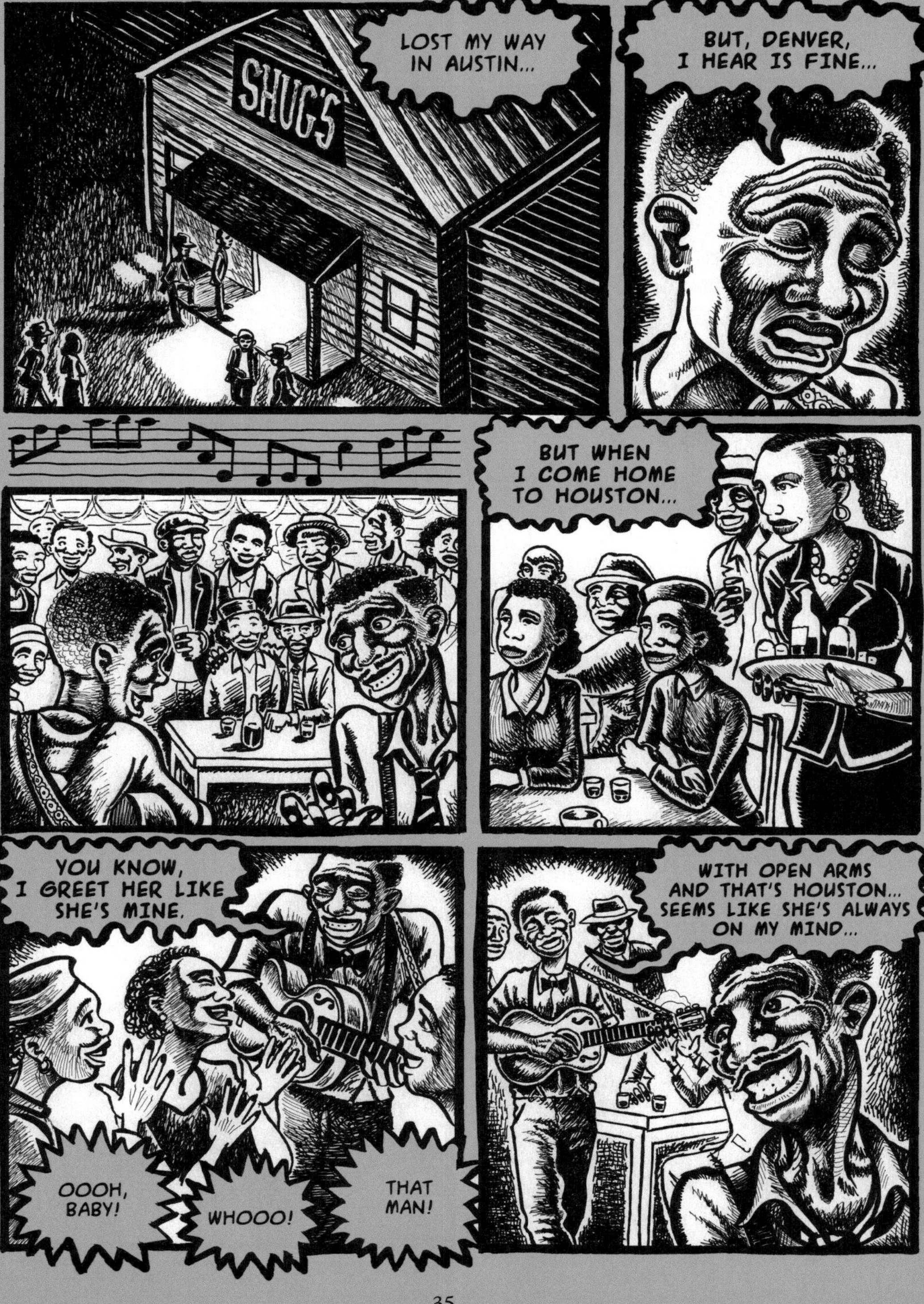
SHUG'S
LOST MY WAY IN AUSTIN...
BUT, DENVER, I HEAR IS FINE...
BUT WHEN I COME HOME TO HOUSTON...
YOU KNOW, I GREET HER LIKE SHE'S MINE.
OOOH, BABY!
WHOOO!
THAT MAN!
WITH OPEN ARMS AND THAT'S HOUSTON... SEEMS LIKE SHE'S ALWAYS ON MY MIND...

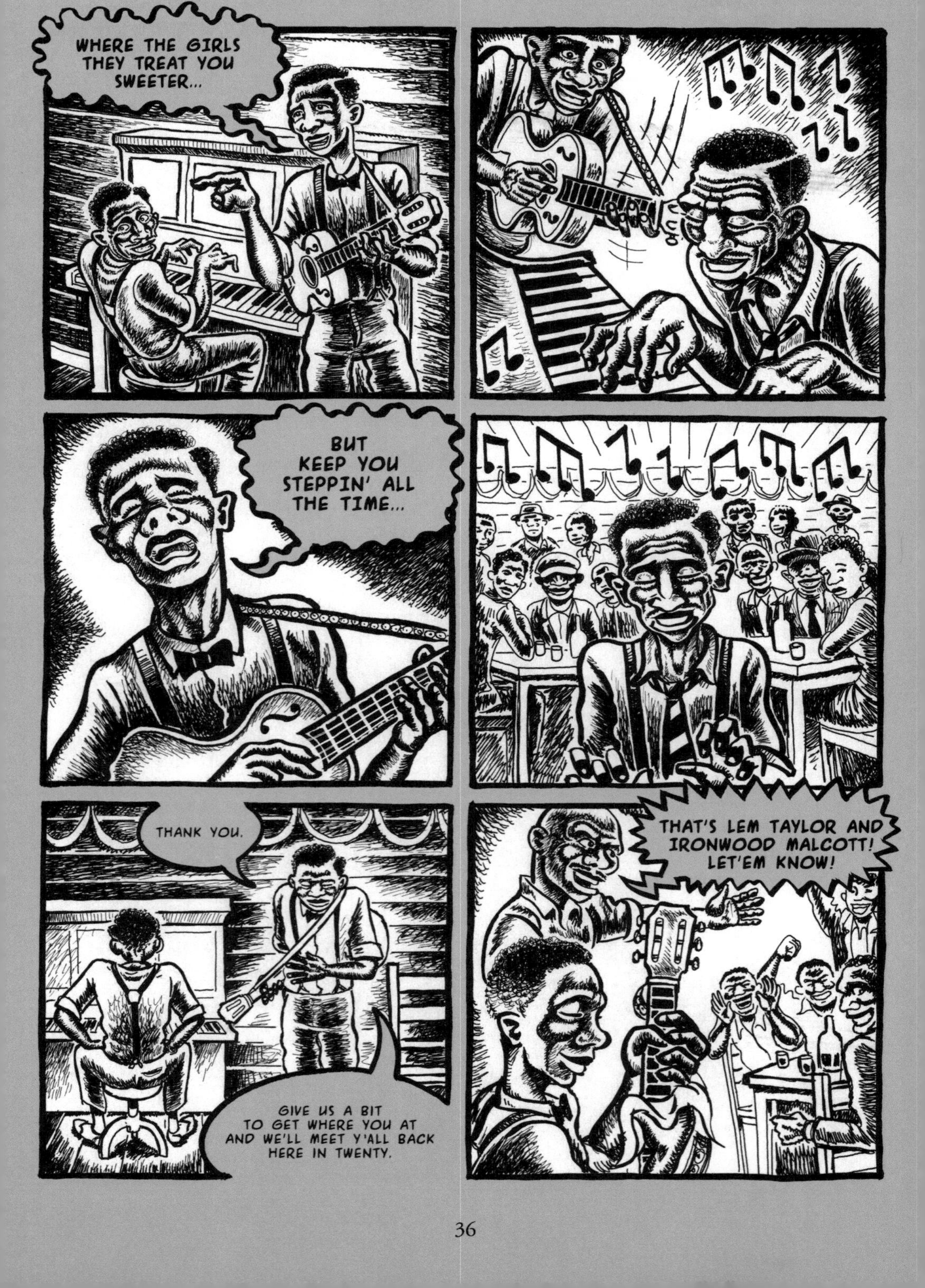
WHERE THE GIRLS THEY TREAT YOU SWEETER...
BUT KEEP YOU STEPPIN' ALL THE TIME...
THANK YOU.
GIVE US A BIT TO GET WHERE YOU AT AND WE'LL MEET Y'ALL BACK HERE IN TWENTY.
THAT'S LEM TAYLOR AND IRONWOOD MALCOTT! LET'EM KNOW!

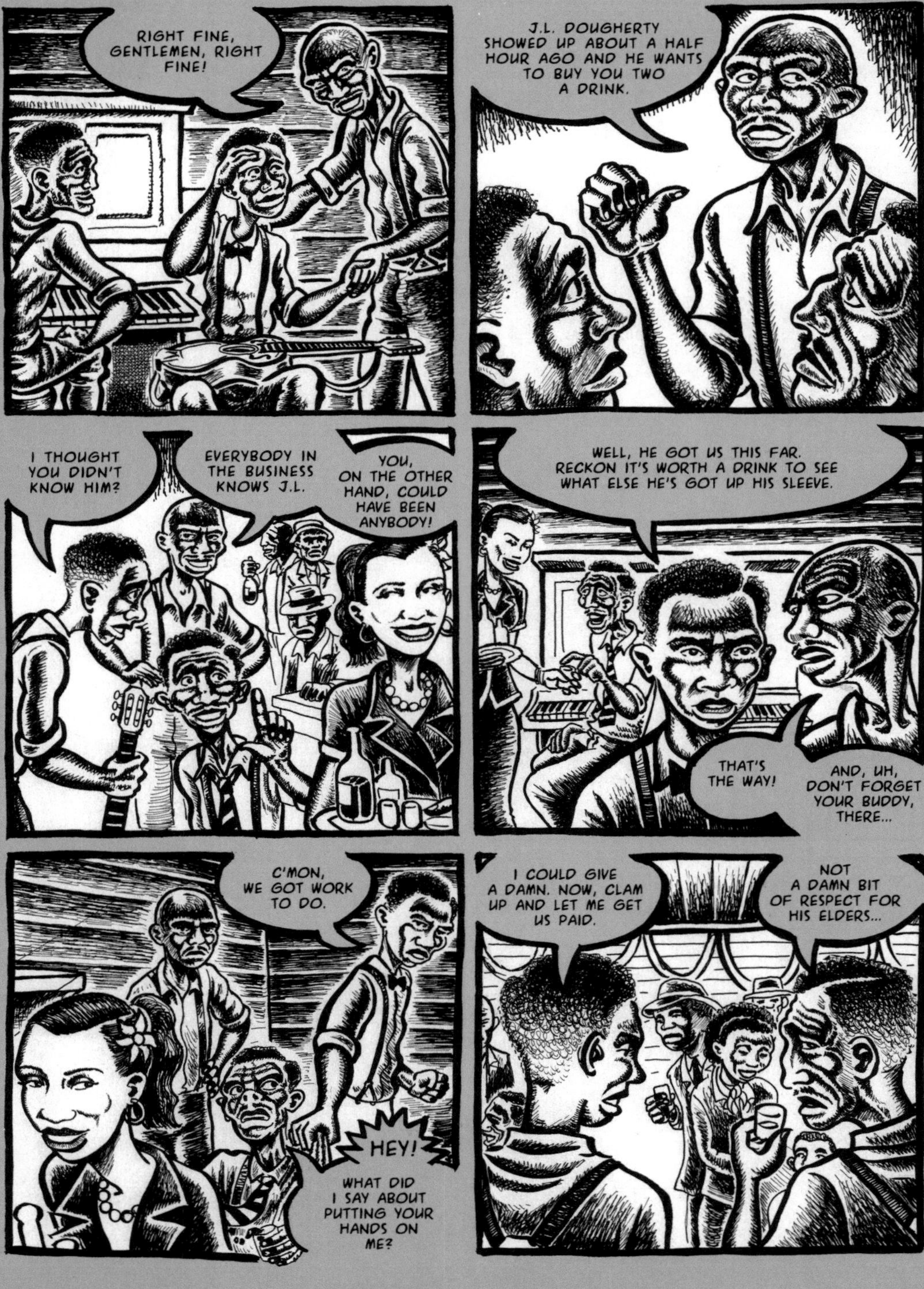
RIGHT FINE, GENTLEMEN, RIGHT FINE!
J.L. DOUGHERTY SHOWED UP ABOUT A HALF HOUR AGO AND HE WANTS TO BUY YOU TWO A DRINK.
I THOUGHT YOU DIDN'T KNOW HIM?
EVERYBODY IN THE BUSINESS KNOWS J.L.
YOU, ON THE OTHER HAND, COULD HAVE BEEN ANYBODY!
WELL, HE GOT US THIS FAR. RECKON IT'S WORTH A DRINK TO SEE WHAT ELSE HE'S GOT UP HIS SLEEVE.
THAT'S THE WAY!
AND, UH, DON'T FORGET YOUR BUDDY, THERE...
C'MON, WE GOT WORK TO DO.
HEY!
WHAT DID I SAY ABOUT PUTTING YOUR HANDS ON ME?
I COULD GIVE A DAMN. NOW, CLAM UP AND LET ME GET US PAID.
NOT A DAMN BIT OF RESPECT FOR HIS ELDERS...

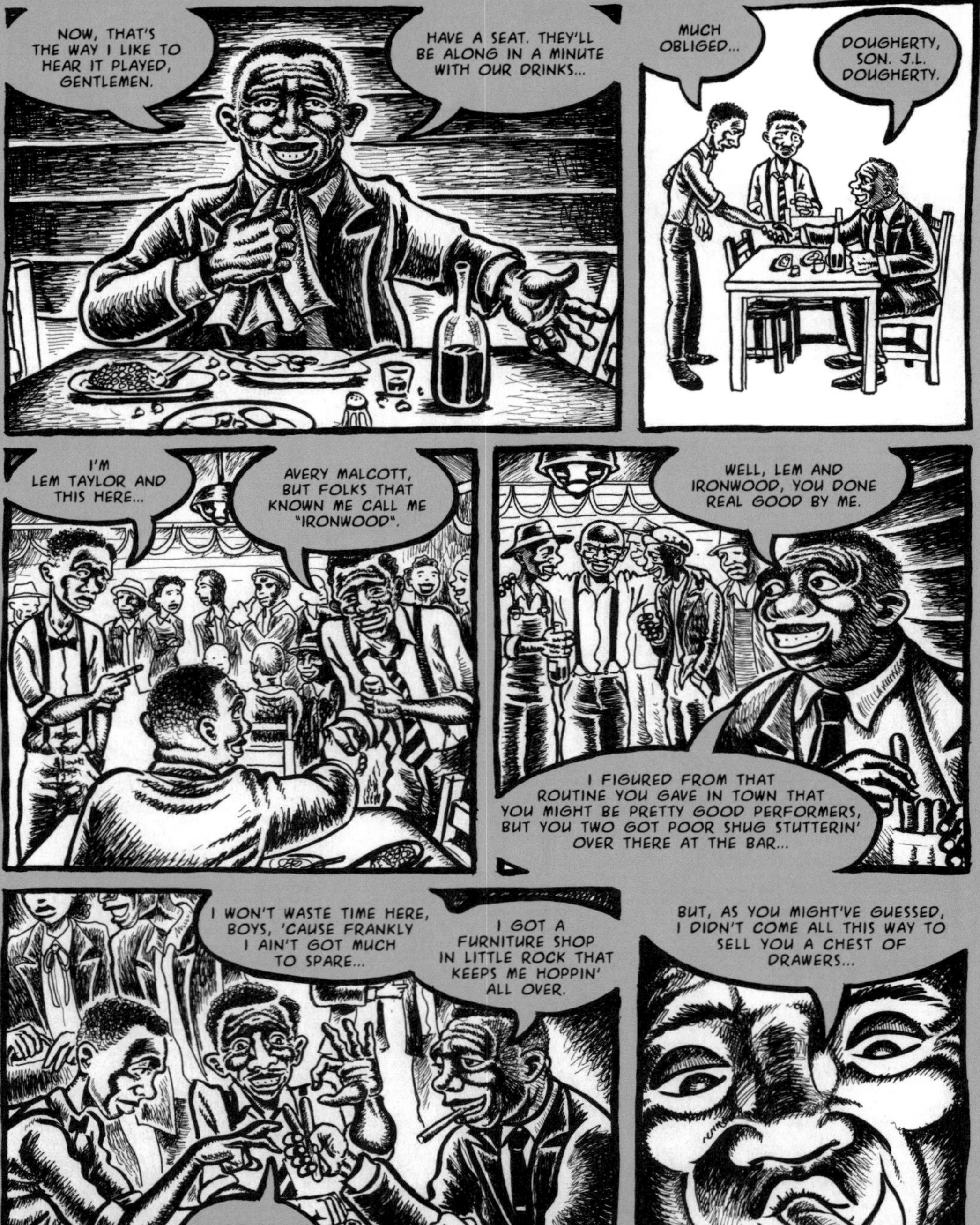
NOW, THAT'S THE WAY I LIKE TO HEAR IT PLAYED, GENTLEMEN.
HAVE A SEAT. THEY'LL BE ALONG IN A MINUTE WITH OUR DRINKS...
MUCH OBLIGED...
DOUGHERTY, SON. J.L. DOUGHERTY.
I'M LEM TAYLOR AND THIS HERE...
AVERY MALCOTT, BUT FOLKS THAT KNOWN ME CALL ME "IRONWOOD".
WELL, LEM AND IRONWOOD, YOU DONE REAL GOOD BY ME.
I FIGURED FROM THAT ROUTINE YOU GAVE IN TOWN THAT YOU MIGHT BE PRETTY GOOD PERFORMERS, BUT YOU TWO GOT POOR SHUG STUTTERIN' OVER THERE AT THE BAR...
I WON'T WASTE TIME HERE, BOYS, 'CAUSE FRANKLY I AIN'T GOT MUCH TO SPARE...
I GOT A FURNITURE SHOP IN LITTLE ROCK THAT KEEPS ME HOPPIN' ALL OVER.
DON'T MIND IF I DO, JL.
BUT, AS YOU MIGHT'VE GUESSED, I DIDN'T COME ALL THIS WAY TO SELL YOU A CHEST OF DRAWERS...

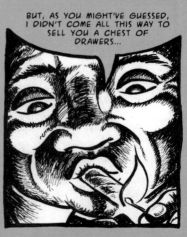

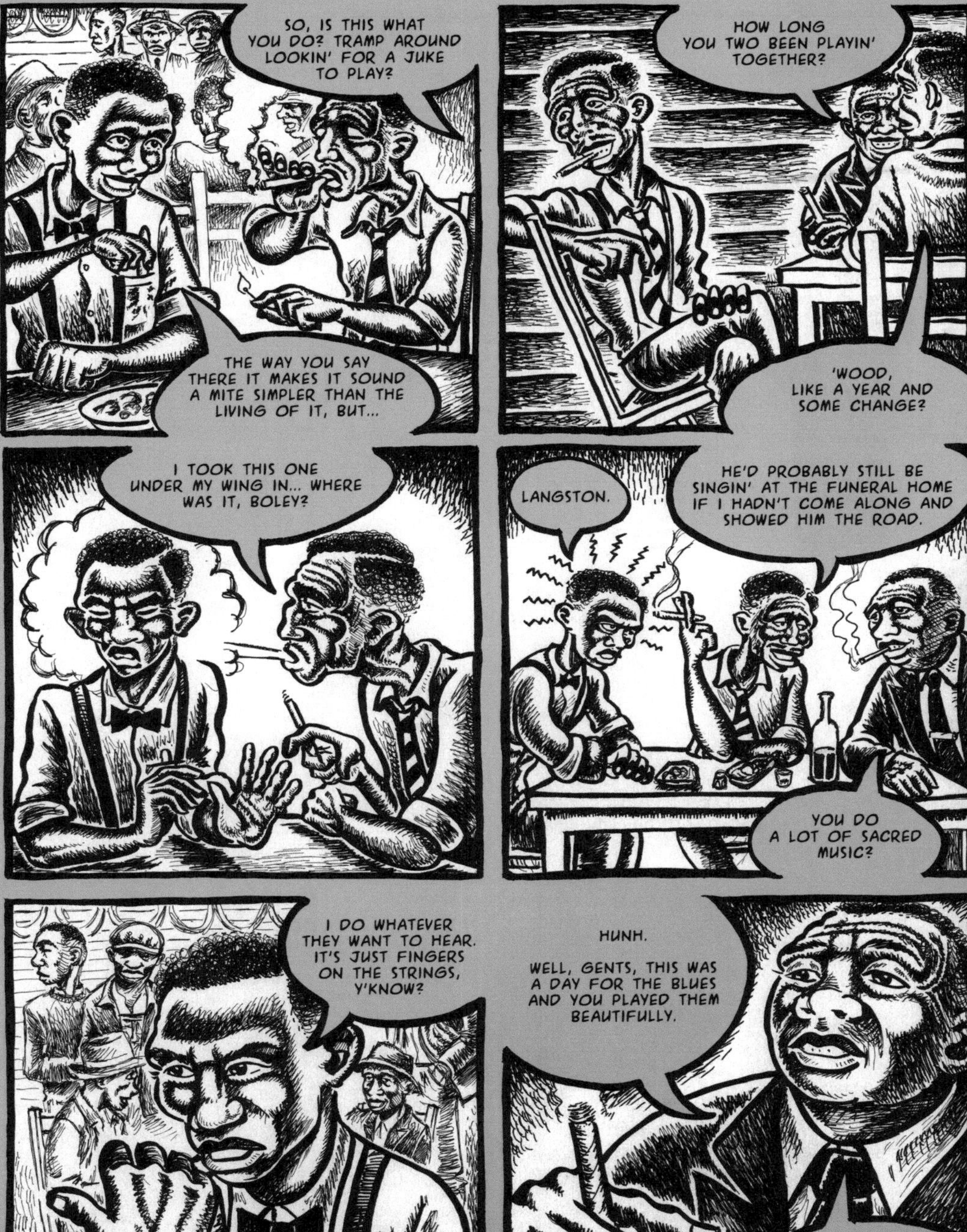
SO, IS THIS WHAT YOU DO? TRAMP AROUND LOOKIN' FOR A JUKE TO PLAY?
THE WAY YOU SAY THERE IT MAKES IT SOUND A MITE SIMPLER THAN THE LIVING OF IT, BUT...
HOW LONG YOU TWO BEEN PLAYIN' TOGETHER?
'WOOD, LIKE A YEAR AND SOME CHANGE?
I TOOK THIS ONE UNDER MY WING IN... WHERE WAS IT, BOLEY?
LANGSTON.
HE'D PROBABLY STILL BE SINGIN' AT THE FUNERAL HOME IF I HADN'T COME ALONG AND SHOWED HIM THE ROAD.
YOU DO A LOT OF SACRED MUSIC?
I DO WHATEVER THEY WANT TO HEAR. IT'S JUST FINGERS ON THE STRINGS, Y'KNOW?
HUNH.
WELL, GENTS, THIS WAS A DAY FOR THE BLUES AND YOU PLAYED THEM BEAUTIFULLY.
NOW, LET ME ASK YOU SOMETHING...

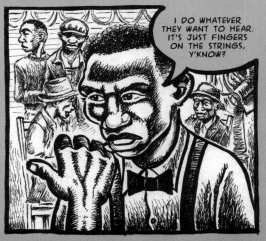

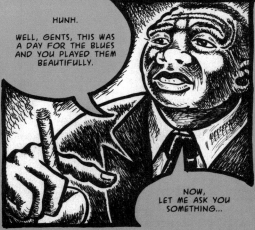

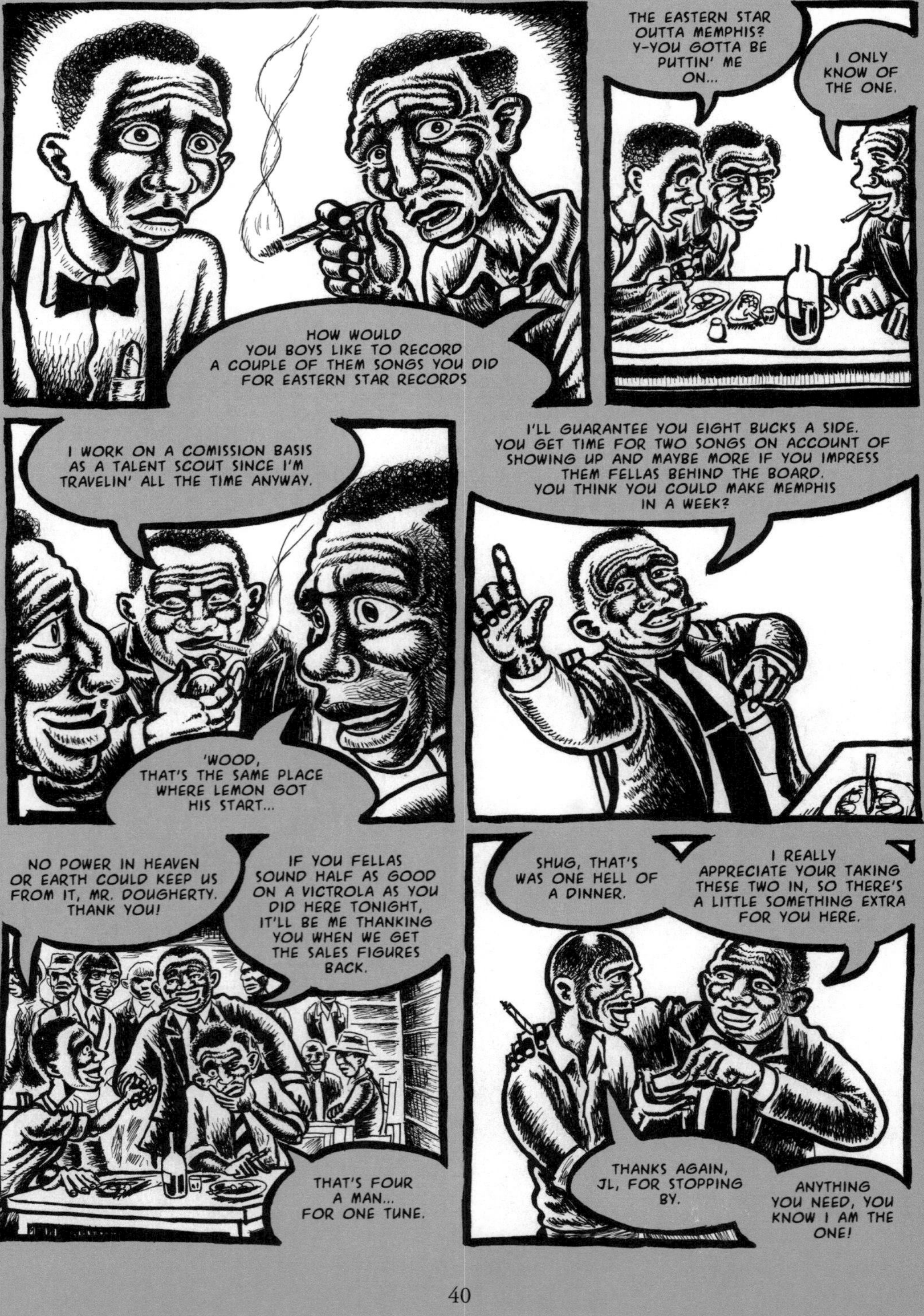
HOW WOULD YOU BOYS LIKE TO RECORD A COUPLE OF THEM SONGS YOU DID FOR EASTERN STAR RECORDS
THE EASTERN STAR OUTTA MEMPHIS? Y-YOU GOTTA BE PUTTIN' ME ON...
I ONLY KNOW OF THE ONE.
I WORK ON A COMISSION BASIS AS A TALENT SCOUT SINCE I'M TRAVELIN' ALL THE TIME ANYWAY.
'WOOD, THAT'S THE SAME PLACE WHERE LEMON GOT HIS START...
I'LL GUARANTEE YOU EIGHT BUCKS A SIDE. YOU GET TIME FOR TWO SONGS ON ACCOUNT OF SHOWING UP AND MAYBE MORE IF YOU IMPRESS THEM FELLAS BEHIND THE BOARD. YOU THINK YOU COULD MAKE MEMPHIS IN A WEEK?
NO POWER IN HEAVEN OR EARTH COULD KEEP US FROM IT, MR. DOUGHERTY. THANK YOU!
IF YOU FELLAS SOUND HALF AS GOOD ON A VICTROLA AS YOU DID HERE TONIGHT, IT'LL BE ME THANKING YOU WHEN WE GET THE SALES FIGURES BACK.
THAT'S FOUR A MAN... FOR ONE TUNE.
SHUG, THAT'S WAS ONE HELL OF A DINNER.
I REALLY APPRECIATE YOUR TAKING THESE TWO IN, SO THERE'S A LITTLE SOMETHING EXTRA FOR YOU HERE.
THANKS AGAIN, JL, FOR STOPPING BY.
ANYTHING YOU NEED, YOU KNOW I AM THE ONE!

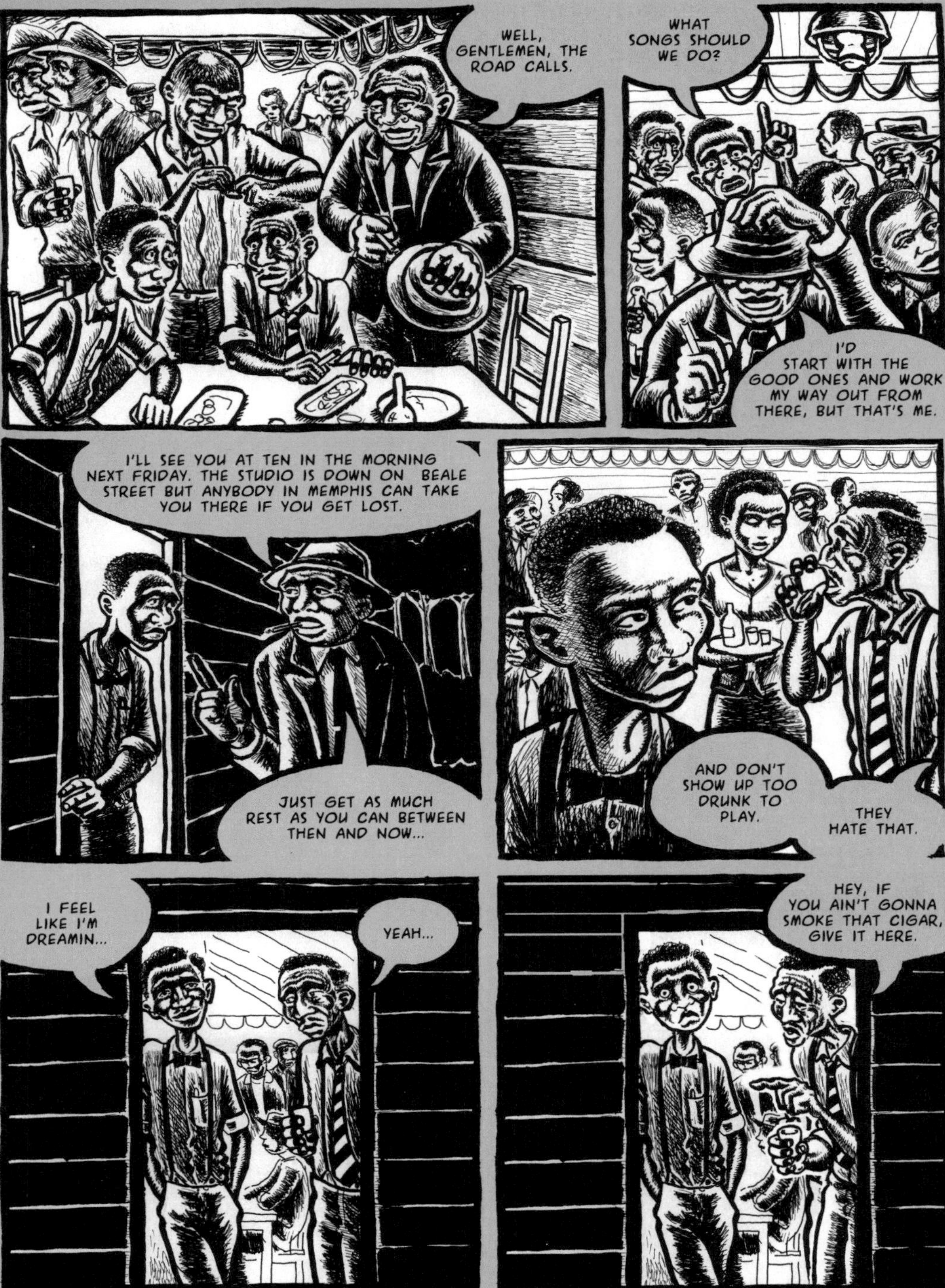
WELL, GENTLEMEN, THE ROAD CALLS.
WHAT SONGS SHOULD WE DO?
I'D START WITH THE GOOD ONES AND WORK MY WAY OUT FROM THERE, BUT THAT'S ME.
I'LL SEE YOU AT TEN IN THE MORNING NEXT FRIDAY. THE STUDIO IS DOWN ON BEALE STREET BUT ANYBODY IN MEMPHIS CAN TAKE YOU THERE IF YOU GET LOST.
JUST GET AS MUCH REST AS YOU CAN BETWEEN THEN AND NOW...
AND DON'T SHOW UP TOO DRUNK TO PLAY.
THEY HATE THAT.
I FEEL LIKE I'M DREAMIN...
YEAH...
HEY, IF YOU AIN'T GONNA SMOKE THAT CIGAR, GIVE IT HERE.

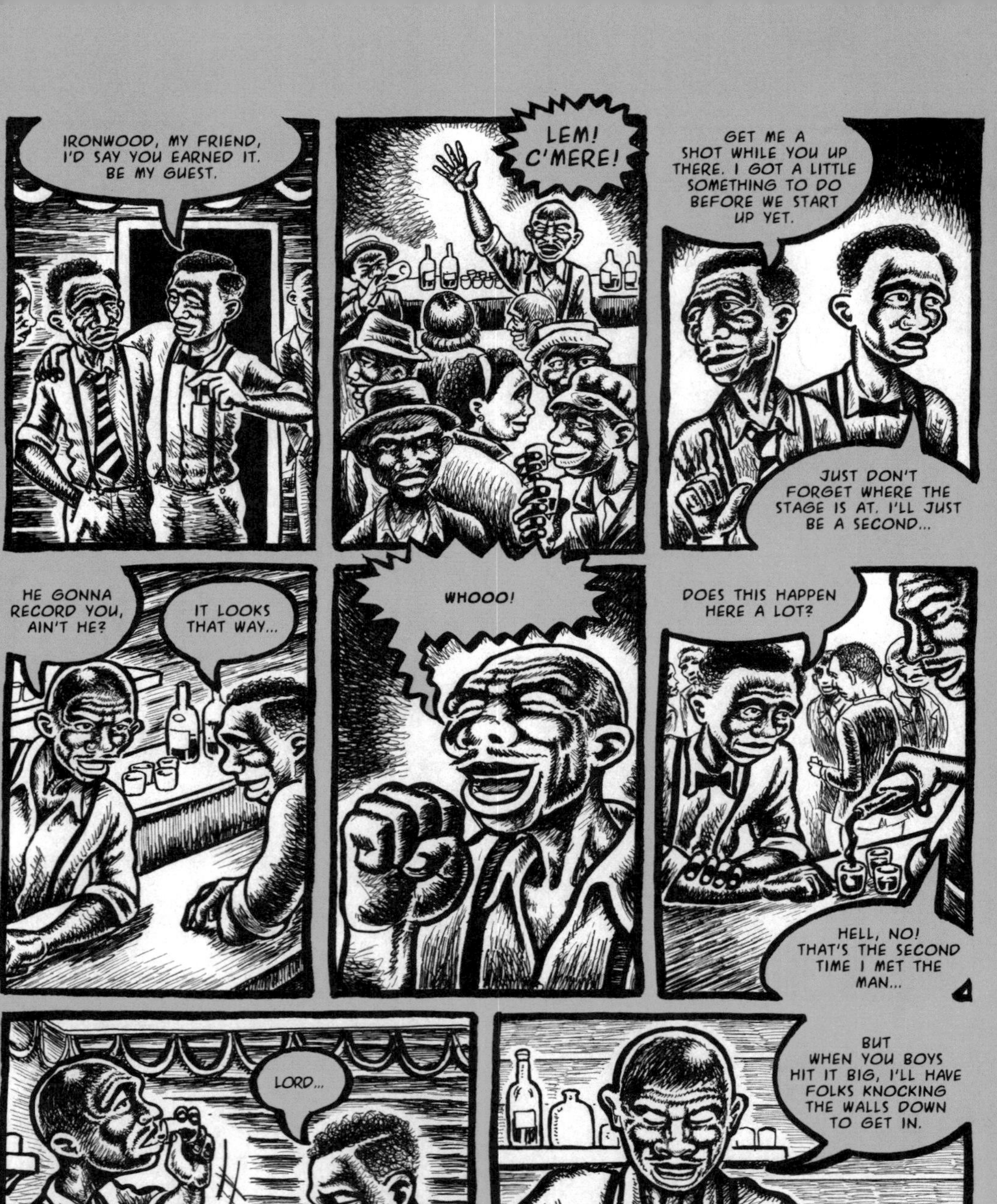

IRONWOOD, MY FRIEND, I'D SAY YOU EARNED IT. BE MY GUEST.
LEM! C'MERE!
GET ME A SHOT WHILE YOU UP THERE. I GOT A LITTLE SOMETHING TO DO BEFORE WE START UP YET.
JUST DON'T FORGET WHERE THE STAGE IS AT. I'LL JUST BE A SECOND...
HE GONNA RECORD YOU, AIN'T HE?
IT LOOKS THAT WAY...
WHOOO!
DOES THIS HAPPEN HERE A LOT?
HELL, NO! THAT'S THE SECOND TIME I MET THE MAN...
LORD...
BUT WHEN YOU BOYS HIT IT BIG, I'LL HAVE FOLKS KNOCKING THE WALLS DOWN TO GET IN.

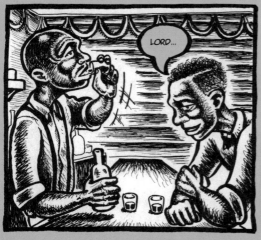

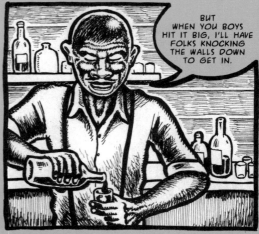

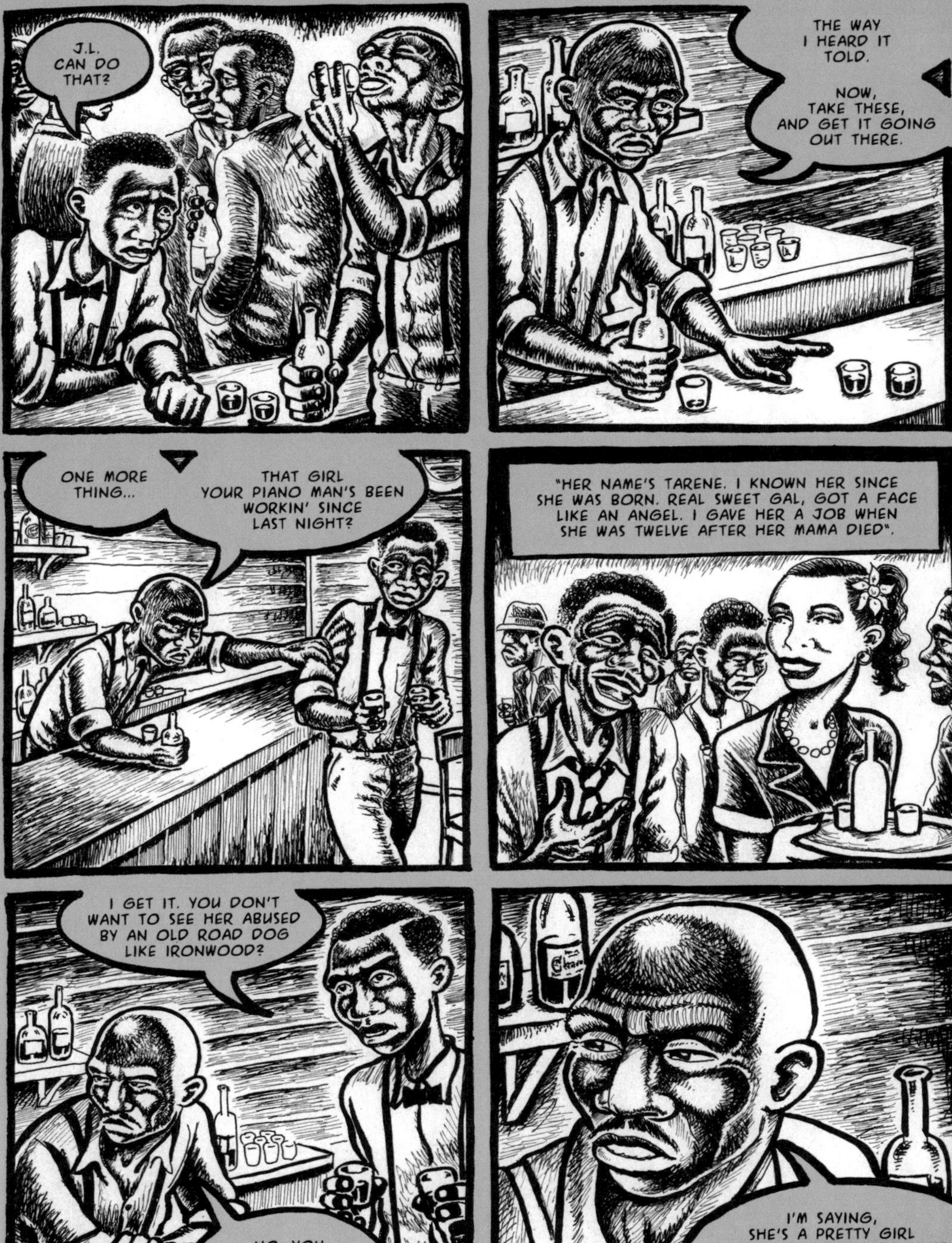
J.L. CAN DO THAT?
THE WAY I HEARD IT TOLD.
NOW, TAKE THESE, AND GET IT GOING OUT THERE.
ONE MORE THING...
THAT GIRL YOUR PIANO MAN'S BEEN WORKIN' SINCE LAST NIGHT?
"HER NAME'S TARENE. I KNOWN HER SINCE SHE WAS BORN. REAL SWEET GAL, GOT A FACE LIKE AN ANGEL. I GAVE HER A JOB WHEN SHE WAS TWELVE AFTER HER MAMA DIED".
I GET IT. YOU DON'T WANT TO SEE HER ABUSED BY AN OLD ROAD DOG LIKE IRONWOOD?
NO, YOU GOT IT ALL TWISTED 'ROUND.
I'M SAYING, SHE'S A PRETTY GIRL AND YOUR BOY THERE AIN'T THE FIRST ONE TO TAKE NOTICE O'THAT...

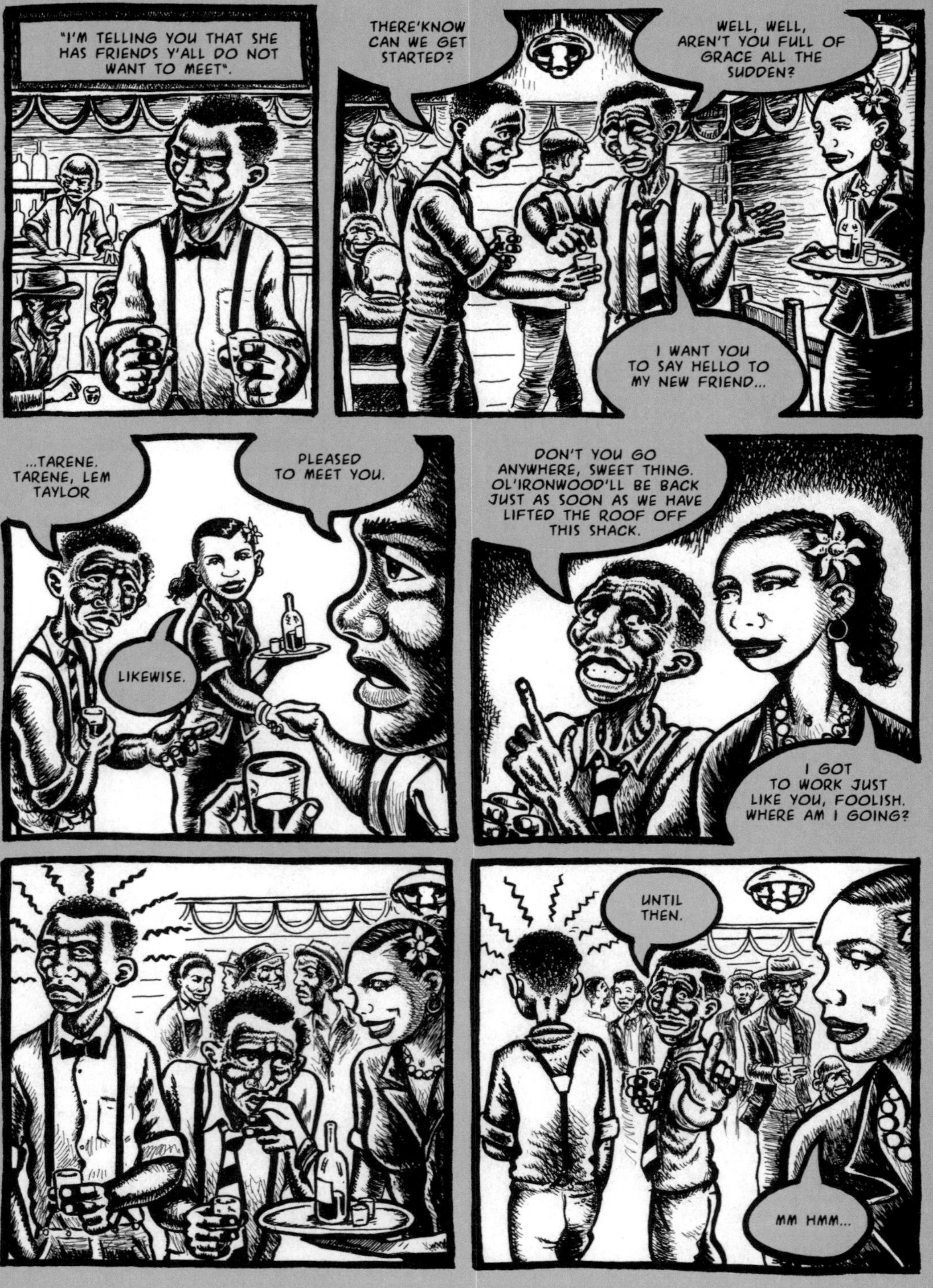
"I'M TELLING YOU THAT SHE HAS FRIENDS Y'ALL DO NOT WANT TO MEET".
THERE'KNOW CAN WE GET STARTED?
WELL, WELL, AREN'T YOU FULL OF GRACE ALL THE SUDDEN?
I WANT YOU TO SAY HELLO TO MY NEW FRIEND...
...TARENE. TARENE, LEM TAYLOR
PLEASED TO MEET YOU.
LIKEWISE.
DON'T YOU GO ANYWHERE, SWEET THING. OL'IRONWOOD'LL BE BACK JUST AS SOON AS WE HAVE LIFTED THE ROOF OFF THIS SHACK.
I GOT TO WORK JUST LIKE YOU, FOOLISH. WHERE AM I GOING?
UNTIL THEN.
MM HMM...

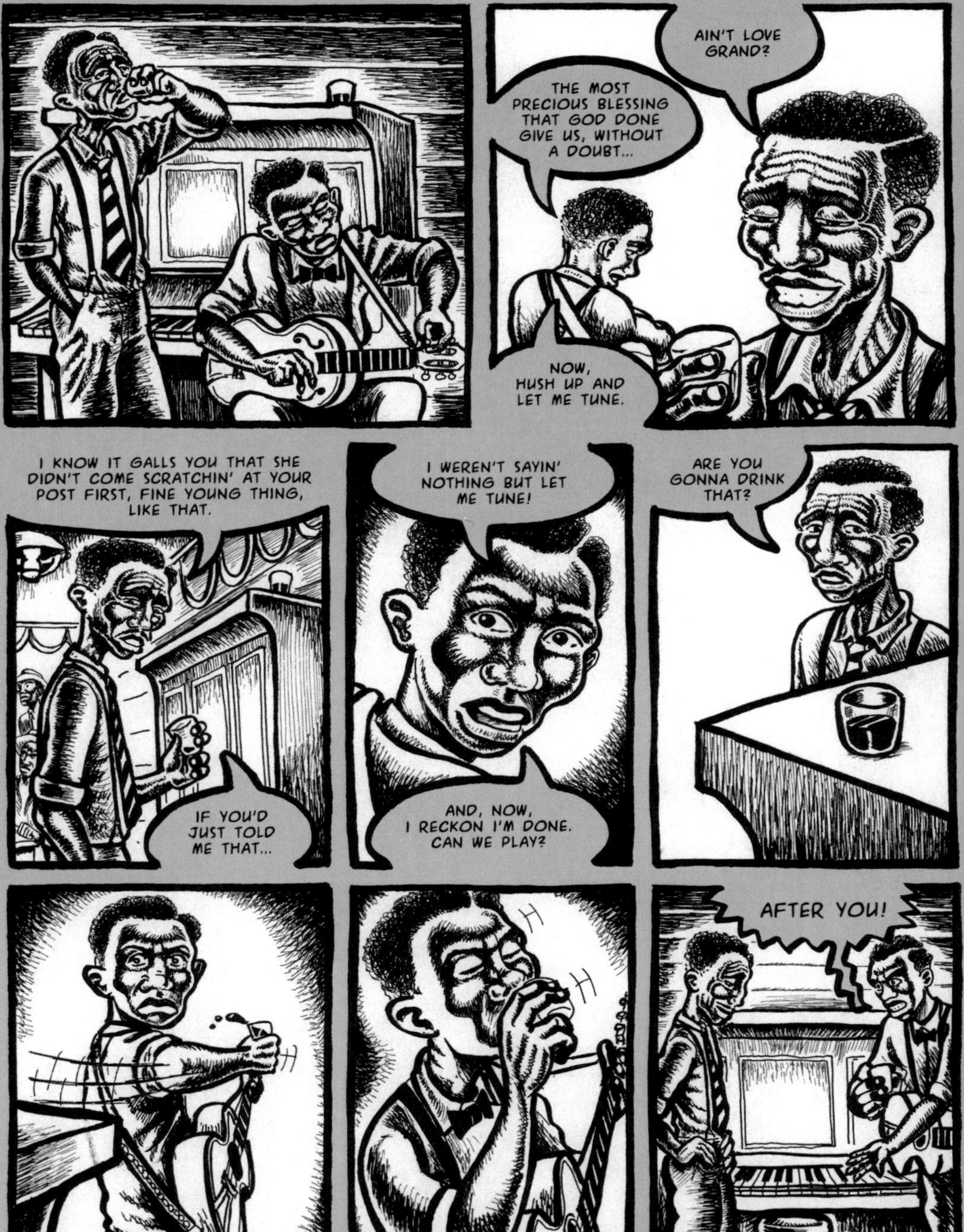
AIN'T LOVE GRAND?
THE MOST PRECIOUS BLESSING THAT GOD DONE GIVE US, WITHOUT A DOUBT...
NOW, HUSH UP AND LET ME TUNE.
I KNOW IT GALLS YOU THAT SHE DIDN'T COME SCRATCHIN' AT YOUR POST FIRST, FINE YOUNG THING, LIKE THAT.
IF YOU'D JUST TOLD ME THAT...
I WEREN'T SAYIN' NOTHING BUT LET ME TUNE!
AND, NOW, I RECKON I'M DONE. CAN WE PLAY?
ARE YOU GONNA DRINK THAT?
AFTER YOU!

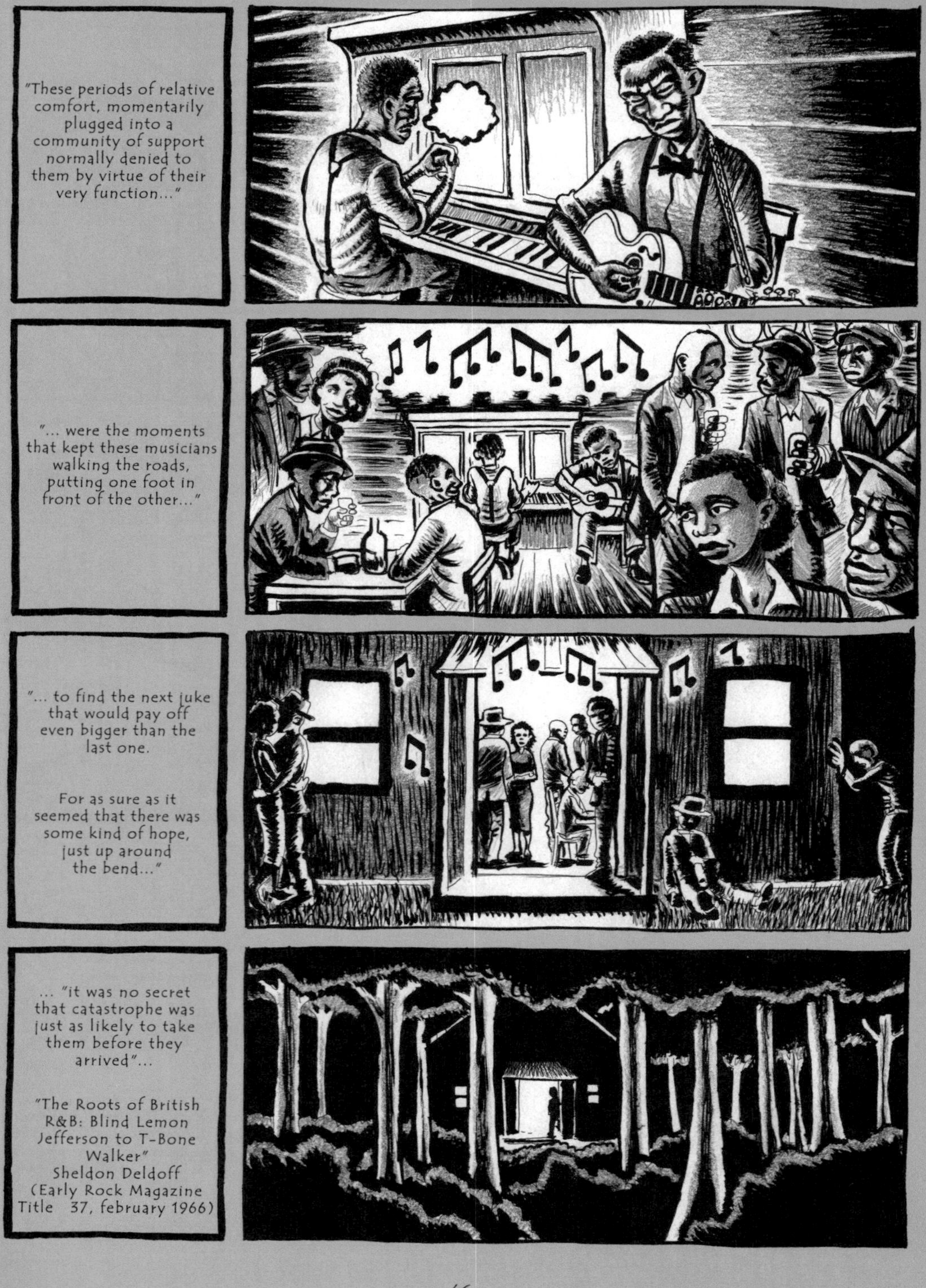
"These periods of relative comfort, momentarily plugged into a community of support normally denied to them by virtue of their very function..."
"... were the moments that kept these musicians walking the roads, putting one foot in front of the other..."
"... to find the next juke that would pay off even bigger than the last one.
For as sure as it seemed that there was some kind of hope, just up around the bend..."
... "it was no secret that catastrophe was just as likely to take them before they arrived"...
"The Roots of British R&B: Blind Lemon Jefferson to T-Bone Walker" Sheldon Deldoff (Early Rock Magazine Title 37, february 1966)

4

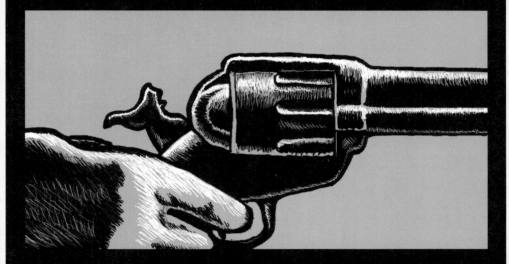

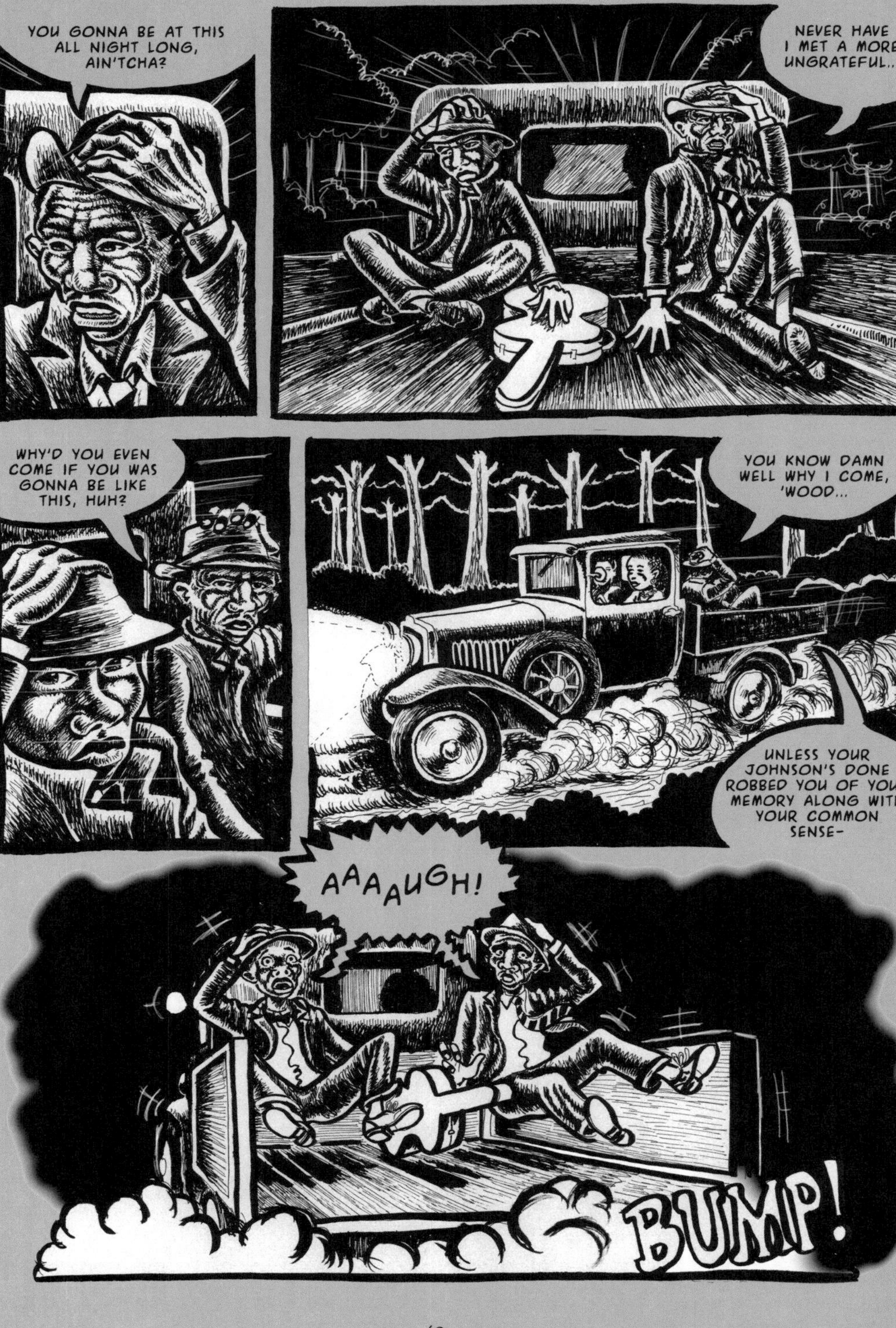
YOU GONNA BE AT THIS ALL NIGHT LONG, AIN'TCHA?
NEVER HAVE I MET A MORE UNGRATEFUL...
WHY'D YOU EVEN COME IF YOU WAS GONNA BE LIKE THIS, HUH?
YOU KNOW DAMN WELL WHY I COME, 'WOOD...
UNLESS YOUR JOHNSON'S DONE ROBBED YOU OF YOUR MEMORY ALONG WITH YOUR COMMON SENSE-
AAAAUGH!
BUMP!

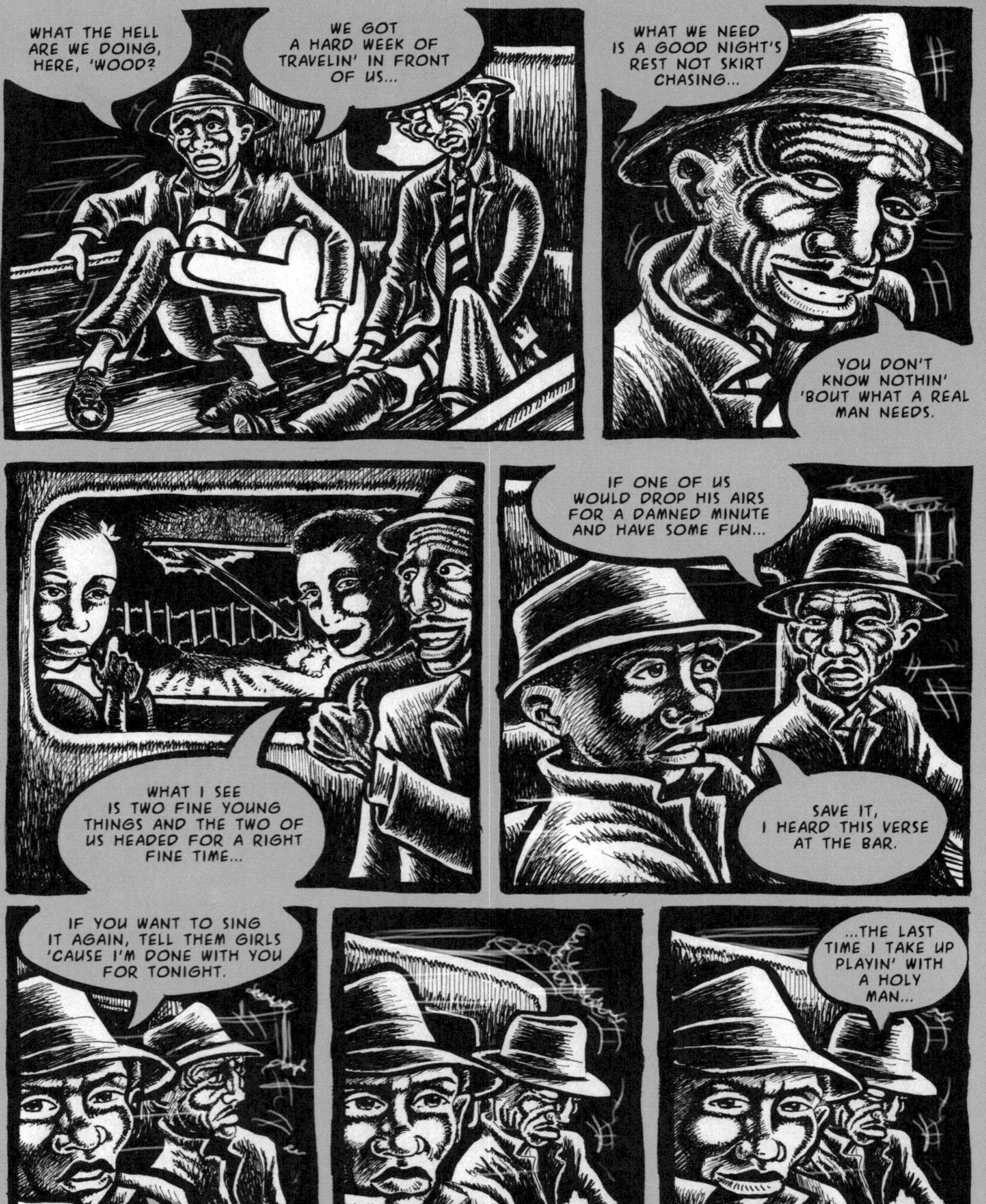

WHAT THE HELL ARE WE DOING, HERE, 'WOOD?
WE GOT A HARD WEEK OF TRAVELIN' IN FRONT OF US...
WHAT WE NEED IS A GOOD NIGHT'S REST NOT SKIRT CHASING...
YOU DON'T KNOW NOTHIN' 'BOUT WHAT A REAL MAN NEEDS.
WHAT I SEE IS TWO FINE YOUNG THINGS AND THE TWO OF US HEADED FOR A RIGHT FINE TIME...
IF ONE OF US WOULD DROP HIS AIRS FOR A DAMNED MINUTE AND HAVE SOME FUN...
SAVE IT, I HEARD THIS VERSE AT THE BAR.
IF YOU WANT TO SING IT AGAIN, TELL THEM GIRLS 'CAUSE I'M DONE WITH YOU FOR TONIGHT.
NOW LEAVE ME BE.
...THE LAST TIME I TAKE UP PLAYIN' WITH A HOLY MAN...

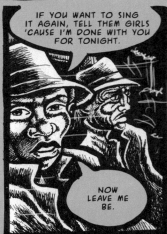

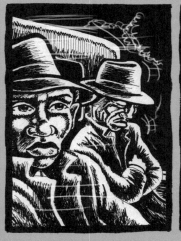

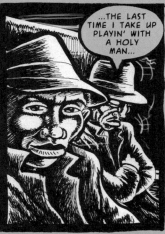

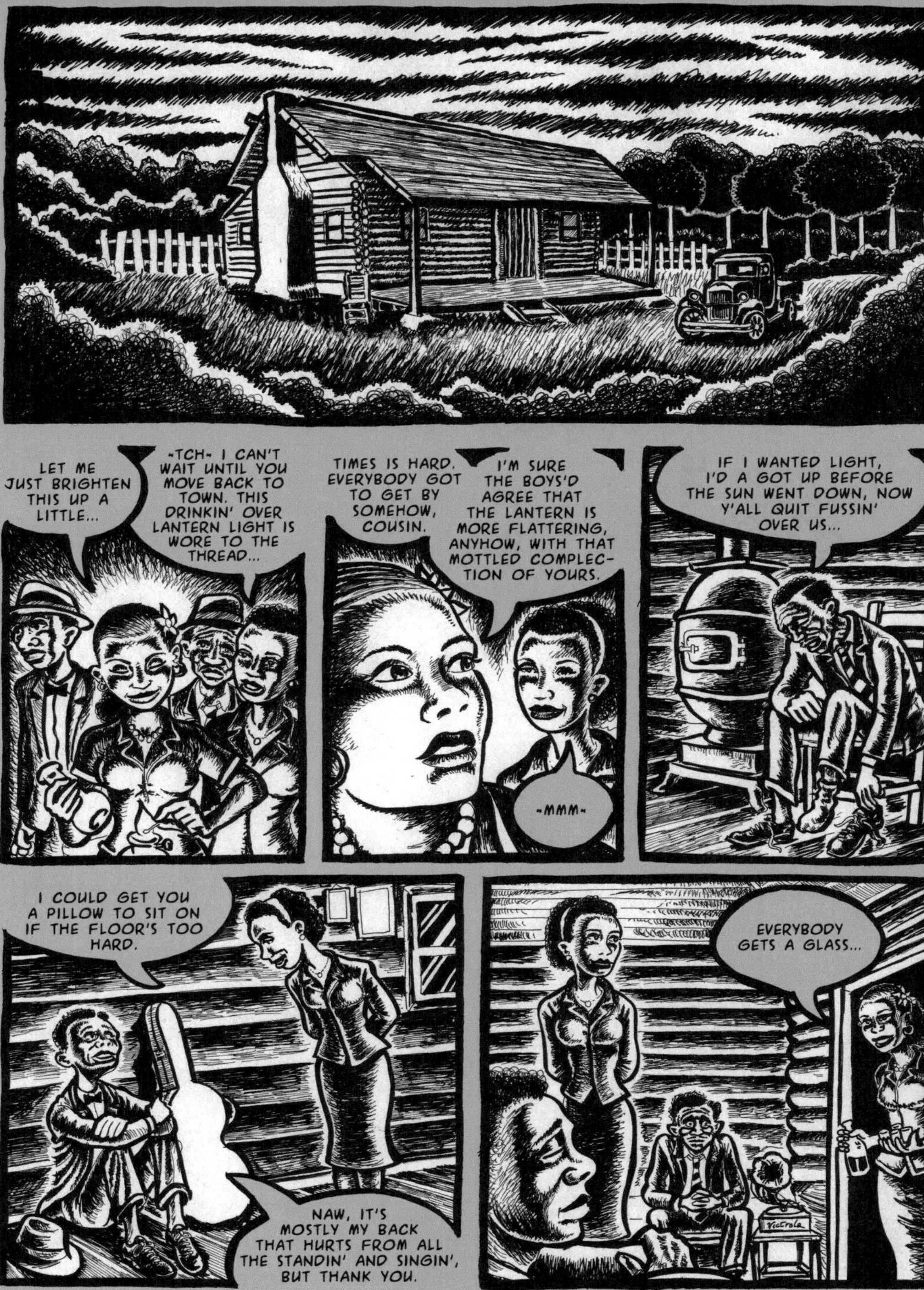
LET ME JUST BRIGHTEN THIS UP A LITTLE...
~TCH~ I CAN'T WAIT UNTIL YOU MOVE BACK TO TOWN. THIS DRINKIN' OVER LANTERN LIGHT IS WORE TO THE THREAD...
TIMES IS HARD. EVERYBODY GOT TO GET BY SOMEHOW, COUSIN.
I'M SURE THE BOYS'D AGREE THAT THE LANTERN IS MORE FLATTERING, ANYHOW, WITH THAT MOTTLED COMPLECTION OF YOURS.
~MMM~
IF I WANTED LIGHT, I'D A GOT UP BEFORE THE SUN WENT DOWN, NOW Y'ALL QUIT FUSSIN' OVER US...
I COULD GET YOU A PILLOW TO SIT ON IF THE FLOOR'S TOO HARD.
NAW, IT'S MOSTLY MY BACK THAT HURTS FROM ALL THE STANDIN' AND SINGIN', BUT THANK YOU.
EVERYBODY GETS A GLASS...
Victrola

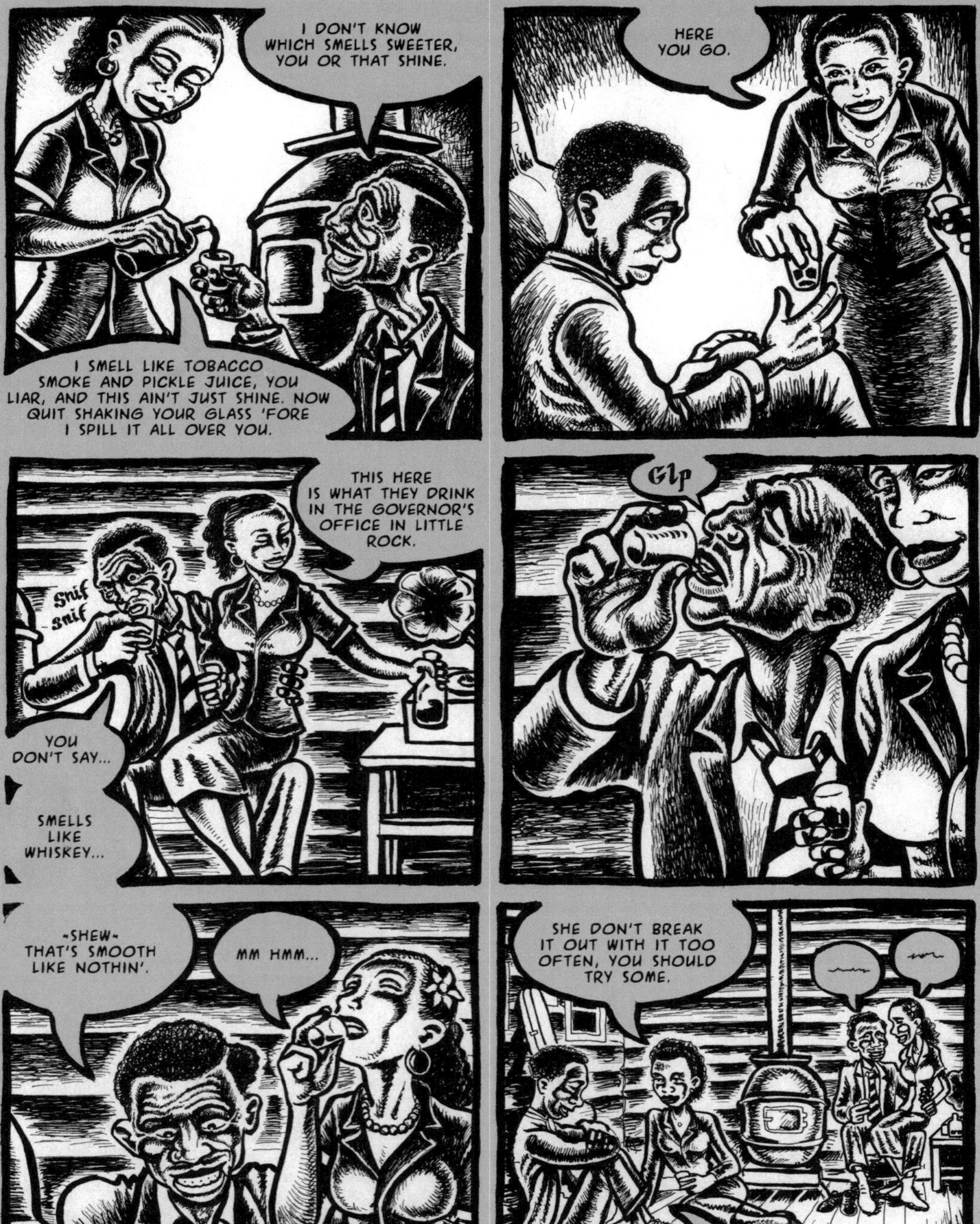
I DON'T KNOW WHICH SMELLS SWEETER, YOU OR THAT SHINE.
I SMELL LIKE TOBACCO SMOKE AND PICKLE JUICE, YOU LIAR, AND THIS AIN'T JUST SHINE. NOW QUIT SHAKING YOUR GLASS 'FORE I SPILL IT ALL OVER YOU.
HERE YOU GO.
THIS HERE IS WHAT THEY DRINK IN THE GOVERNOR'S OFFICE IN LITTLE ROCK.
Snif snif
YOU DON'T SAY...
SMELLS LIKE WHISKEY...
Glp
~SHEW~ THAT'S SMOOTH LIKE NOTHIN'.
MM HMM...
SHE DON'T BREAK IT OUT WITH IT TOO OFTEN, YOU SHOULD TRY SOME.
IT'S ALL I CAN DO TO KEEP MY EYES OPEN. I DON'T EVEN KNOW IF I CAN LIFT MY ARM.

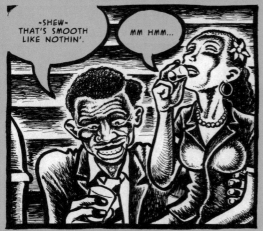

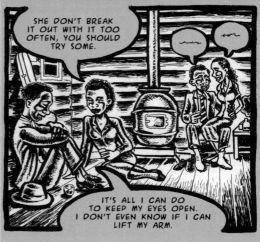

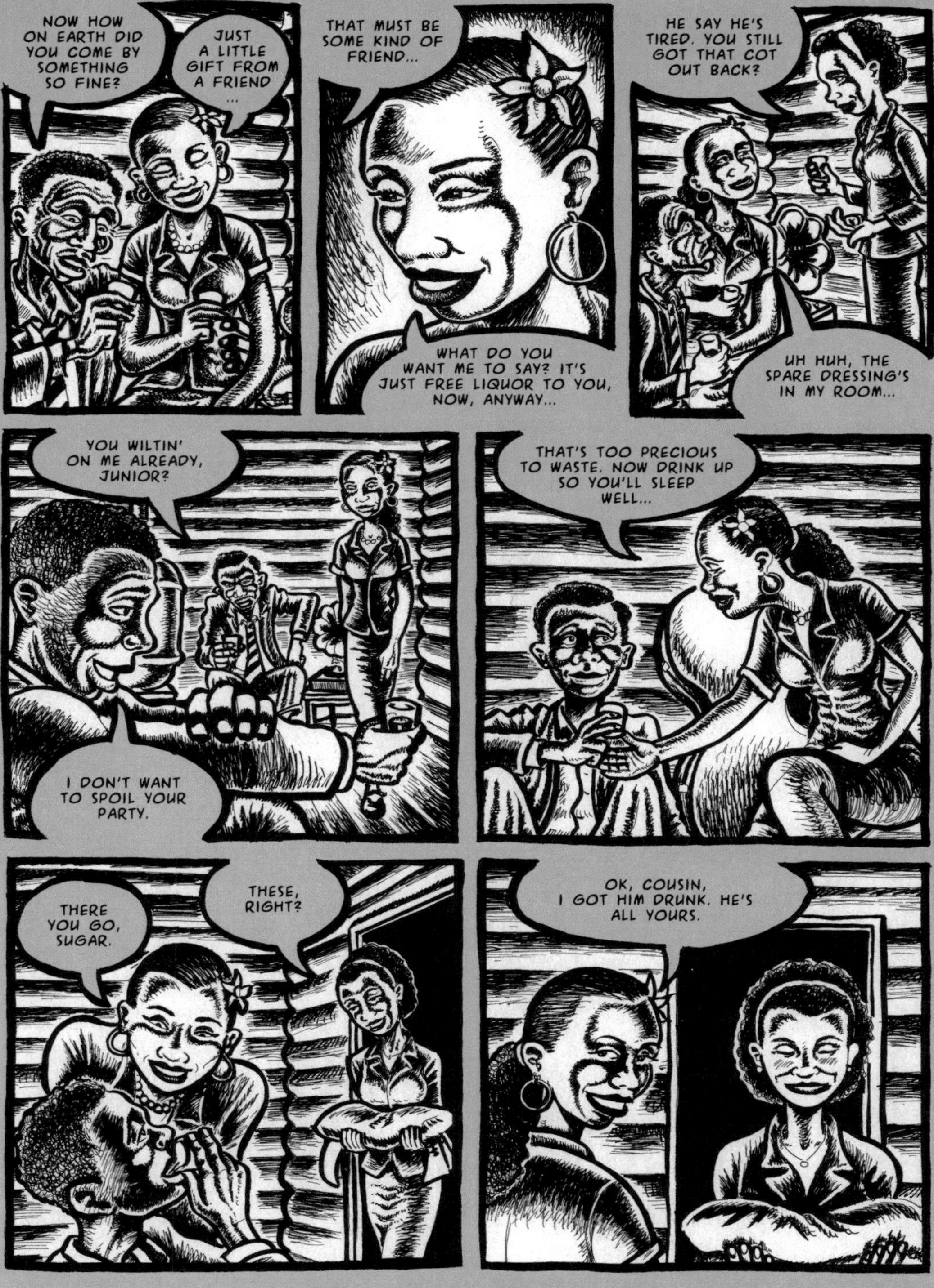
NOW HOW ON EARTH DID YOU COME BY SOMETHING SO FINE?
JUST A LITTLE GIFT FROM A FRIEND ...
THAT MUST BE SOME KIND OF FRIEND...
WHAT DO YOU WANT ME TO SAY? IT'S JUST FREE LIQUOR TO YOU, NOW, ANYWAY...
HE SAY HE'S TIRED. YOU STILL GOT THAT COT OUT BACK?
UH HUH, THE SPARE DRESSING'S IN MY ROOM...
YOU WILTIN' ON ME ALREADY, JUNIOR?
I DON'T WANT TO SPOIL YOUR PARTY.
THAT'S TOO PRECIOUS TO WASTE. NOW DRINK UP SO YOU'LL SLEEP WELL...
THERE YOU GO, SUGAR.
THESE, RIGHT?
OK, COUSIN, I GOT HIM DRUNK. HE'S ALL YOURS.

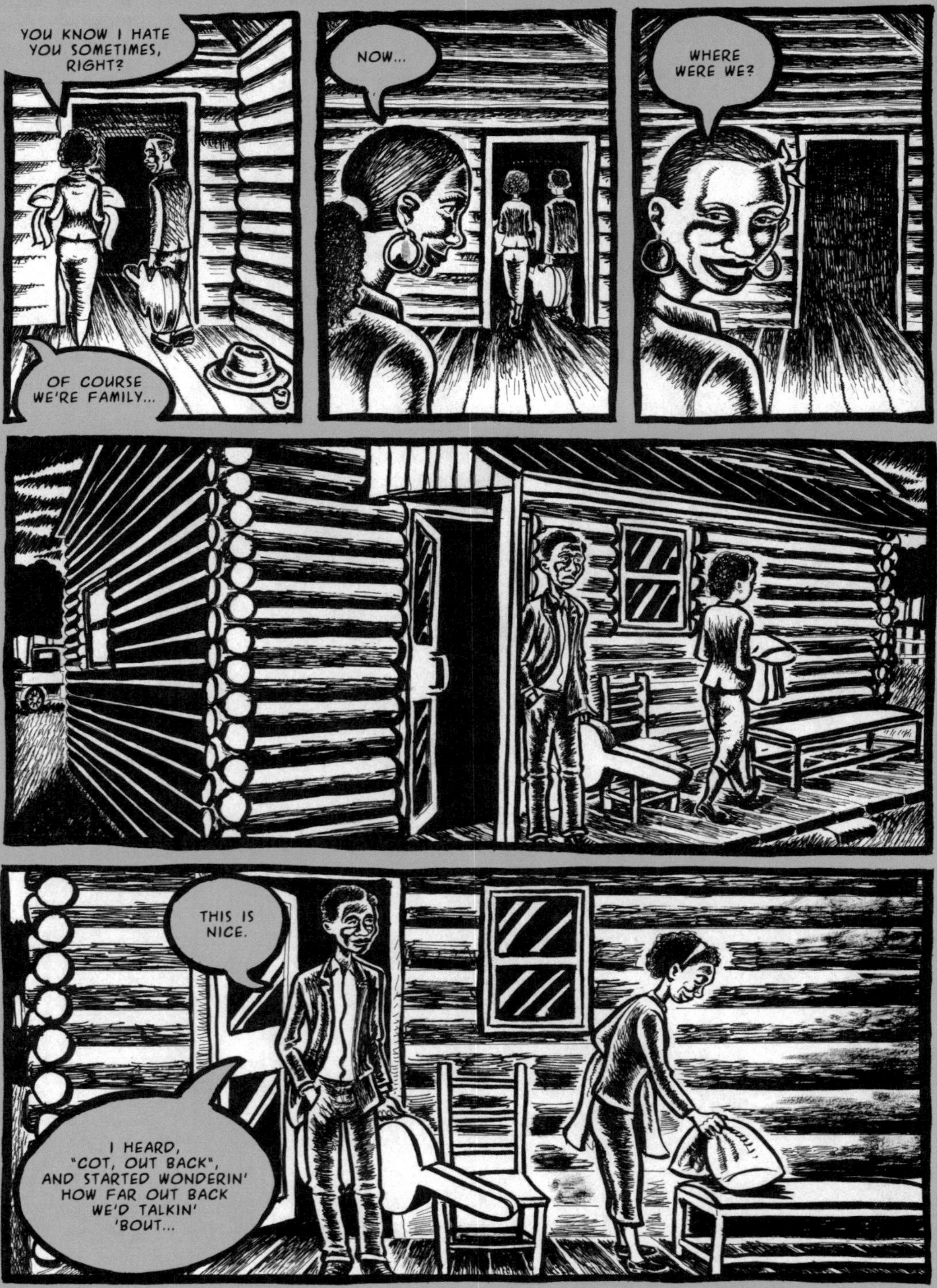
YOU KNOW I HATE YOU SOMETIMES, RIGHT?
OF COURSE WE'RE FAMILY...
NOW...
WHERE WERE WE?
THIS IS NICE.
I HEARD, "COT, OUT BACK", AND STARTED WONDERIN' HOW FAR OUT BACK WE'D TALKIN' 'BOUT...

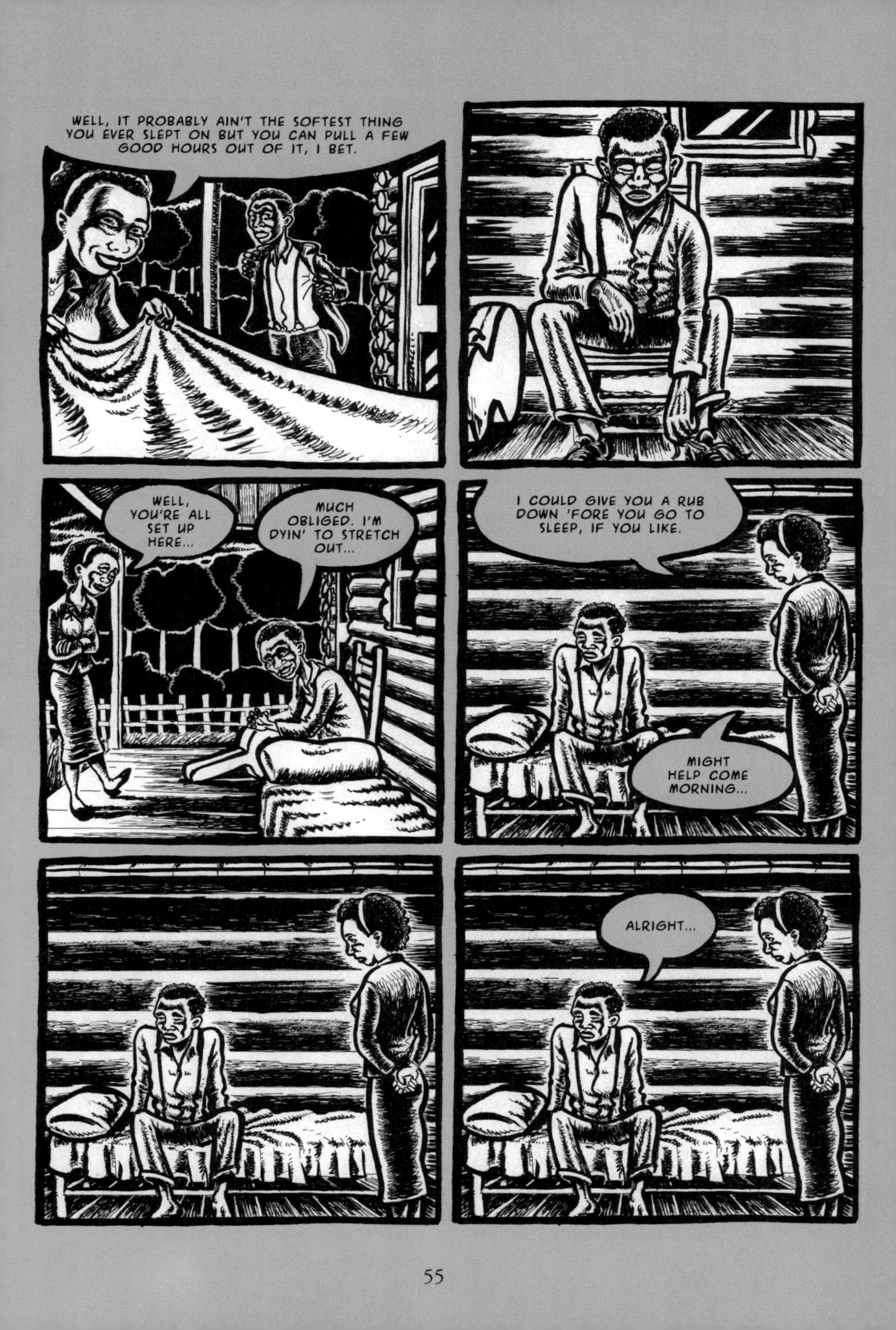
WELL, IT PROBABLY AIN'T THE SOFTEST THING YOU EVER SLEPT ON BUT YOU CAN PULL A FEW GOOD HOURS OUT OF IT, I BET.
WELL, YOU'RE ALL SET UP HERE...
MUCH OBLIGED. I'M DYIN' TO STRETCH OUT...
I COULD GIVE YOU A RUB DOWN 'FORE YOU GO TO SLEEP, IF YOU LIKE.
MIGHT HELP COME MORNING...
ALRIGHT...

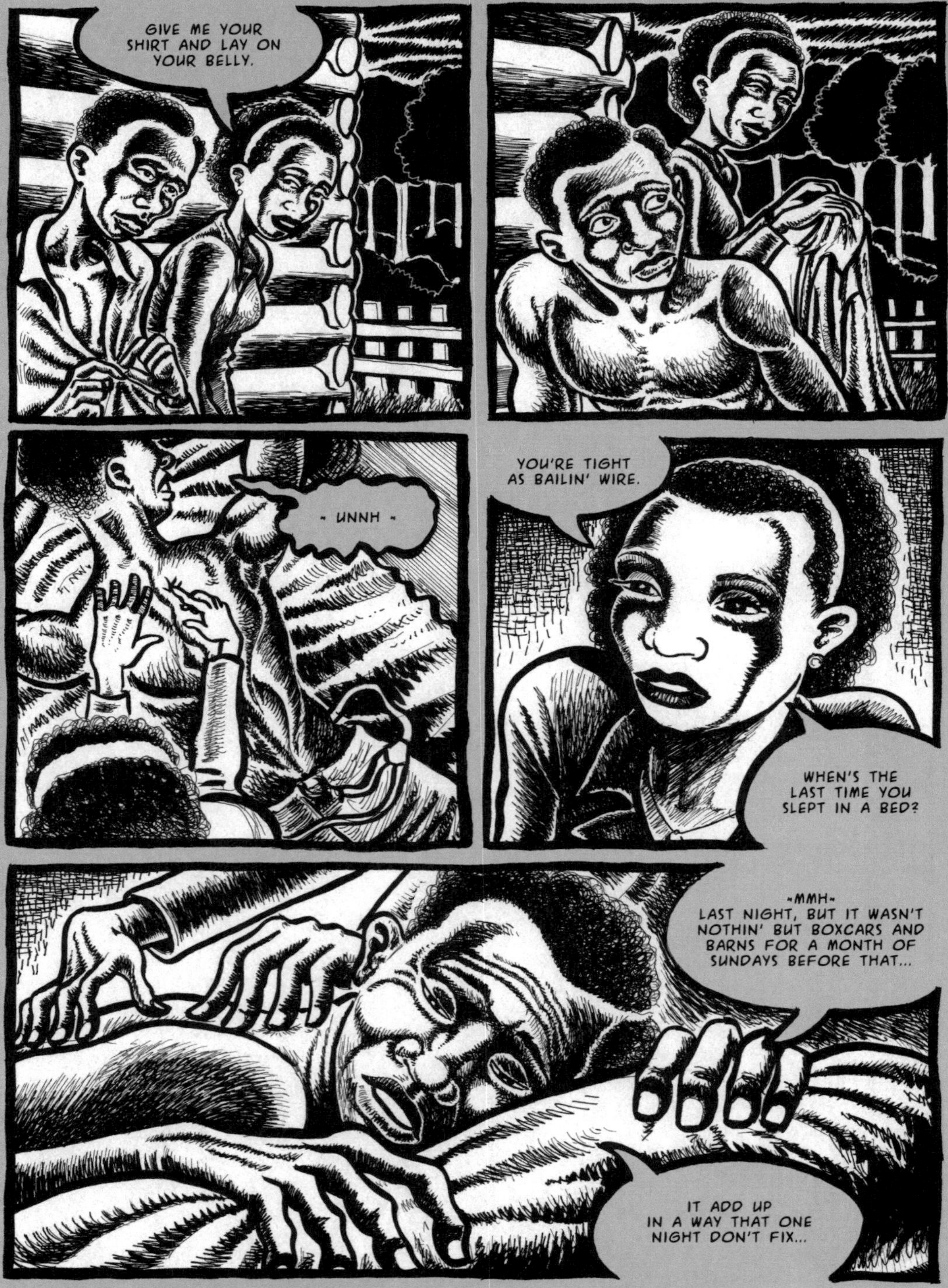
GIVE ME YOUR SHIRT AND LAY ON YOUR BELLY.
~ UNNH ~
YOU'RE TIGHT AS BAILIN' WIRE.
WHEN'S THE LAST TIME YOU SLEPT IN A BED?
~MMH~
LAST NIGHT, BUT IT WASN'T NOTHIN' BUT BOXCARS AND BARNS FOR A MONTH OF SUNDAYS BEFORE THAT...
IT ADD UP IN A WAY THAT ONE NIGHT DON'T FIX...

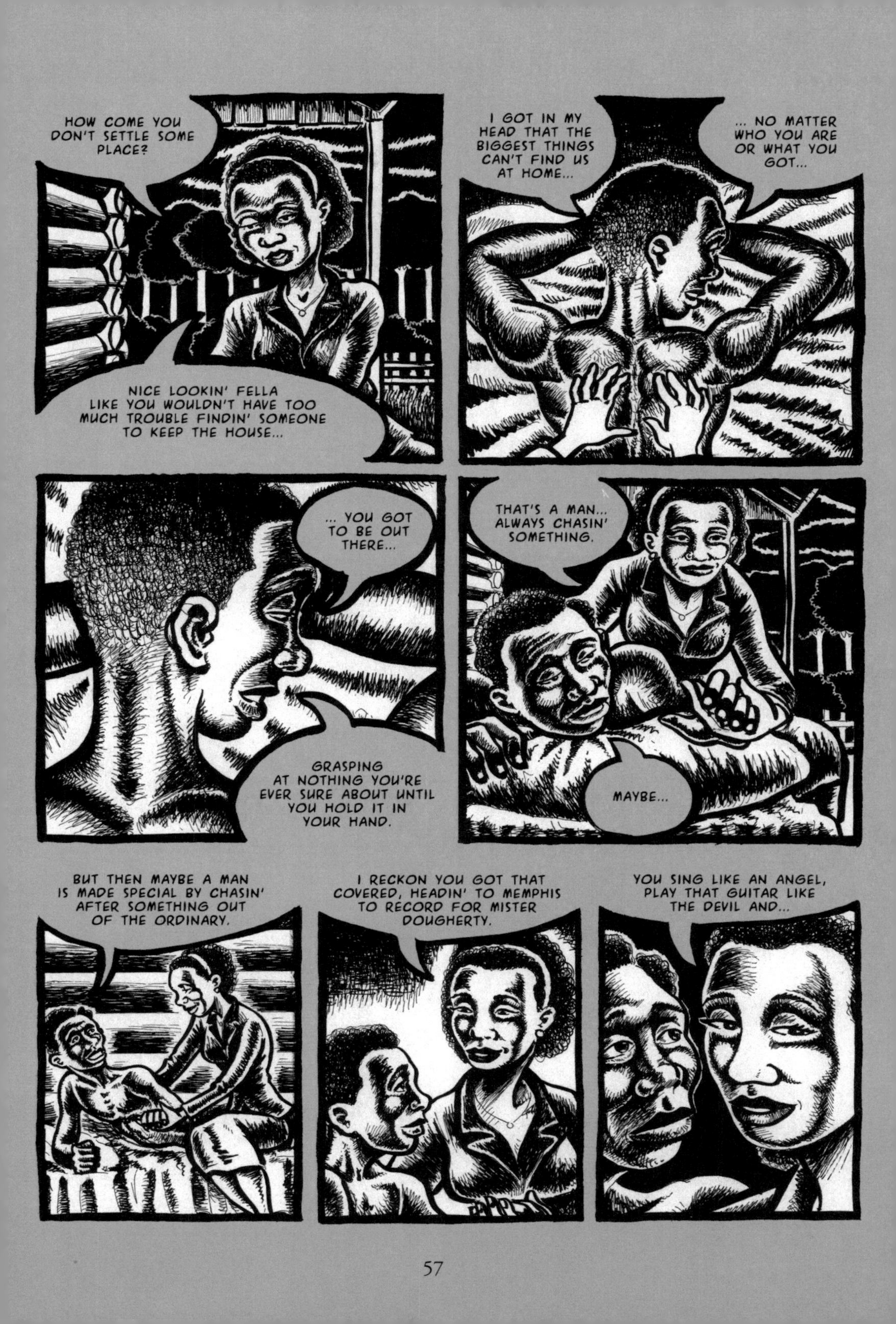
HOW COME YOU DON'T SETTLE SOME PLACE?
NICE LOOKIN' FELLA LIKE YOU WOULDN'T HAVE TOO MUCH TROUBLE FINDIN' SOMEONE TO KEEP THE HOUSE...
I GOT IN MY HEAD THAT THE BIGGEST THINGS CAN'T FIND US AT HOME...
... NO MATTER WHO YOU ARE OR WHAT YOU GOT...
... YOU GOT TO BE OUT THERE...
GRASPING AT NOTHING YOU'RE EVER SURE ABOUT UNTIL YOU HOLD IT IN YOUR HAND.
THAT'S A MAN... ALWAYS CHASIN' SOMETHING.
MAYBE...
BUT THEN MAYBE A MAN IS MADE SPECIAL BY CHASIN' AFTER SOMETHING OUT OF THE ORDINARY.
I RECKON YOU GOT THAT COVERED, HEADIN' TO MEMPHIS TO RECORD FOR MISTER DOUGHERTY.
YOU SING LIKE AN ANGEL, PLAY THAT GUITAR LIKE THE DEVIL AND...

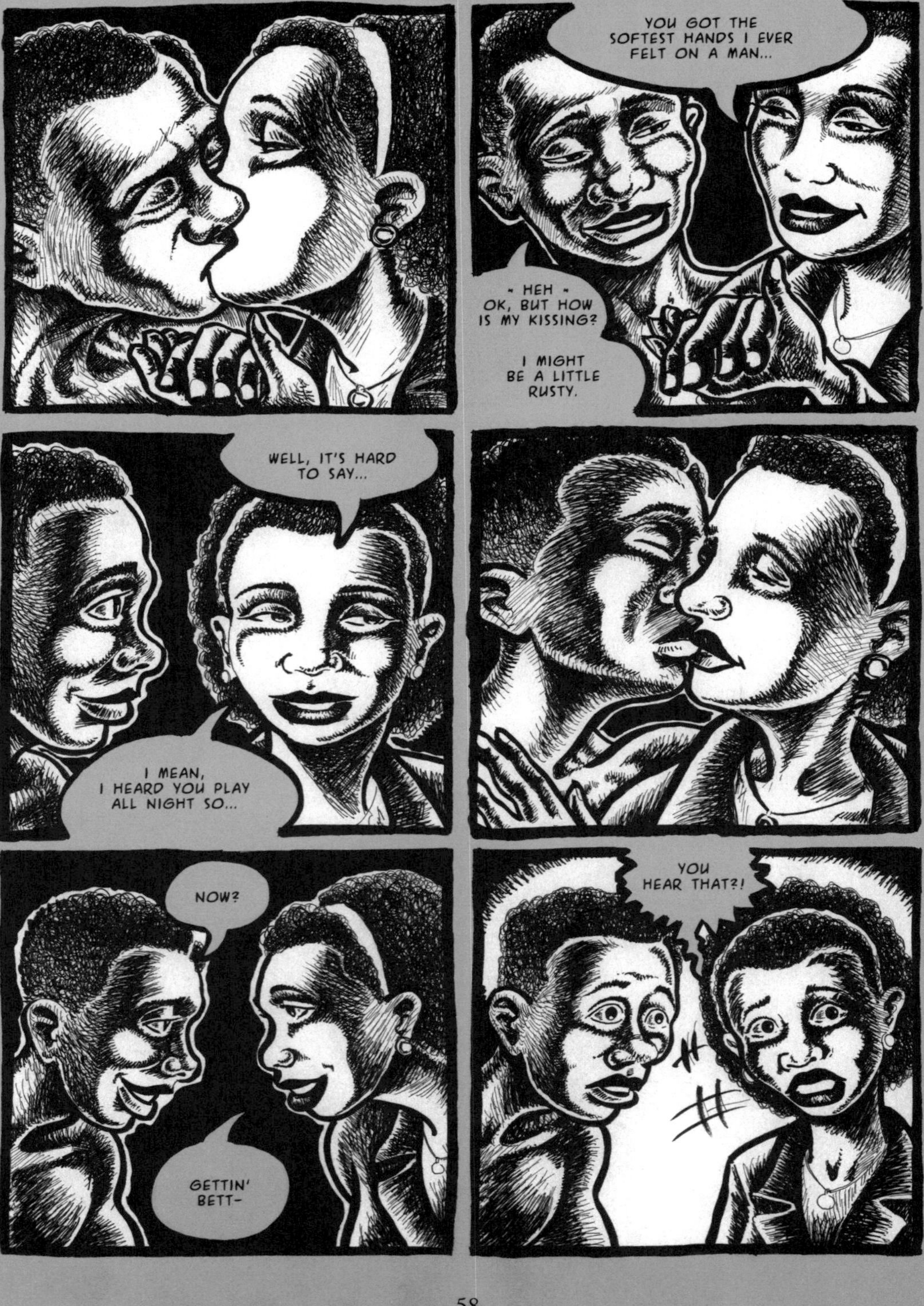
YOU GOT THE SOFTEST HANDS I EVER FELT ON A MAN...
• HEH • OK, BUT HOW IS MY KISSING?
I MIGHT BE A LITTLE RUSTY.
WELL, IT'S HARD TO SAY...
I MEAN, I HEARD YOU PLAY ALL NIGHT SO...
NOW?
GETTIN' BETT-
YOU HEAR THAT?!

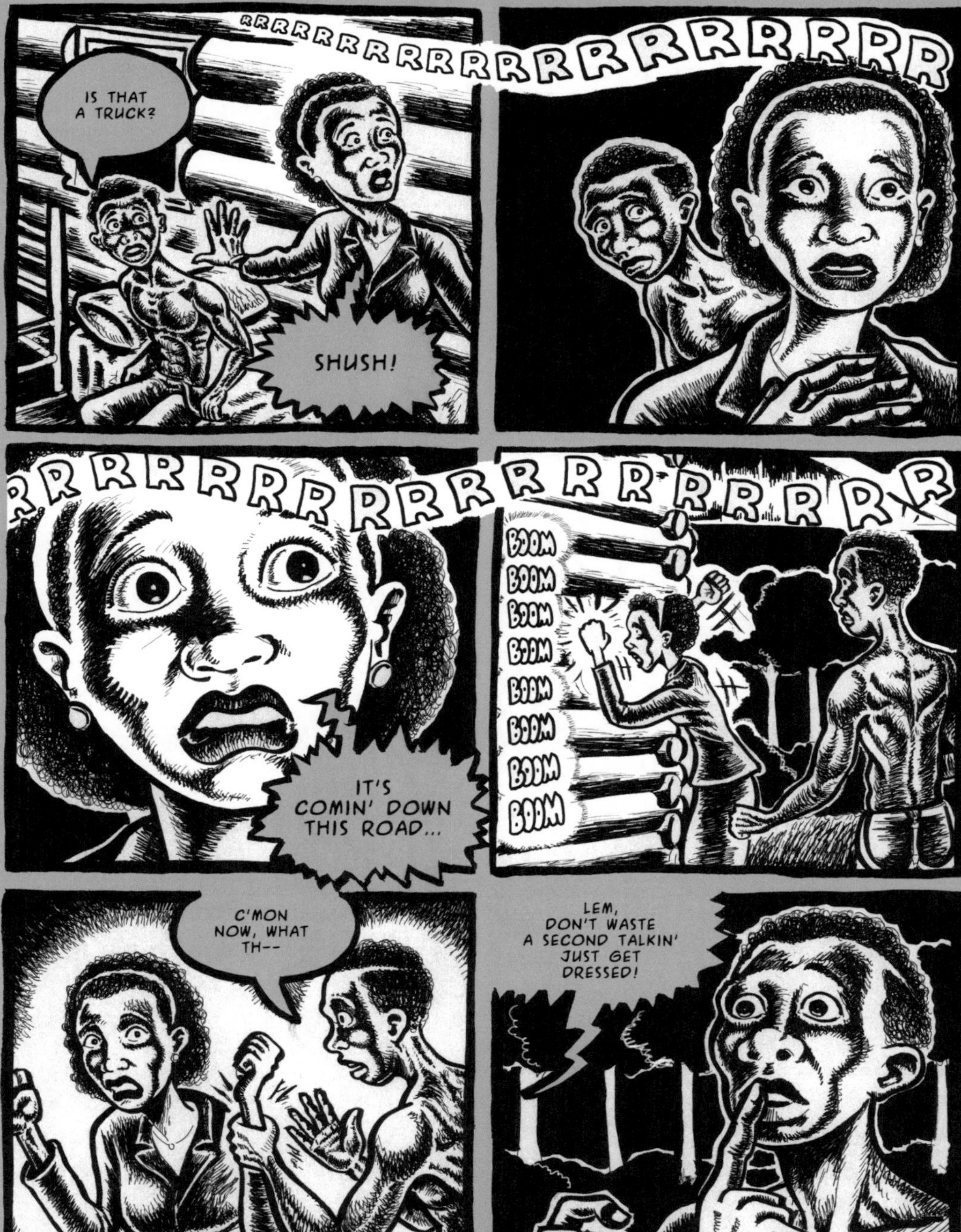
RRRRRRRRRRRRRRRRRRRR
IS THAT A TRUCK?
SHUSH!
RRRRRRRRRRRRRRRRRRR
IT'S COMIN' DOWN THIS ROAD...
BOOM BOOM BOOM BOOM BOOM BOOM BOOM BOOM
C'MON NOW, WHAT TH--
LEM, DON'T WASTE A SECOND TALKIN' JUST GET DRESSED!

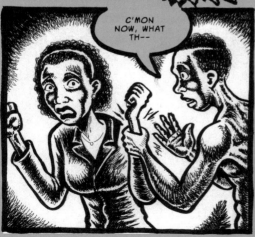

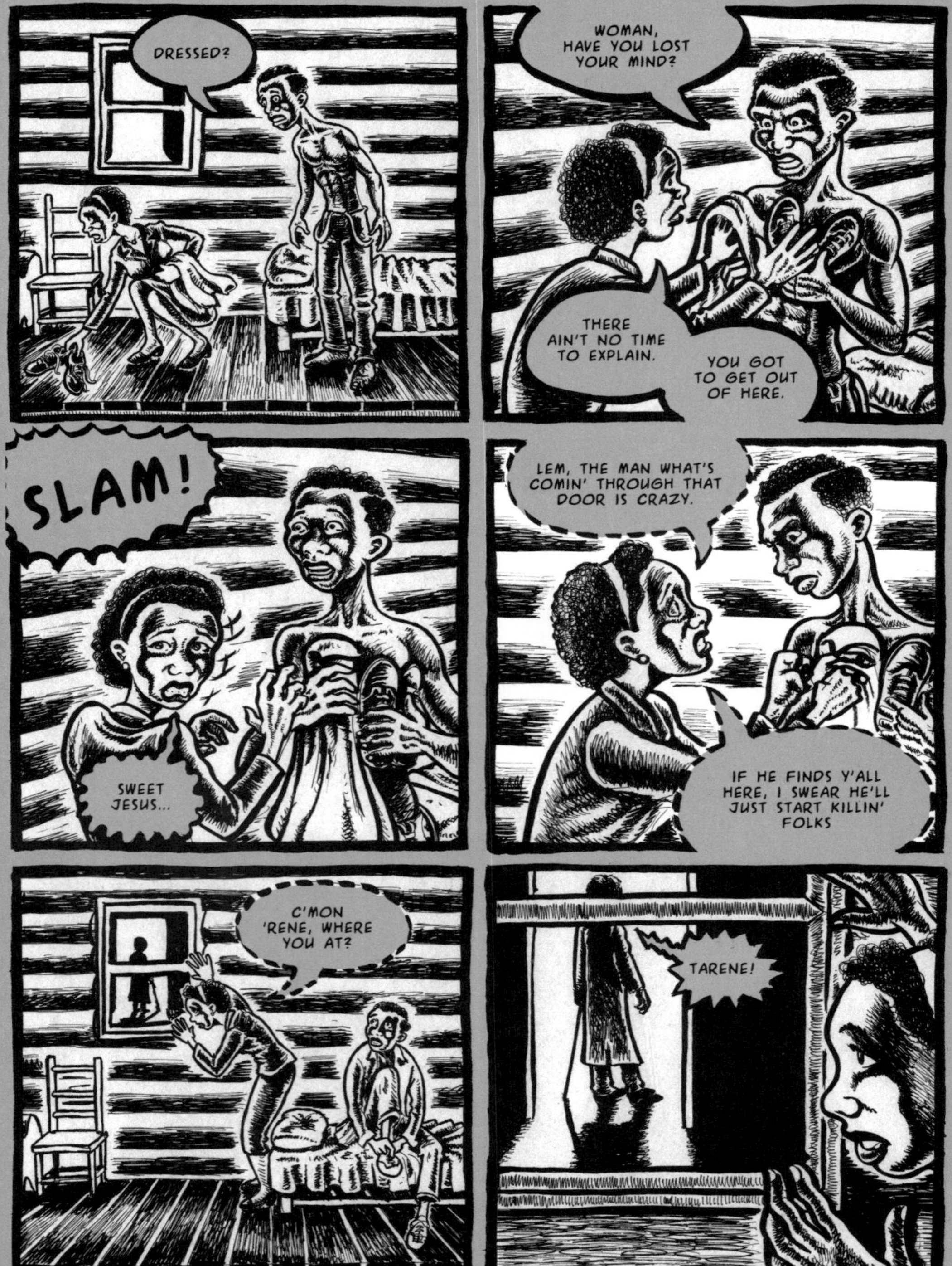
DRESSED?
WOMAN, HAVE YOU LOST YOUR MIND?
THERE AIN'T NO TIME TO EXPLAIN.
YOU GOT TO GET OUT OF HERE.
SLAM!
SWEET JESUS...
LEM, THE MAN WHAT'S COMIN' THROUGH THAT DOOR IS CRAZY.
IF HE FINDS Y'ALL HERE, I SWEAR HE'LL JUST START KILLIN' FOLKS
C'MON 'RENE, WHERE YOU AT?
TARENE!

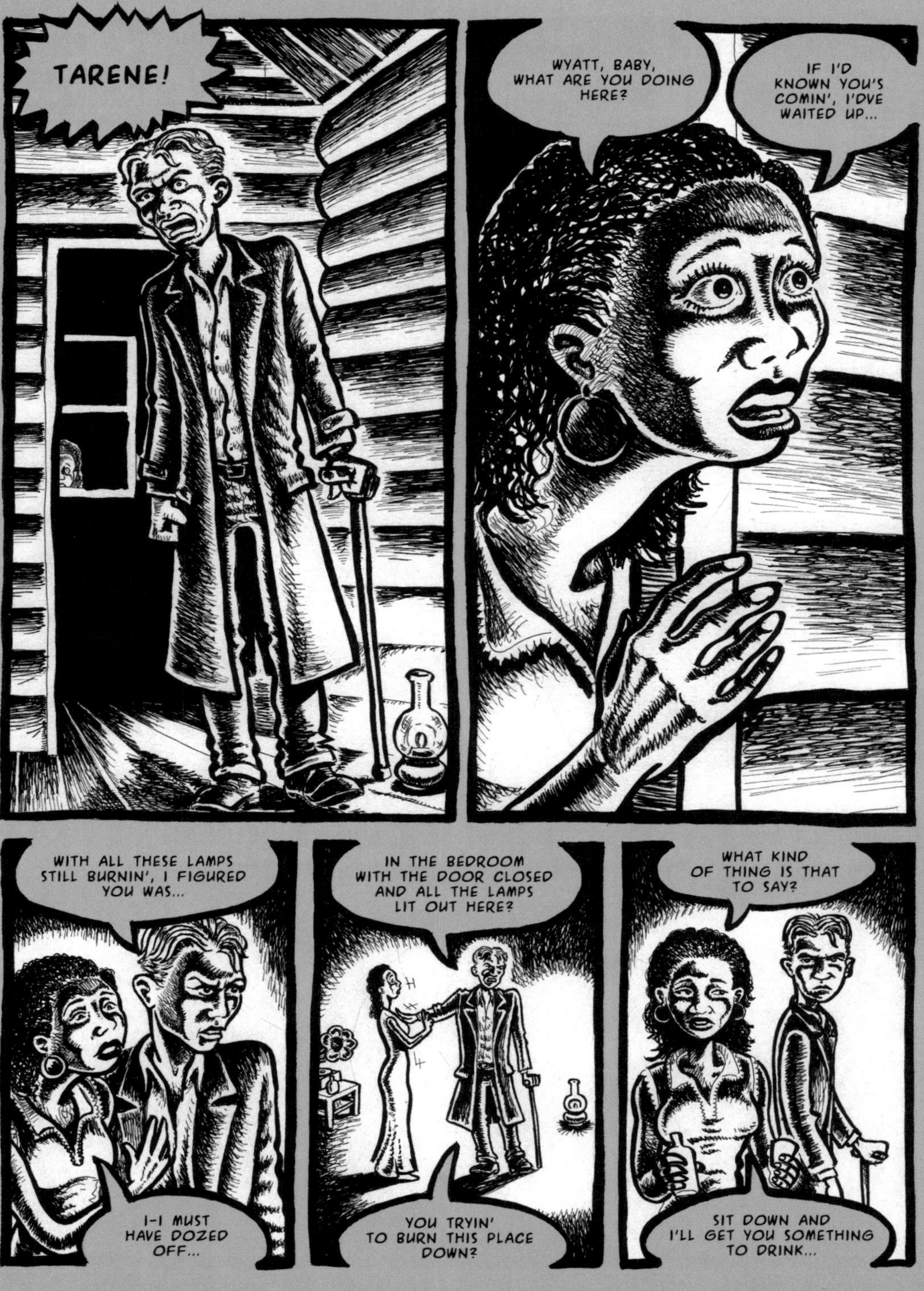
TARENE!
WYATT, BABY, WHAT ARE YOU DOING HERE?
IF I'D KNOWN YOU'S COMIN', I'DVE WAITED UP...
WITH ALL THESE LAMPS STILL BURNIN', I FIGURED YOU WAS...
I-I MUST HAVE DOZED OFF...
IN THE BEDROOM WITH THE DOOR CLOSED AND ALL THE LAMPS LIT OUT HERE?
YOU TRYIN' TO BURN THIS PLACE DOWN?
WHAT KIND OF THING IS THAT TO SAY?
SIT DOWN AND I'LL GET YOU SOMETHING TO DRINK...

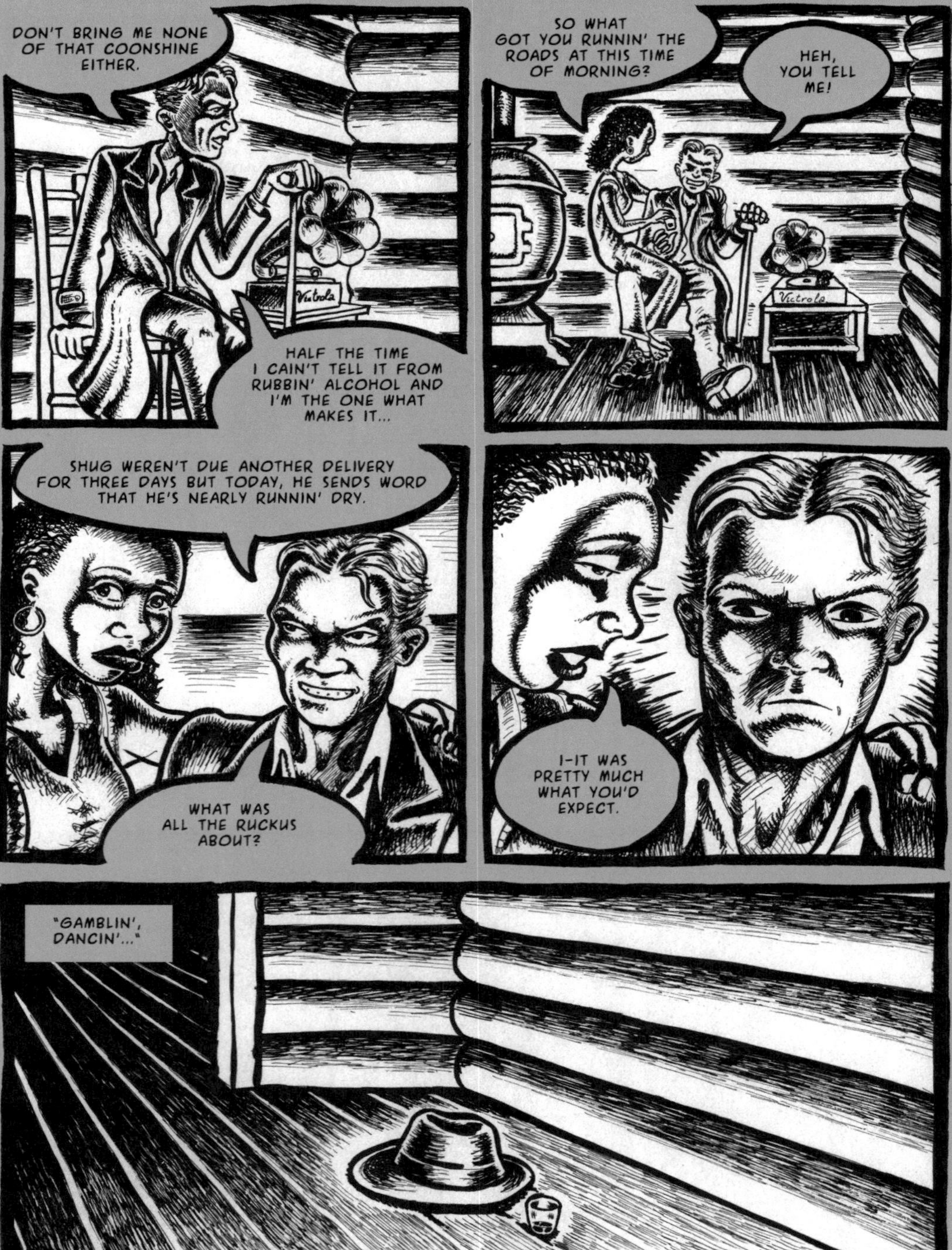
DON'T BRING ME NONE OF THAT COONSHINE EITHER.
Victrola
HALF THE TIME I CAIN'T TELL IT FROM RUBBIN' ALCOHOL AND I'M THE ONE WHAT MAKES IT...
SO WHAT GOT YOU RUNNIN' THE ROADS AT THIS TIME OF MORNING?
HEH, YOU TELL ME!
Victrola
SHUG WEREN'T DUE ANOTHER DELIVERY FOR THREE DAYS BUT TODAY, HE SENDS WORD THAT HE'S NEARLY RUNNIN' DRY.
WHAT WAS ALL THE RUCKUS ABOUT?
I-IT WAS PRETTY MUCH WHAT YOU'D EXPECT.
"GAMBLIN', DANCIN'..."

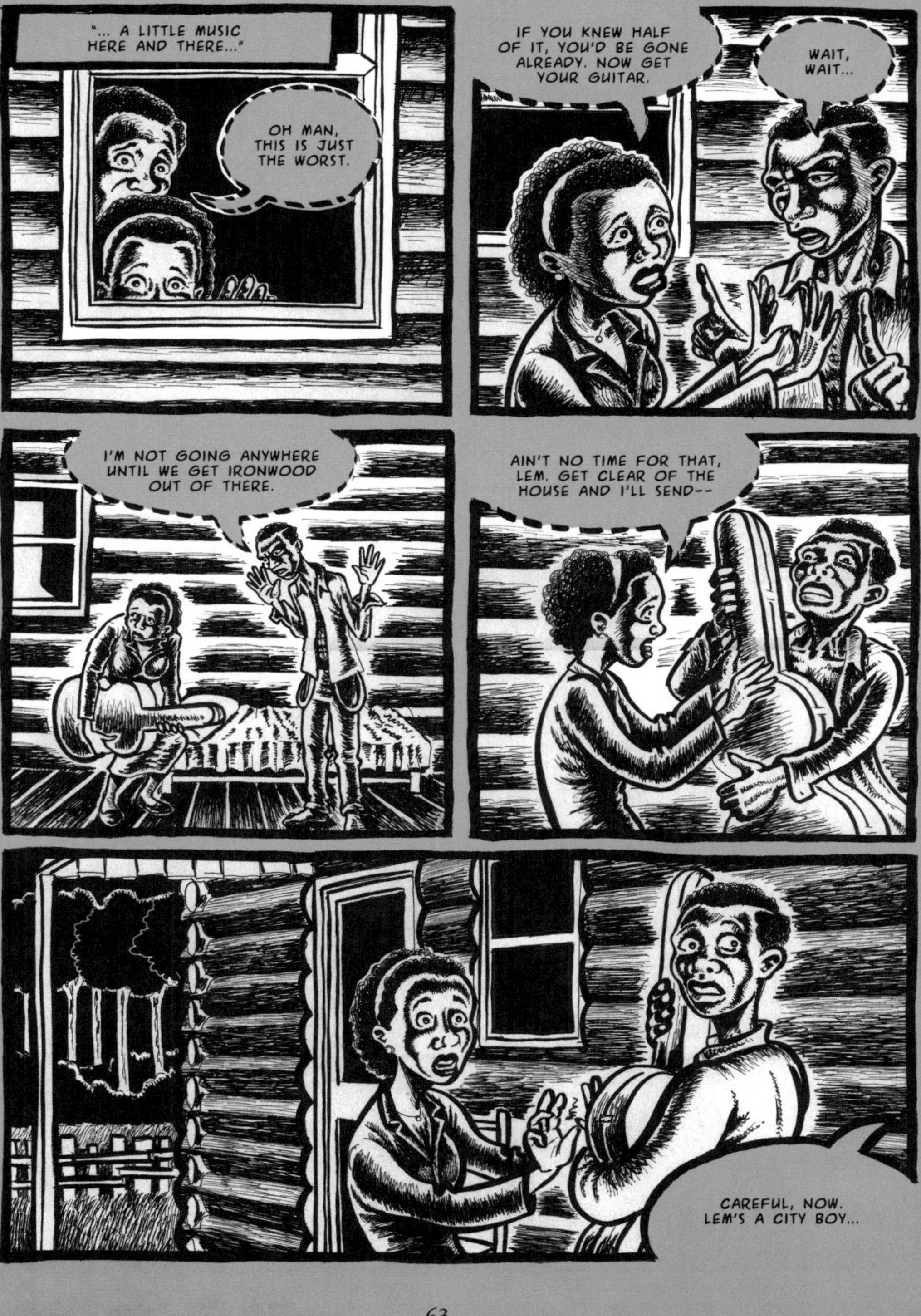
"... A LITTLE MUSIC HERE AND THERE..."
OH MAN, THIS IS JUST THE WORST.
IF YOU KNEW HALF OF IT, YOU'D BE GONE ALREADY. NOW GET YOUR GUITAR.
WAIT, WAIT...
I'M NOT GOING ANYWHERE UNTIL WE GET IRONWOOD OUT OF THERE.
AIN'T NO TIME FOR THAT, LEM. GET CLEAR OF THE HOUSE AND I'LL SEND--
CAREFUL, NOW. LEM'S A CITY BOY...

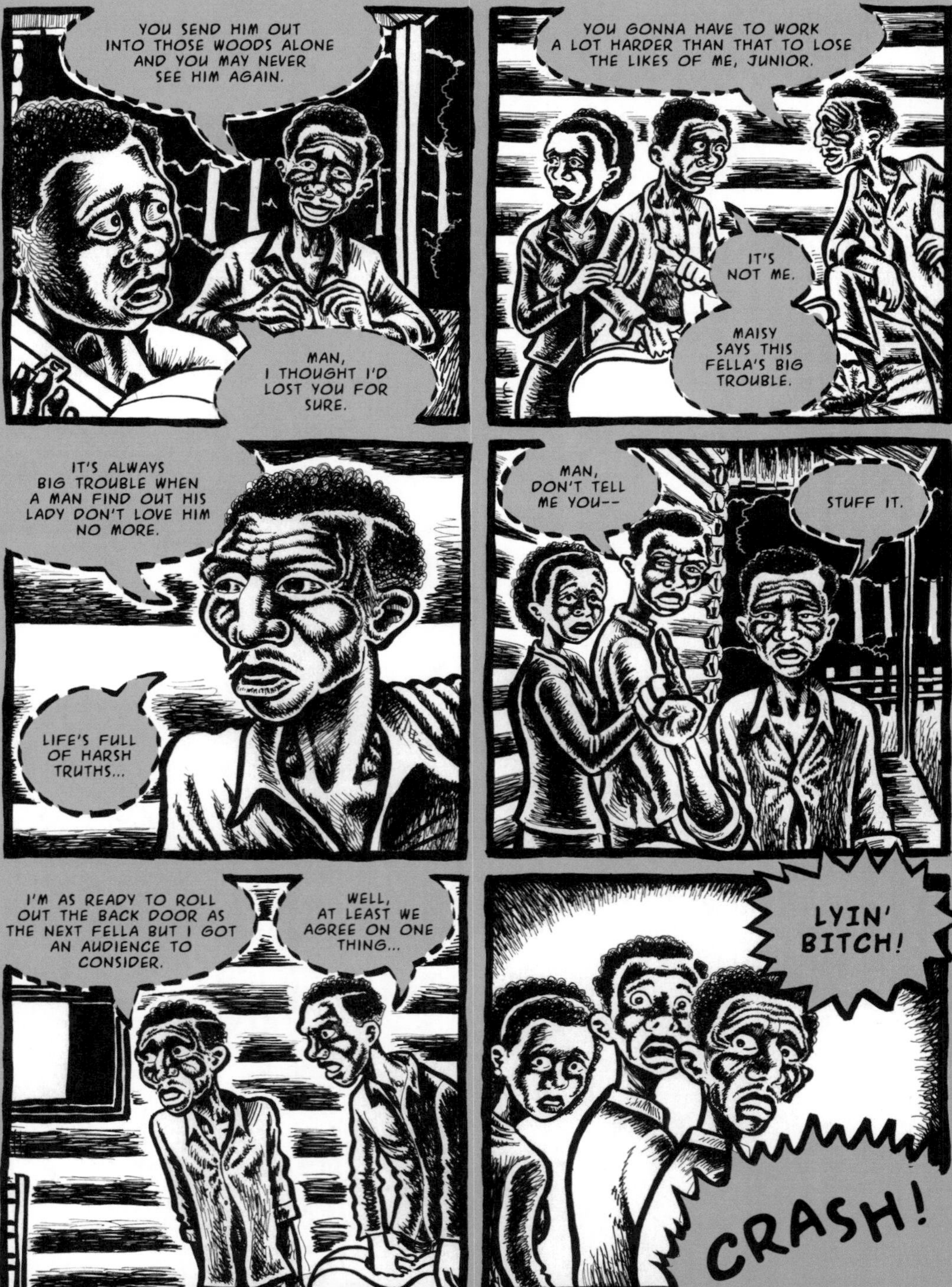
YOU SEND HIM OUT INTO THOSE WOODS ALONE AND YOU MAY NEVER SEE HIM AGAIN.
MAN, I THOUGHT I'D LOST YOU FOR SURE.
YOU GONNA HAVE TO WORK A LOT HARDER THAN THAT TO LOSE THE LIKES OF ME, JUNIOR.
IT'S NOT ME.
MAISY SAYS THIS FELLA'S BIG TROUBLE.
IT'S ALWAYS BIG TROUBLE WHEN A MAN FIND OUT HIS LADY DON'T LOVE HIM NO MORE.
LIFE'S FULL OF HARSH TRUTHS...
MAN, DON'T TELL ME YOU--
STUFF IT.
I'M AS READY TO ROLL OUT THE BACK DOOR AS THE NEXT FELLA BUT I GOT AN AUDIENCE TO CONSIDER.
WELL, AT LEAST WE AGREE ON ONE THING...
LYIN' BITCH!
CRASH!

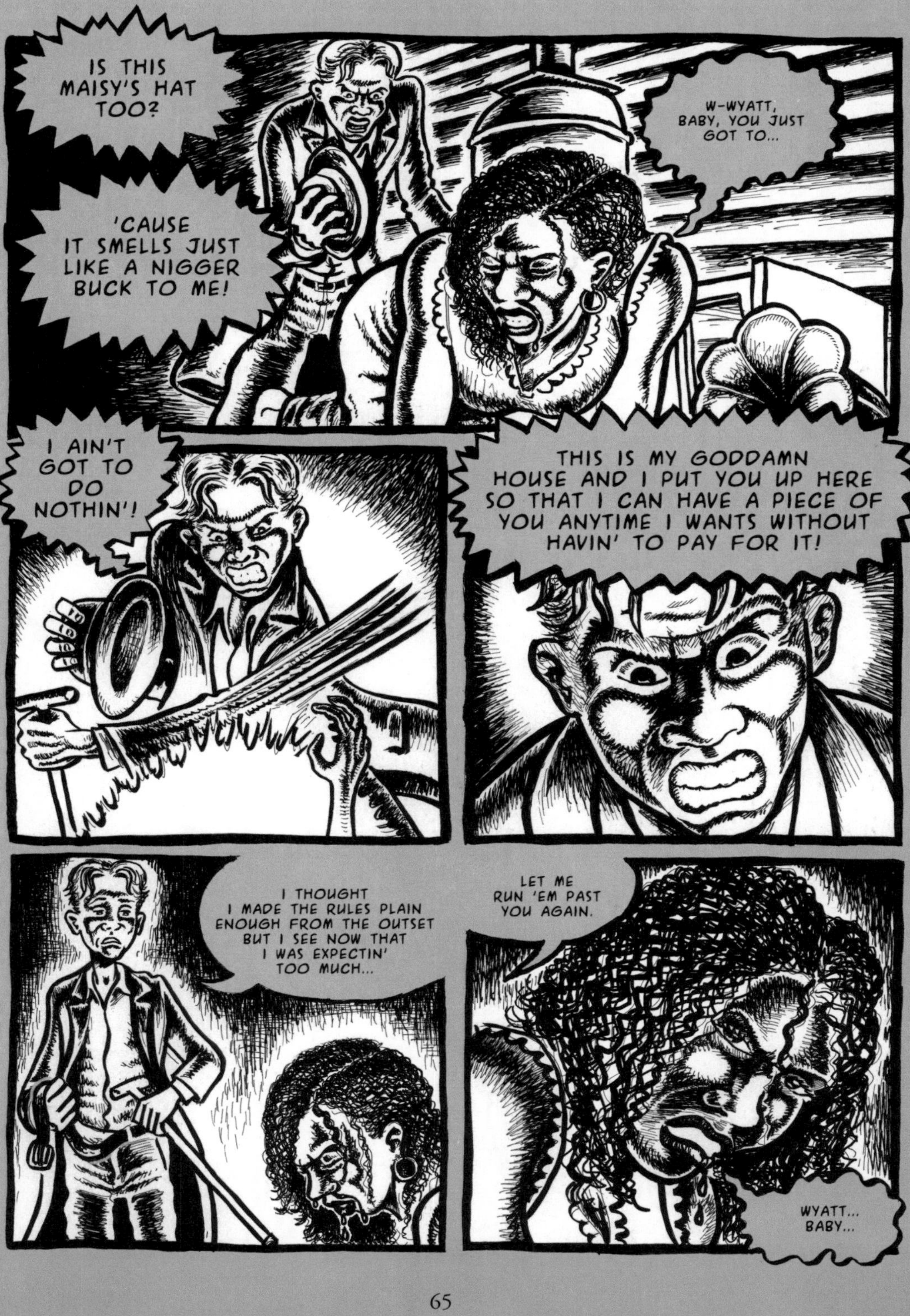

IS THIS MAISY'S HAT TOO?
'CAUSE IT SMELLS JUST LIKE A NIGGER BUCK TO ME!
W-WYATT, BABY, YOU JUST GOT TO...
I AIN'T GOT TO DO NOTHIN'!
THIS IS MY GODDAMN HOUSE AND I PUT YOU UP HERE SO THAT I CAN HAVE A PIECE OF YOU ANYTIME I WANTS WITHOUT HAVIN' TO PAY FOR IT!
I THOUGHT I MADE THE RULES PLAIN ENOUGH FROM THE OUTSET BUT I SEE NOW THAT I WAS EXPECTIN' TOO MUCH...
LET ME RUN 'EM PAST YOU AGAIN.
WYATT... BABY...

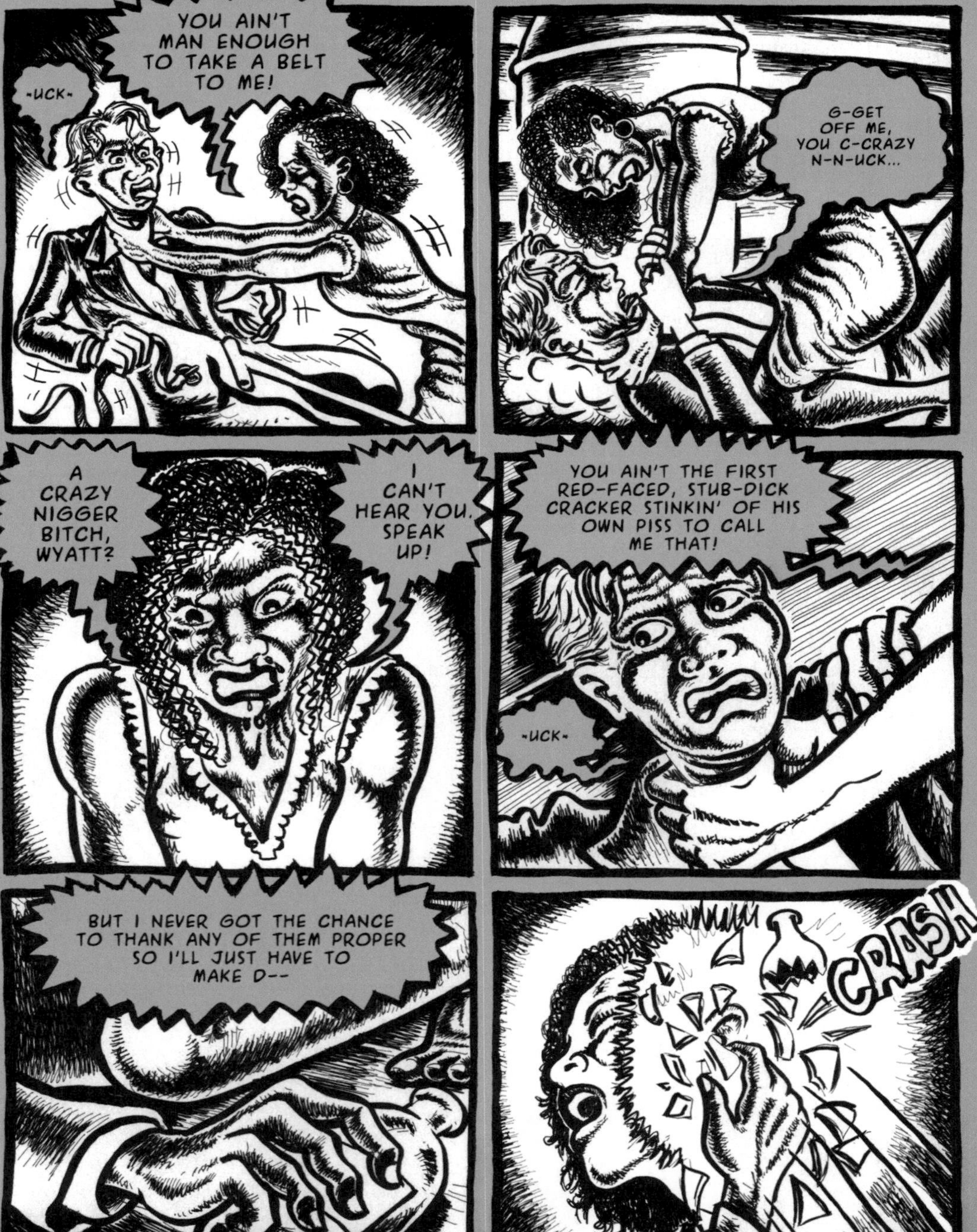
YOU AIN'T MAN ENOUGH TO TAKE A BELT TO ME!
~UCK~
G-GET OFF ME, YOU C-CRAZY N-N-UCK...
A CRAZY NIGGER BITCH, WYATT?
I CAN'T HEAR YOU. SPEAK UP!
YOU AIN'T THE FIRST RED-FACED, STUB-DICK CRACKER STINKIN' OF HIS OWN PISS TO CALL ME THAT!
~UCK~
BUT I NEVER GOT THE CHANCE TO THANK ANY OF THEM PROPER SO I'LL JUST HAVE TO MAKE D--
CRASH

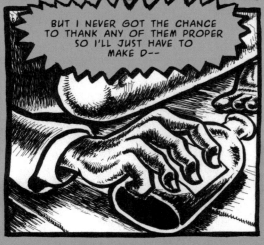

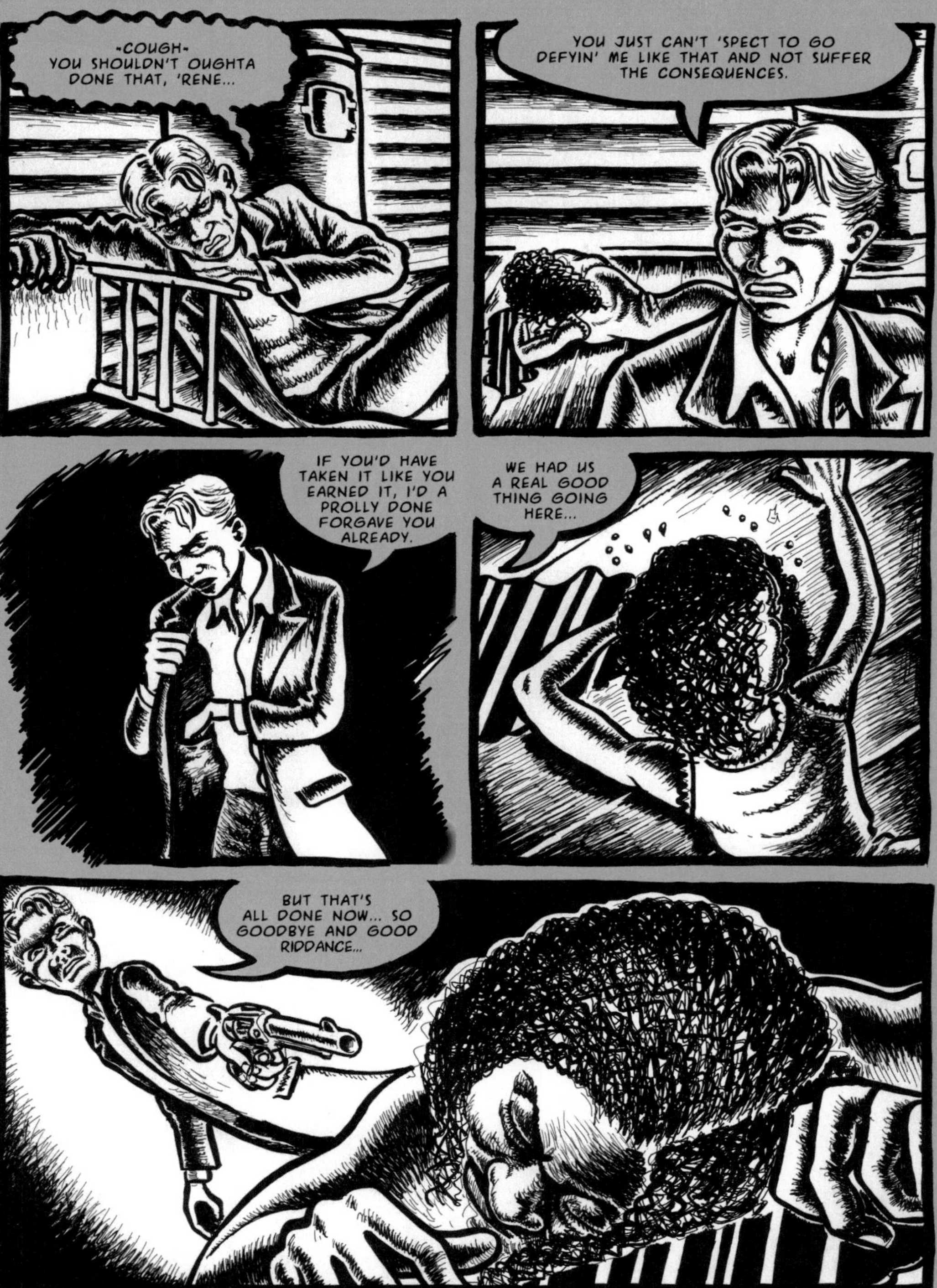
-COUGH-
YOU SHOULDN'T OUGHTA DONE THAT, 'RENE...
YOU JUST CAN'T 'SPECT TO GO DEFYIN' ME LIKE THAT AND NOT SUFFER THE CONSEQUENCES.
IF YOU'D HAVE TAKEN IT LIKE YOU EARNED IT, I'D A PROLLY DONE FORGAVE YOU ALREADY.
WE HAD US A REAL GOOD THING GOING HERE...
BUT THAT'S ALL DONE NOW... SO GOODBYE AND GOOD RIDDANCE...

'WOOD!
WHA-?
YAAAAAAGH!
~ GUCKK ~
I-
BAMM
'W-WOOD?

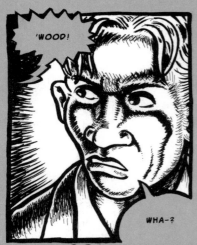

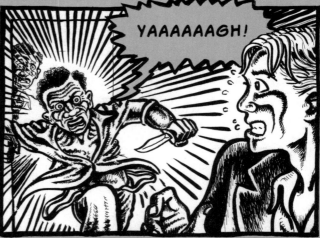

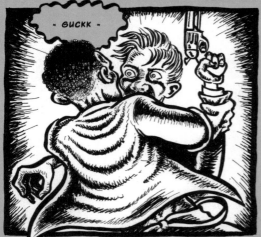

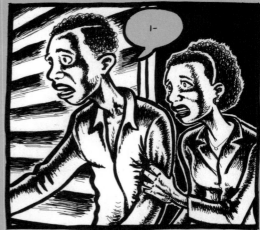

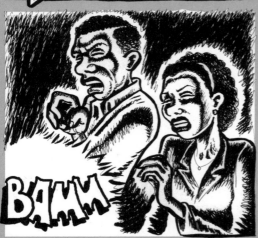

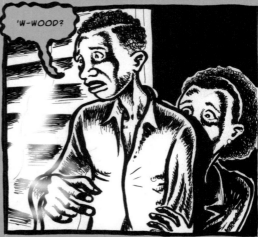

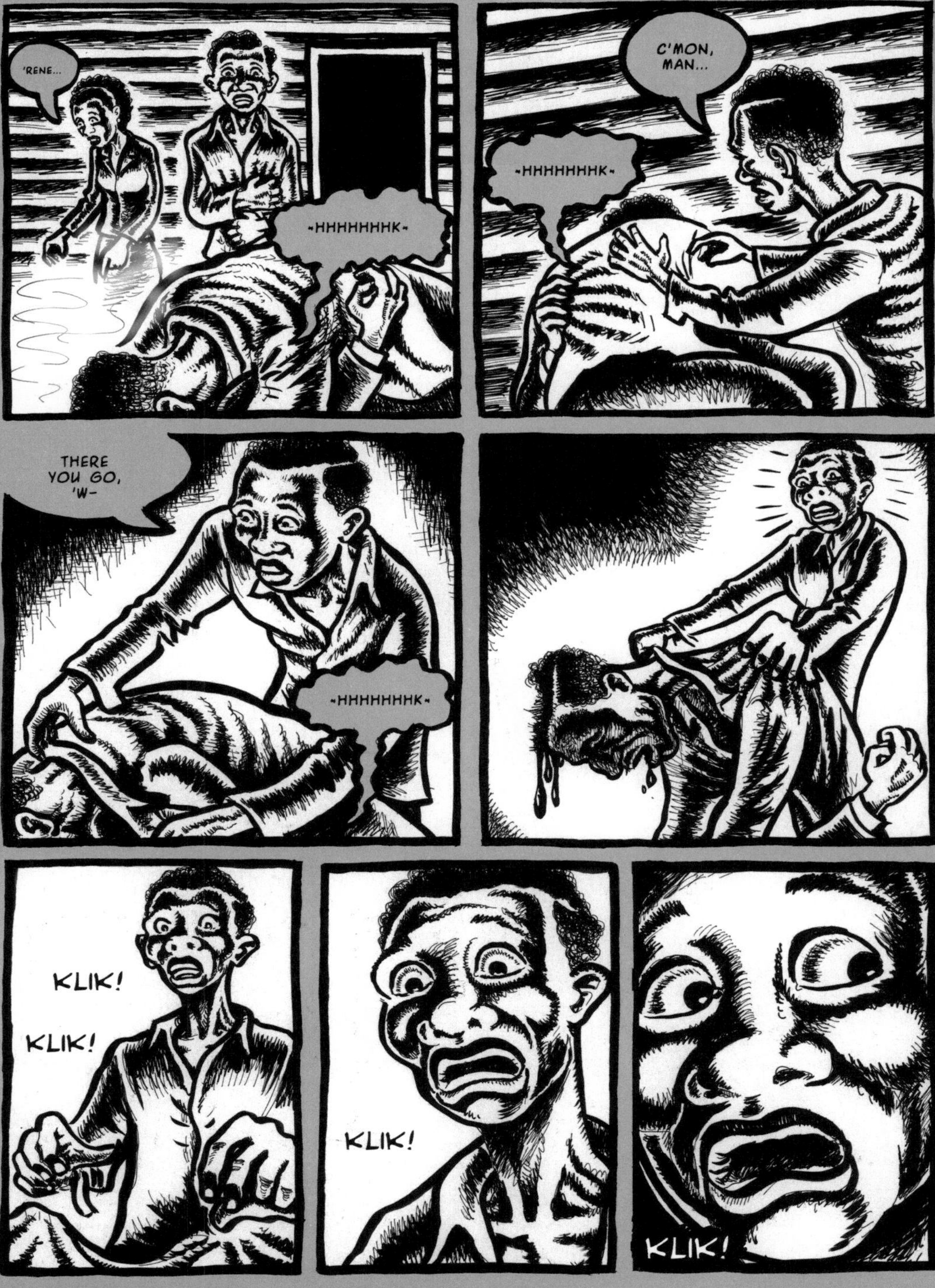
'RENE...
-HHHHHHHK-
C'MON, MAN...
-HHHHHHHK-
THERE YOU GO, 'W-
-HHHHHHHK-
KLIK!
KLIK!
KLIK!
KLIK!

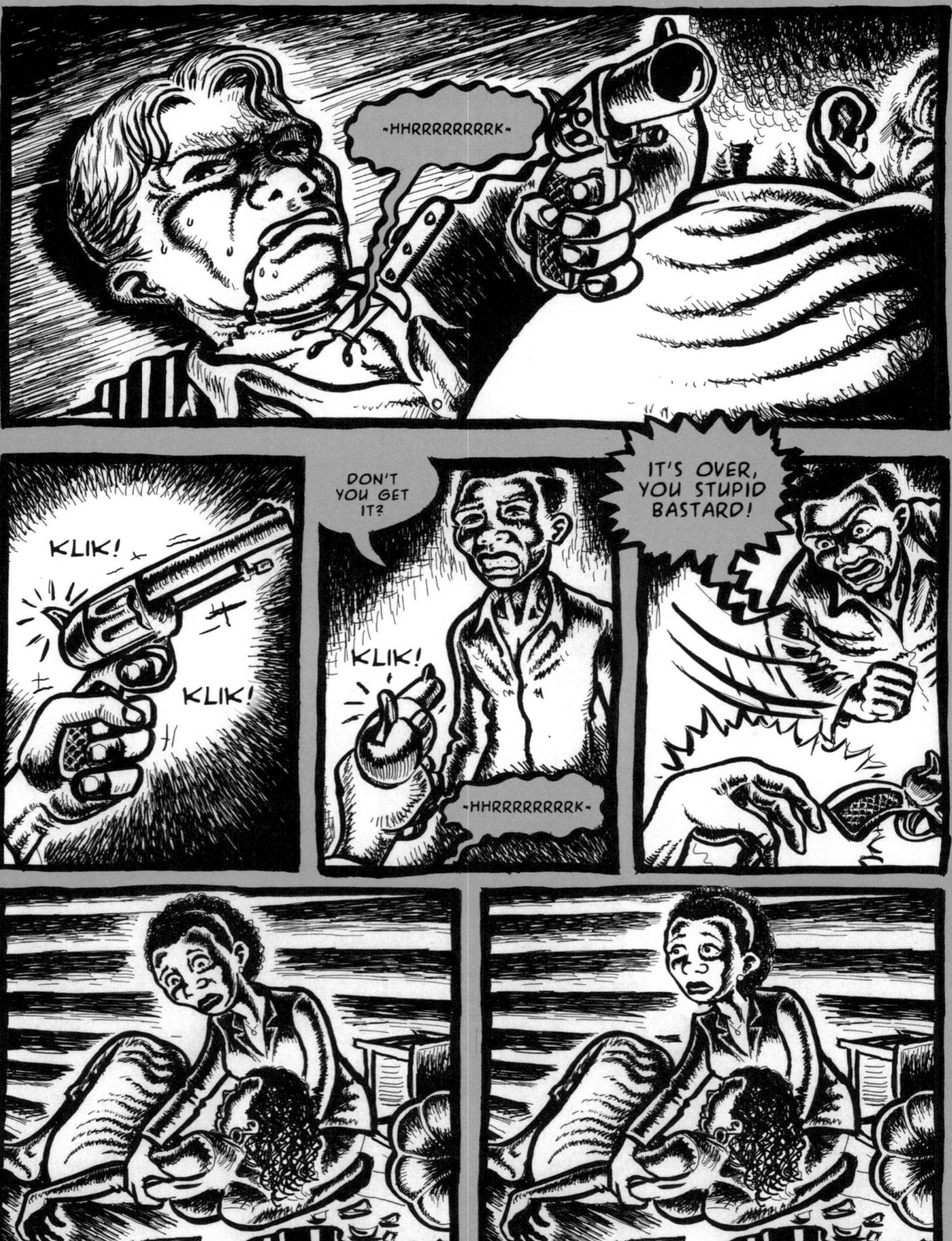
~HHRRRRRRRRK~
KLIK!
KLIK!
DON'T YOU GET IT?
KLIK!
~HHRRRRRRRRK~
IT'S OVER, YOU STUPID BASTARD!
RRRR

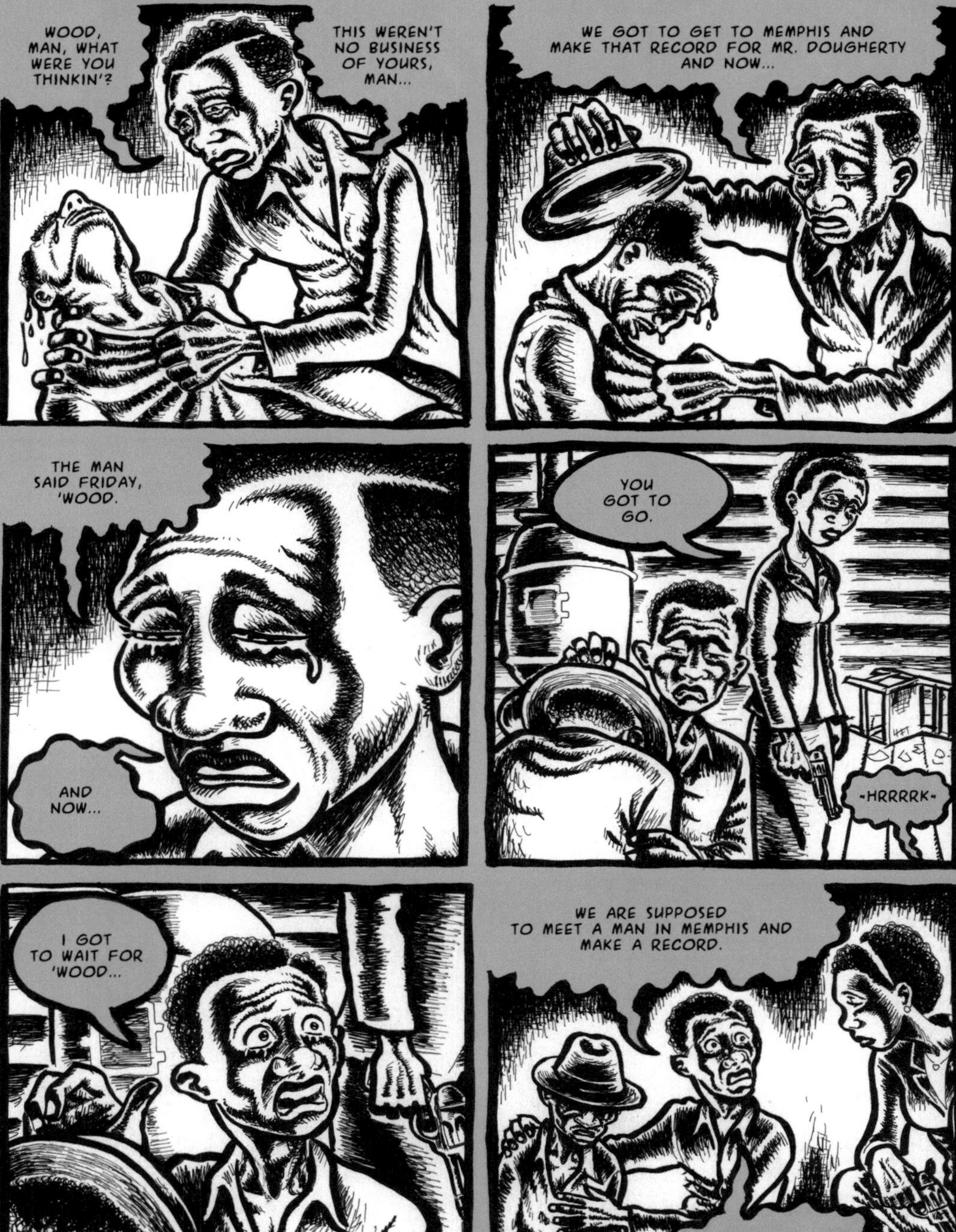
WOOD, MAN, WHAT WERE YOU THINKIN'?
THIS WEREN'T NO BUSINESS OF YOURS, MAN...
WE GOT TO GET TO MEMPHIS AND MAKE THAT RECORD FOR MR. DOUGHERTY AND NOW...
THE MAN SAID FRIDAY, 'WOOD.
AND NOW...
YOU GOT TO GO.
»HRRRRK«
I GOT TO WAIT FOR 'WOOD...
WE ARE SUPPOSED TO MEET A MAN IN MEMPHIS AND MAKE A RECORD.
AND THE MAN SAID FRIDAY...

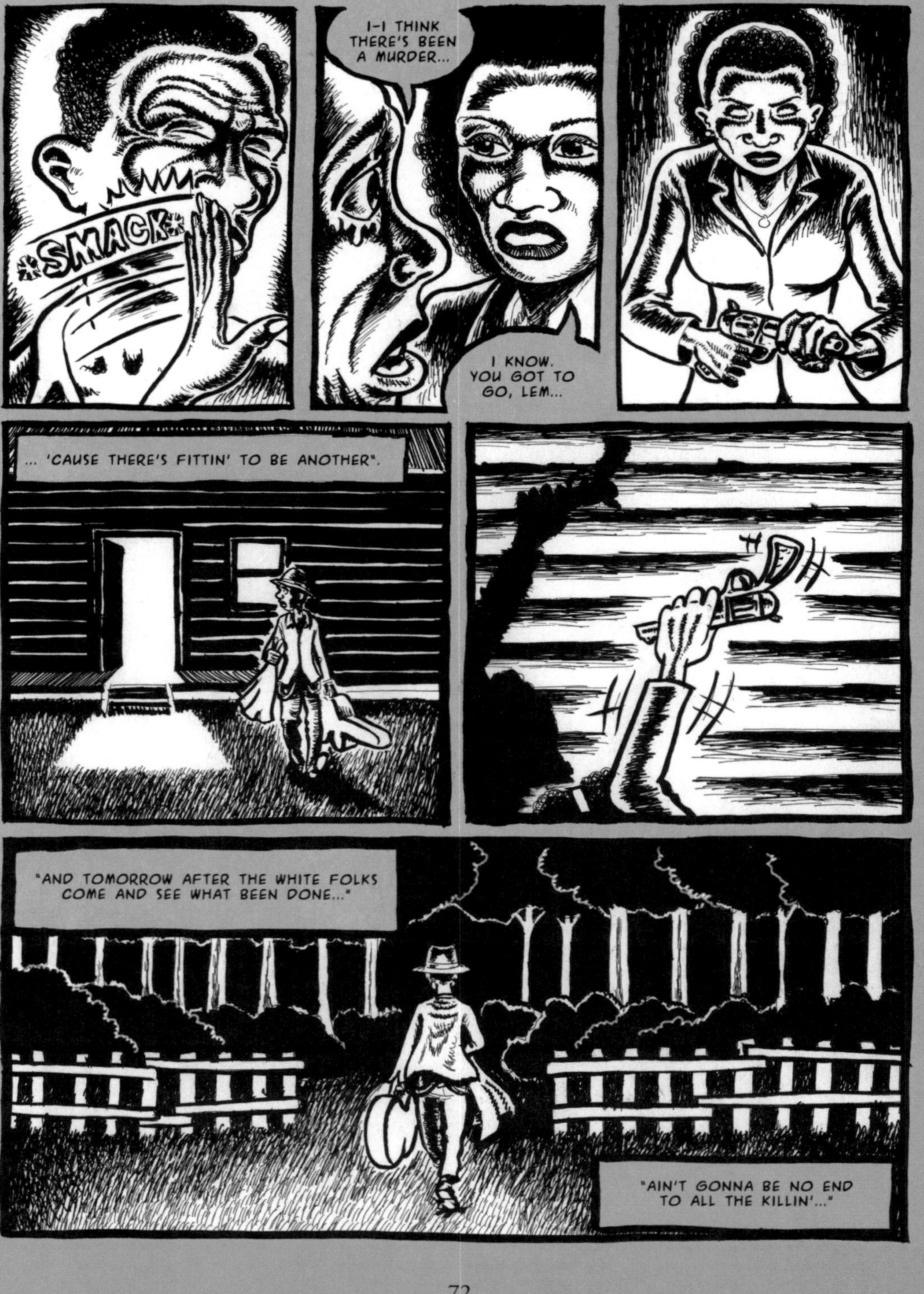
SMACK
I-I THINK THERE'S BEEN A MURDER...
I KNOW. YOU GOT TO GO, LEM...
... 'CAUSE THERE'S FITTIN' TO BE ANOTHER".
"AND TOMORROW AFTER THE WHITE FOLKS COME AND SEE WHAT BEEN DONE..."
"AIN'T GONNA BE NO END TO ALL THE KILLIN'..."

5

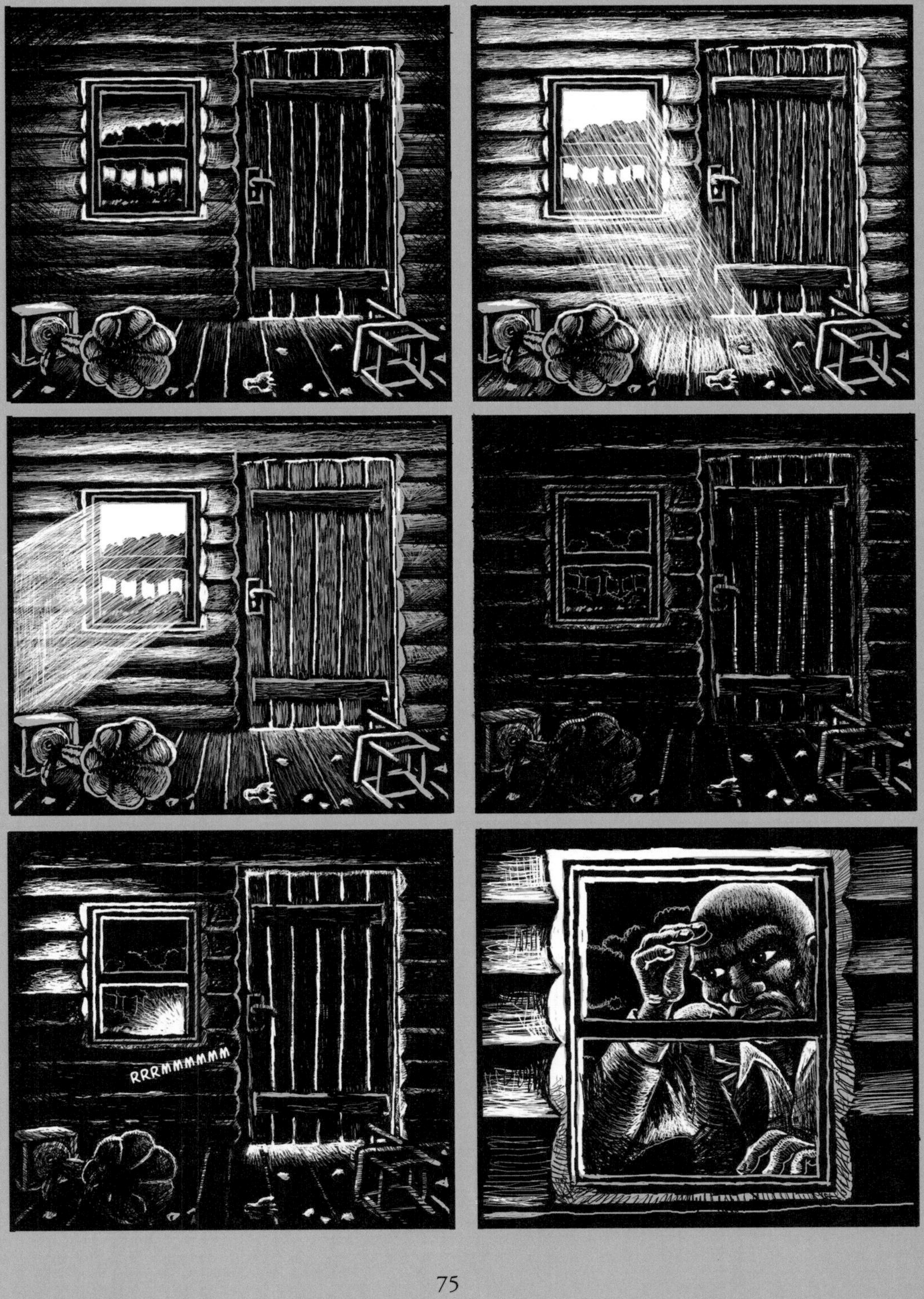
RRRMMMMMMM

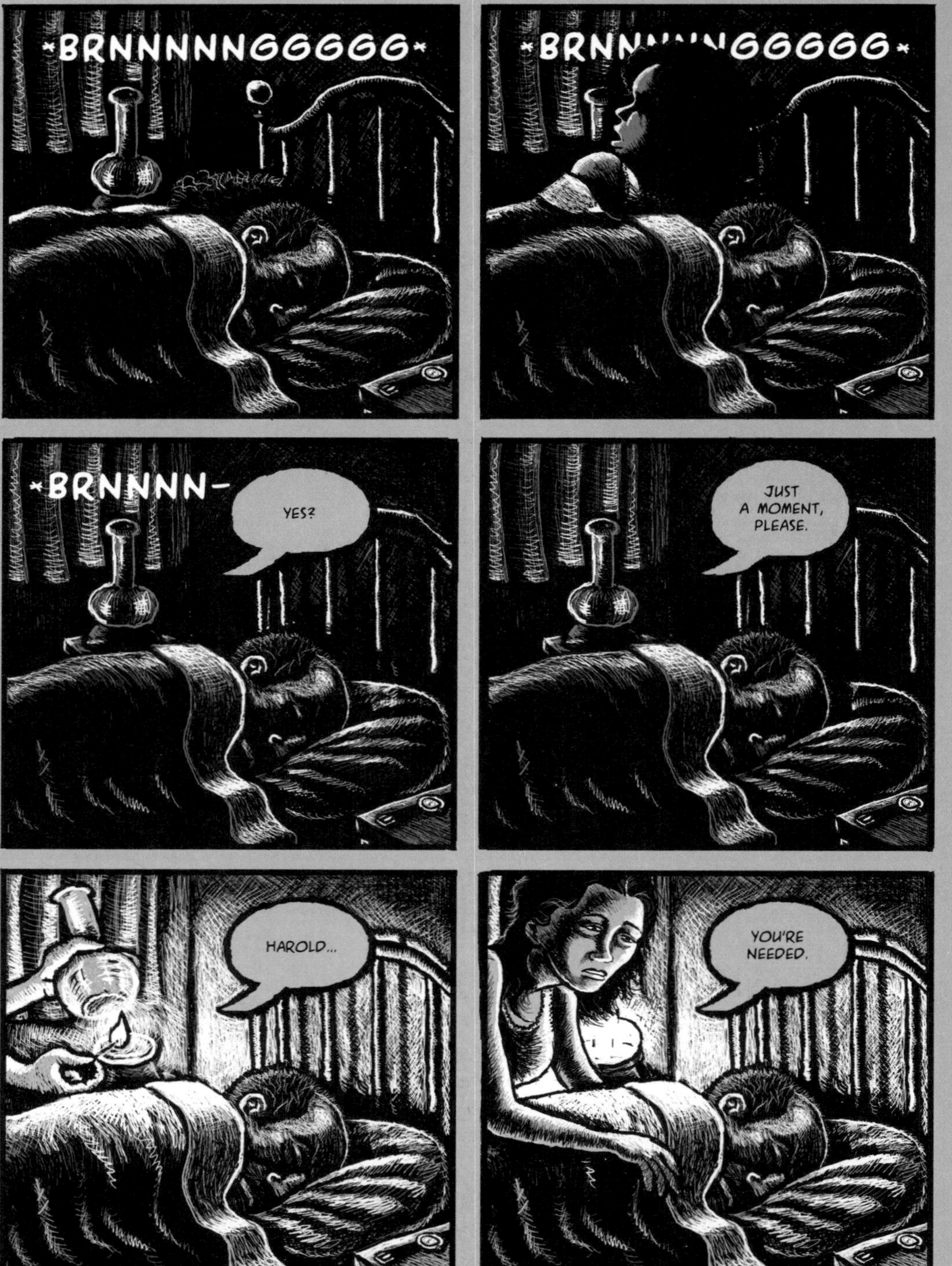
BRNNNNNGGGGG
BRNNNNNGGGGG
*BRNNNN-
YES?
JUST A MOMENT, PLEASE.
HAROLD...
YOU'RE NEEDED.

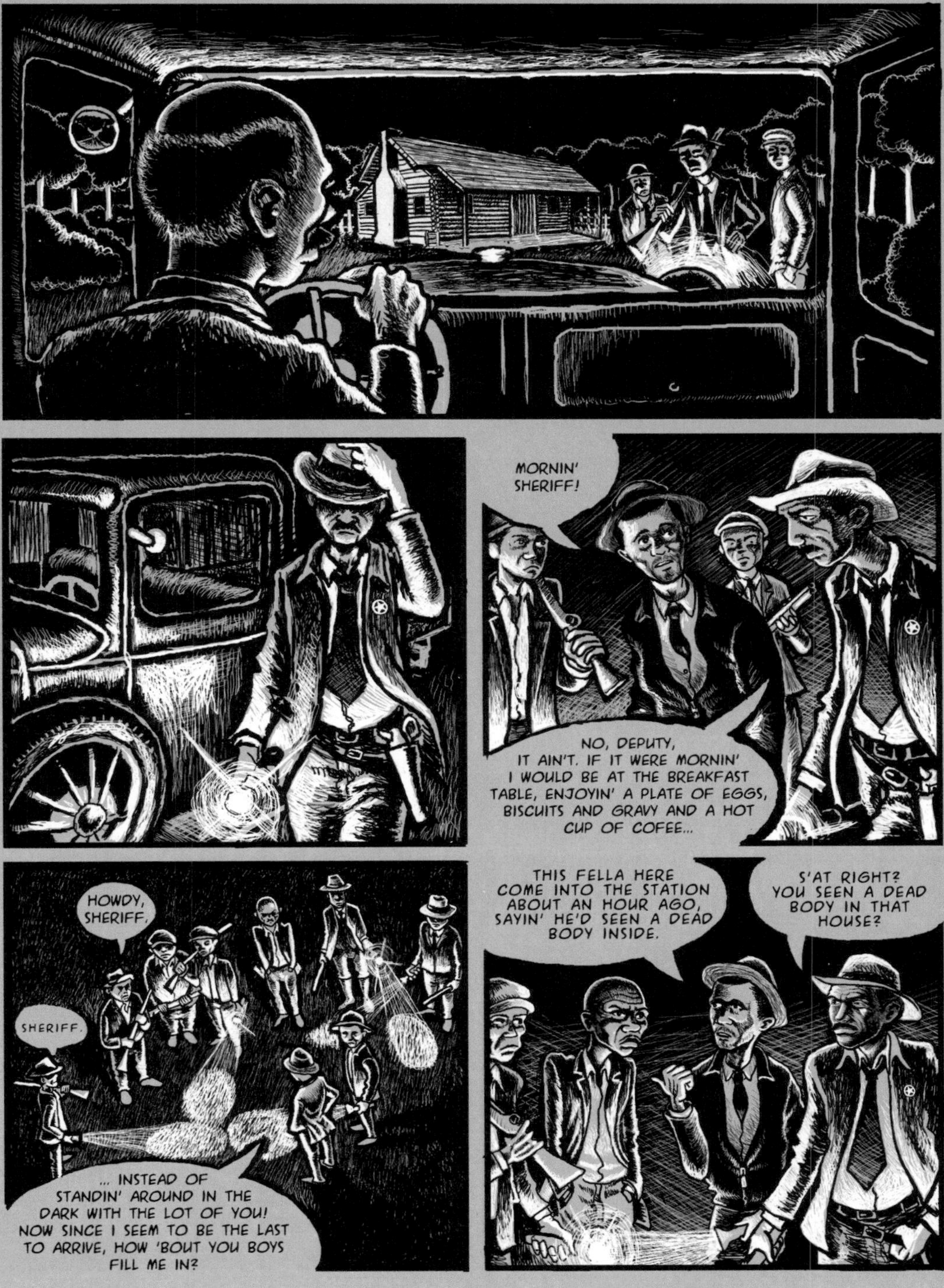

MORNIN' SHERIFF!
NO, DEPUTY, IT AIN'T. IF IT WERE MORNIN' I WOULD BE AT THE BREAKFAST TABLE, ENJOYIN' A PLATE OF EGGS, BISCUITS AND GRAVY AND A HOT CUP OF COFEE...
HOWDY, SHERIFF.
SHERIFF.
... INSTEAD OF STANDIN' AROUND IN THE DARK WITH THE LOT OF YOU! NOW SINCE I SEEM TO BE THE LAST TO ARRIVE, HOW 'BOUT YOU BOYS FILL ME IN?
THIS FELLA HERE COME INTO THE STATION ABOUT AN HOUR AGO, SAYIN' HE'D SEEN A DEAD BODY INSIDE.
S'AT RIGHT? YOU SEEN A DEAD BODY IN THAT HOUSE?

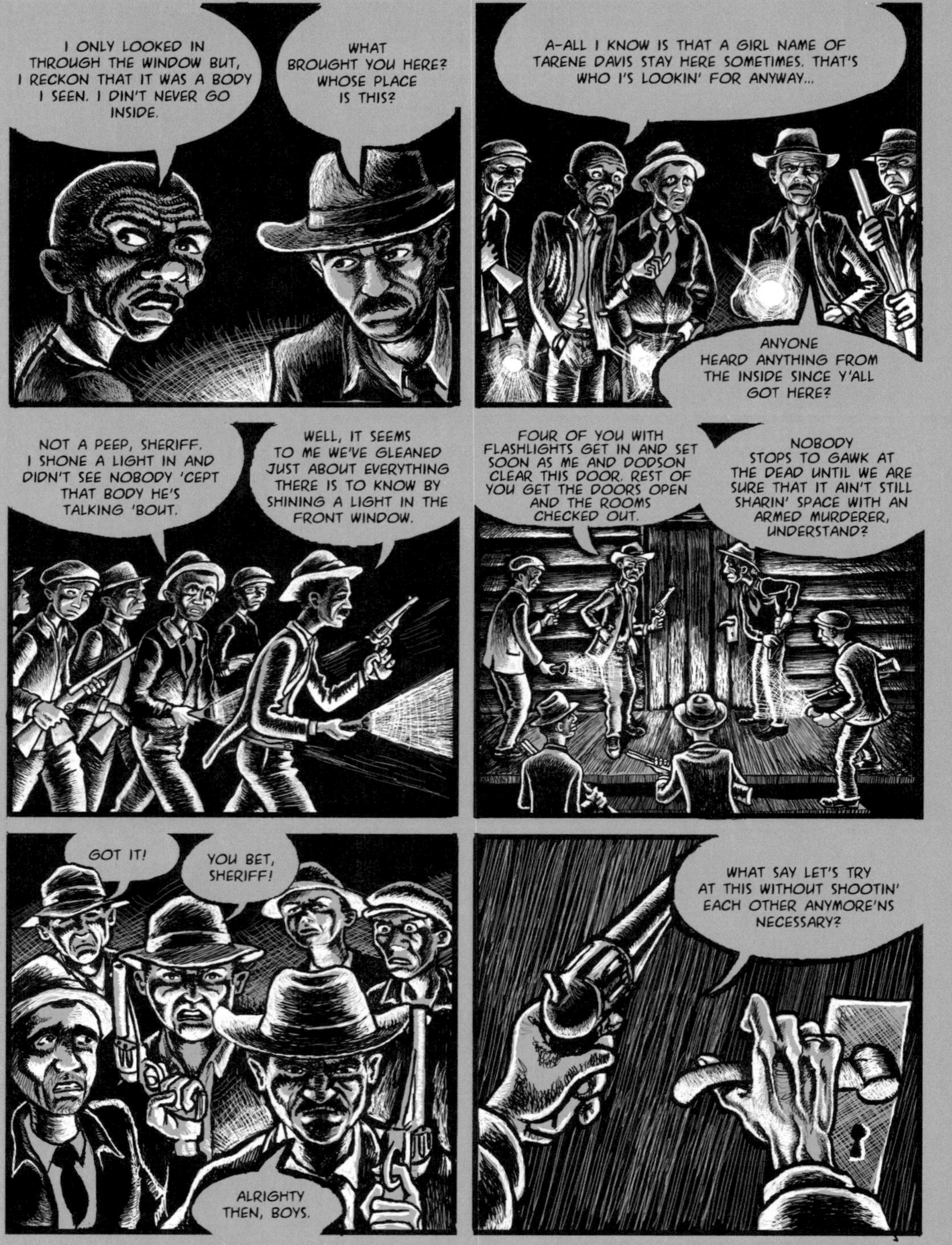
I ONLY LOOKED IN THROUGH THE WINDOW BUT, I RECKON THAT IT WAS A BODY I SEEN. I DIN'T NEVER GO INSIDE.
WHAT BROUGHT YOU HERE? WHOSE PLACE IS THIS?
A-ALL I KNOW IS THAT A GIRL NAME OF TARENE DAVIS STAY HERE SOMETIMES. THAT'S WHO I'S LOOKIN' FOR ANYWAY...
ANYONE HEARD ANYTHING FROM THE INSIDE SINCE Y'ALL GOT HERE?
NOT A PEEP, SHERIFF. I SHONE A LIGHT IN AND DIDN'T SEE NOBODY 'CEPT THAT BODY HE'S TALKING 'BOUT.
WELL, IT SEEMS TO ME WE'VE GLEANED JUST ABOUT EVERYTHING THERE IS TO KNOW BY SHINING A LIGHT IN THE FRONT WINDOW.
FOUR OF YOU WITH FLASHLIGHTS GET IN AND SET SOON AS ME AND DODSON CLEAR THIS DOOR. REST OF YOU GET THE DOORS OPEN AND THE ROOMS CHECKED OUT.
NOBODY STOPS TO GAWK AT THE DEAD UNTIL WE ARE SURE THAT IT AIN'T STILL SHARIN' SPACE WITH AN ARMED MURDERER, UNDERSTAND?
GOT IT!
YOU BET, SHERIFF!
ALRIGHTY THEN, BOYS.
WHAT SAY LET'S TRY AT THIS WITHOUT SHOOTIN' EACH OTHER ANYMORE'NS NECESSARY?

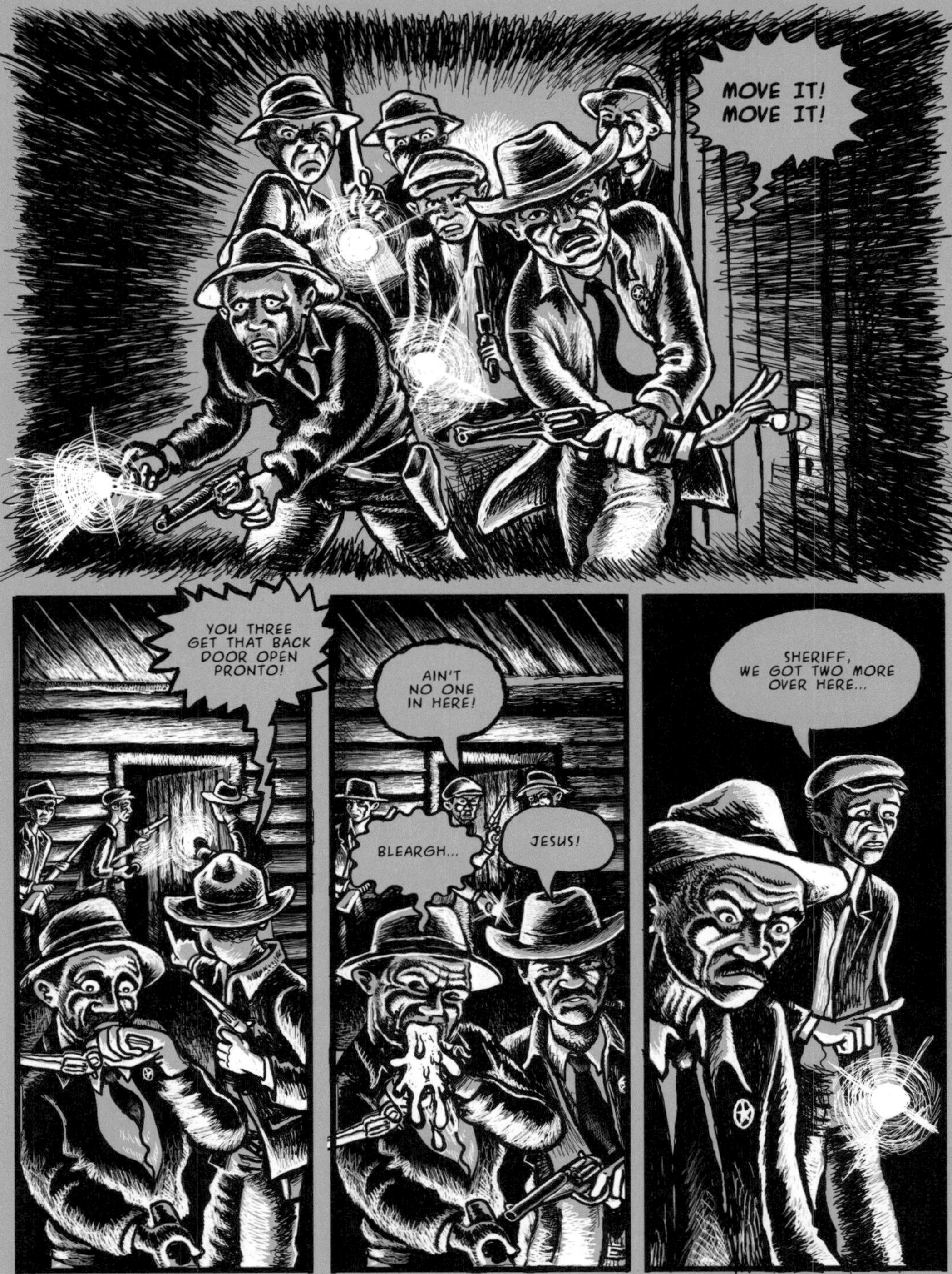
MOVE IT! MOVE IT!
YOU THREE GET THAT BACK DOOR OPEN PRONTO!
AIN'T NO ONE IN HERE!
BLEARGH...
JESUS!
SHERIFF, WE GOT TWO MORE OVER HERE...

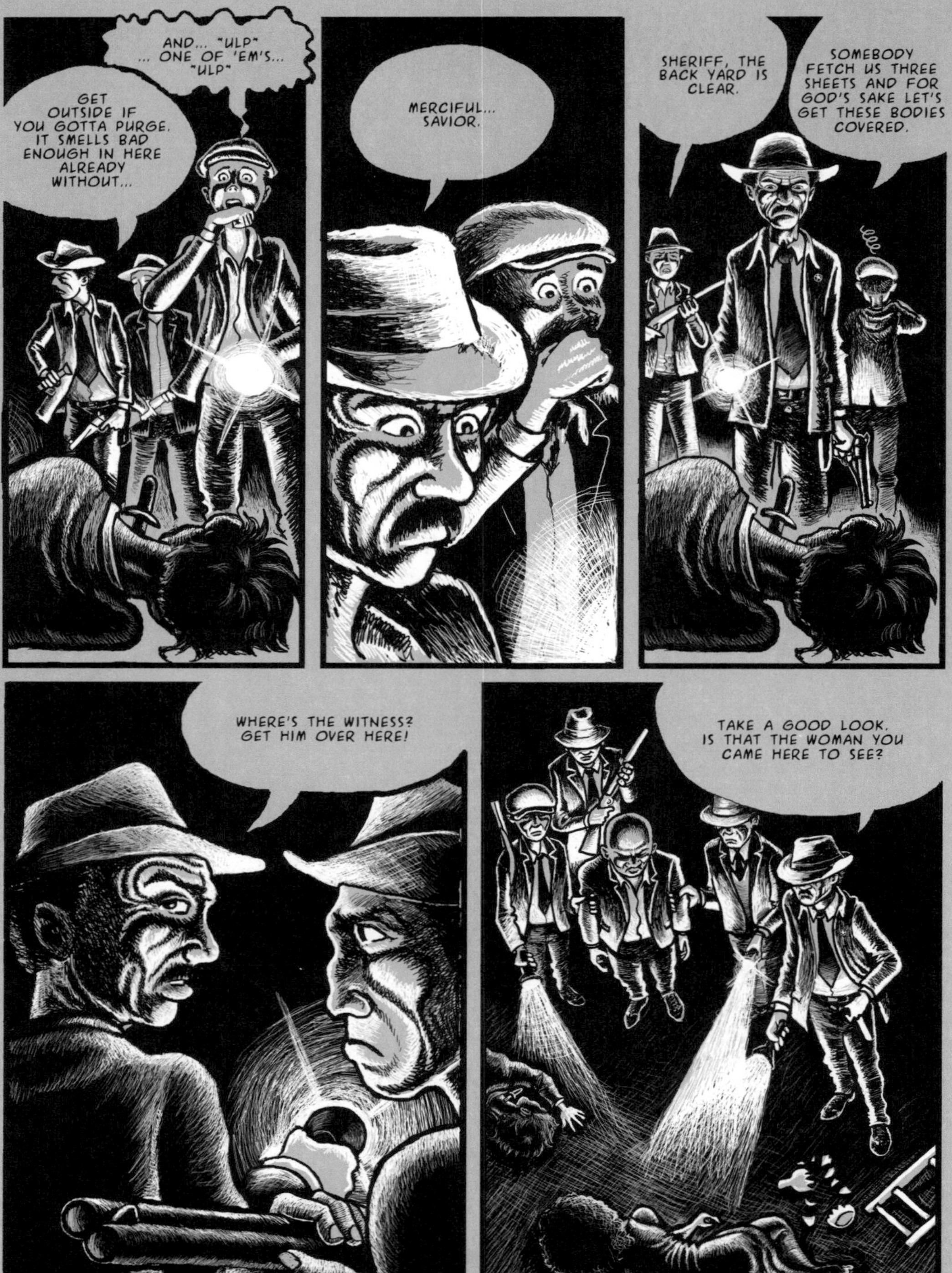
AND... "ULP" ... ONE OF 'EM'S... "ULP"
GET OUTSIDE IF YOU GOTTA PURGE. IT SMELLS BAD ENOUGH IN HERE ALREADY WITHOUT...
MERCIFUL... SAVIOR.
SHERIFF, THE BACK YARD IS CLEAR.
SOMEBODY FETCH US THREE SHEETS AND FOR GOD'S SAKE LET'S GET THESE BODIES COVERED.
WHERE'S THE WITNESS? GET HIM OVER HERE!
TAKE A GOOD LOOK. IS THAT THE WOMAN YOU CAME HERE TO SEE?

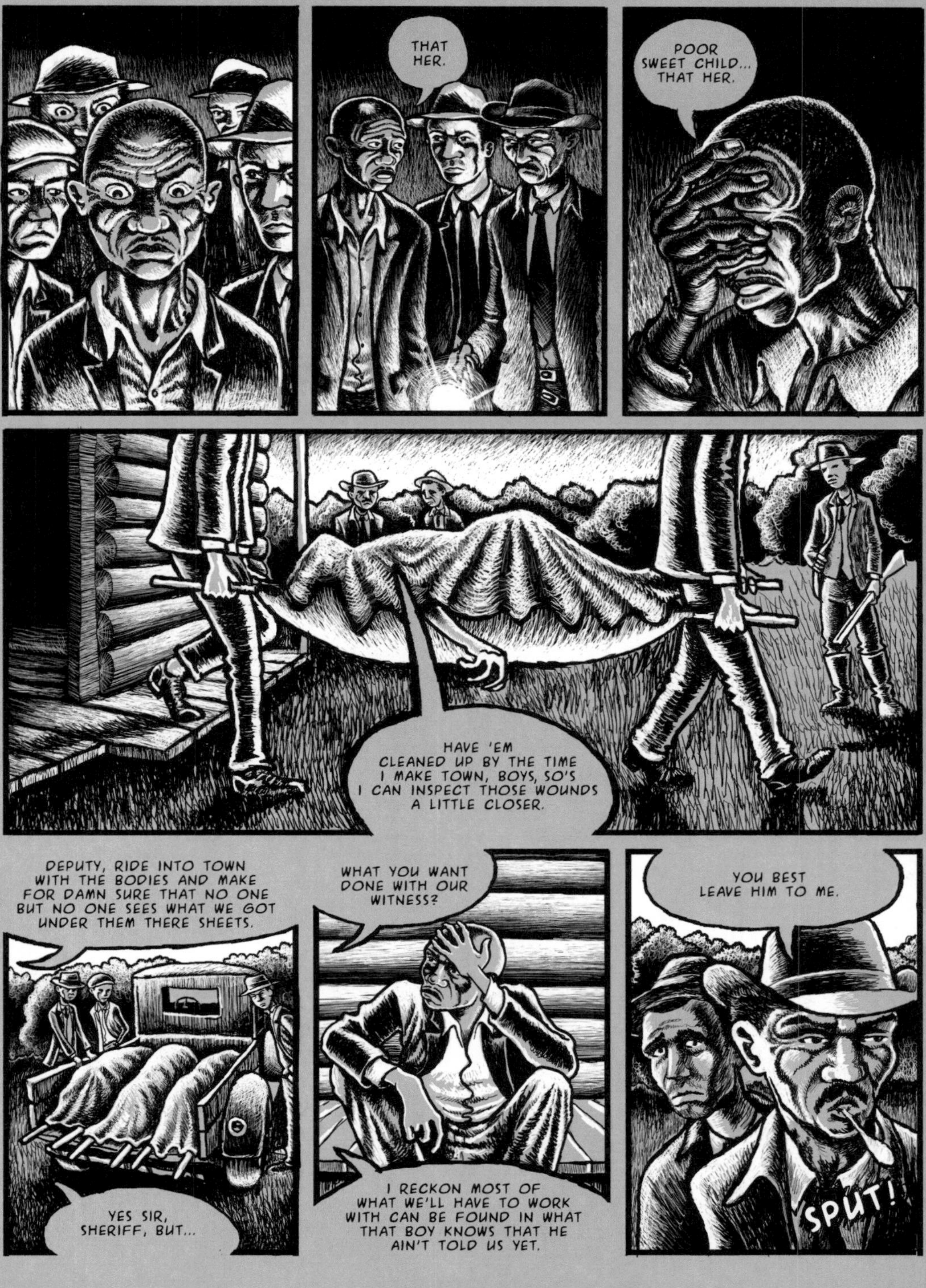
THAT HER.
POOR SWEET CHILD... THAT HER.
HAVE 'EM CLEANED UP BY THE TIME I MAKE TOWN, BOYS, SO'S I CAN INSPECT THOSE WOUNDS A LITTLE CLOSER.
DEPUTY, RIDE INTO TOWN WITH THE BODIES AND MAKE FOR DAMN SURE THAT NO ONE BUT NO ONE SEES WHAT WE GOT UNDER THEM THERE SHEETS.
YES SIR, SHERIFF, BUT...
WHAT YOU WANT DONE WITH OUR WITNESS?
I RECKON MOST OF WHAT WE'LL HAVE TO WORK WITH CAN BE FOUND IN WHAT THAT BOY KNOWS THAT HE AIN'T TOLD US YET.
YOU BEST LEAVE HIM TO ME.
SPUT!

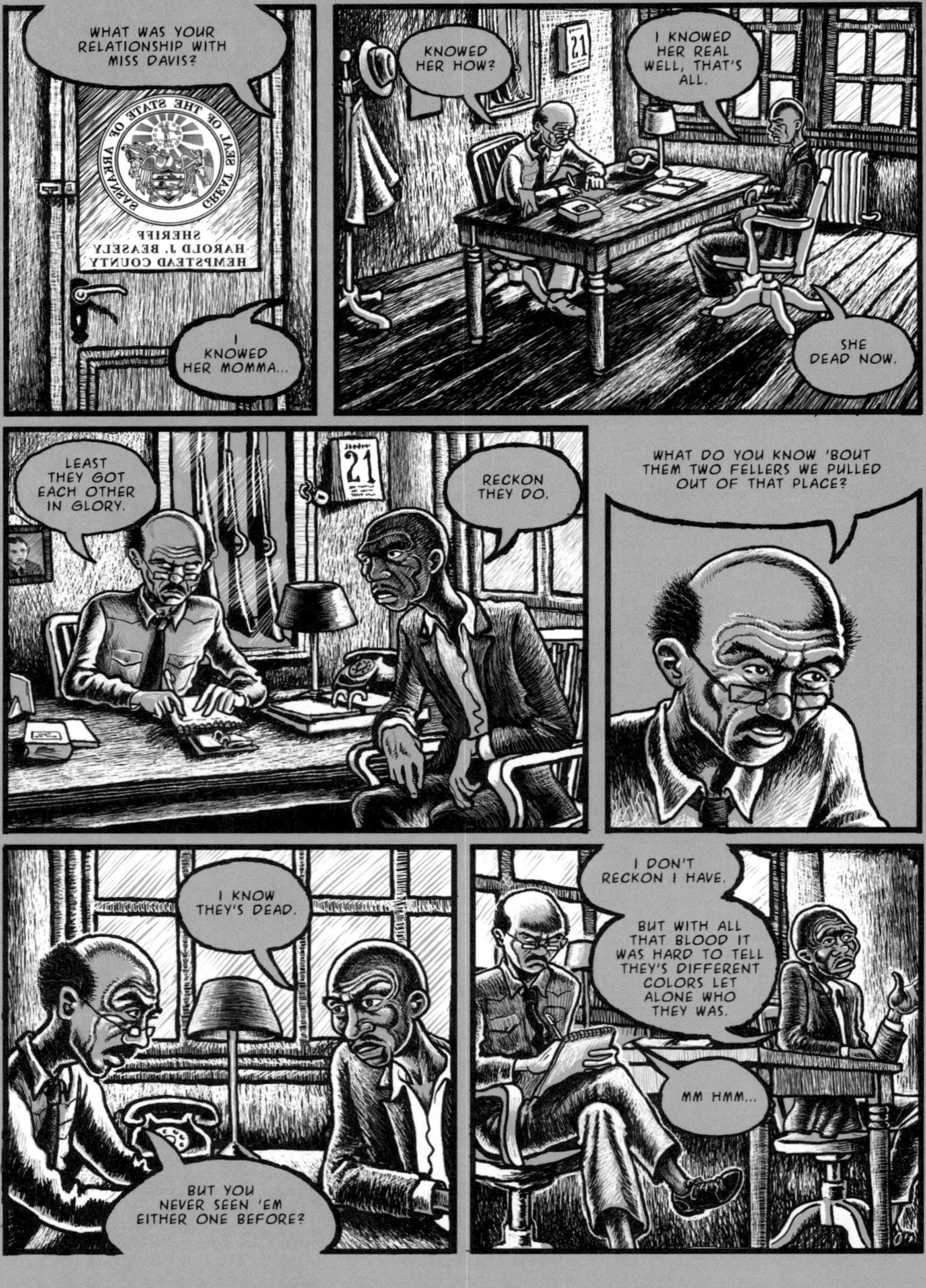
WHAT WAS YOUR RELATIONSHIP WITH MISS DAVIS?
SEAL OF THE STATE OF ARKANSAS
SHERIFF HAROLD J. BEASLY HEMPSTEAD COUNTY
I KNOWED HER MOMMA...
KNOWED HER HOW?
21
I KNOWED HER REAL WELL, THAT'S ALL.
SHE DEAD NOW.
LEAST THEY GOT EACH OTHER IN GLORY.
21
RECKON THEY DO.
WHAT DO YOU KNOW 'BOUT THEM TWO FELLERS WE PULLED OUT OF THAT PLACE?
I KNOW THEY'S DEAD.
BUT YOU NEVER SEEN 'EM EITHER ONE BEFORE?
I DON'T RECKON I HAVE.
BUT WITH ALL THAT BLOOD IT WAS HARD TO TELL THEY'S DIFFERENT COLORS LET ALONE WHO THEY WAS.
MM HMM...

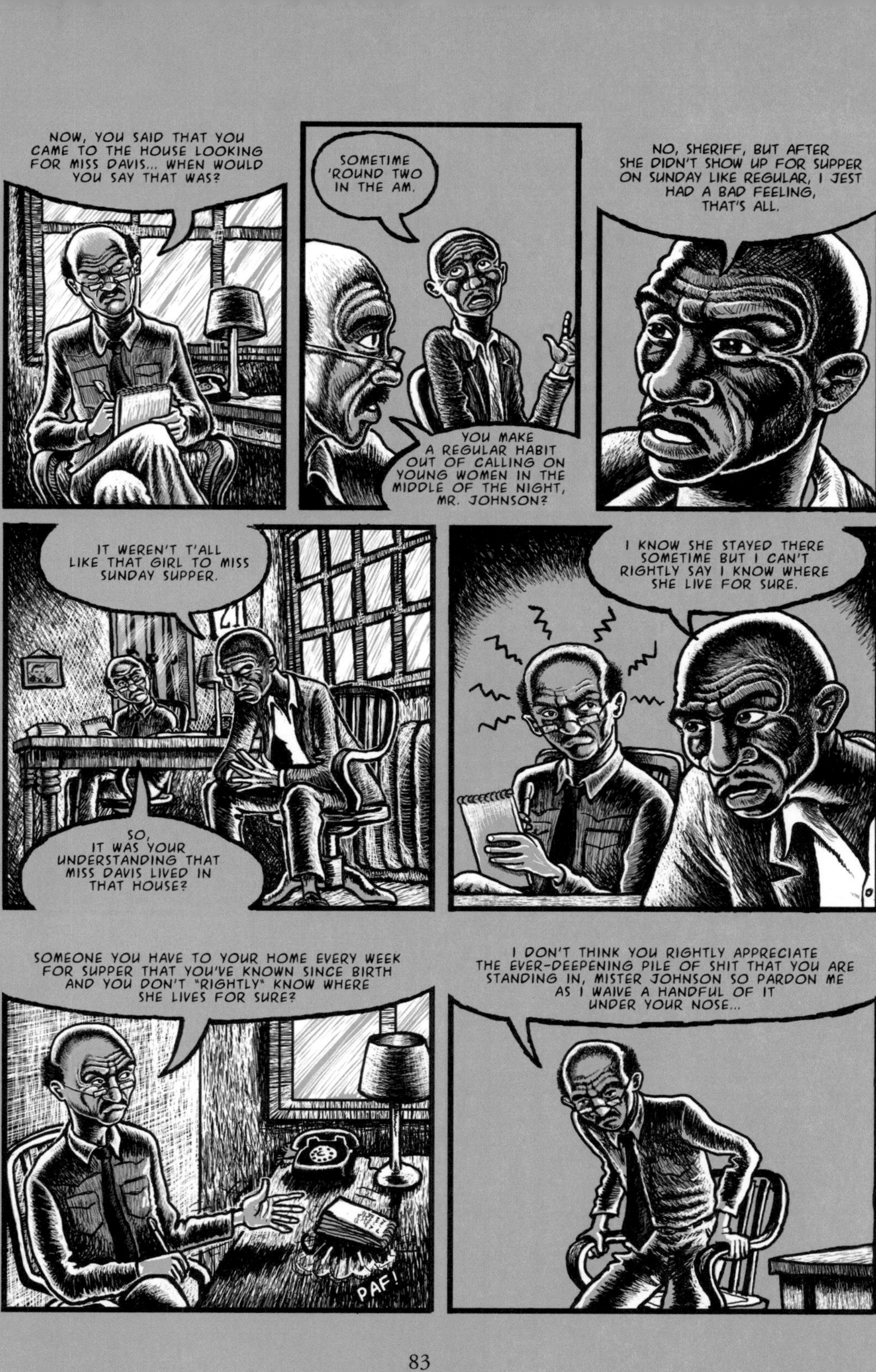

NOW, YOU SAID THAT YOU CAME TO THE HOUSE LOOKING FOR MISS DAVIS... WHEN WOULD YOU SAY THAT WAS?
SOMETIME 'ROUND TWO IN THE AM.
YOU MAKE A REGULAR HABIT OUT OF CALLING ON YOUNG WOMEN IN THE MIDDLE OF THE NIGHT, MR. JOHNSON?
NO, SHERIFF, BUT AFTER SHE DIDN'T SHOW UP FOR SUPPER ON SUNDAY LIKE REGULAR, I JEST HAD A BAD FEELING, THAT'S ALL.
IT WEREN'T T'ALL LIKE THAT GIRL TO MISS SUNDAY SUPPER.
SO, IT WAS YOUR UNDERSTANDING THAT MISS DAVIS LIVED IN THAT HOUSE?
I KNOW SHE STAYED THERE SOMETIME BUT I CAN'T RIGHTLY SAY I KNOW WHERE SHE LIVE FOR SURE.
SOMEONE YOU HAVE TO YOUR HOME EVERY WEEK FOR SUPPER THAT YOU'VE KNOWN SINCE BIRTH AND YOU DON'T "RIGHTLY" KNOW WHERE SHE LIVES FOR SURE?
PAF!
I DON'T THINK YOU RIGHTLY APPRECIATE THE EVER-DEEPENING PILE OF SHIT THAT YOU ARE STANDING IN, MISTER JOHNSON SO PARDON ME AS I WAIVE A HANDFUL OF IT UNDER YOUR NOSE...

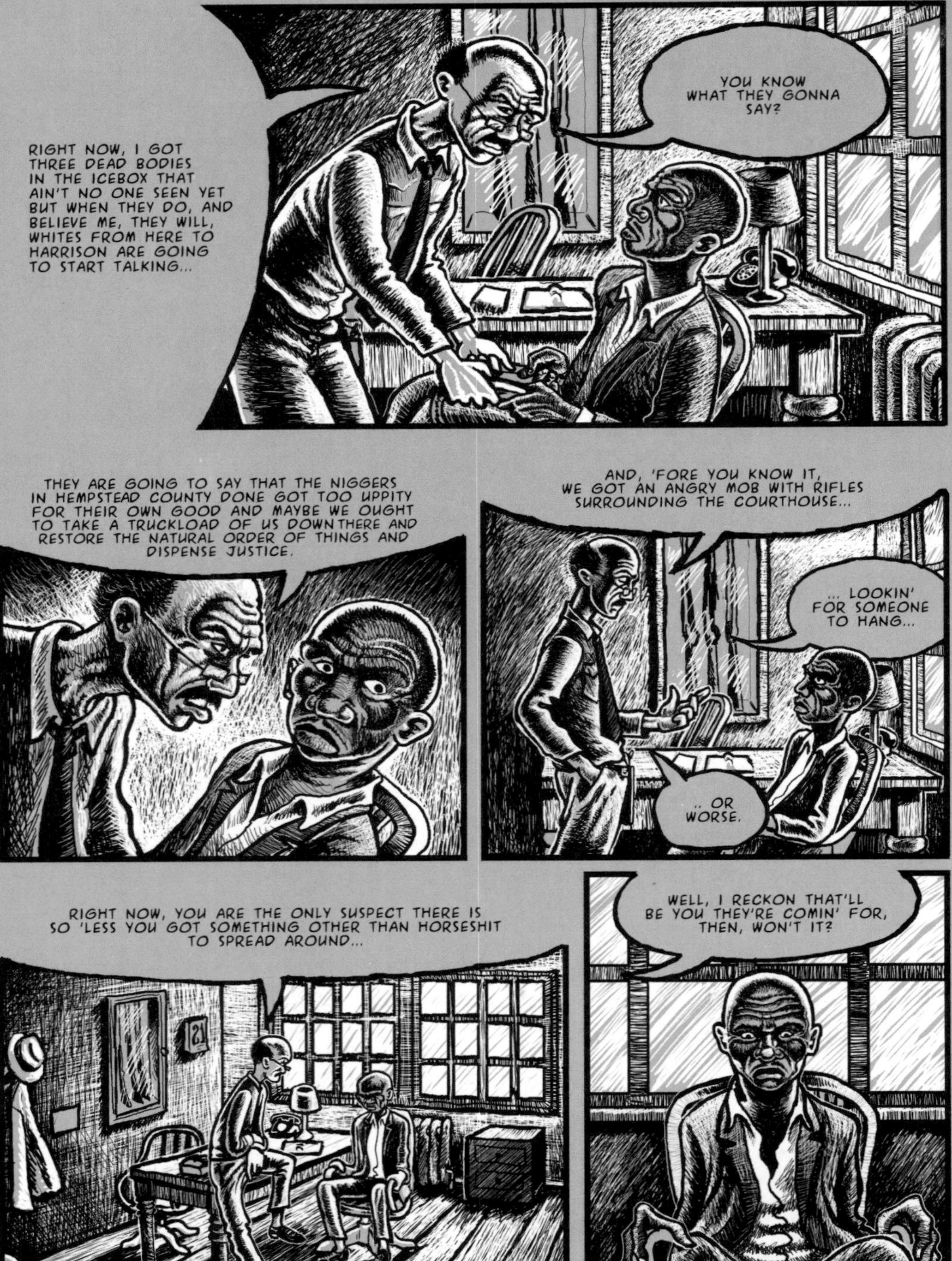
RIGHT NOW, I GOT THREE DEAD BODIES IN THE ICEBOX THAT AIN'T NO ONE SEEN YET BUT WHEN THEY DO, AND BELIEVE ME, THEY WILL, WHITES FROM HERE TO HARRISON ARE GOING TO START TALKING...
YOU KNOW WHAT THEY GONNA SAY?
THEY ARE GOING TO SAY THAT THE NIGGERS IN HEMPSTEAD COUNTY DONE GOT TOO UPPITY FOR THEIR OWN GOOD AND MAYBE WE OUGHT TO TAKE A TRUCKLOAD OF US DOWN THERE AND RESTORE THE NATURAL ORDER OF THINGS AND DISPENSE JUSTICE.
AND, 'FORE YOU KNOW IT, WE GOT AN ANGRY MOB WITH RIFLES SURROUNDING THE COURTHOUSE...
... LOOKIN' FOR SOMEONE TO HANG...
.. OR WORSE.
RIGHT NOW, YOU ARE THE ONLY SUSPECT THERE IS SO 'LESS YOU GOT SOMETHING OTHER THAN HORSESHIT TO SPREAD AROUND...
WELL, I RECKON THAT'LL BE YOU THEY'RE COMIN' FOR, THEN, WON'T IT?

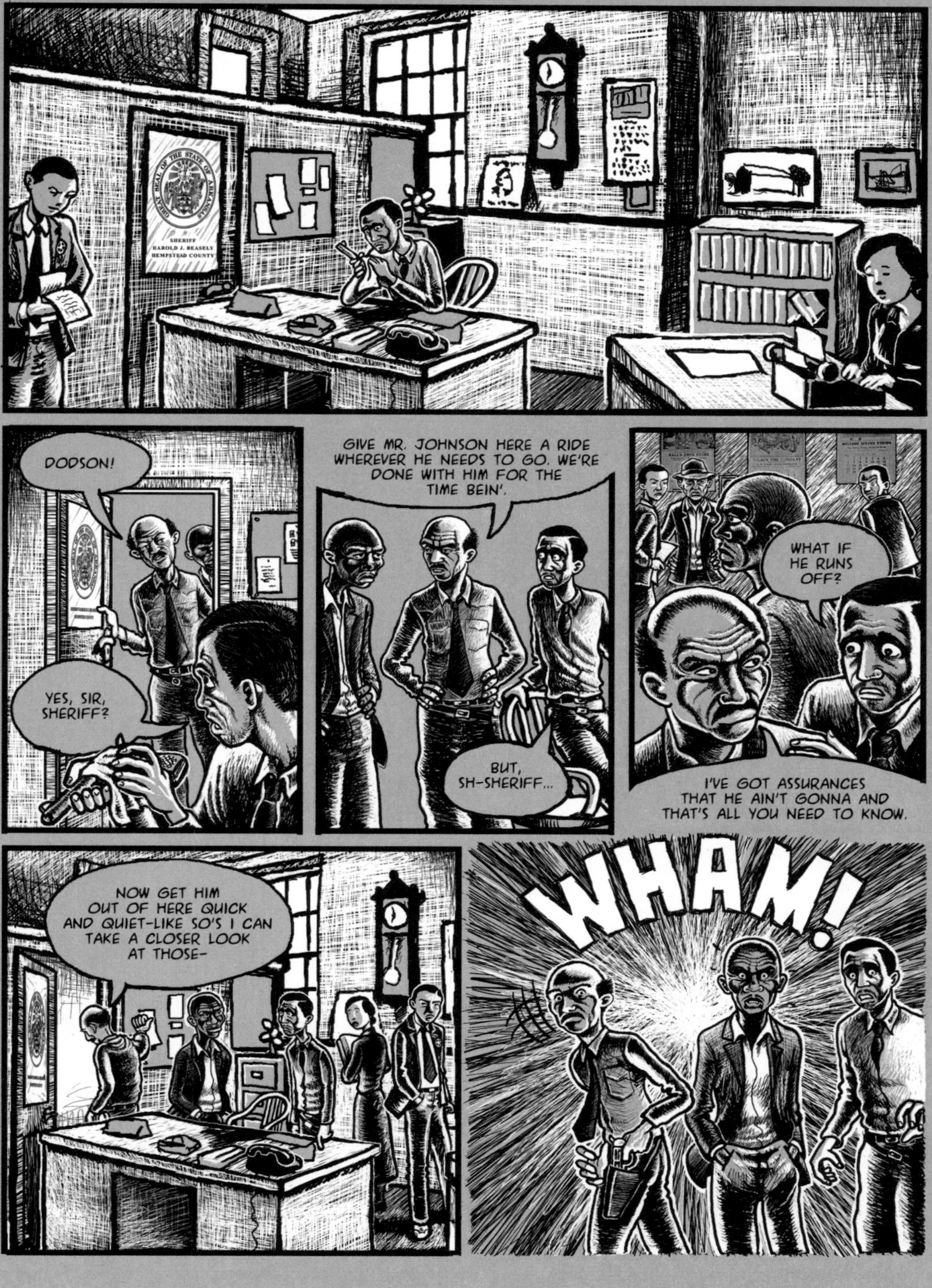
SHERIFF
HAROLD J. BEASELY
HEMPSTEAD COUNTY
DODSON!
YES, SIR, SHERIFF?
GIVE MR. JOHNSON HERE A RIDE WHEREVER HE NEEDS TO GO. WE'RE DONE WITH HIM FOR THE TIME BEIN'.
BUT, SH-SHERIFF...
WHAT IF HE RUNS OFF?
I'VE GOT ASSURANCES THAT HE AIN'T GONNA AND THAT'S ALL YOU NEED TO KNOW.
NOW GET HIM OUT OF HERE QUICK AND QUIET-LIKE SO'S I CAN TAKE A CLOSER LOOK AT THOSE-
WHAM!

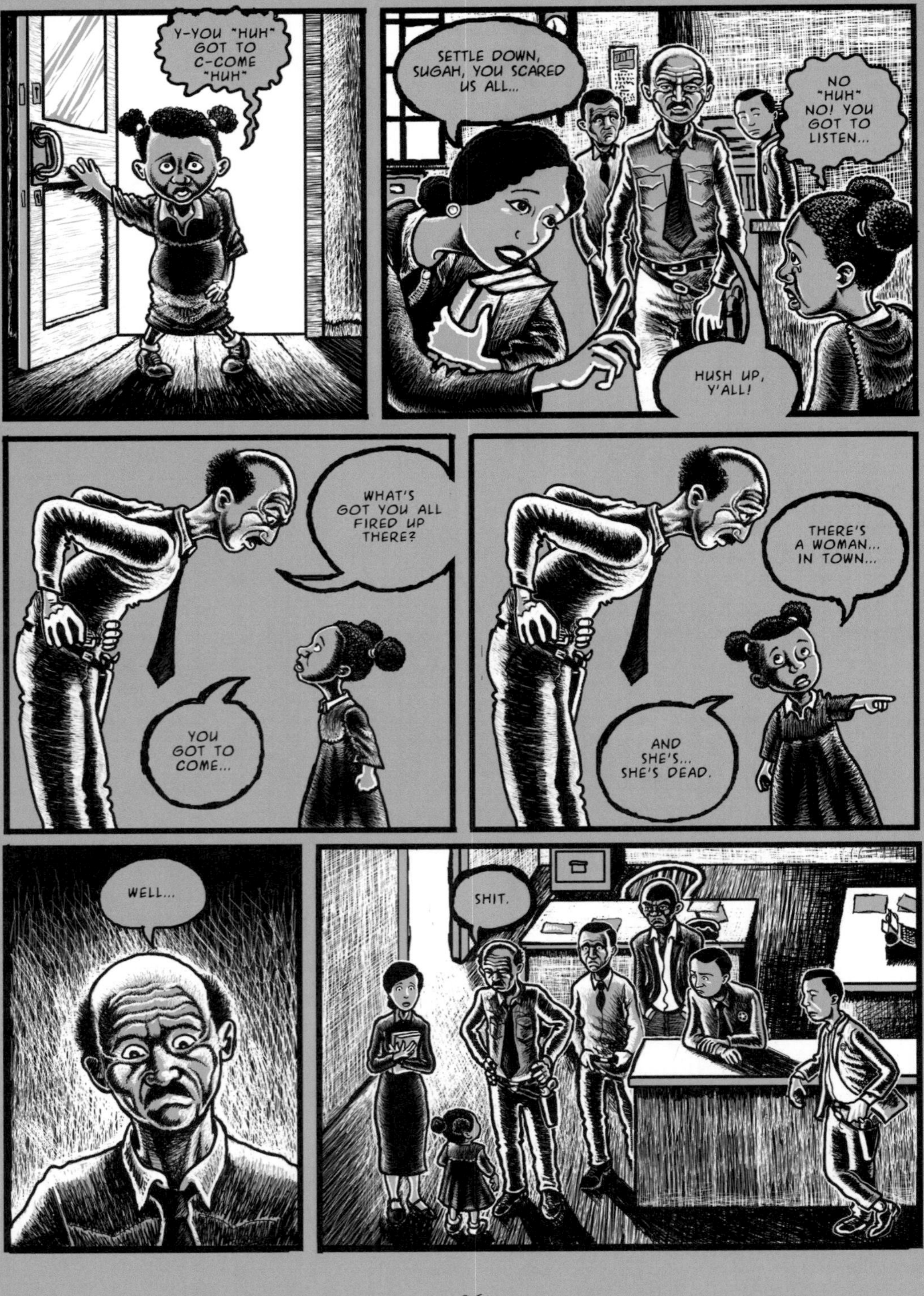
Y-YOU "HUH" GOT TO C-COME "HUH"
SETTLE DOWN, SUGAH, YOU SCARED US ALL...
NO "HUH" NO! YOU GOT TO LISTEN...
HUSH UP, Y'ALL!
WHAT'S GOT YOU ALL FIRED UP THERE?
YOU GOT TO COME...
THERE'S A WOMAN... IN TOWN...
AND SHE'S... SHE'S DEAD.
WELL...
SHIT.

6

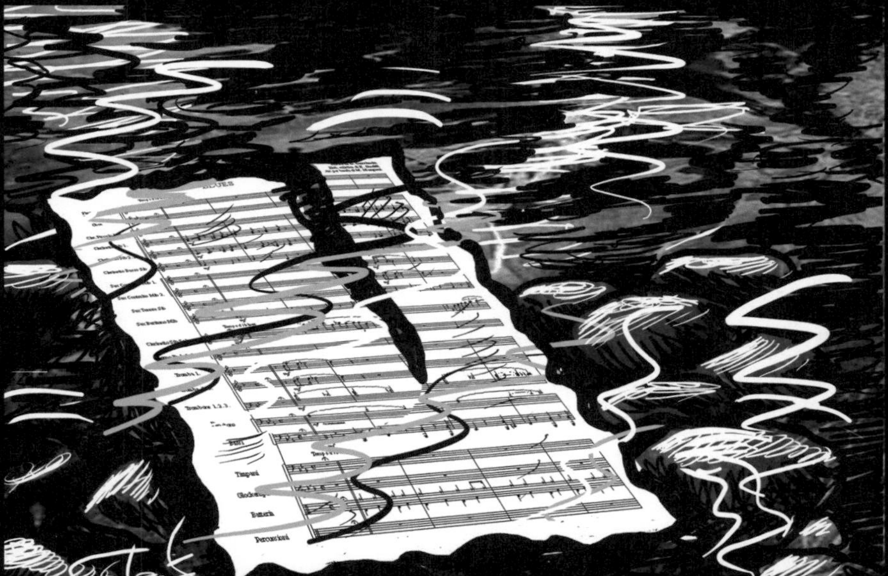
BLUES
Trombone 1.2.3.
Timpani
Batteria
Percussioni

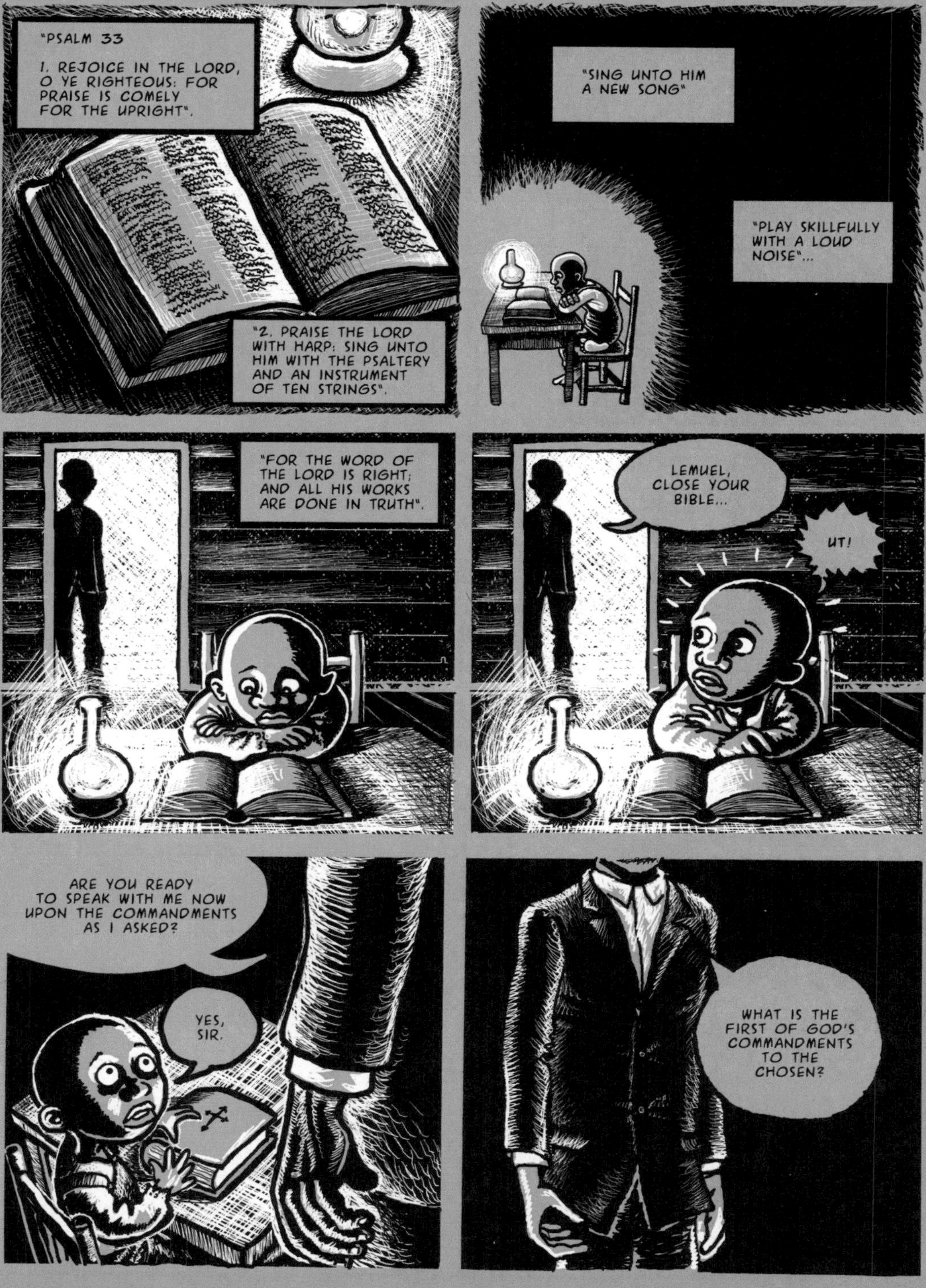
"PSALM 33
1. REJOICE IN THE LORD, O YE RIGHTEOUS: FOR PRAISE IS COMELY FOR THE UPRIGHT".
"2. PRAISE THE LORD WITH HARP: SING UNTO HIM WITH THE PSALTERY AND AN INSTRUMENT OF TEN STRINGS".
"SING UNTO HIM A NEW SONG"
"PLAY SKILLFULLY WITH A LOUD NOISE"...
"FOR THE WORD OF THE LORD IS RIGHT; AND ALL HIS WORKS ARE DONE IN TRUTH".
LEMUEL, CLOSE YOUR BIBLE...
UT!
ARE YOU READY TO SPEAK WITH ME NOW UPON THE COMMANDMENTS AS I ASKED?
YES, SIR.
WHAT IS THE FIRST OF GOD'S COMMANDMENTS TO THE CHOSEN?

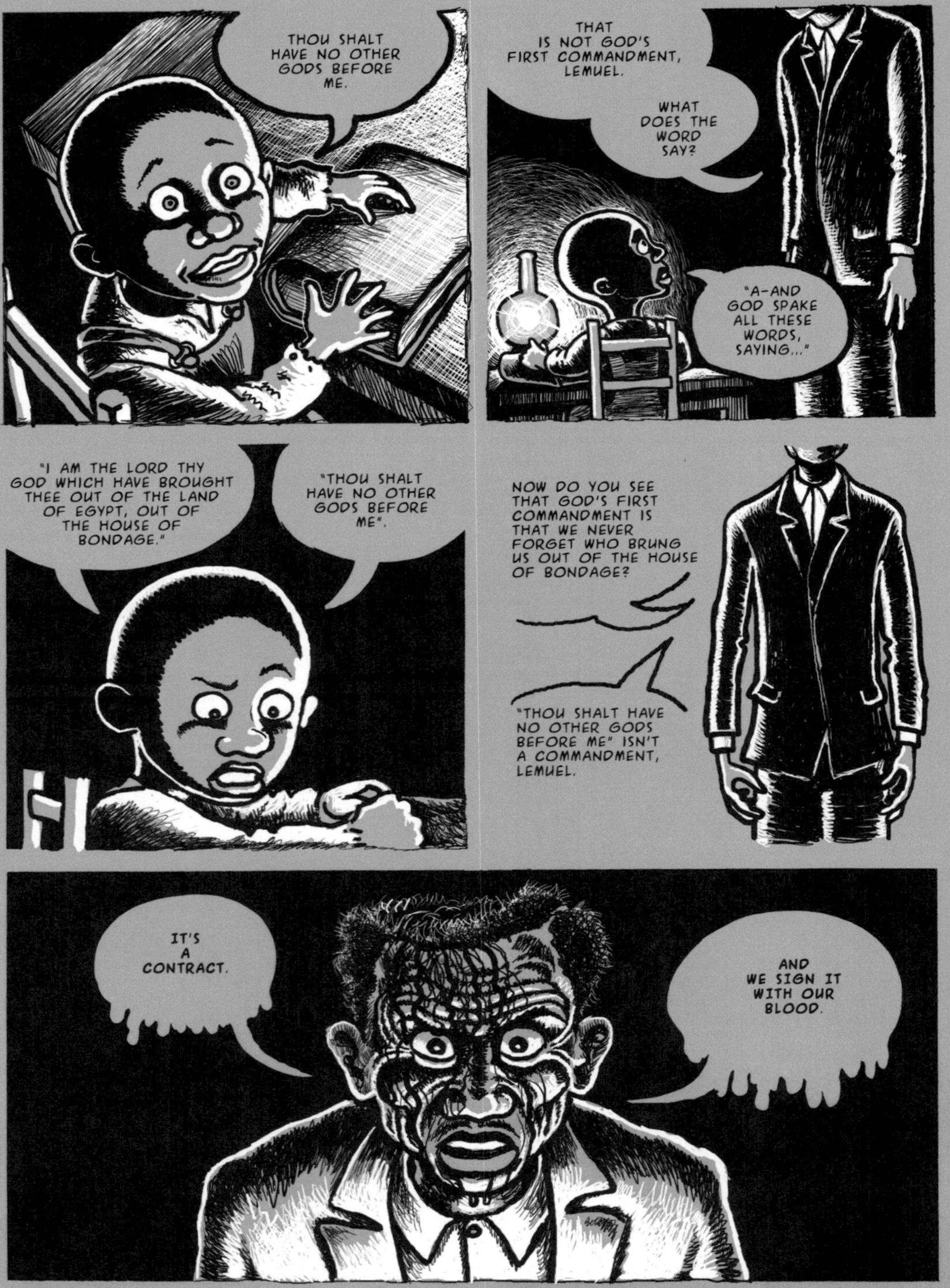
THOU SHALT HAVE NO OTHER GODS BEFORE ME.
THAT IS NOT GOD'S FIRST COMMANDMENT, LEMUEL.
WHAT DOES THE WORD SAY?
"A-AND GOD SPAKE ALL THESE WORDS, SAYING..."
"I AM THE LORD THY GOD WHICH HAVE BROUGHT THEE OUT OF THE LAND OF EGYPT, OUT OF THE HOUSE OF BONDAGE."
"THOU SHALT HAVE NO OTHER GODS BEFORE ME".
NOW DO YOU SEE THAT GOD'S FIRST COMMANDMENT IS THAT WE NEVER FORGET WHO BRUNG US OUT OF THE HOUSE OF BONDAGE?
"THOU SHALT HAVE NO OTHER GODS BEFORE ME" ISN'T A COMMANDMENT, LEMUEL.
IT'S A CONTRACT.
AND WE SIGN IT WITH OUR BLOOD.

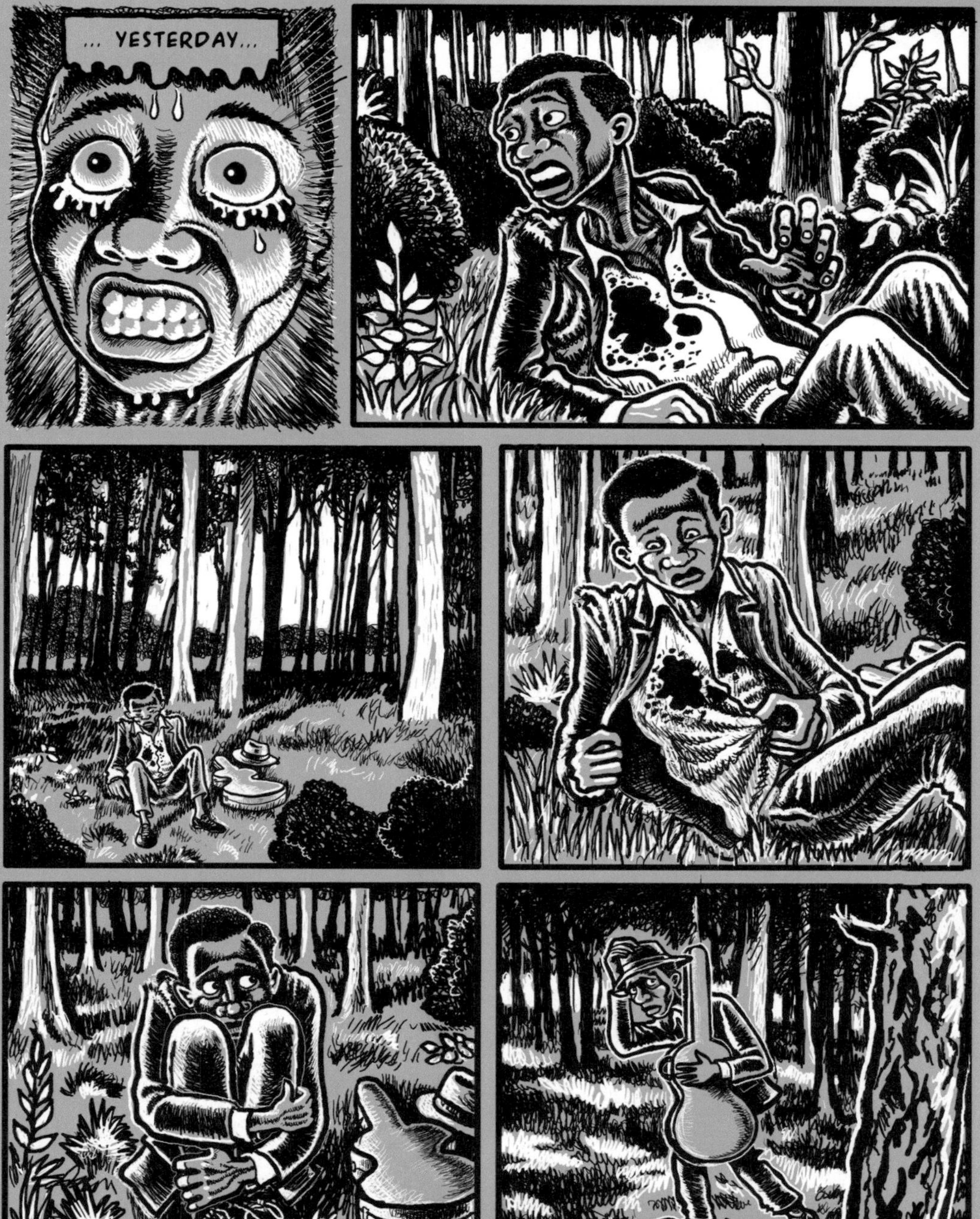
... YESTERDAY...

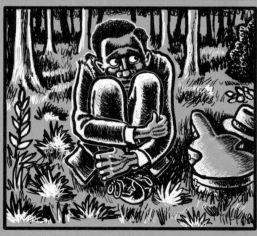

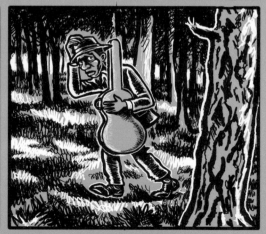

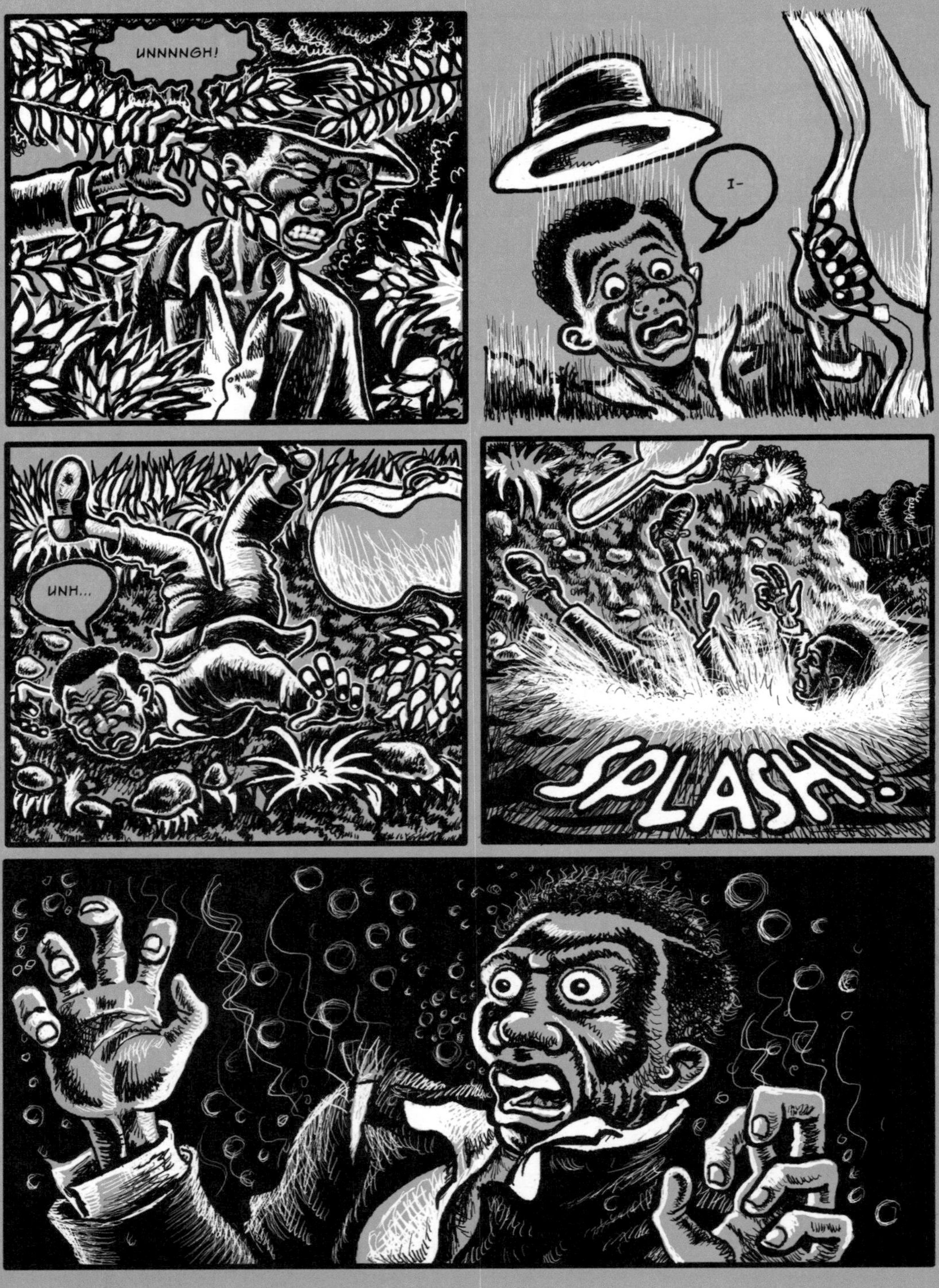
UNNNNGH!
I-
UNH...
SPLASH!

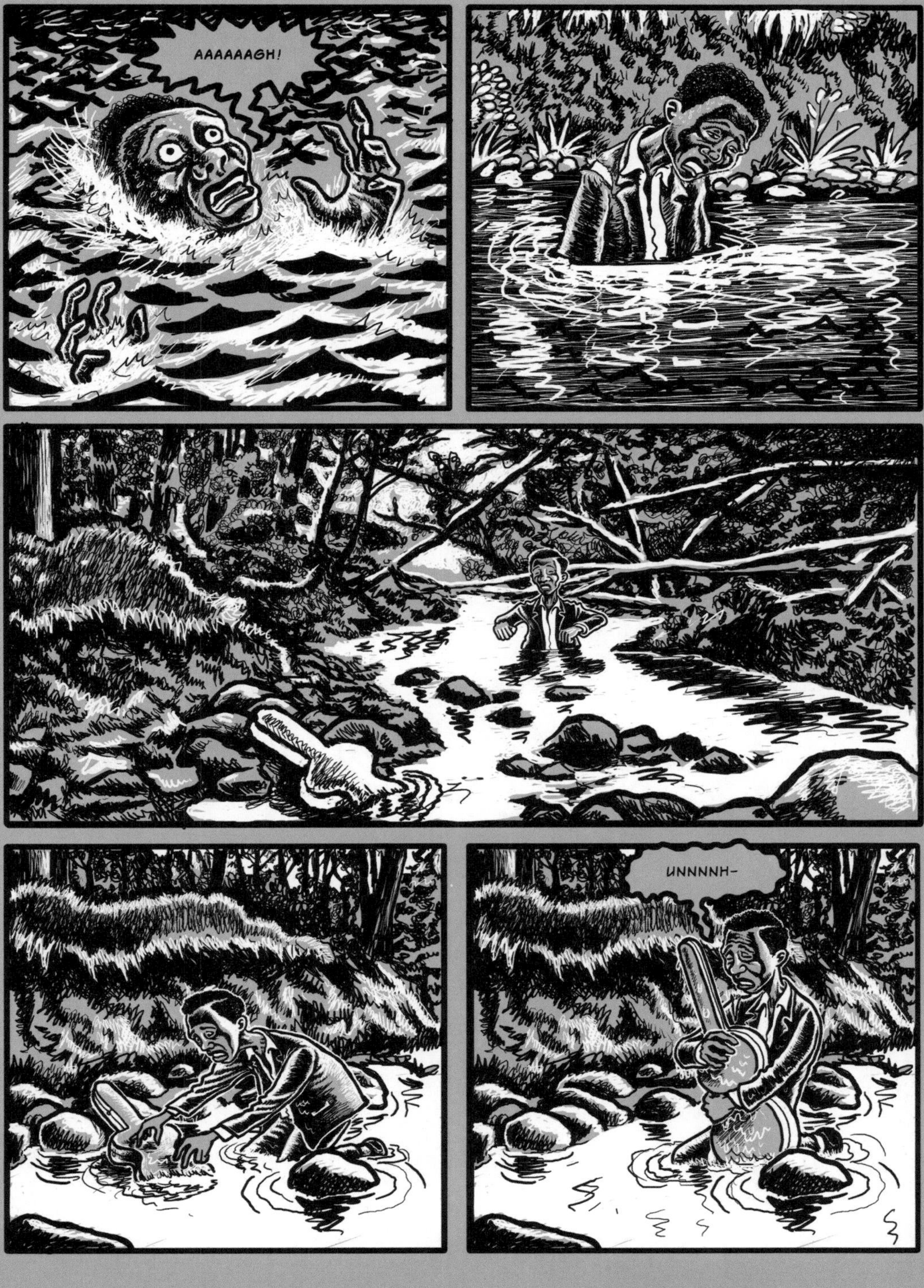
AAAAAAGH!
UNNNNH-

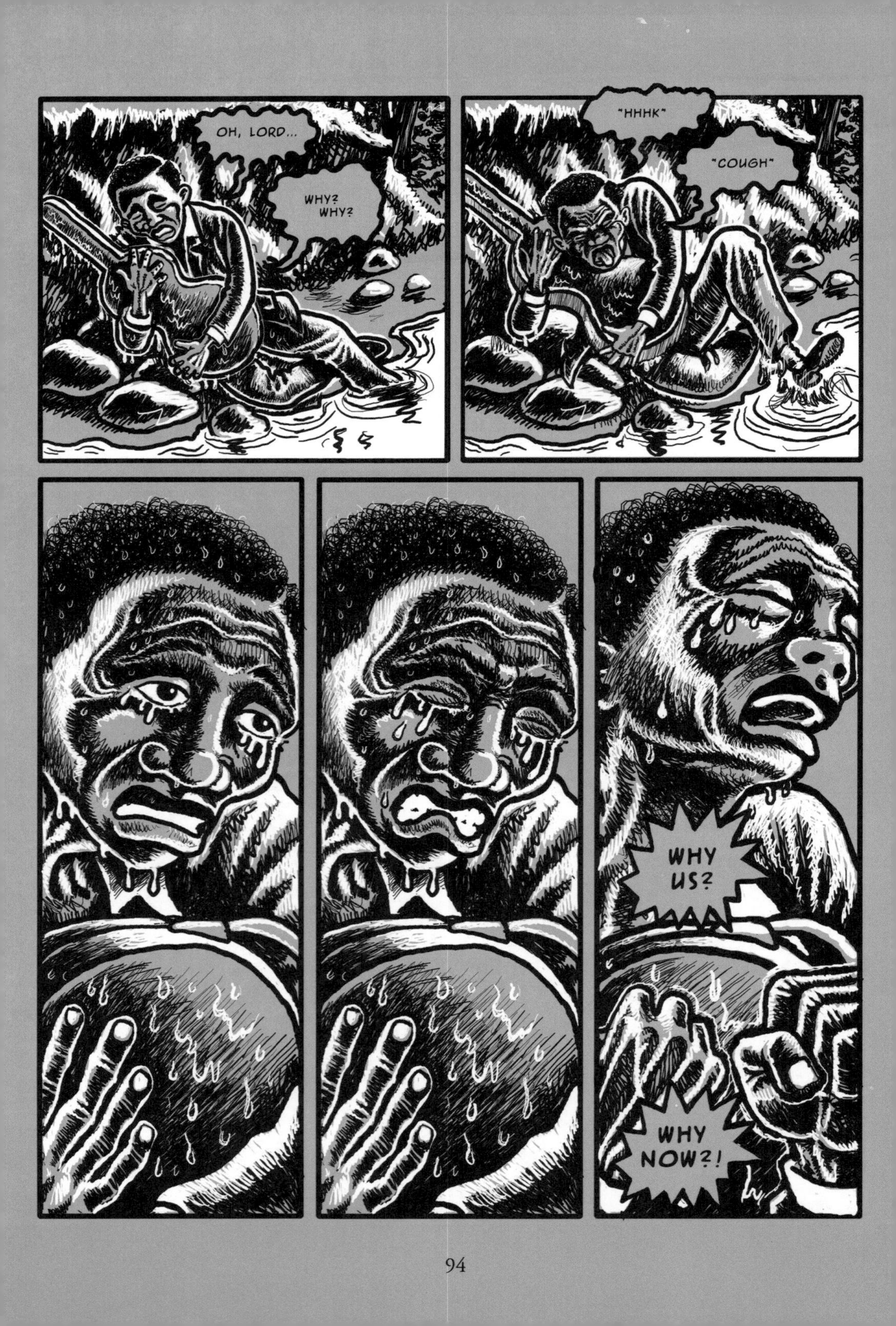
OH, LORD...
WHY? WHY?
"HHHK"
"COUGH"
WHY US?
WHY NOW?!

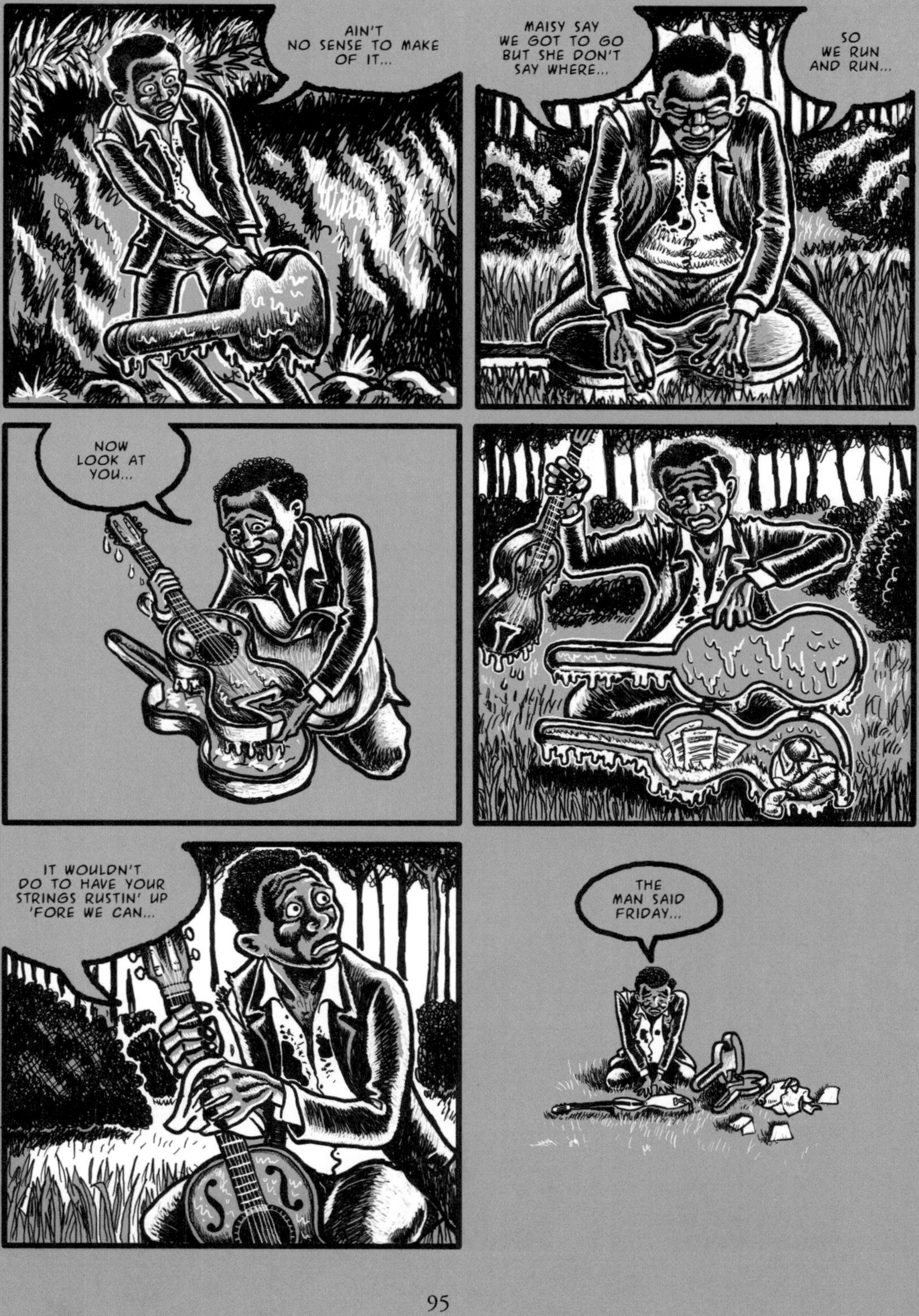
AIN'T NO SENSE TO MAKE OF IT...
MAISY SAY WE GOT TO GO BUT SHE DON'T SAY WHERE...
SO WE RUN AND RUN...
NOW LOOK AT YOU...
IT WOULDN'T DO TO HAVE YOUR STRINGS RUSTIN' UP 'FORE WE CAN...
THE MAN SAID FRIDAY...

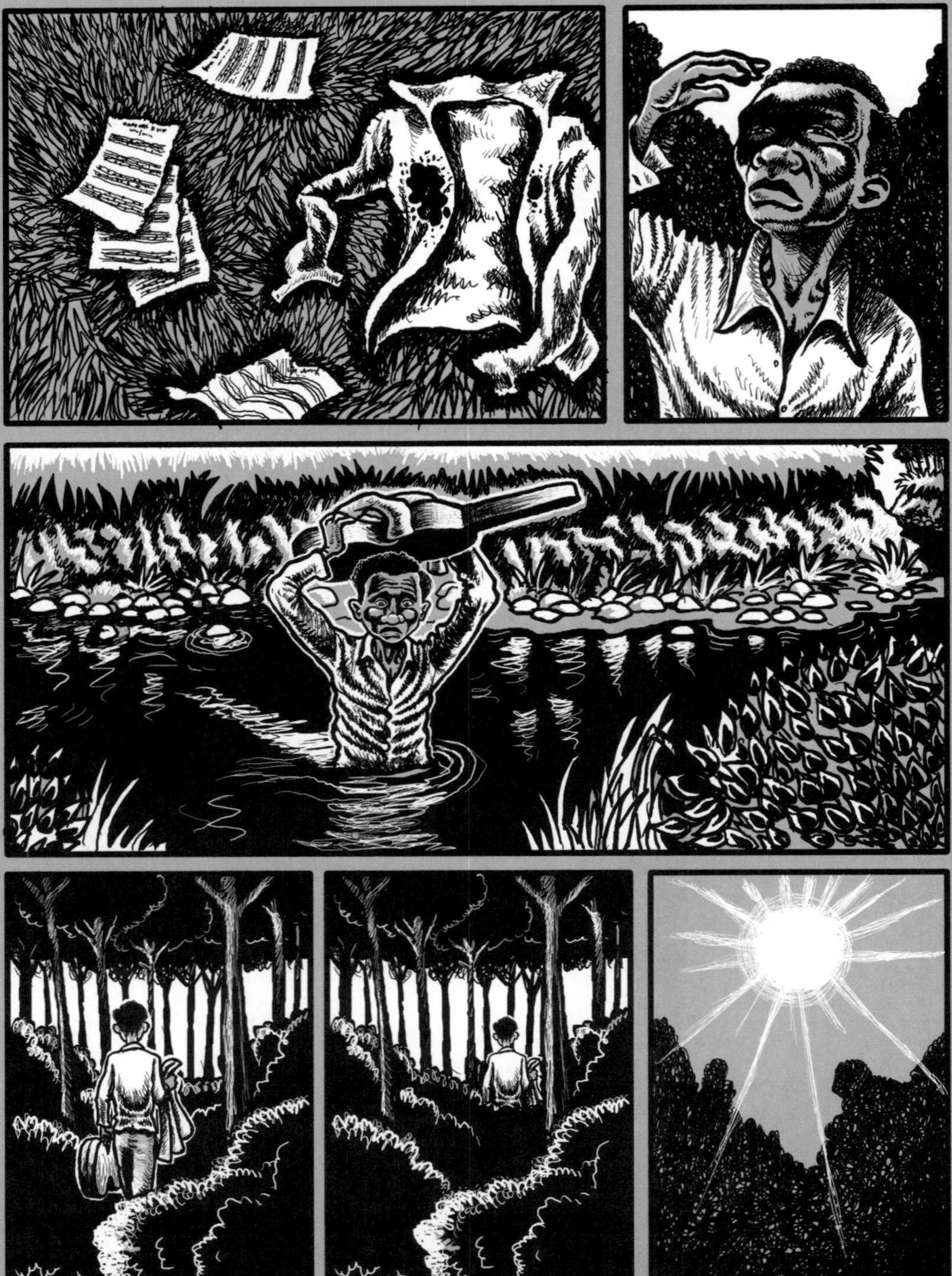

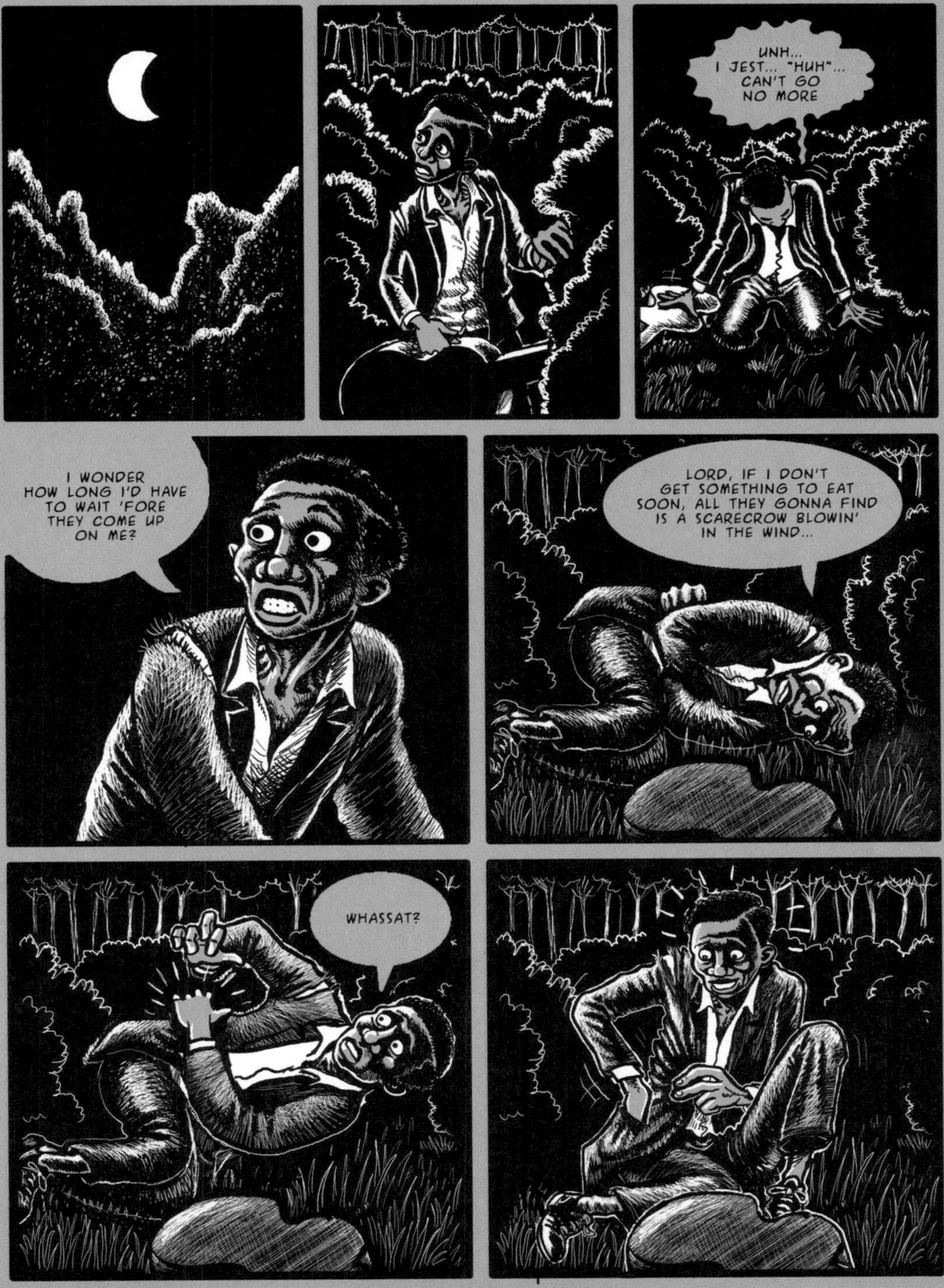
UNH... I JEST... "HUH"... CAN'T GO NO MORE
I WONDER HOW LONG I'D HAVE TO WAIT 'FORE THEY COME UP ON ME?
LORD, IF I DON'T GET SOMETHING TO EAT SOON, ALL THEY GONNA FIND IS A SCARECROW BLOWIN' IN THE WIND...
WHASSAT?

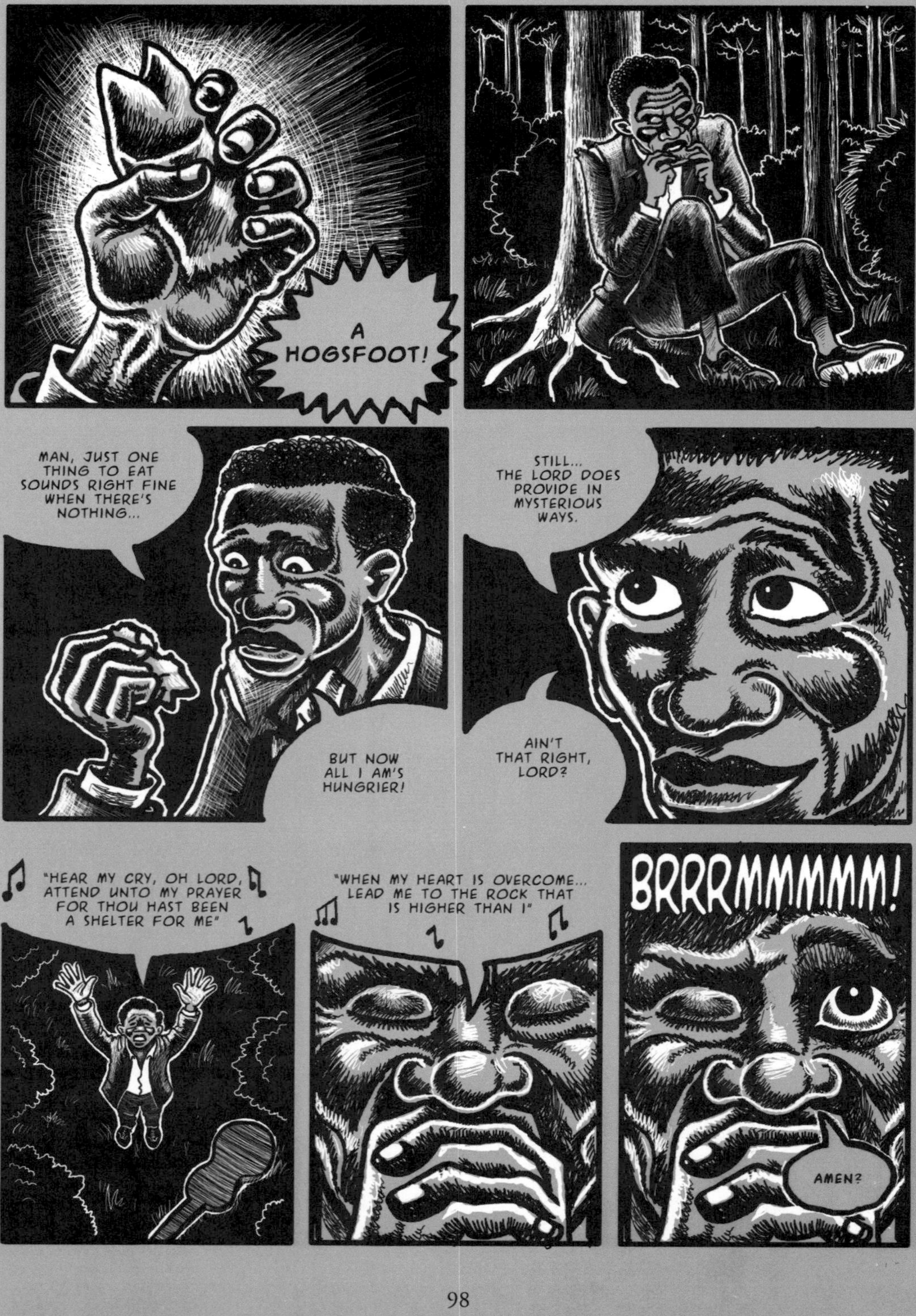
A HOGSFOOT!
MAN, JUST ONE THING TO EAT SOUNDS RIGHT FINE WHEN THERE'S NOTHING...
BUT NOW ALL I AM'S HUNGRIER!
STILL... THE LORD DOES PROVIDE IN MYSTERIOUS WAYS.
AIN'T THAT RIGHT, LORD?
"HEAR MY CRY, OH LORD, ATTEND UNTO MY PRAYER FOR THOU HAST BEEN A SHELTER FOR ME"
"WHEN MY HEART IS OVERCOME... LEAD ME TO THE ROCK THAT IS HIGHER THAN I"
BRRRMMMMM!
AMEN?

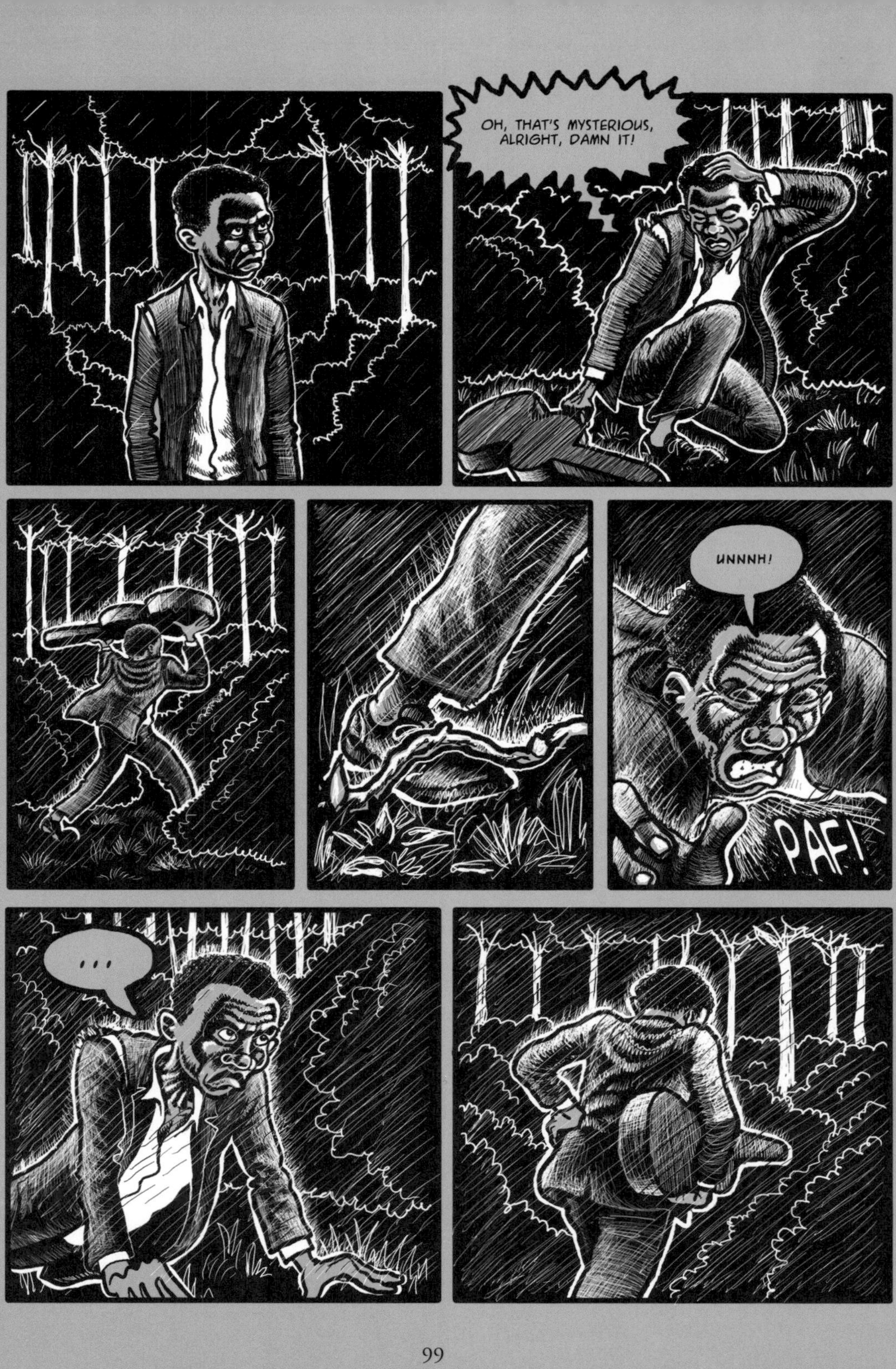
OH, THAT'S MYSTERIOUS, ALRIGHT, DAMN IT!
UNNNH!
PAF!
...

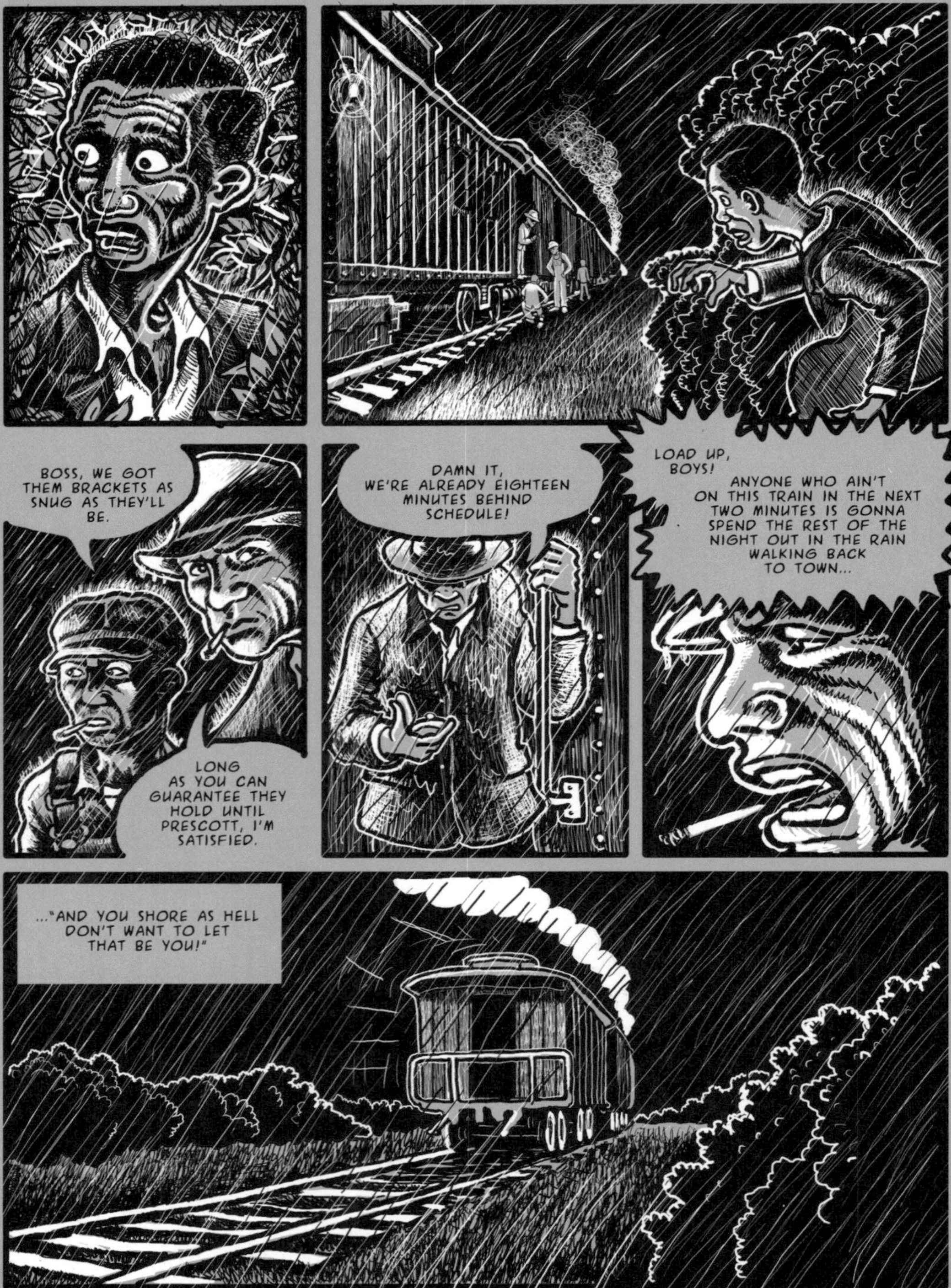
BOSS, WE GOT THEM BRACKETS AS SNUG AS THEY'LL BE.
LONG AS YOU CAN GUARANTEE THEY HOLD UNTIL PRESCOTT, I'M SATISFIED.
DAMN IT, WE'RE ALREADY EIGHTEEN MINUTES BEHIND SCHEDULE!
LOAD UP, BOYS!
ANYONE WHO AIN'T ON THIS TRAIN IN THE NEXT TWO MINUTES IS GONNA SPEND THE REST OF THE NIGHT OUT IN THE RAIN WALKING BACK TO TOWN...
..."AND YOU SHORE AS HELL DON'T WANT TO LET THAT BE YOU!"

7

WE...
"AHEM"

SORRY...
THE OFFICERS, ARRIVED
AT APPROXIMATELY
10:30 AM.

UPON ENTERING THE HOUSE AT 312 "A" STREET,
OFFICERS VERIFIED EARLIER REPORTS OF ONE
MAISY ABRAMS, AGED 20 YRS AND LOCAL
TO HOPE, DEAD IN HER HOME.

Goodman
Funeral home
12 West End
Hope

"SHE WAS HUNG,
PROBABLE SUICIDE".

"SHE WAS COVERED IN BLOOD
THAT WASN'T HER OWN AND HAIR
THAT MATCHED OUR WHITE VICTIM
IN THE OTHER MURDER"...

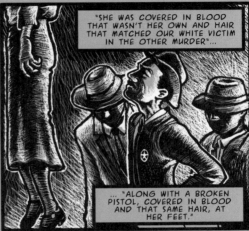

... "ALONG WITH A BROKEN
PISTOL, COVERED IN BLOOD
AND THAT SAME HAIR, AT
HER FEET."

WE FOUND OUT BY TALKING TO LOCAL RESIDENTS
THAT ABRAMS WAS OF DEFINITE RELATION TO TARENE
DAVIS, OUR OTHER KNOWN VICTIM
AT THIS TIME.

THIS BRINGS
THE TOTAL NUMBER OF DEAD BODIES
TO TURN UP WITHOUT WARNING IN
THE LAST 48 HOURS TO FOUR.

103

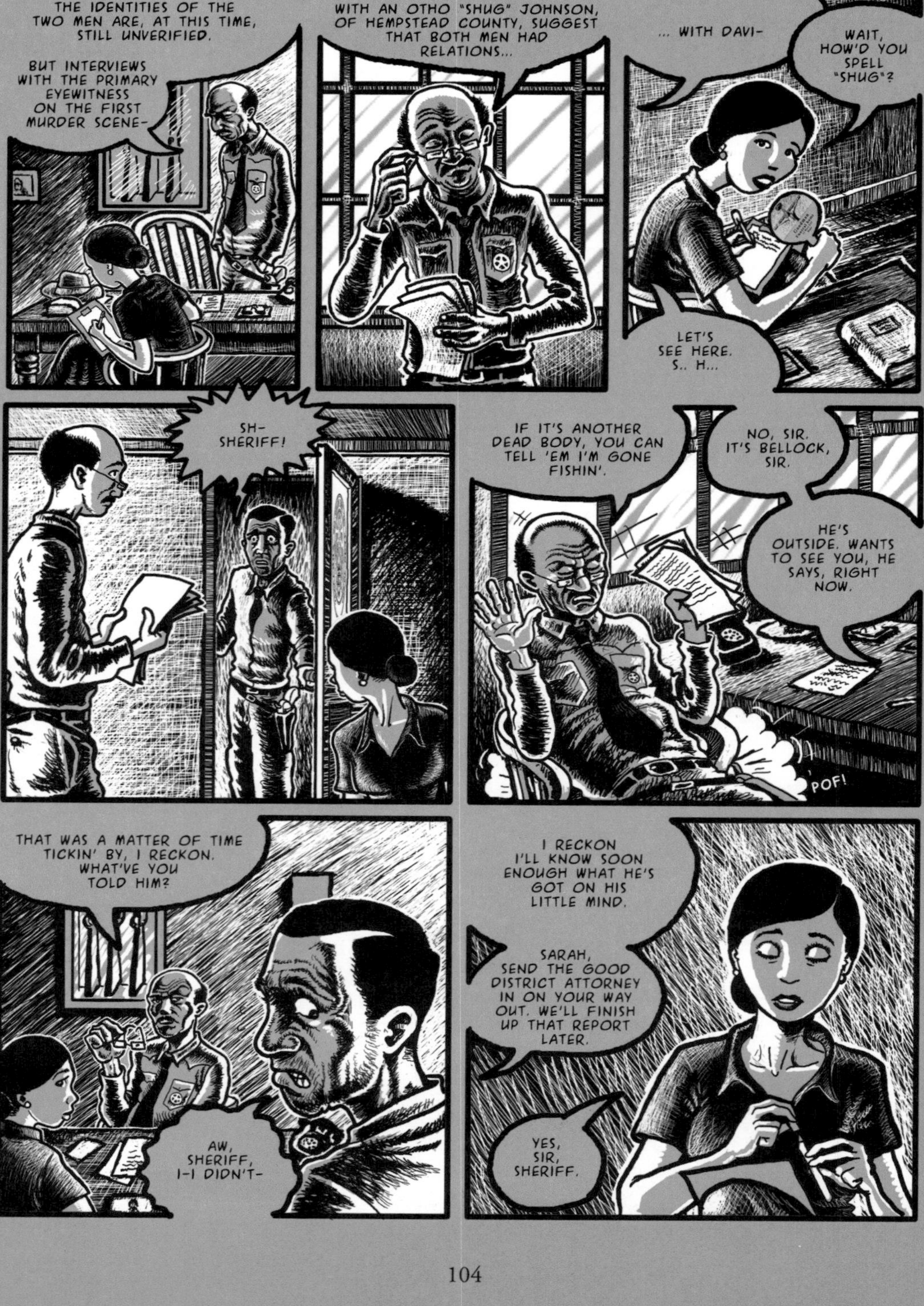
THE IDENTITIES OF THE TWO MEN ARE, AT THIS TIME, STILL UNVERIFIED.
BUT INTERVIEWS WITH THE PRIMARY EYEWITNESS ON THE FIRST MURDER SCENE-
WITH AN OTHO "SHUG" JOHNSON, OF HEMPSTEAD COUNTY, SUGGEST THAT BOTH MEN HAD RELATIONS...
... WITH DAVI-
WAIT, HOW'D YOU SPELL "SHUG"?
LET'S SEE HERE. S.. H...
SH- SHERIFF!
IF IT'S ANOTHER DEAD BODY, YOU CAN TELL 'EM I'M GONE FISHIN'.
NO, SIR. IT'S BELLOCK, SIR.
HE'S OUTSIDE. WANTS TO SEE YOU, HE SAYS, RIGHT NOW.
POF!
THAT WAS A MATTER OF TIME TICKIN' BY, I RECKON. WHAT'VE YOU TOLD HIM?
AW, SHERIFF, I-I DIDN'T-
I RECKON I'LL KNOW SOON ENOUGH WHAT HE'S GOT ON HIS LITTLE MIND.
SARAH, SEND THE GOOD DISTRICT ATTORNEY IN ON YOUR WAY OUT. WE'LL FINISH UP THAT REPORT LATER.
YES, SIR, SHERIFF.

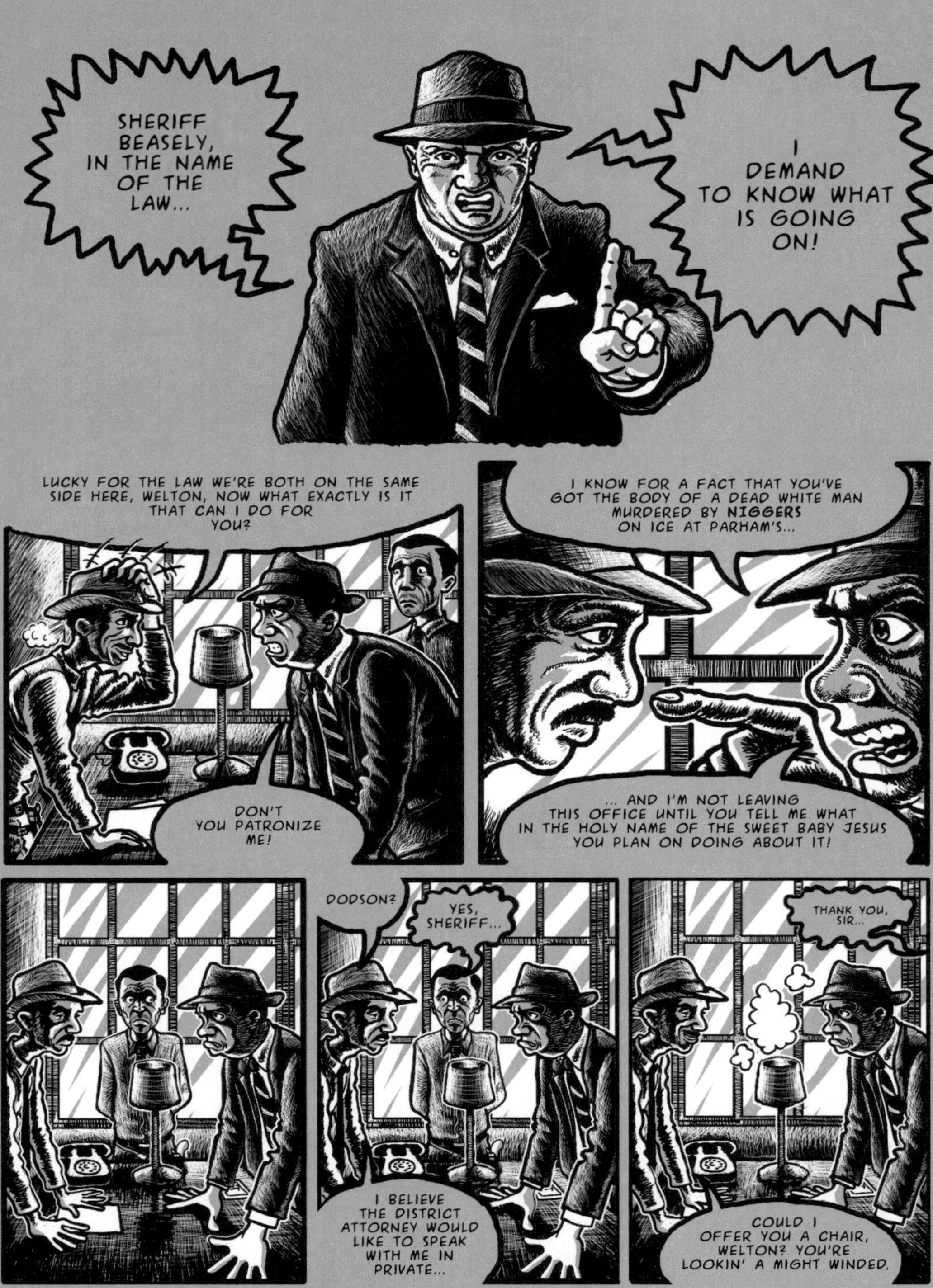
SHERIFF BEASELY, IN THE NAME OF THE LAW...
I DEMAND TO KNOW WHAT IS GOING ON!
LUCKY FOR THE LAW WE'RE BOTH ON THE SAME SIDE HERE, WELTON, NOW WHAT EXACTLY IS IT THAT CAN I DO FOR YOU?
DON'T YOU PATRONIZE ME!
I KNOW FOR A FACT THAT YOU'VE GOT THE BODY OF A DEAD WHITE MAN MURDERED BY NIGGERS ON ICE AT PARHAM'S...
... AND I'M NOT LEAVING THIS OFFICE UNTIL YOU TELL ME WHAT IN THE HOLY NAME OF THE SWEET BABY JESUS YOU PLAN ON DOING ABOUT IT!
DODSON?
YES, SHERIFF...
I BELIEVE THE DISTRICT ATTORNEY WOULD LIKE TO SPEAK WITH ME IN PRIVATE...
THANK YOU, SIR...
COULD I OFFER YOU A CHAIR, WELTON? YOU'RE LOOKIN' A MIGHT WINDED.

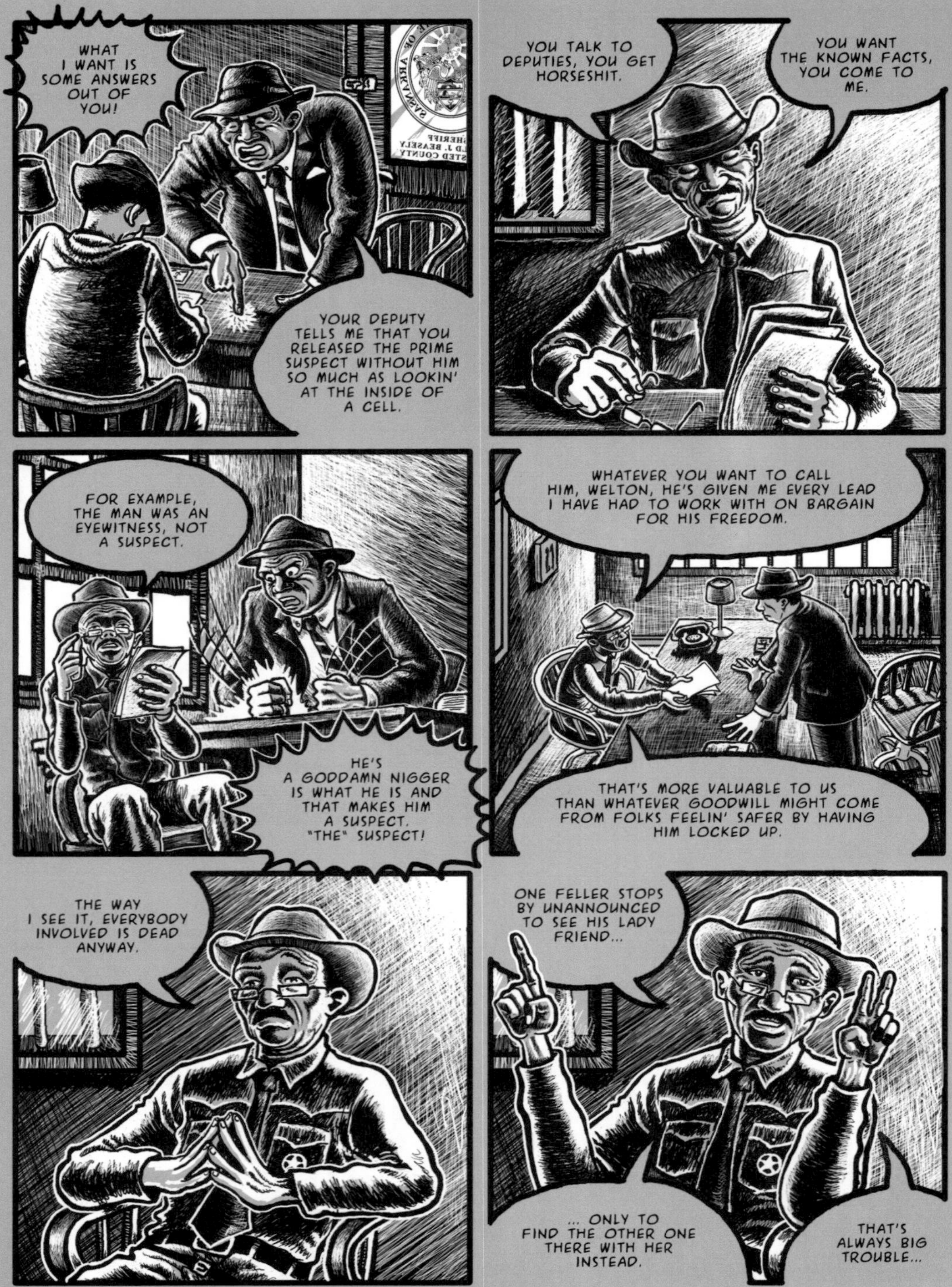
WHAT I WANT IS SOME ANSWERS OUT OF YOU!
YOUR DEPUTY TELLS ME THAT YOU RELEASED THE PRIME SUSPECT WITHOUT HIM SO MUCH AS LOOKIN' AT THE INSIDE OF A CELL.
YOU TALK TO DEPUTIES, YOU GET HORSESHIT.
YOU WANT THE KNOWN FACTS, YOU COME TO ME.
FOR EXAMPLE, THE MAN WAS AN EYEWITNESS, NOT A SUSPECT.
HE'S A GODDAMN NIGGER IS WHAT HE IS AND THAT MAKES HIM A SUSPECT. "THE" SUSPECT!
WHATEVER YOU WANT TO CALL HIM, WELTON, HE'S GIVEN ME EVERY LEAD I HAVE HAD TO WORK WITH ON BARGAIN FOR HIS FREEDOM.
THAT'S MORE VALUABLE TO US THAN WHATEVER GOODWILL MIGHT COME FROM FOLKS FEELIN' SAFER BY HAVING HIM LOCKED UP.
THE WAY I SEE IT, EVERYBODY INVOLVED IS DEAD ANYWAY.
ONE FELLER STOPS BY UNANNOUNCED TO SEE HIS LADY FRIEND...
... ONLY TO FIND THE OTHER ONE THERE WITH HER INSTEAD.
THAT'S ALWAYS BIG TROUBLE...

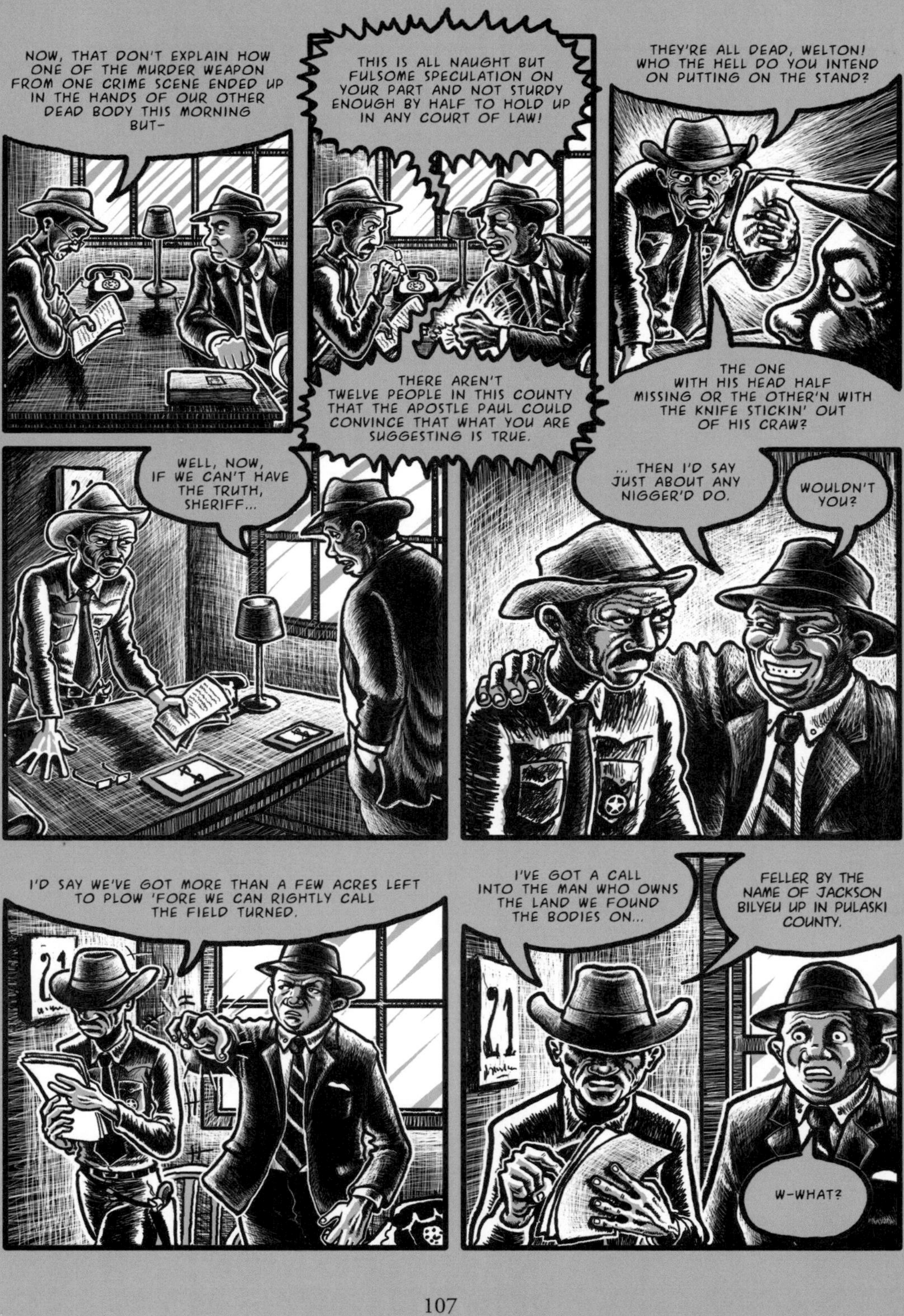

NOW, THAT DON'T EXPLAIN HOW ONE OF THE MURDER WEAPON FROM ONE CRIME SCENE ENDED UP IN THE HANDS OF OUR OTHER DEAD BODY THIS MORNING BUT–
THIS IS ALL NAUGHT BUT FULSOME SPECULATION ON YOUR PART AND NOT STURDY ENOUGH BY HALF TO HOLD UP IN ANY COURT OF LAW!
THERE AREN'T TWELVE PEOPLE IN THIS COUNTY THAT THE APOSTLE PAUL COULD CONVINCE THAT WHAT YOU ARE SUGGESTING IS TRUE.
THEY'RE ALL DEAD, WELTON! WHO THE HELL DO YOU INTEND ON PUTTING ON THE STAND?
THE ONE WITH HIS HEAD HALF MISSING OR THE OTHER'N WITH THE KNIFE STICKIN' OUT OF HIS CRAW?
WELL, NOW, IF WE CAN'T HAVE THE TRUTH, SHERIFF...
... THEN I'D SAY JUST ABOUT ANY NIGGER'D DO.
WOULDN'T YOU?
I'D SAY WE'VE GOT MORE THAN A FEW ACRES LEFT TO PLOW 'FORE WE CAN RIGHTLY CALL THE FIELD TURNED.
I'VE GOT A CALL INTO THE MAN WHO OWNS THE LAND WE FOUND THE BODIES ON...
FELLER BY THE NAME OF JACKSON BILYEU UP IN PULASKI COUNTY.
W-WHAT?

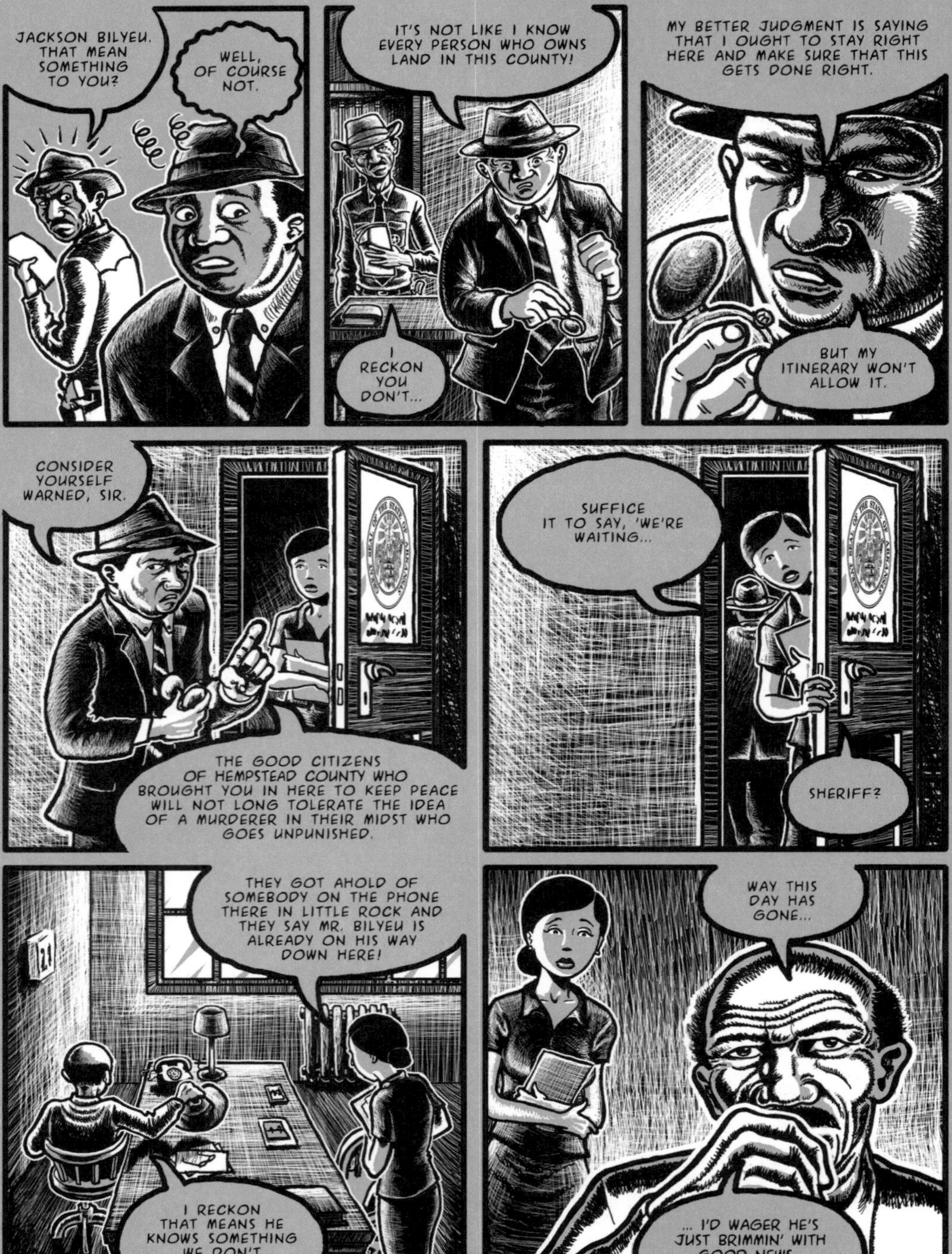
JACKSON BILYEU. THAT MEAN SOMETHING TO YOU?
WELL, OF COURSE NOT.
IT'S NOT LIKE I KNOW EVERY PERSON WHO OWNS LAND IN THIS COUNTY!
I RECKON YOU DON'T...
MY BETTER JUDGMENT IS SAYING THAT I OUGHT TO STAY RIGHT HERE AND MAKE SURE THAT THIS GETS DONE RIGHT.
BUT MY ITINERARY WON'T ALLOW IT.
CONSIDER YOURSELF WARNED, SIR.
THE GOOD CITIZENS OF HEMPSTEAD COUNTY WHO BROUGHT YOU IN HERE TO KEEP PEACE WILL NOT LONG TOLERATE THE IDEA OF A MURDERER IN THEIR MIDST WHO GOES UNPUNISHED.
SUFFICE IT TO SAY, 'WE'RE WAITING...
SHERIFF?
THEY GOT AHOLD OF SOMEBODY ON THE PHONE THERE IN LITTLE ROCK AND THEY SAY MR. BILYEU IS ALREADY ON HIS WAY DOWN HERE!
I RECKON THAT MEANS HE KNOWS SOMETHING WE DON'T
WAY THIS DAY HAS GONE...
... I'D WAGER HE'S JUST BRIMMIN' WITH GOOD NEWS...

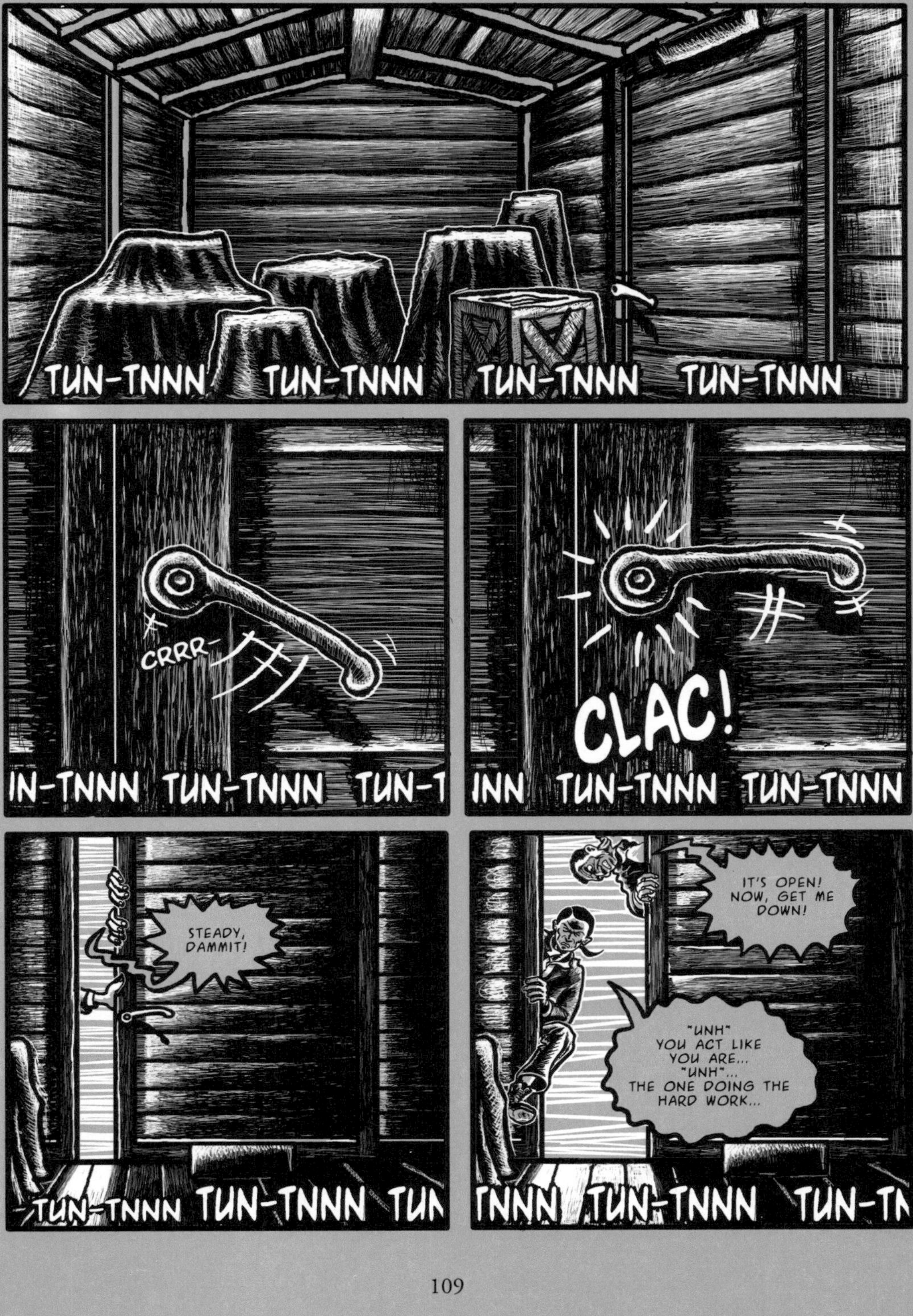
TUN-TNNN TUN-TNNN TUN-TNNN TUN-TNNN
CRRR-
IN-TNNN TUN-TNNN TUN-T
CLAC!
INN TUN-TNNN TUN-TNNN
STEADY, DAMMIT!
-TUN-TNNN TUN-TNNN TUN
IT'S OPEN! NOW, GET ME DOWN!
"UNH" YOU ACT LIKE YOU ARE... "UNH"... THE ONE DOING THE HARD WORK...
TNNN TUN-TNNN TUN-TN

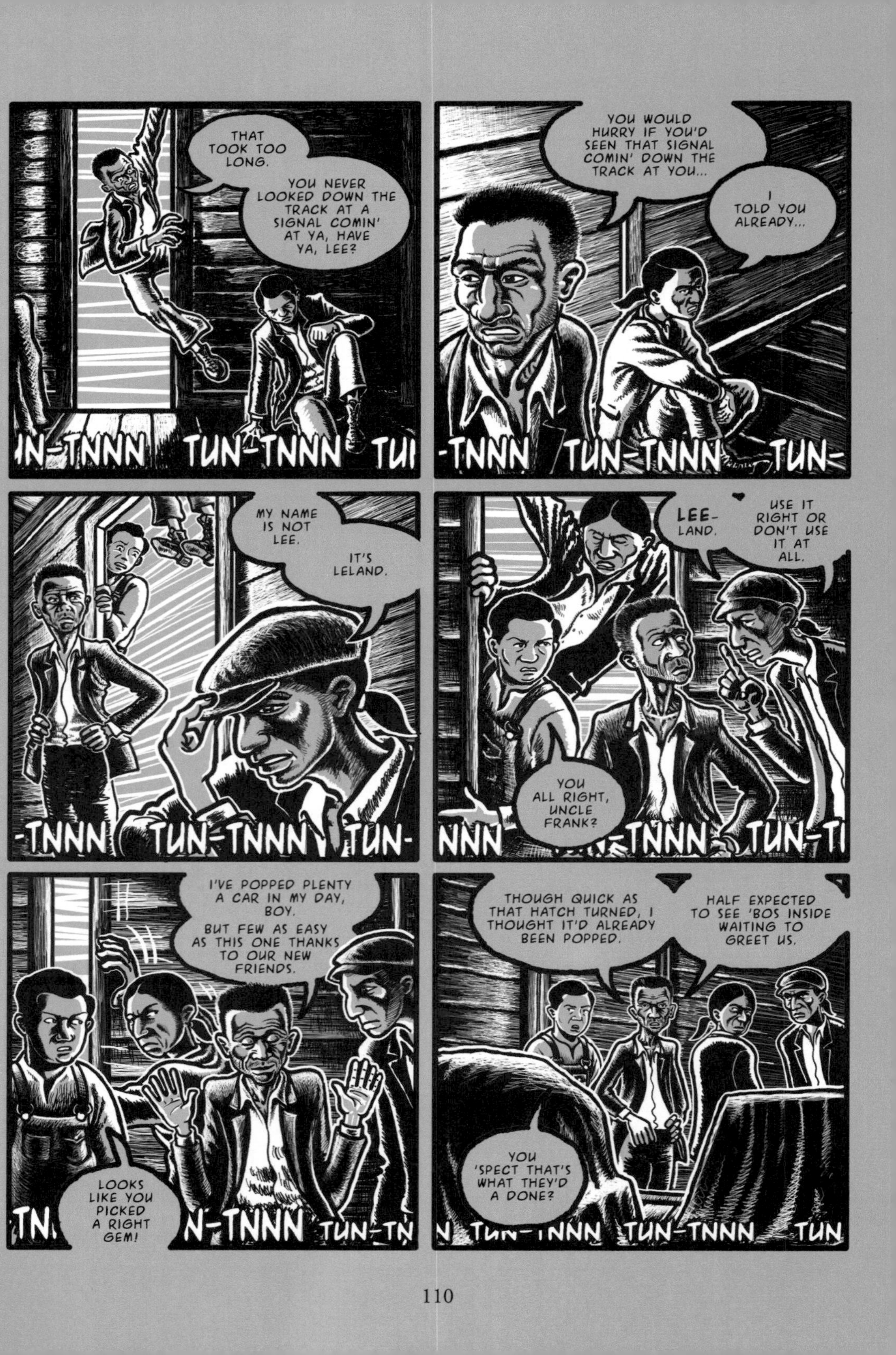
THAT TOOK TOO LONG.
YOU NEVER LOOKED DOWN THE TRACK AT A SIGNAL COMIN' AT YA, HAVE YA, LEE?
N-TNNN TUN-TNNN TU
YOU WOULD HURRY IF YOU'D SEEN THAT SIGNAL COMIN' DOWN THE TRACK AT YOU...
I TOLD YOU ALREADY...
-TNNN TUN-TNNN TUN-
MY NAME IS NOT LEE.
IT'S LELAND.
-TNNN TUN-TNNN TUN-
LEE-LAND.
USE IT RIGHT OR DON'T USE IT AT ALL.
YOU ALL RIGHT, UNCLE FRANK?
NNN -TNNN TUN-T
I'VE POPPED PLENTY A CAR IN MY DAY, BOY.
BUT FEW AS EASY AS THIS ONE THANKS TO OUR NEW FRIENDS.
LOOKS LIKE YOU PICKED A RIGHT GEM!
TN N-TNNN TUN-TN
THOUGH QUICK AS THAT HATCH TURNED, I THOUGHT IT'D ALREADY BEEN POPPED.
HALF EXPECTED TO SEE 'BOS INSIDE WAITING TO GREET US.
YOU 'SPECT THAT'S WHAT THEY'D A DONE?
N TUN-TNNN TUN-TNNN TUN

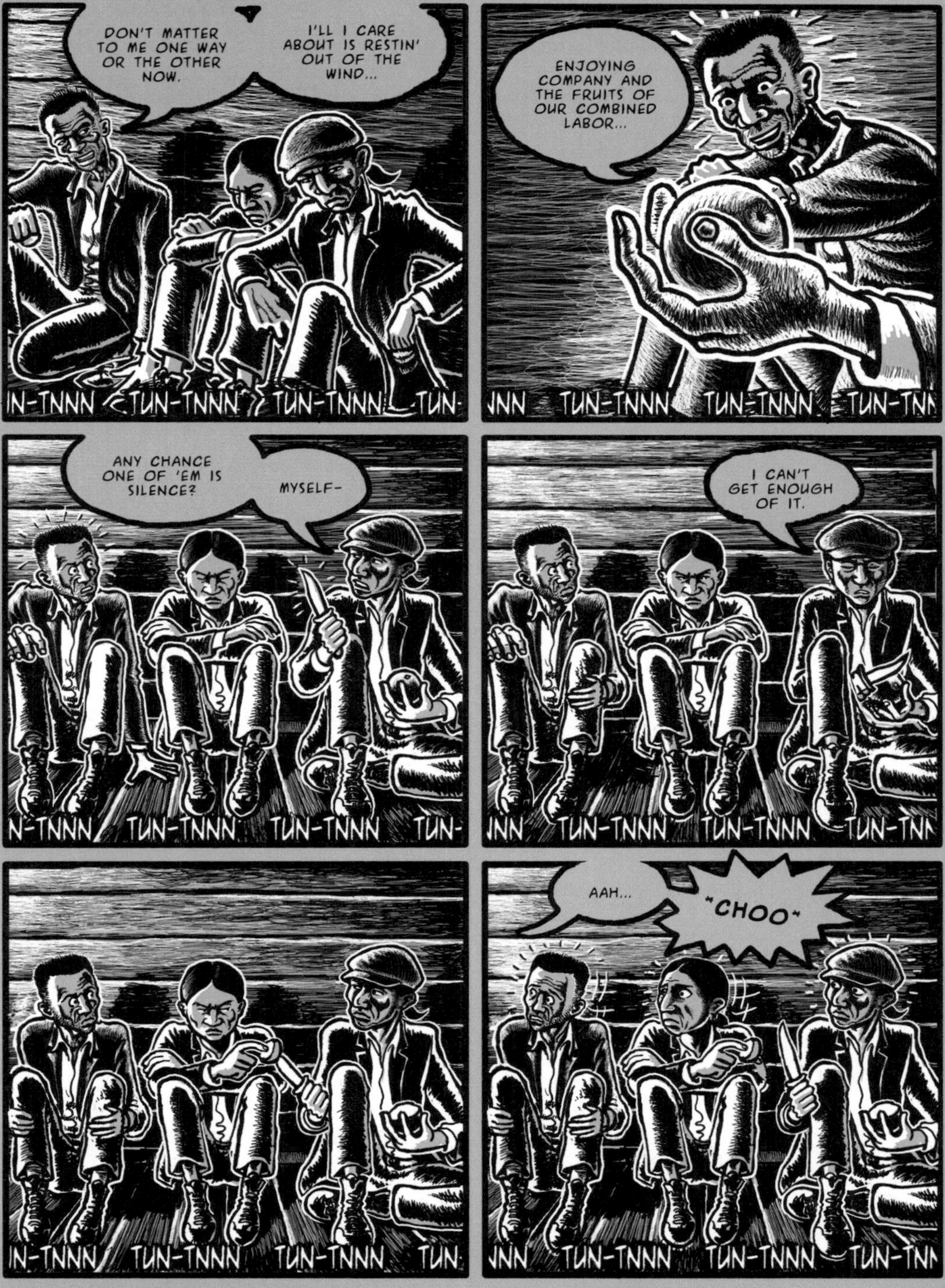
DON'T MATTER TO ME ONE WAY OR THE OTHER NOW.
I'LL I CARE ABOUT IS RESTIN' OUT OF THE WIND...
TUN-TNNN TUN-TNNN TUN-TNNN
ENJOYING COMPANY AND THE FRUITS OF OUR COMBINED LABOR...
TUN-TNNN TUN-TNNN TUN-TNNN
ANY CHANCE ONE OF 'EM IS SILENCE?
MYSELF-
TUN-TNNN TUN-TNNN
I CAN'T GET ENOUGH OF IT.
TUN-TNNN TUN-TNNN
TUN-TNNN TUN-TNNN
AAH...
CHOO
TUN-TNNN TUN-TNNN

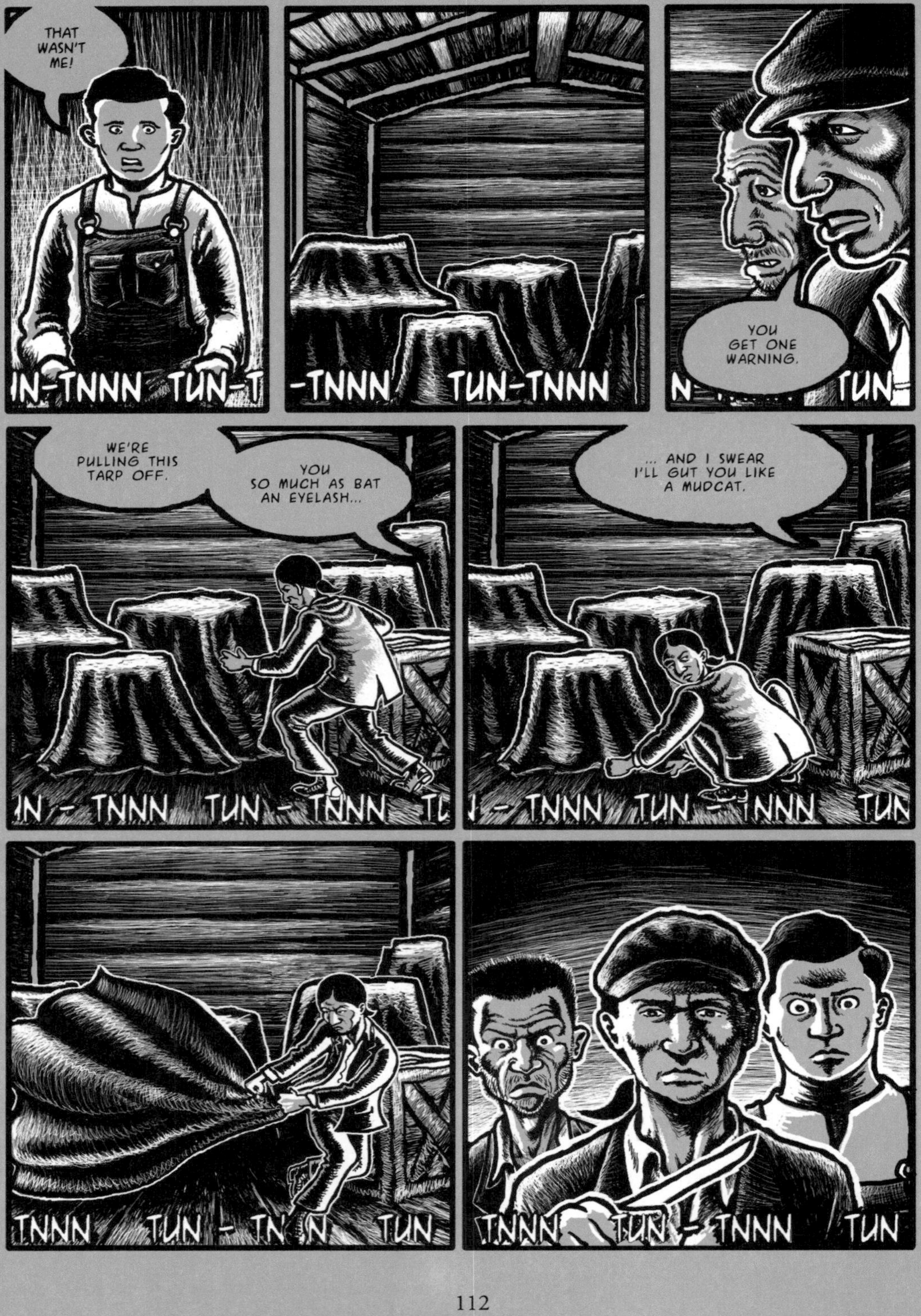
THAT WASN'T ME!
N-TNNN TUN-T
-TNNN TUN-TNNN
YOU GET ONE WARNING.
N TUN
WE'RE PULLING THIS TARP OFF.
YOU SO MUCH AS BAT AN EYELASH...
N - TNNN TUN - TNNN TU
... AND I SWEAR I'LL GUT YOU LIKE A MUDCAT.
N - TNNN TUN - TNNN TUN
TNNN TUN - TN N TUN
TNNN TUN - TNNN TUN

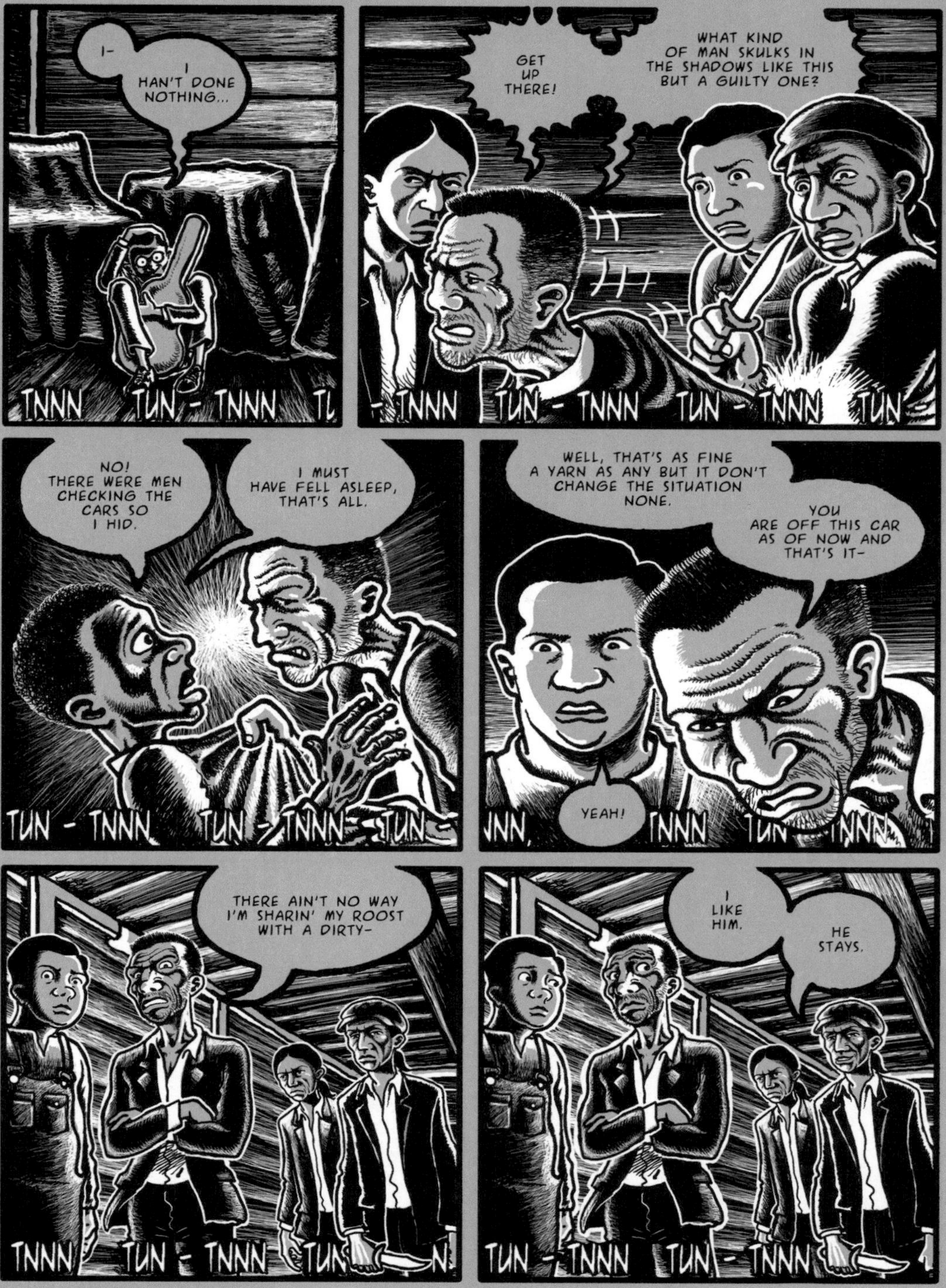
I-
I HAN'T DONE NOTHING...
TNNN TUN - TNNN TU
GET UP THERE!
WHAT KIND OF MAN SKULKS IN THE SHADOWS LIKE THIS BUT A GUILTY ONE?
- TNNN TUN - TNNN TUN - TNNN TUN -
NO! THERE WERE MEN CHECKING THE CARS SO I HID.
I MUST HAVE FELL ASLEEP, THAT'S ALL.
TUN - TNNN TUN - TNNN - TUN -
WELL, THAT'S AS FINE A YARN AS ANY BUT IT DON'T CHANGE THE SITUATION NONE.
YOU ARE OFF THIS CAR AS OF NOW AND THAT'S IT-
YEAH!
NNN TNNN TUN - TNNN
THERE AIN'T NO WAY I'M SHARIN' MY ROOST WITH A DIRTY-
TNNN TUN - TNNN TUN
I LIKE HIM.
HE STAYS.
TUN - TNNN TUN - TNNN

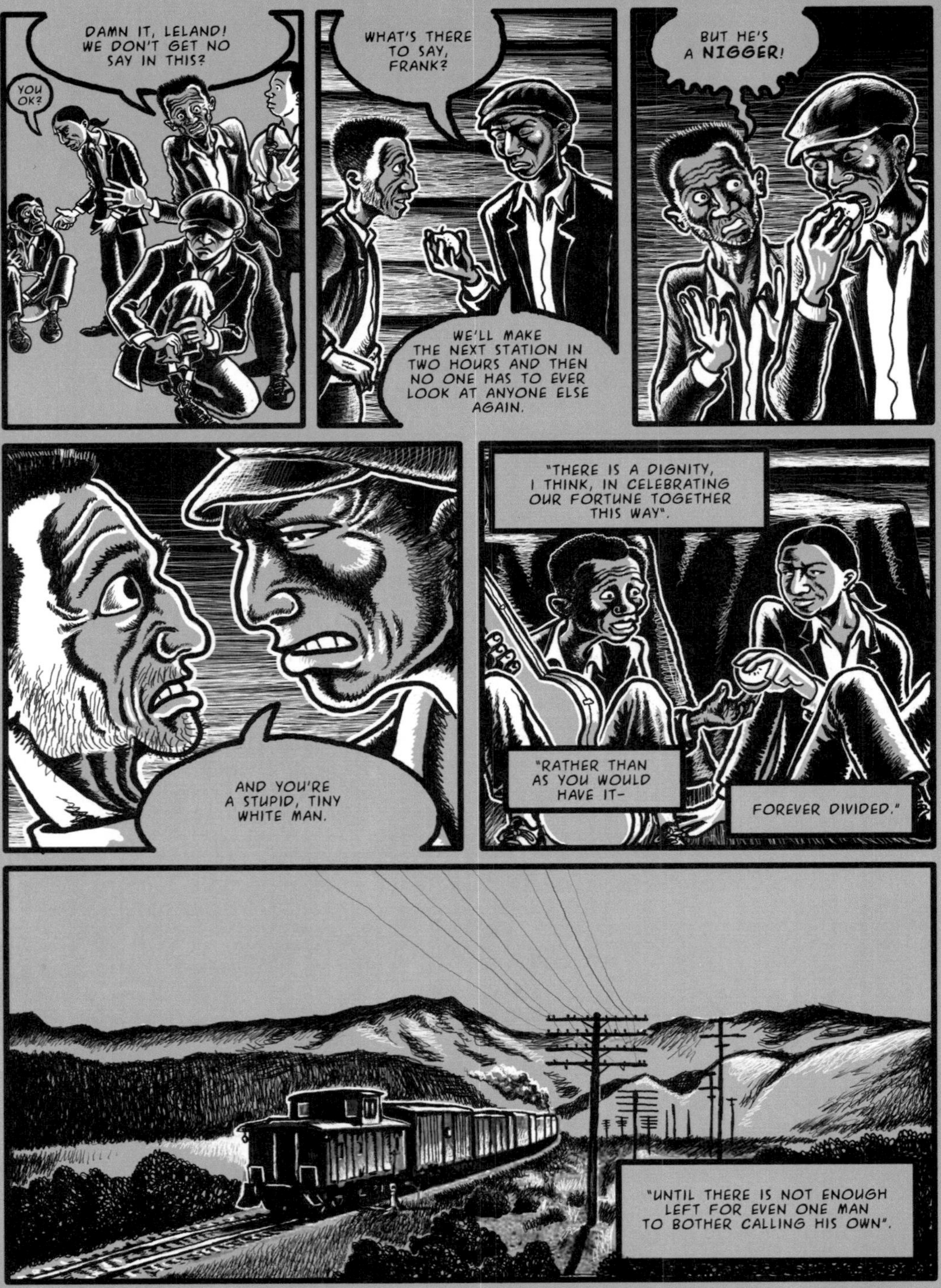
DAMN IT, LELAND! WE DON'T GET NO SAY IN THIS?
YOU OK?
WHAT'S THERE TO SAY, FRANK?
WE'LL MAKE THE NEXT STATION IN TWO HOURS AND THEN NO ONE HAS TO EVER LOOK AT ANYONE ELSE AGAIN.
BUT HE'S A **NIGGER**!
AND YOU'RE A STUPID, TINY WHITE MAN.
"THERE IS A DIGNITY, I THINK, IN CELEBRATING OUR FORTUNE TOGETHER THIS WAY".
"RATHER THAN AS YOU WOULD HAVE IT-
FOREVER DIVIDED."
"UNTIL THERE IS NOT ENOUGH LEFT FOR EVEN ONE MAN TO BOTHER CALLING HIS OWN".

8

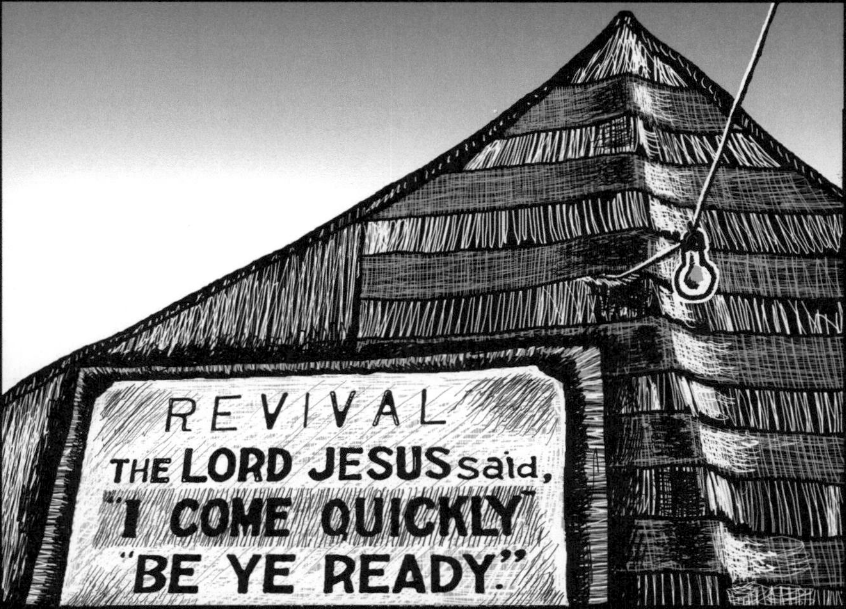
REVIVAL
THE LORD JESUS said,
"I COME QUICKLY"
"BE YE READY."

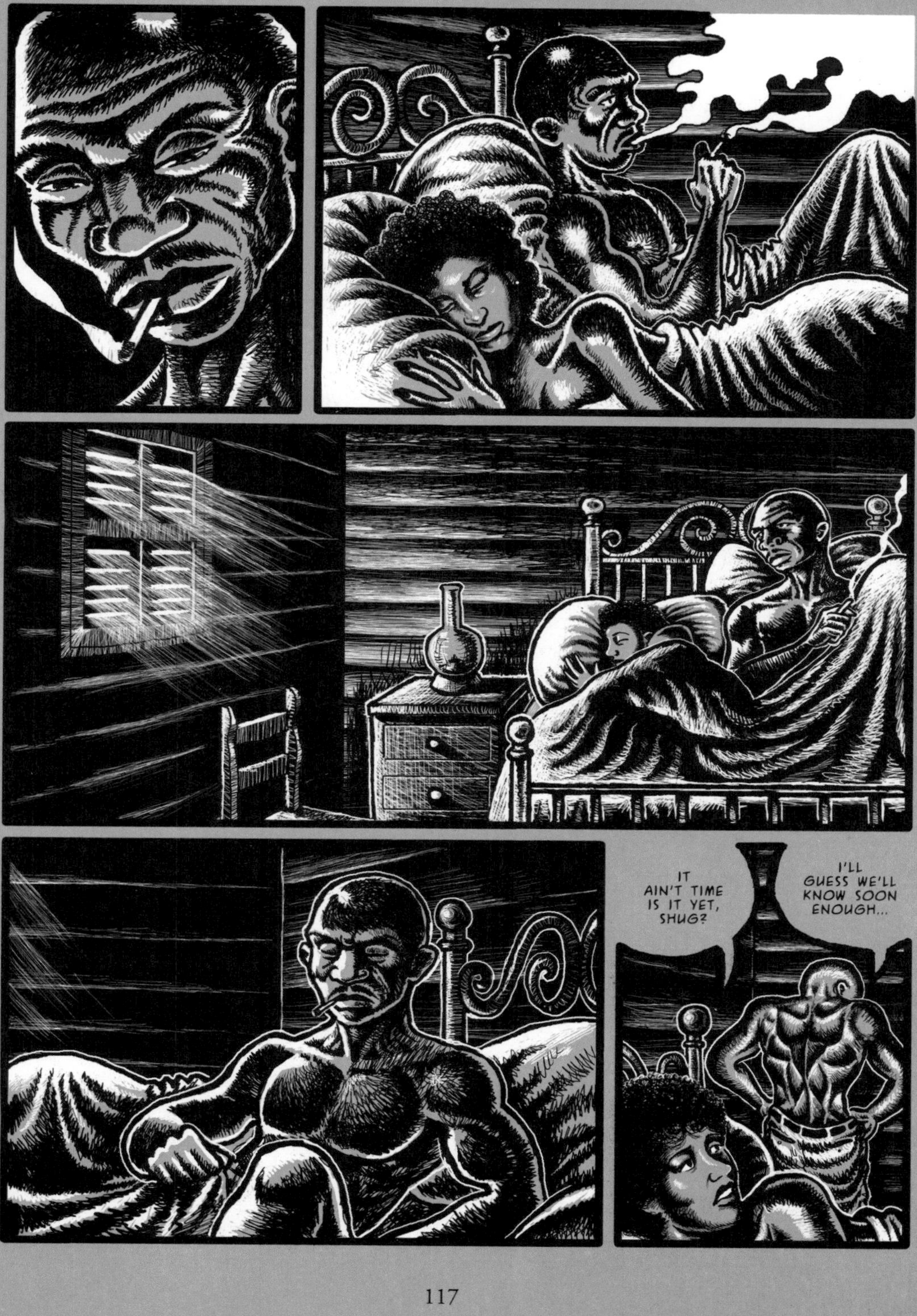
IT AIN'T TIME IS IT YET, SHUG?
I'LL GUESS WE'LL KNOW SOON ENOUGH...

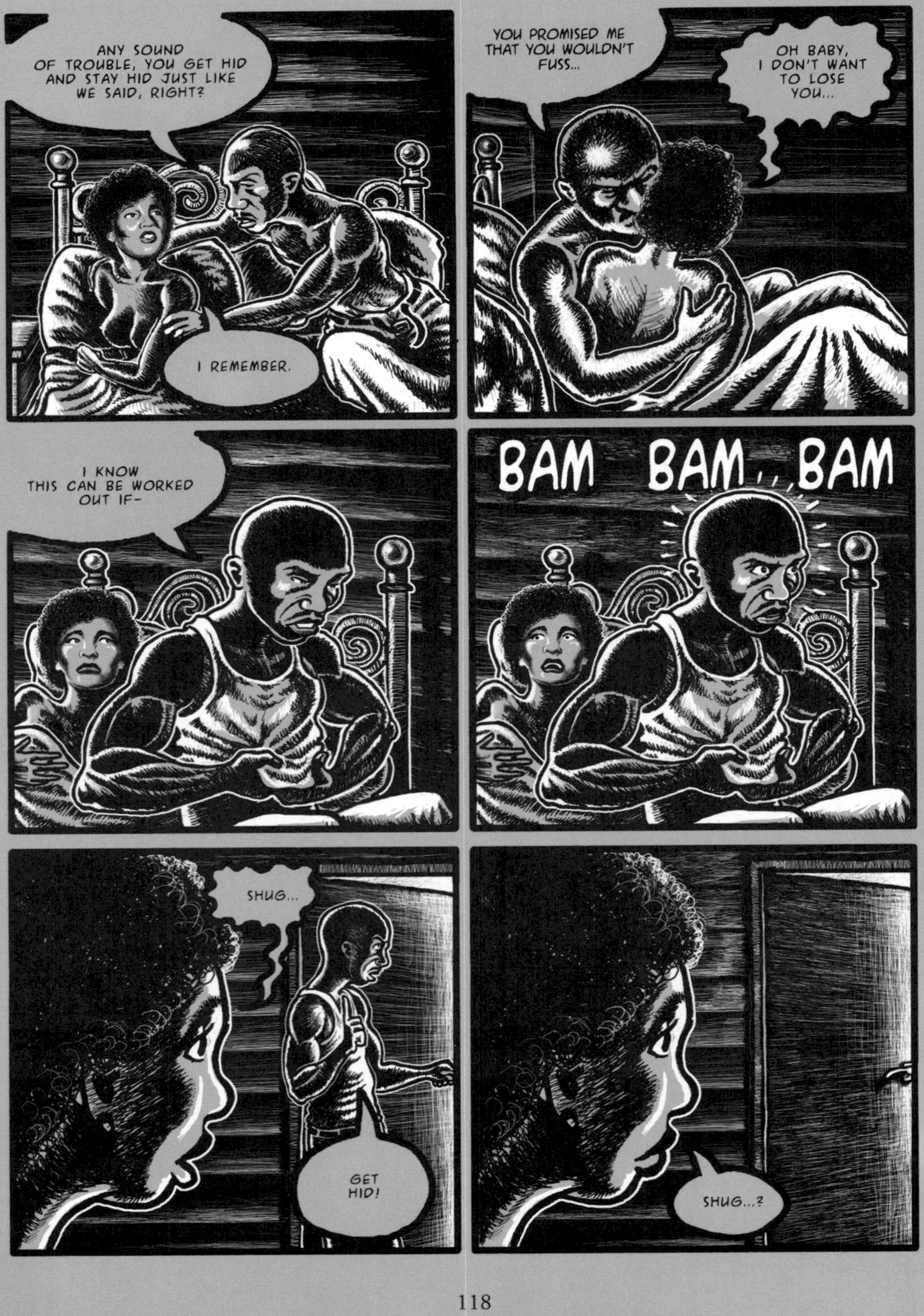
ANY SOUND OF TROUBLE, YOU GET HID AND STAY HID JUST LIKE WE SAID, RIGHT?
I REMEMBER.
YOU PROMISED ME THAT YOU WOULDN'T FUSS...
OH BABY, I DON'T WANT TO LOSE YOU...
I KNOW THIS CAN BE WORKED OUT IF-
BAM BAM BAM
SHUG...
GET HID!
SHUG...?

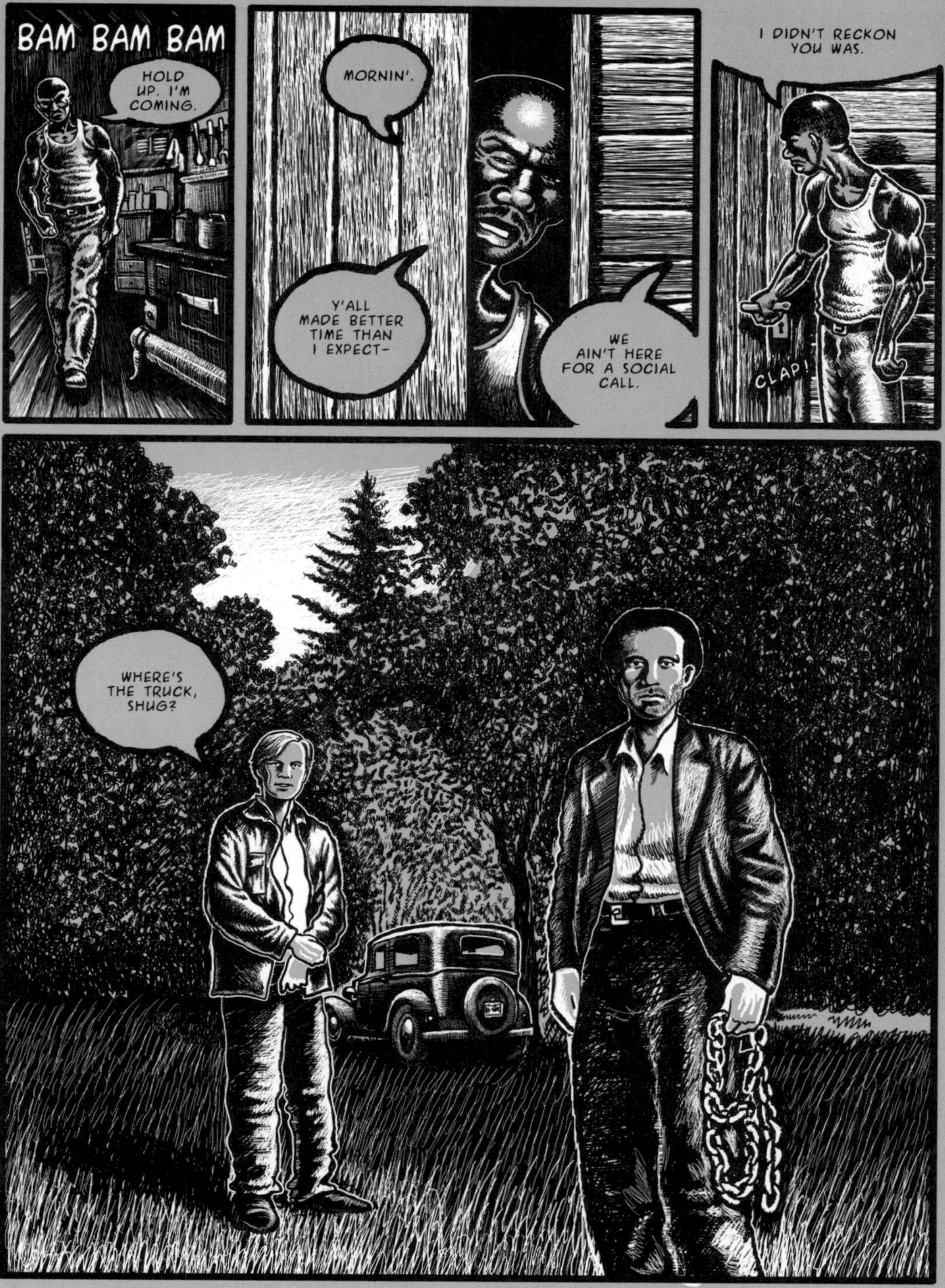
BAM BAM BAM
HOLD UP. I'M COMING.
MORNIN'.
Y'ALL MADE BETTER TIME THAN I EXPECT-
WE AIN'T HERE FOR A SOCIAL CALL.
I DIDN'T RECKON YOU WAS.
CLAP!
WHERE'S THE TRUCK, SHUG?

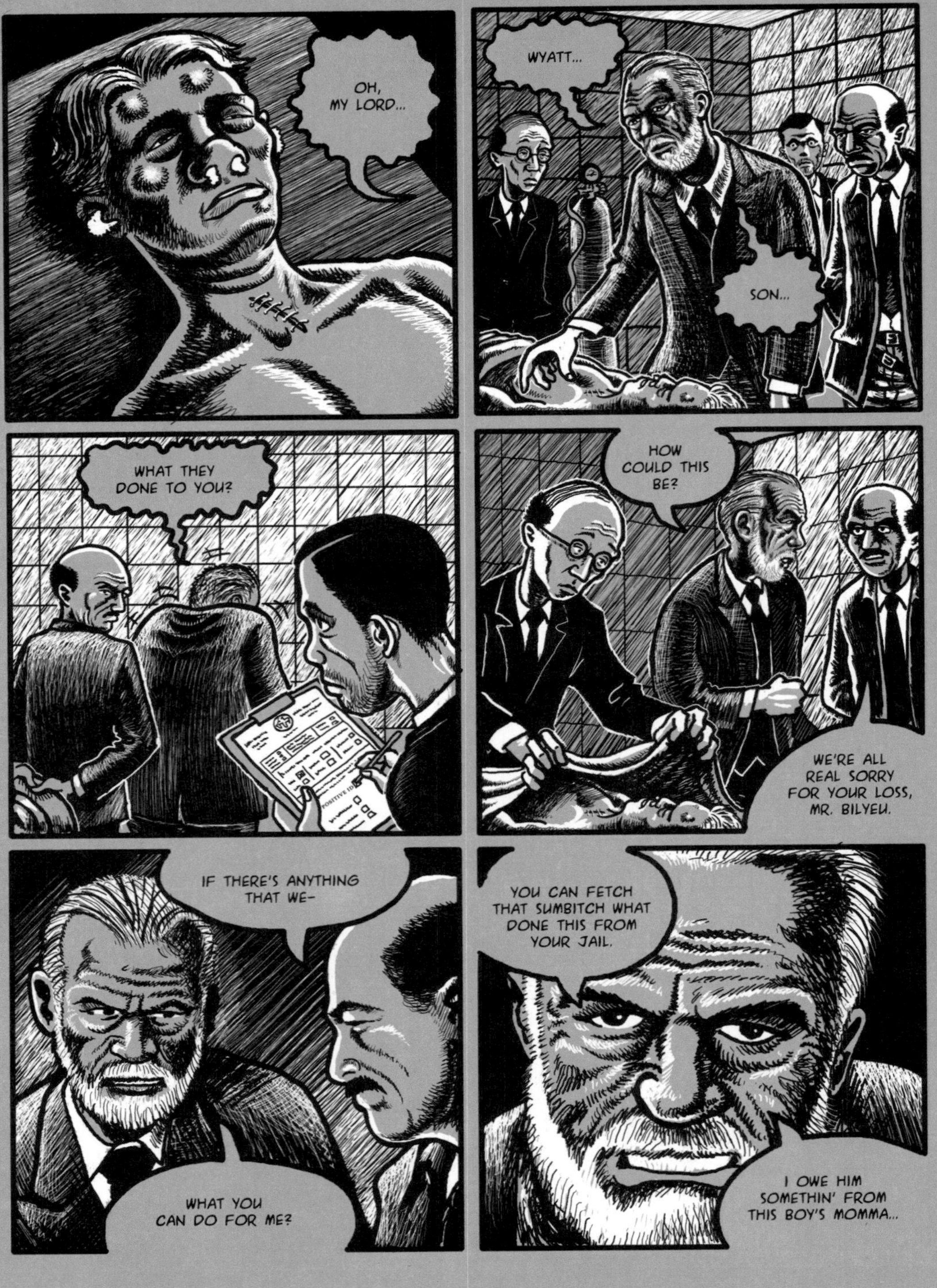
OH, MY LORD...
WYATT...
SON...
WHAT THEY DONE TO YOU?
POSITIVE ID
HOW COULD THIS BE?
WE'RE ALL REAL SORRY FOR YOUR LOSS, MR. BILYEU.
IF THERE'S ANYTHING THAT WE-
WHAT YOU CAN DO FOR ME?
YOU CAN FETCH THAT SUMBITCH WHAT DONE THIS FROM YOUR JAIL.
I OWE HIM SOMETHIN' FROM THIS BOY'S MOMMA...

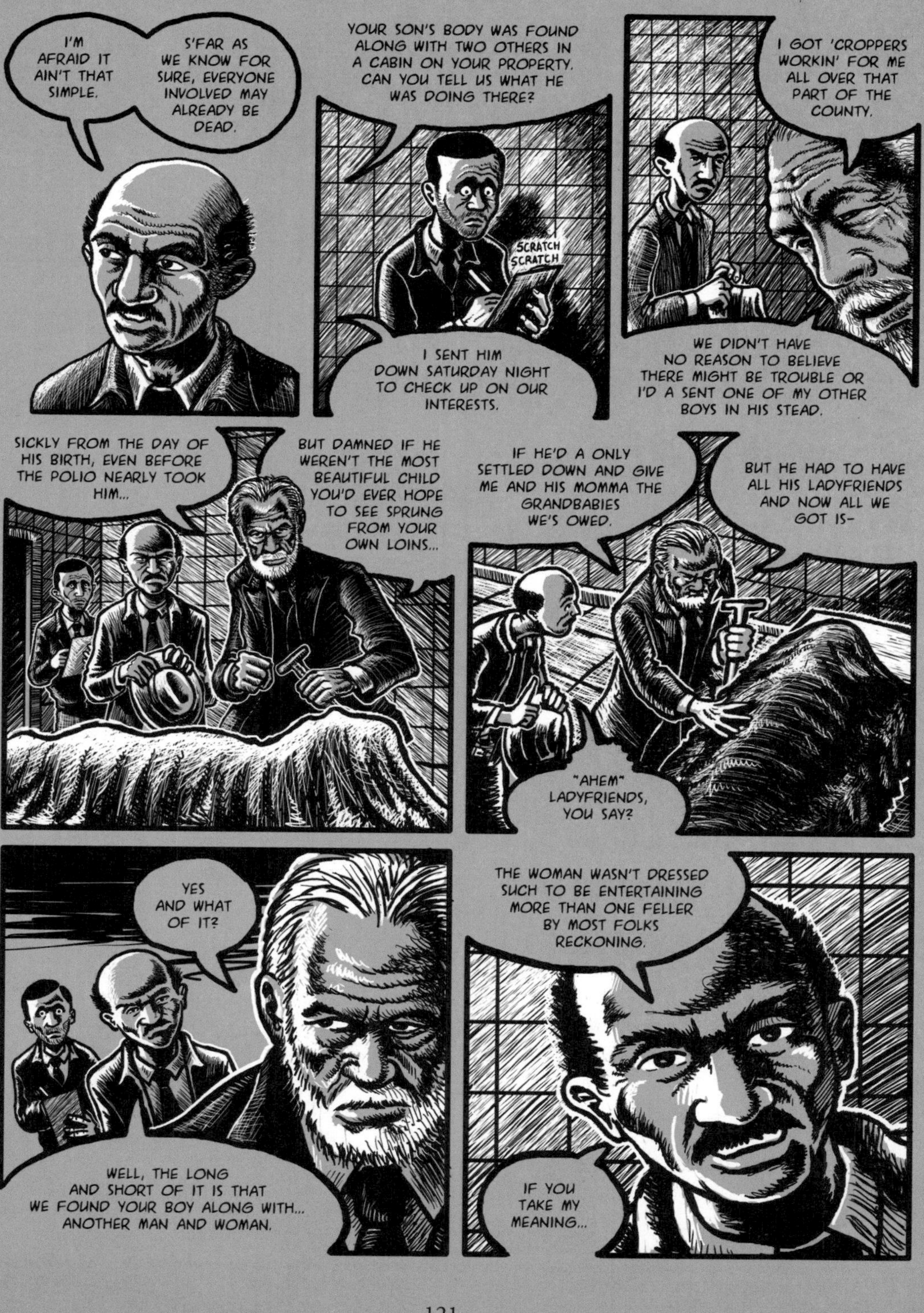
I'M AFRAID IT AIN'T THAT SIMPLE.
S'FAR AS WE KNOW FOR SURE, EVERYONE INVOLVED MAY ALREADY BE DEAD.
YOUR SON'S BODY WAS FOUND ALONG WITH TWO OTHERS IN A CABIN ON YOUR PROPERTY. CAN YOU TELL US WHAT HE WAS DOING THERE?
SCRATCH SCRATCH
I SENT HIM DOWN SATURDAY NIGHT TO CHECK UP ON OUR INTERESTS.
I GOT 'CROPPERS WORKIN' FOR ME ALL OVER THAT PART OF THE COUNTY.
WE DIDN'T HAVE NO REASON TO BELIEVE THERE MIGHT BE TROUBLE OR I'D A SENT ONE OF MY OTHER BOYS IN HIS STEAD.
SICKLY FROM THE DAY OF HIS BIRTH, EVEN BEFORE THE POLIO NEARLY TOOK HIM...
BUT DAMNED IF HE WEREN'T THE MOST BEAUTIFUL CHILD YOU'D EVER HOPE TO SEE SPRUNG FROM YOUR OWN LOINS...
IF HE'D A ONLY SETTLED DOWN AND GIVE ME AND HIS MOMMA THE GRANDBABIES WE'S OWED.
BUT HE HAD TO HAVE ALL HIS LADYFRIENDS AND NOW ALL WE GOT IS-
"AHEM" LADYFRIENDS, YOU SAY?
YES AND WHAT OF IT?
WELL, THE LONG AND SHORT OF IT IS THAT WE FOUND YOUR BOY ALONG WITH... ANOTHER MAN AND WOMAN.
THE WOMAN WASN'T DRESSED SUCH TO BE ENTERTAINING MORE THAN ONE FELLER BY MOST FOLKS RECKONING.
IF YOU TAKE MY MEANING...

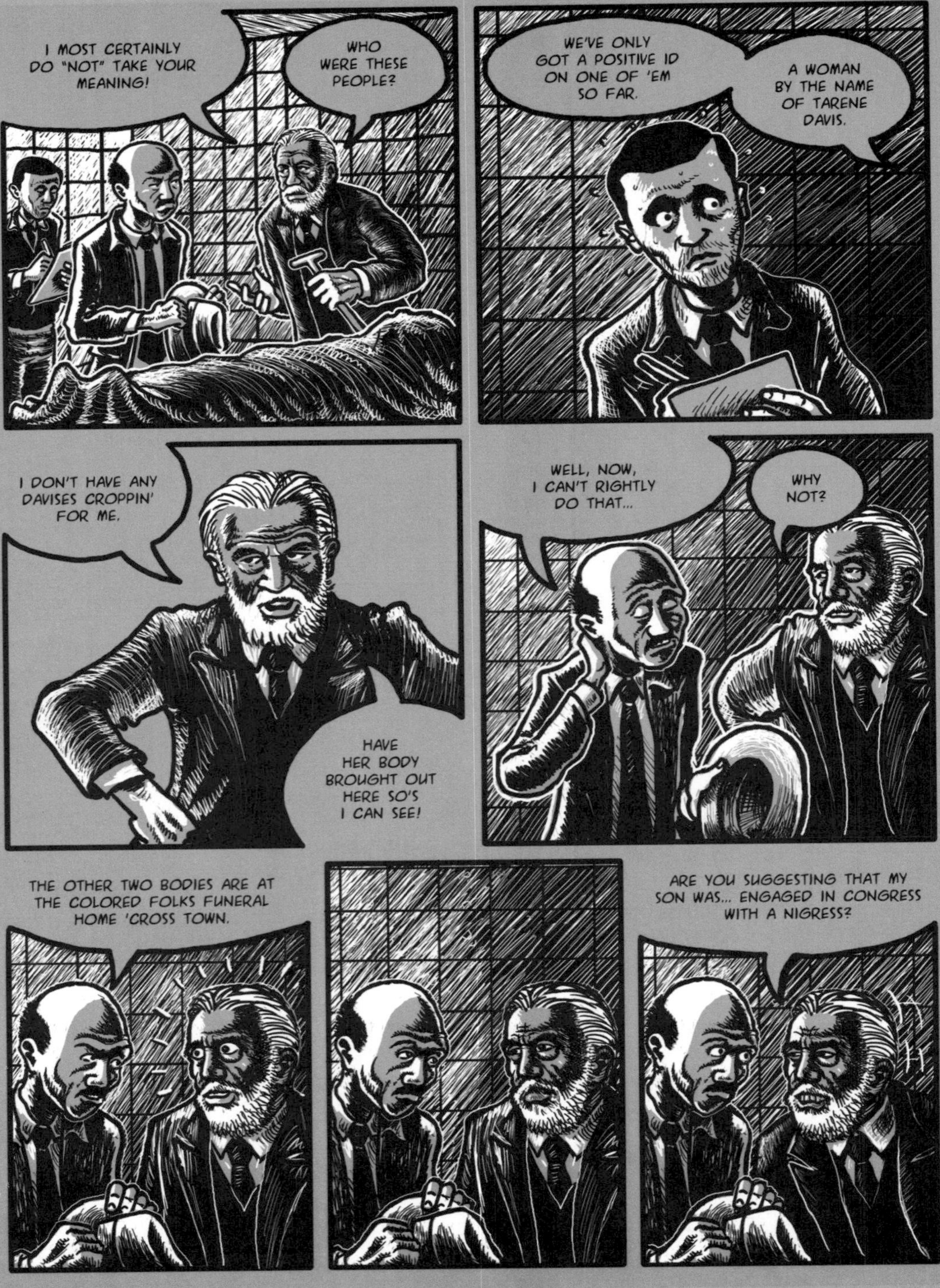
I MOST CERTAINLY DO "NOT" TAKE YOUR MEANING!
WHO WERE THESE PEOPLE?
WE'VE ONLY GOT A POSITIVE ID ON ONE OF 'EM SO FAR.
A WOMAN BY THE NAME OF TARENE DAVIS.
I DON'T HAVE ANY DAVISES CROPPIN' FOR ME.
HAVE HER BODY BROUGHT OUT HERE SO'S I CAN SEE!
WELL, NOW, I CAN'T RIGHTLY DO THAT...
WHY NOT?
THE OTHER TWO BODIES ARE AT THE COLORED FOLKS FUNERAL HOME 'CROSS TOWN.
ARE YOU SUGGESTING THAT MY SON WAS... ENGAGED IN CONGRESS WITH A NIGRESS?

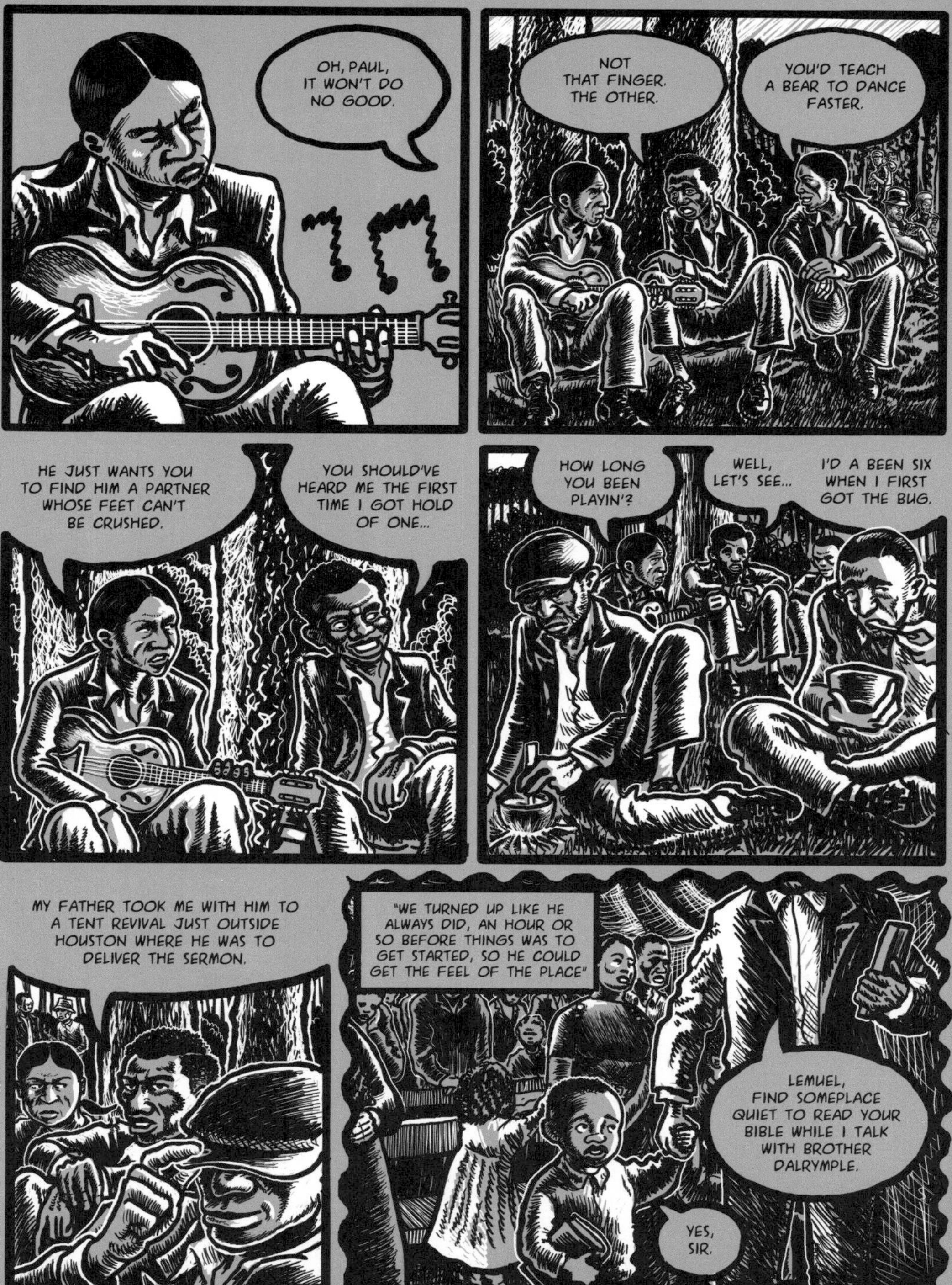
OH, PAUL, IT WON'T DO NO GOOD.
NOT THAT FINGER. THE OTHER.
YOU'D TEACH A BEAR TO DANCE FASTER.
HE JUST WANTS YOU TO FIND HIM A PARTNER WHOSE FEET CAN'T BE CRUSHED.
YOU SHOULD'VE HEARD ME THE FIRST TIME I GOT HOLD OF ONE...
HOW LONG YOU BEEN PLAYIN'?
WELL, LET'S SEE...
I'D A BEEN SIX WHEN I FIRST GOT THE BUG.
MY FATHER TOOK ME WITH HIM TO A TENT REVIVAL JUST OUTSIDE HOUSTON WHERE HE WAS TO DELIVER THE SERMON.
"WE TURNED UP LIKE HE ALWAYS DID, AN HOUR OR SO BEFORE THINGS WAS TO GET STARTED, SO HE COULD GET THE FEEL OF THE PLACE"
LEMUEL, FIND SOMEPLACE QUIET TO READ YOUR BIBLE WHILE I TALK WITH BROTHER DALRYMPLE.
YES, SIR.

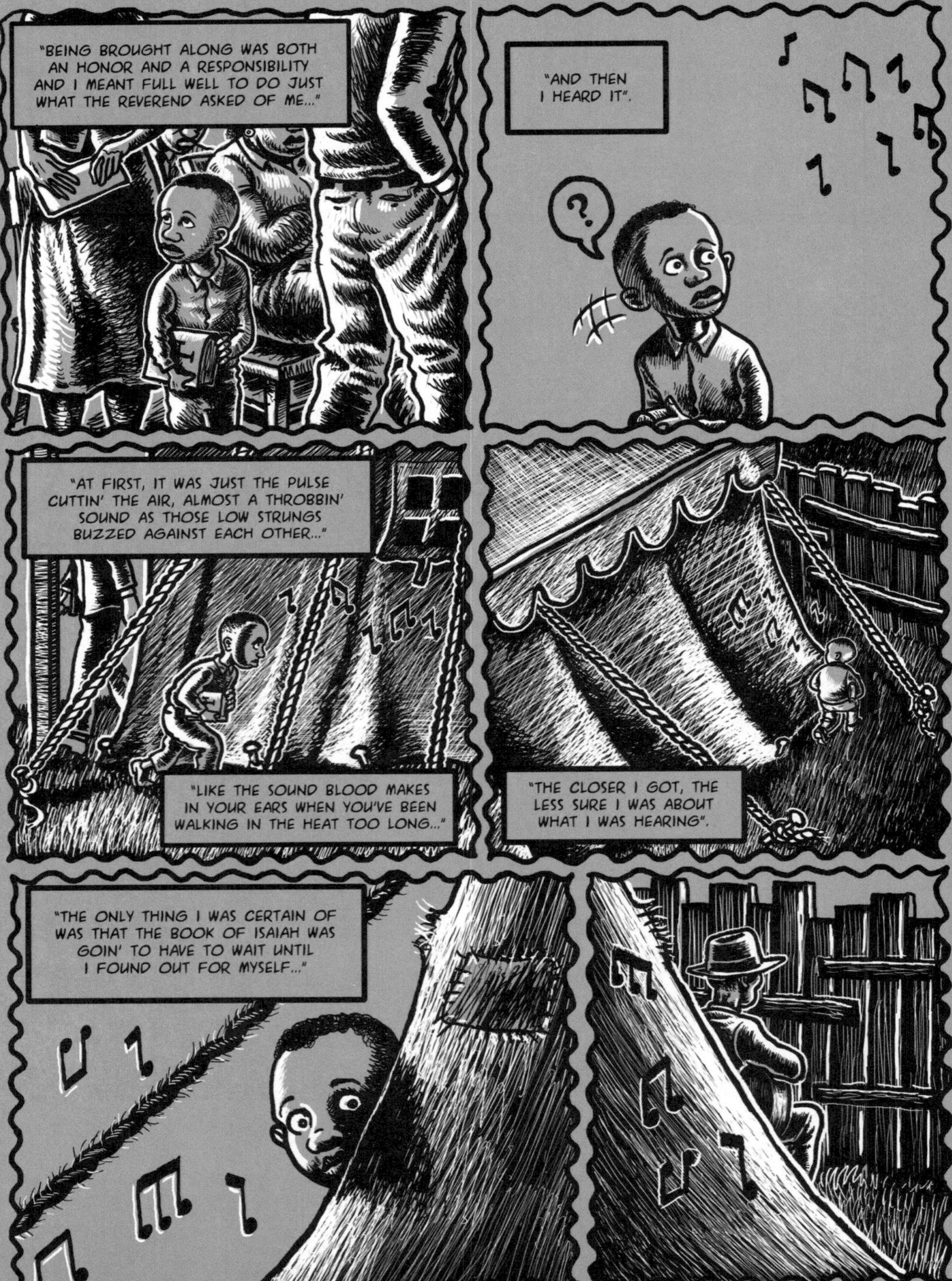
"BEING BROUGHT ALONG WAS BOTH AN HONOR AND A RESPONSIBILITY AND I MEANT FULL WELL TO DO JUST WHAT THE REVEREND ASKED OF ME..."
"AND THEN I HEARD IT".
?
"AT FIRST, IT WAS JUST THE PULSE CUTTIN' THE AIR, ALMOST A THROBBIN' SOUND AS THOSE LOW STRUNGS BUZZED AGAINST EACH OTHER..."
"LIKE THE SOUND BLOOD MAKES IN YOUR EARS WHEN YOU'VE BEEN WALKING IN THE HEAT TOO LONG..."
"THE CLOSER I GOT, THE LESS SURE I WAS ABOUT WHAT I WAS HEARING".
"THE ONLY THING I WAS CERTAIN OF WAS THAT THE BOOK OF ISAIAH WAS GOIN' TO HAVE TO WAIT UNTIL I FOUND OUT FOR MYSELF..."

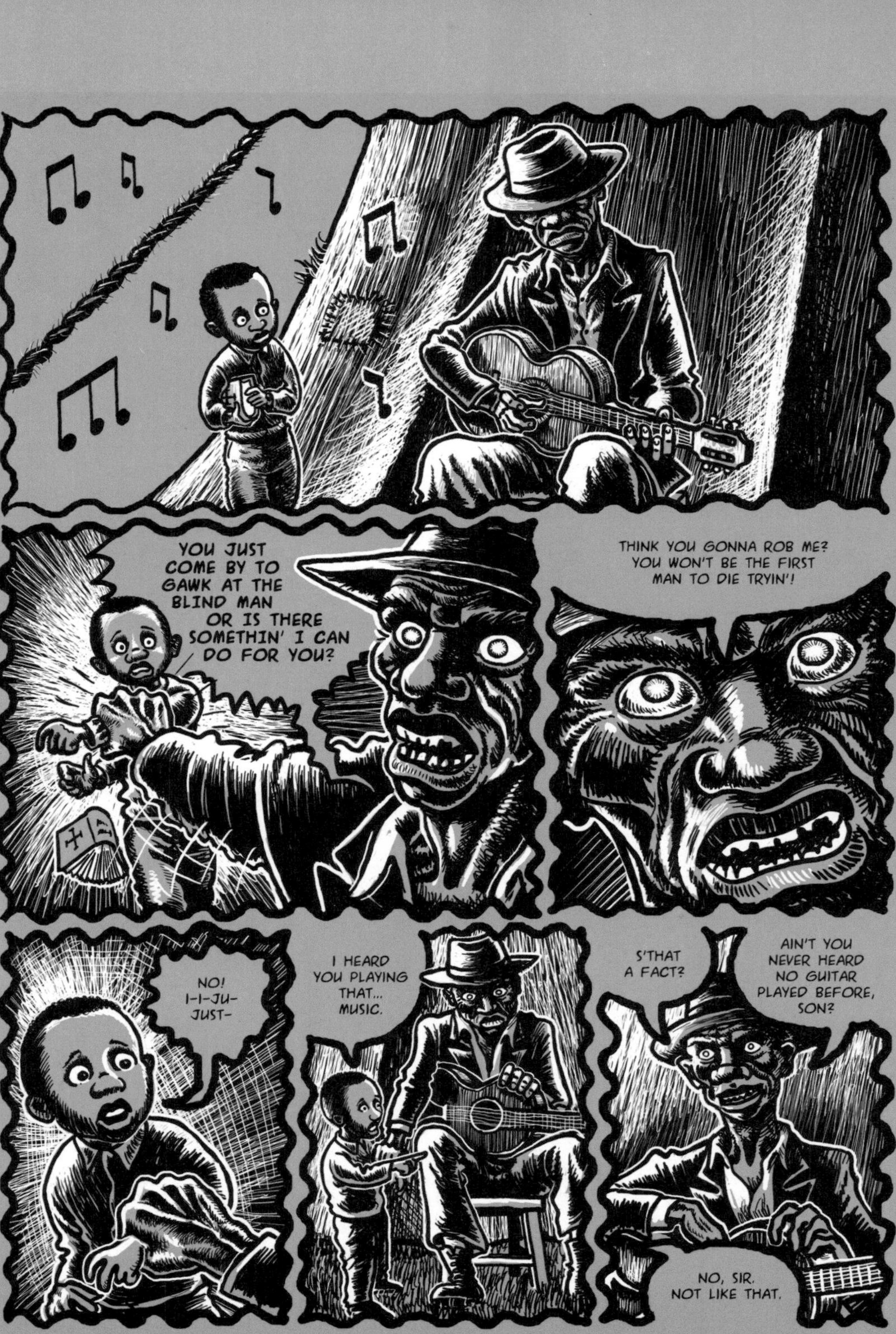
YOU JUST COME BY TO GAWK AT THE BLIND MAN OR IS THERE SOMETHIN' I CAN DO FOR YOU?
THINK YOU GONNA ROB ME? YOU WON'T BE THE FIRST MAN TO DIE TRYIN'!
NO! I-I-JU-JUST-
I HEARD YOU PLAYING THAT... MUSIC.
S'THAT A FACT?
AIN'T YOU NEVER HEARD NO GUITAR PLAYED BEFORE, SON?
NO, SIR. NOT LIKE THAT.

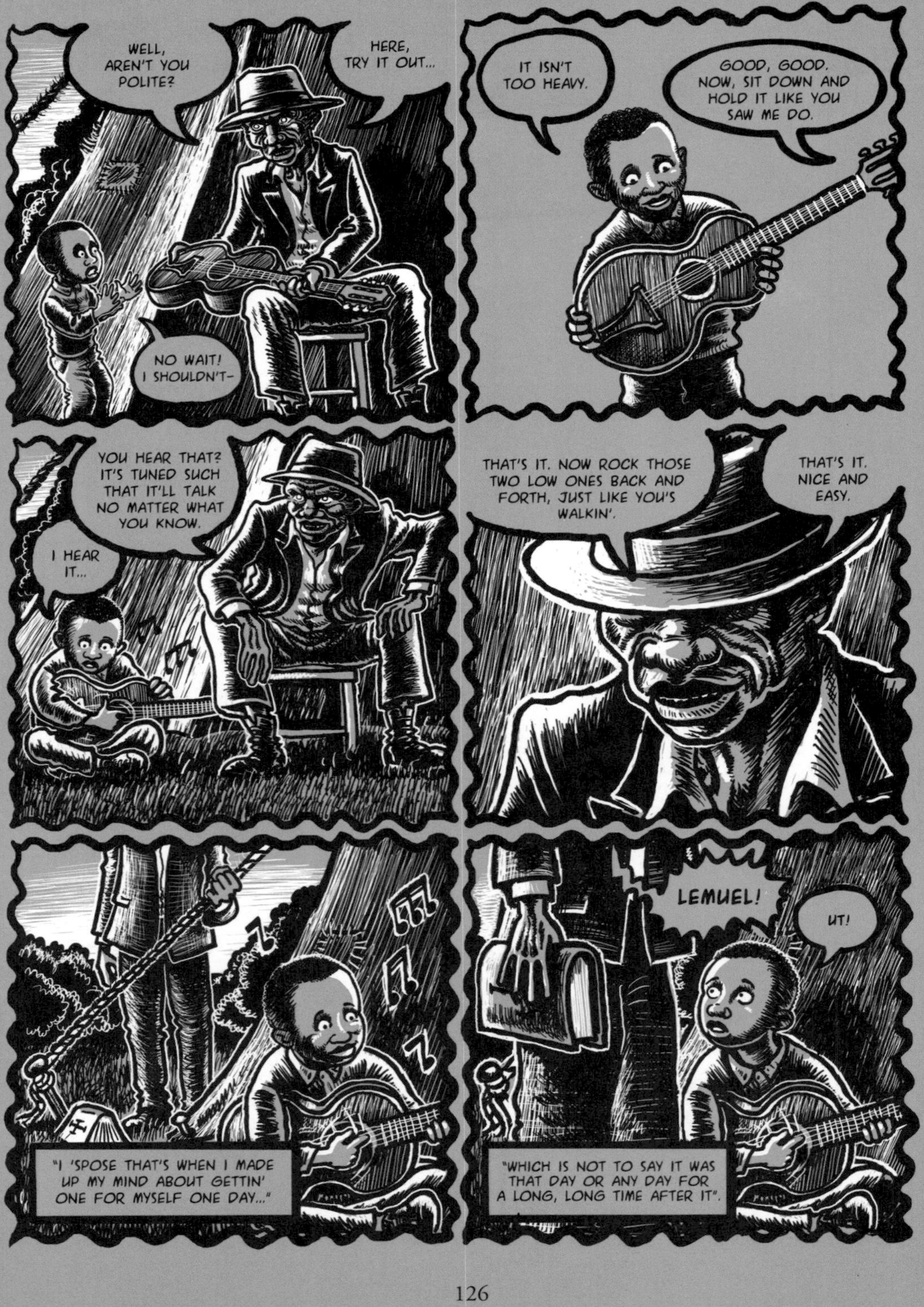
WELL, AREN'T YOU POLITE?
HERE, TRY IT OUT...
NO WAIT! I SHOULDN'T-
IT ISN'T TOO HEAVY.
GOOD, GOOD. NOW, SIT DOWN AND HOLD IT LIKE YOU SAW ME DO.
YOU HEAR THAT? IT'S TUNED SUCH THAT IT'LL TALK NO MATTER WHAT YOU KNOW.
I HEAR IT...
THAT'S IT. NOW ROCK THOSE TWO LOW ONES BACK AND FORTH, JUST LIKE YOU'S WALKIN'.
THAT'S IT. NICE AND EASY.
"I 'SPOSE THAT'S WHEN I MADE UP MY MIND ABOUT GETTIN' ONE FOR MYSELF ONE DAY..."
LEMUEL!
UT!
"WHICH IS NOT TO SAY IT WAS THAT DAY OR ANY DAY FOR A LONG, LONG TIME AFTER IT".

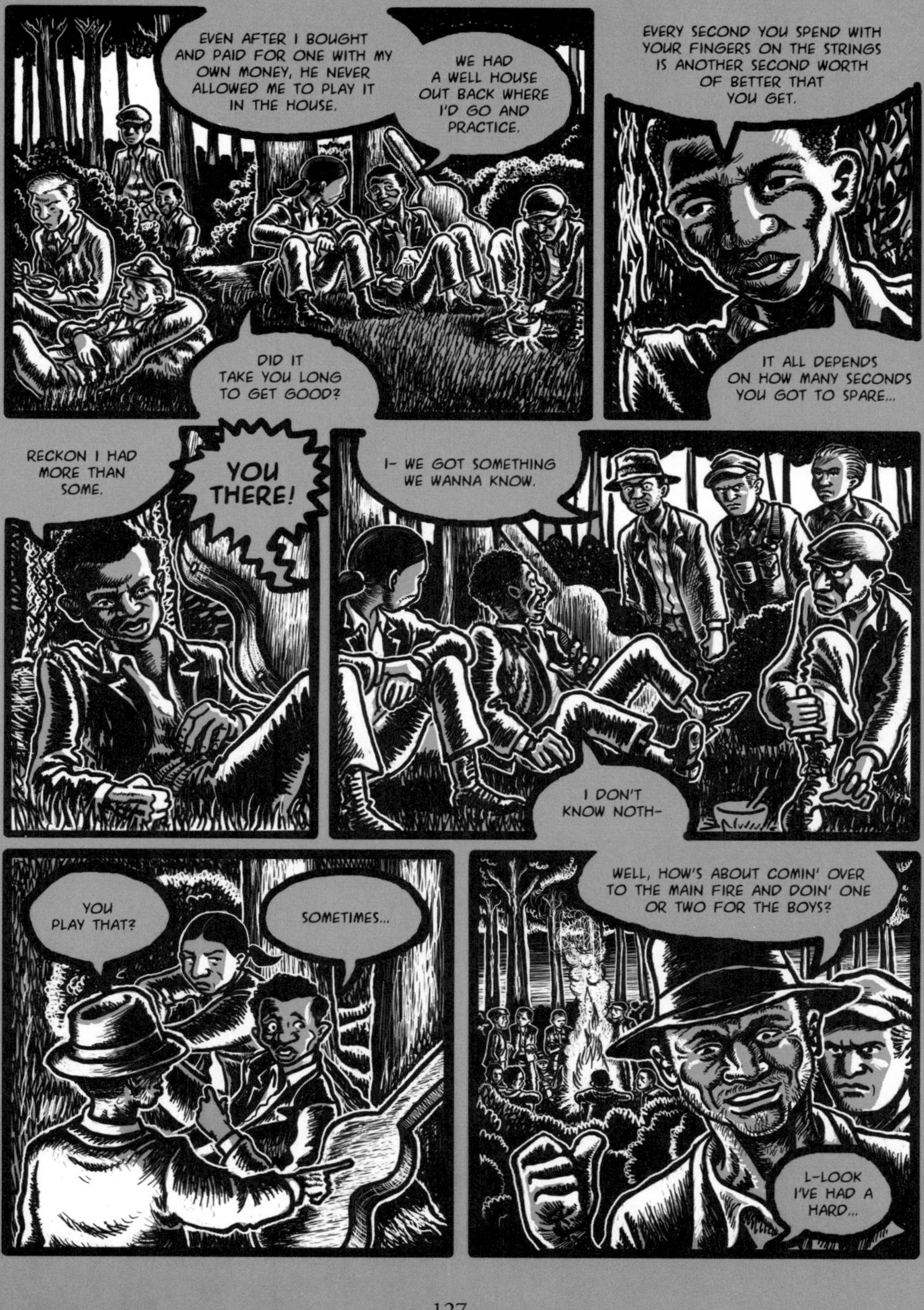
EVEN AFTER I BOUGHT AND PAID FOR ONE WITH MY OWN MONEY, HE NEVER ALLOWED ME TO PLAY IT IN THE HOUSE.
WE HAD A WELL HOUSE OUT BACK WHERE I'D GO AND PRACTICE.
DID IT TAKE YOU LONG TO GET GOOD?
EVERY SECOND YOU SPEND WITH YOUR FINGERS ON THE STRINGS IS ANOTHER SECOND WORTH OF BETTER THAT YOU GET.
IT ALL DEPENDS ON HOW MANY SECONDS YOU GOT TO SPARE...
RECKON I HAD MORE THAN SOME.
YOU THERE!
I- WE GOT SOMETHING WE WANNA KNOW.
I DON'T KNOW NOTH-
YOU PLAY THAT?
SOMETIMES...
WELL, HOW'S ABOUT COMIN' OVER TO THE MAIN FIRE AND DOIN' ONE OR TWO FOR THE BOYS?
L-LOOK I'VE HAD A HARD...

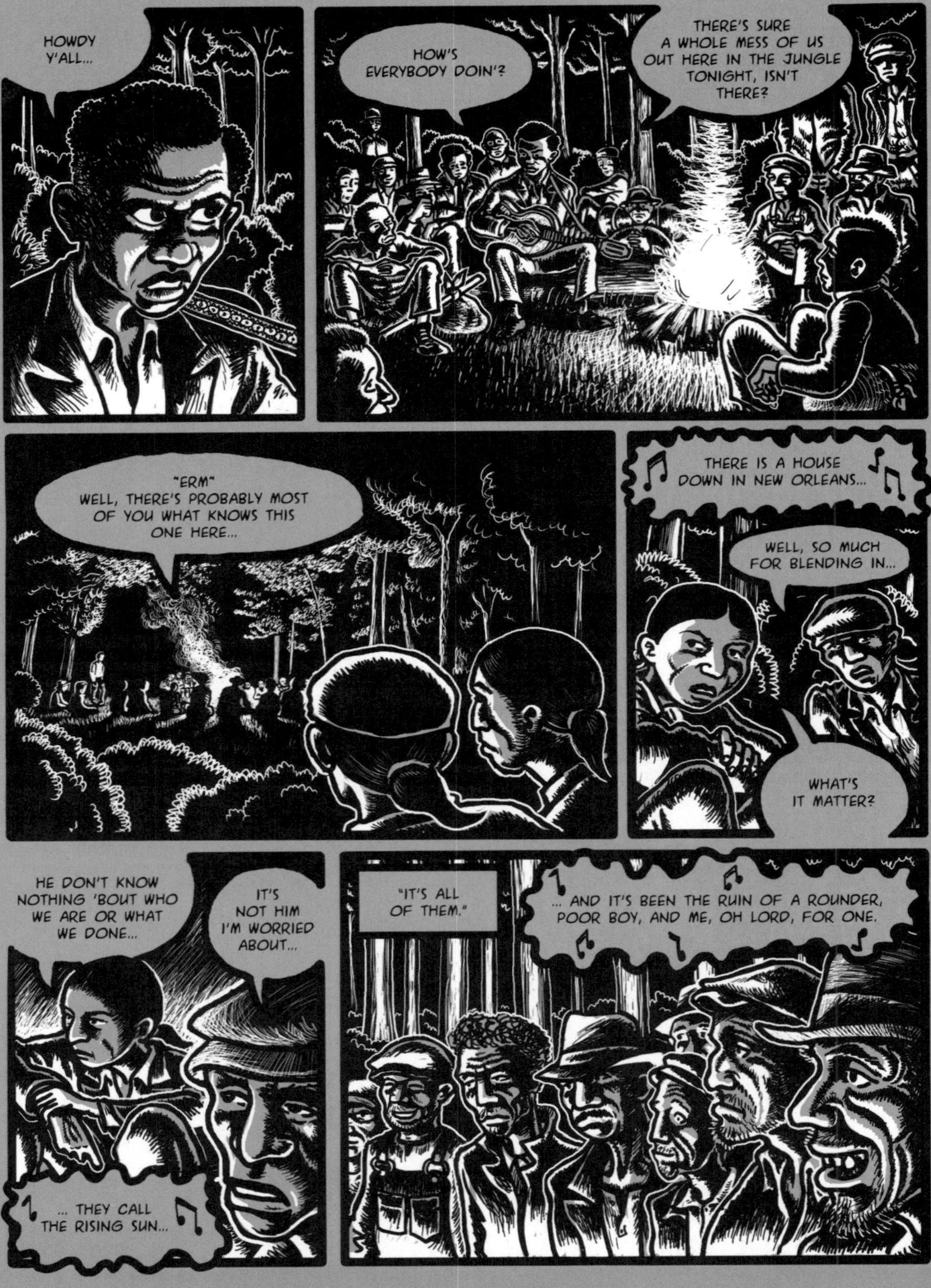
HOWDY Y'ALL...
HOW'S EVERYBODY DOIN'?
THERE'S SURE A WHOLE MESS OF US OUT HERE IN THE JUNGLE TONIGHT, ISN'T THERE?
"ERM" WELL, THERE'S PROBABLY MOST OF YOU WHAT KNOWS THIS ONE HERE...
THERE IS A HOUSE DOWN IN NEW ORLEANS...
WELL, SO MUCH FOR BLENDING IN...
WHAT'S IT MATTER?
HE DON'T KNOW NOTHING 'BOUT WHO WE ARE OR WHAT WE DONE...
IT'S NOT HIM I'M WORRIED ABOUT...
... THEY CALL THE RISING SUN...
"IT'S ALL OF THEM."
... AND IT'S BEEN THE RUIN OF A ROUNDER, POOR BOY, AND ME, OH LORD, FOR ONE.

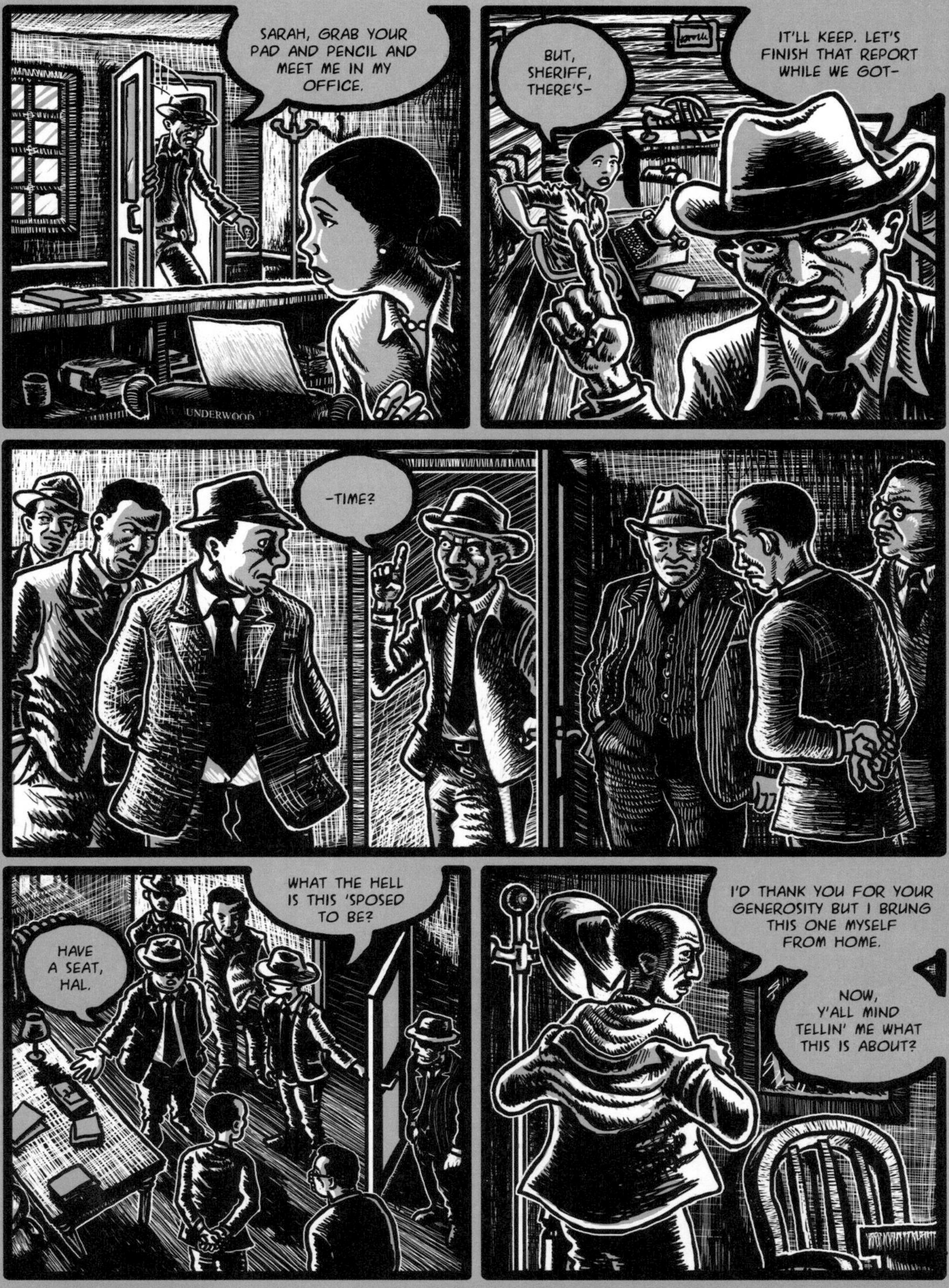
SARAH, GRAB YOUR PAD AND PENCIL AND MEET ME IN MY OFFICE.
UNDERWOOD
BUT, SHERIFF, THERE'S–
IT'LL KEEP. LET'S FINISH THAT REPORT WHILE WE GOT–
–TIME?
WHAT THE HELL IS THIS 'SPOSED TO BE?
HAVE A SEAT, HAL.
I'D THANK YOU FOR YOUR GENEROSITY BUT I BRUNG THIS ONE MYSELF FROM HOME.
NOW, Y'ALL MIND TELLIN' ME WHAT THIS IS ABOUT?

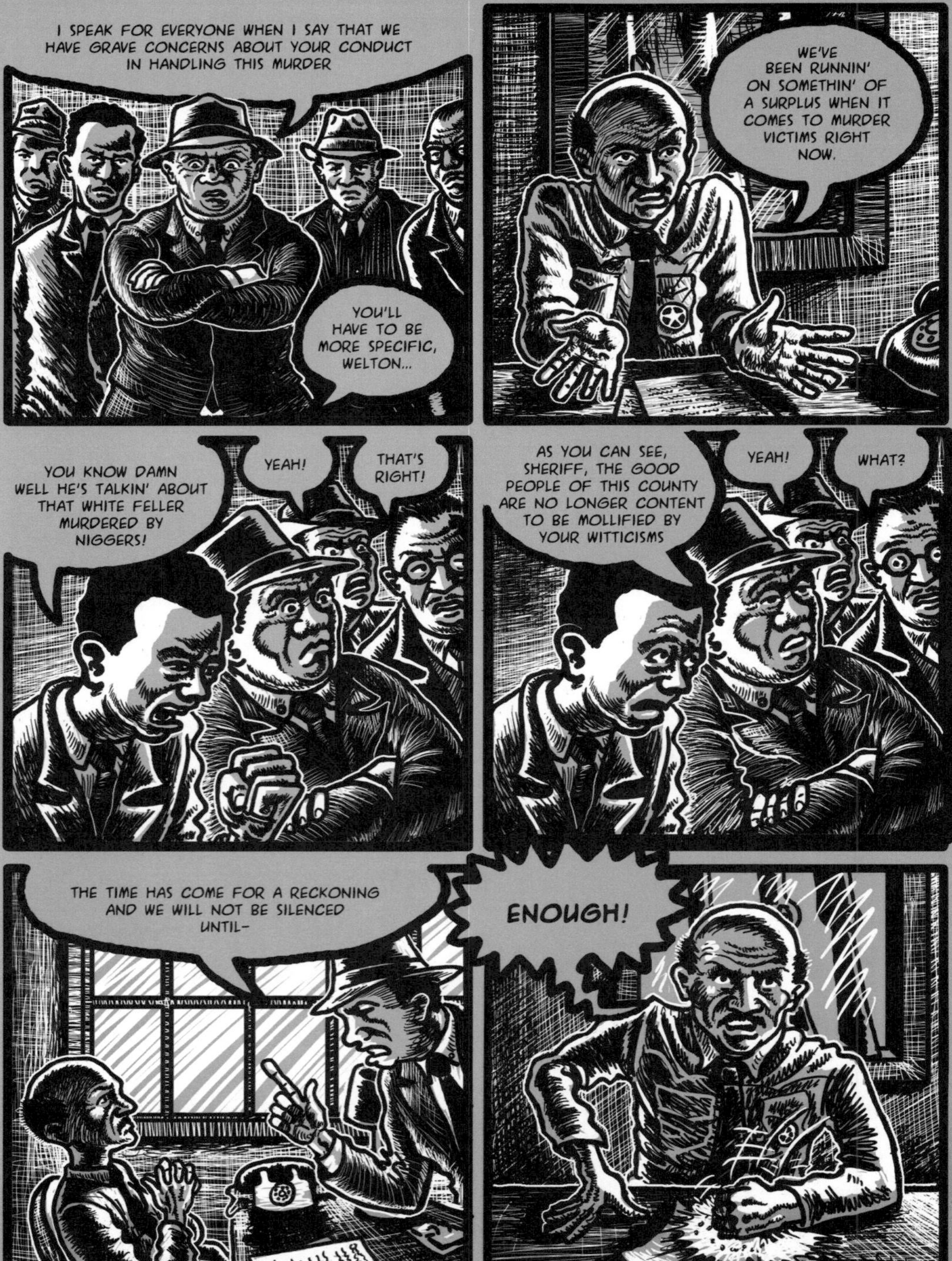
I SPEAK FOR EVERYONE WHEN I SAY THAT WE HAVE GRAVE CONCERNS ABOUT YOUR CONDUCT IN HANDLING THIS MURDER
YOU'LL HAVE TO BE MORE SPECIFIC, WELTON...
WE'VE BEEN RUNNIN' ON SOMETHIN' OF A SURPLUS WHEN IT COMES TO MURDER VICTIMS RIGHT NOW.
YOU KNOW DAMN WELL HE'S TALKIN' ABOUT THAT WHITE FELLER MURDERED BY NIGGERS!
YEAH!
THAT'S RIGHT!
AS YOU CAN SEE, SHERIFF, THE GOOD PEOPLE OF THIS COUNTY ARE NO LONGER CONTENT TO BE MOLLIFIED BY YOUR WITTICISMS
YEAH!
WHAT?
THE TIME HAS COME FOR A RECKONING AND WE WILL NOT BE SILENCED UNTIL-
ENOUGH!

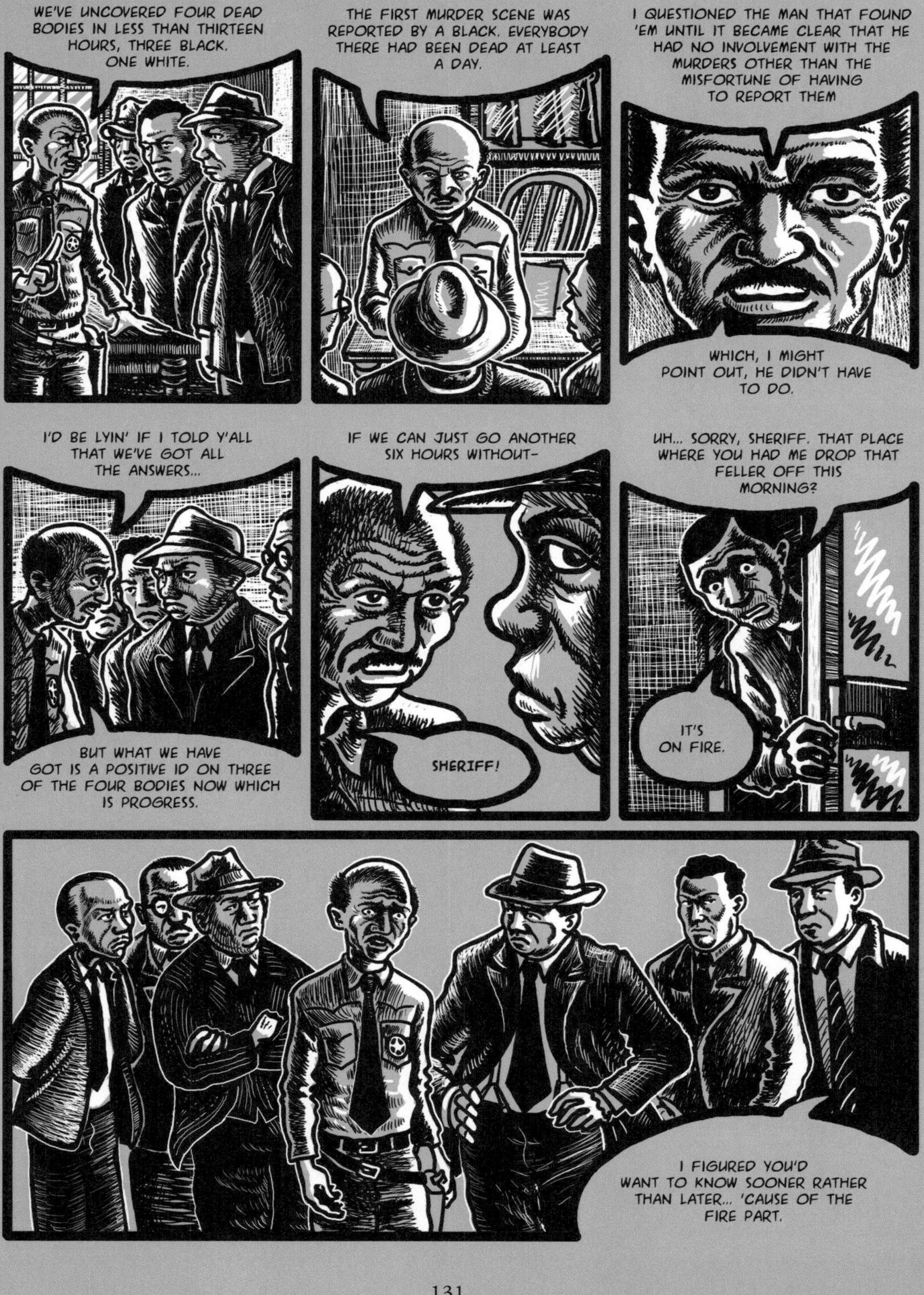

WE'VE UNCOVERED FOUR DEAD BODIES IN LESS THAN THIRTEEN HOURS, THREE BLACK, ONE WHITE.
THE FIRST MURDER SCENE WAS REPORTED BY A BLACK. EVERYBODY THERE HAD BEEN DEAD AT LEAST A DAY.
I QUESTIONED THE MAN THAT FOUND 'EM UNTIL IT BECAME CLEAR THAT HE HAD NO INVOLVEMENT WITH THE MURDERS OTHER THAN THE MISFORTUNE OF HAVING TO REPORT THEM
WHICH, I MIGHT POINT OUT, HE DIDN'T HAVE TO DO.
I'D BE LYIN' IF I TOLD Y'ALL THAT WE'VE GOT ALL THE ANSWERS...
BUT WHAT WE HAVE GOT IS A POSITIVE ID ON THREE OF THE FOUR BODIES NOW WHICH IS PROGRESS.
IF WE CAN JUST GO ANOTHER SIX HOURS WITHOUT-
SHERIFF!
UH... SORRY, SHERIFF. THAT PLACE WHERE YOU HAD ME DROP THAT FELLER OFF THIS MORNING?
IT'S ON FIRE.
I FIGURED YOU'D WANT TO KNOW SOONER RATHER THAN LATER... 'CAUSE OF THE FIRE PART.

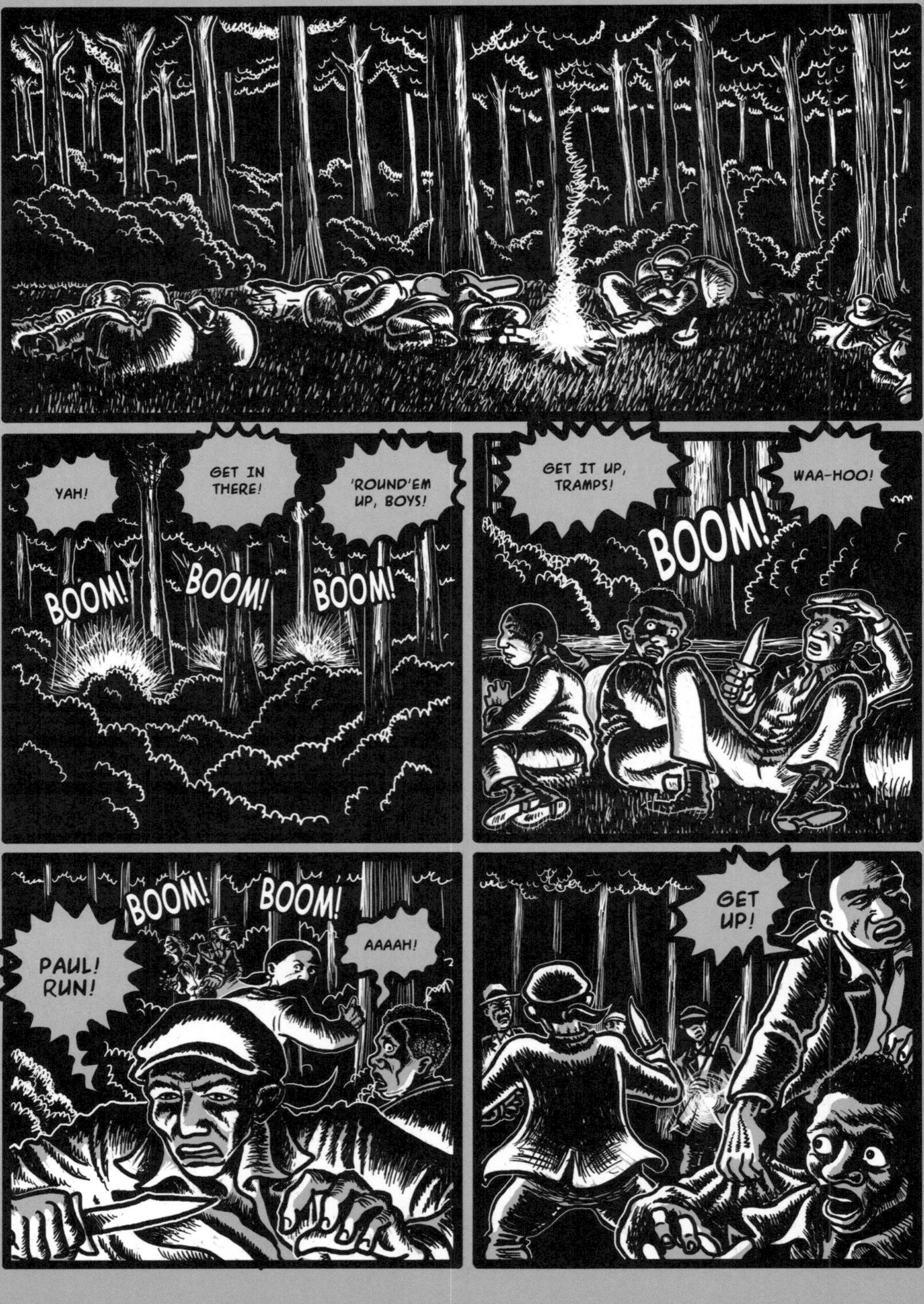
YAH!
GET IN THERE!
'ROUND'EM UP, BOYS!
BOOM!
BOOM!
BOOM!
GET IT UP, TRAMPS!
WAA-HOO!
BOOM!
BOOM!
BOOM!
PAUL! RUN!
AAAAH!
GET UP!

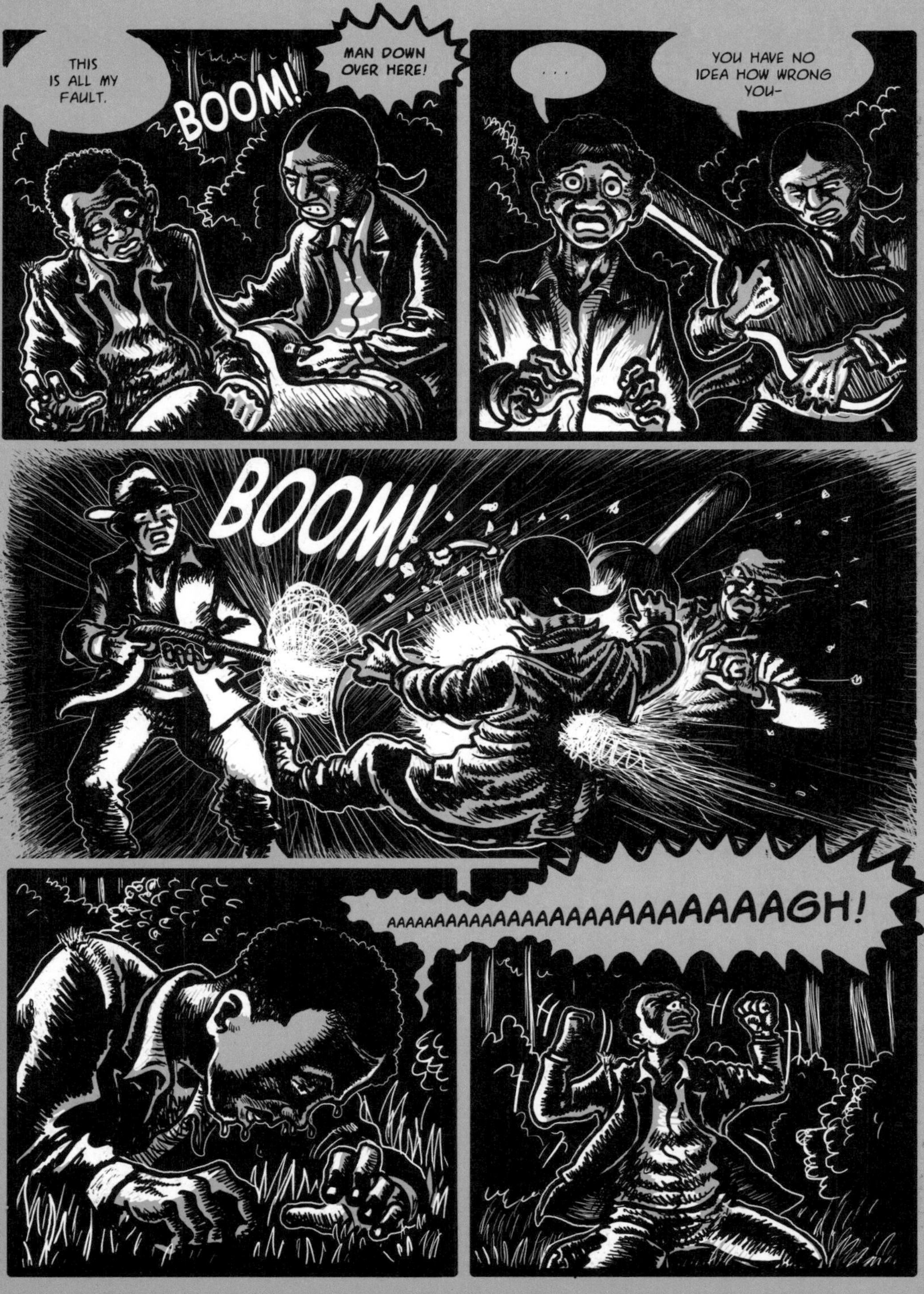
THIS IS ALL MY FAULT.
BOOM!
MAN DOWN OVER HERE!
. . .
YOU HAVE NO IDEA HOW WRONG YOU-
BOOM!
AAAAAAAAAAAAAAAAAAAAAAAAAAGH!

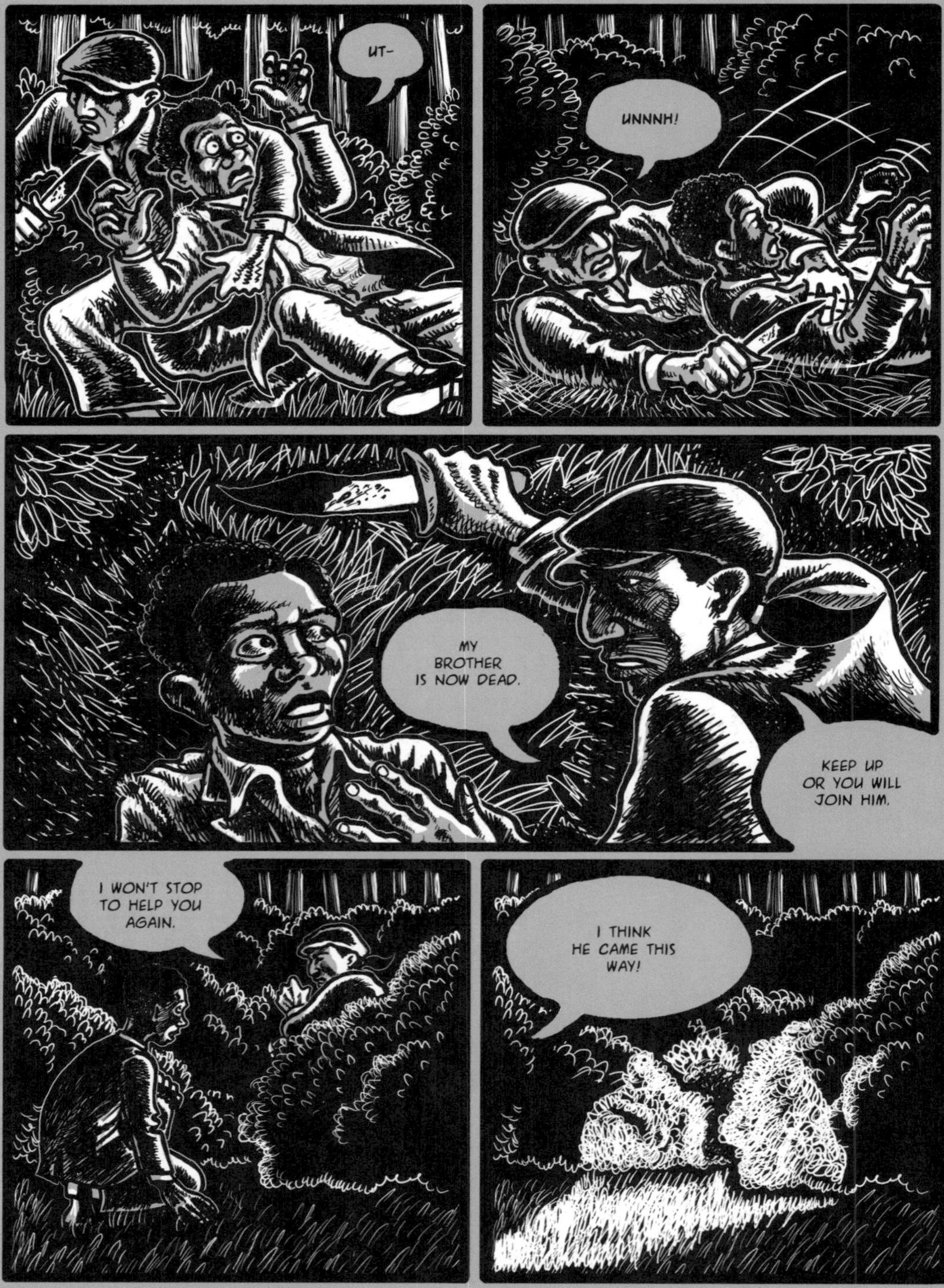
UT-
UNNNH!
MY BROTHER IS NOW DEAD.
KEEP UP OR YOU WILL JOIN HIM.
I WON'T STOP TO HELP YOU AGAIN.
I THINK HE CAME THIS WAY!

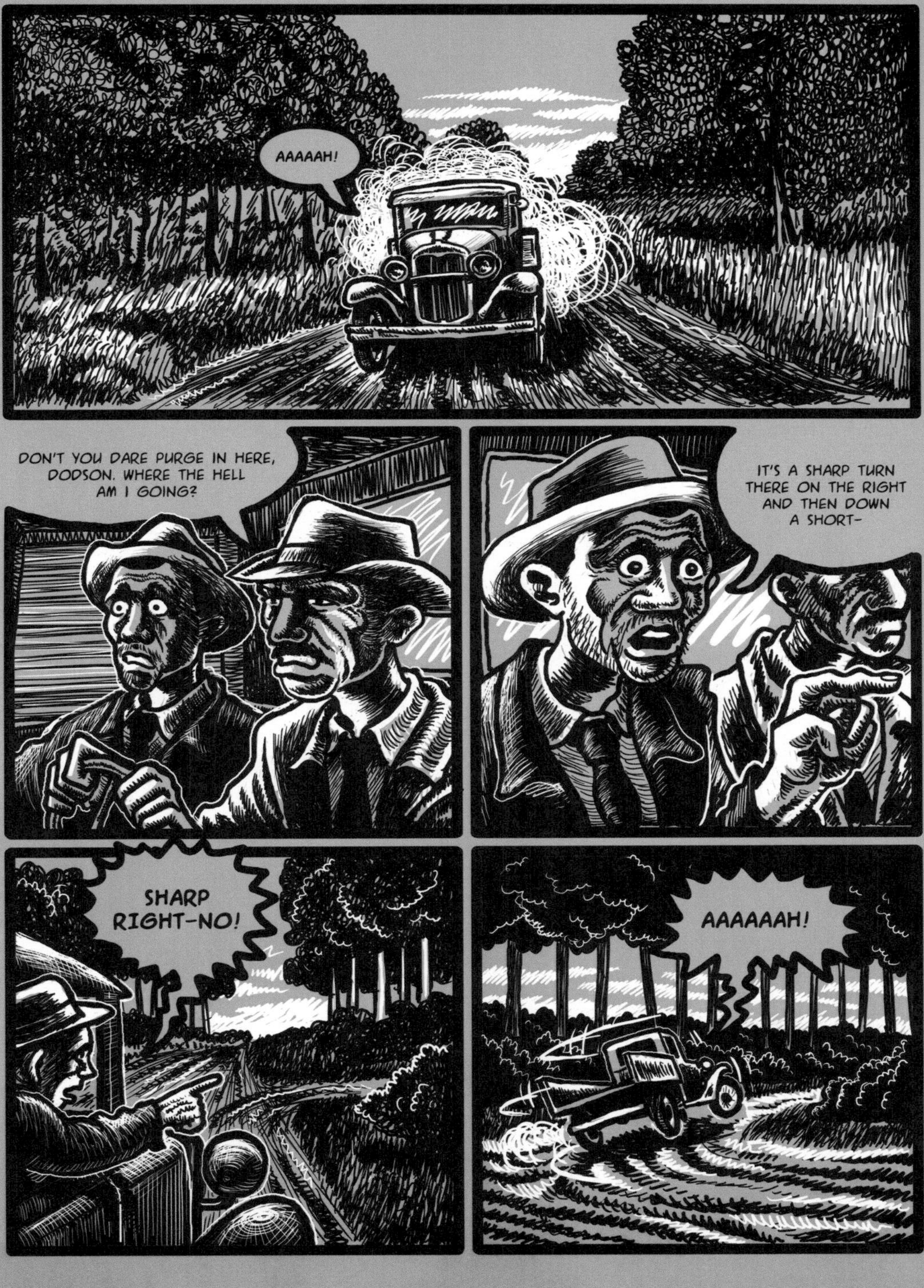
AAAAAH!
DON'T YOU DARE PURGE IN HERE, DODSON. WHERE THE HELL AM I GOING?
IT'S A SHARP TURN THERE ON THE RIGHT AND THEN DOWN A SHORT-
SHARP RIGHT-NO!
AAAAAAH!

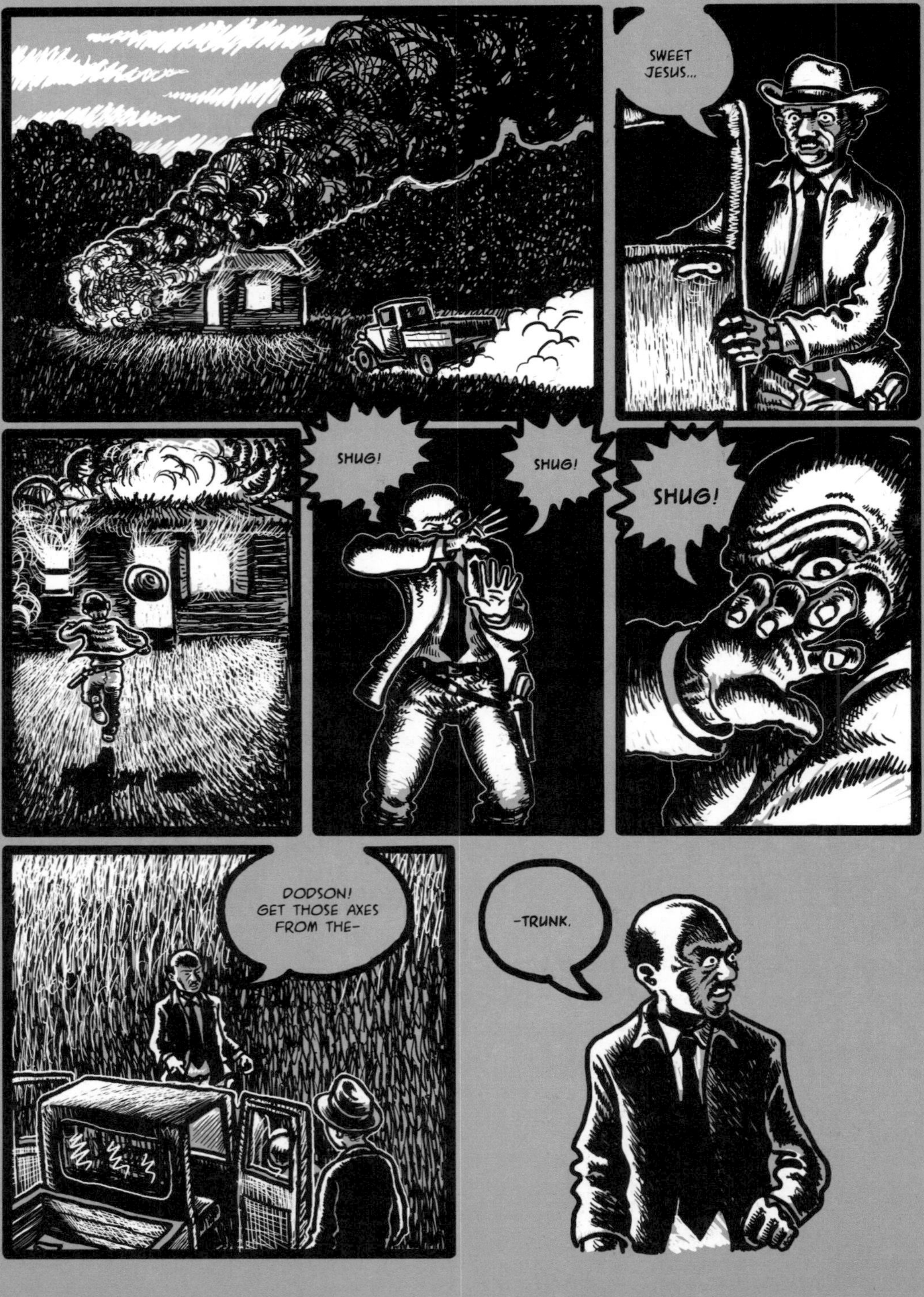
SWEET JESUS...
SHUG!
SHUG!
SHUG!
DODSON! GET THOSE AXES FROM THE-
-TRUNK.

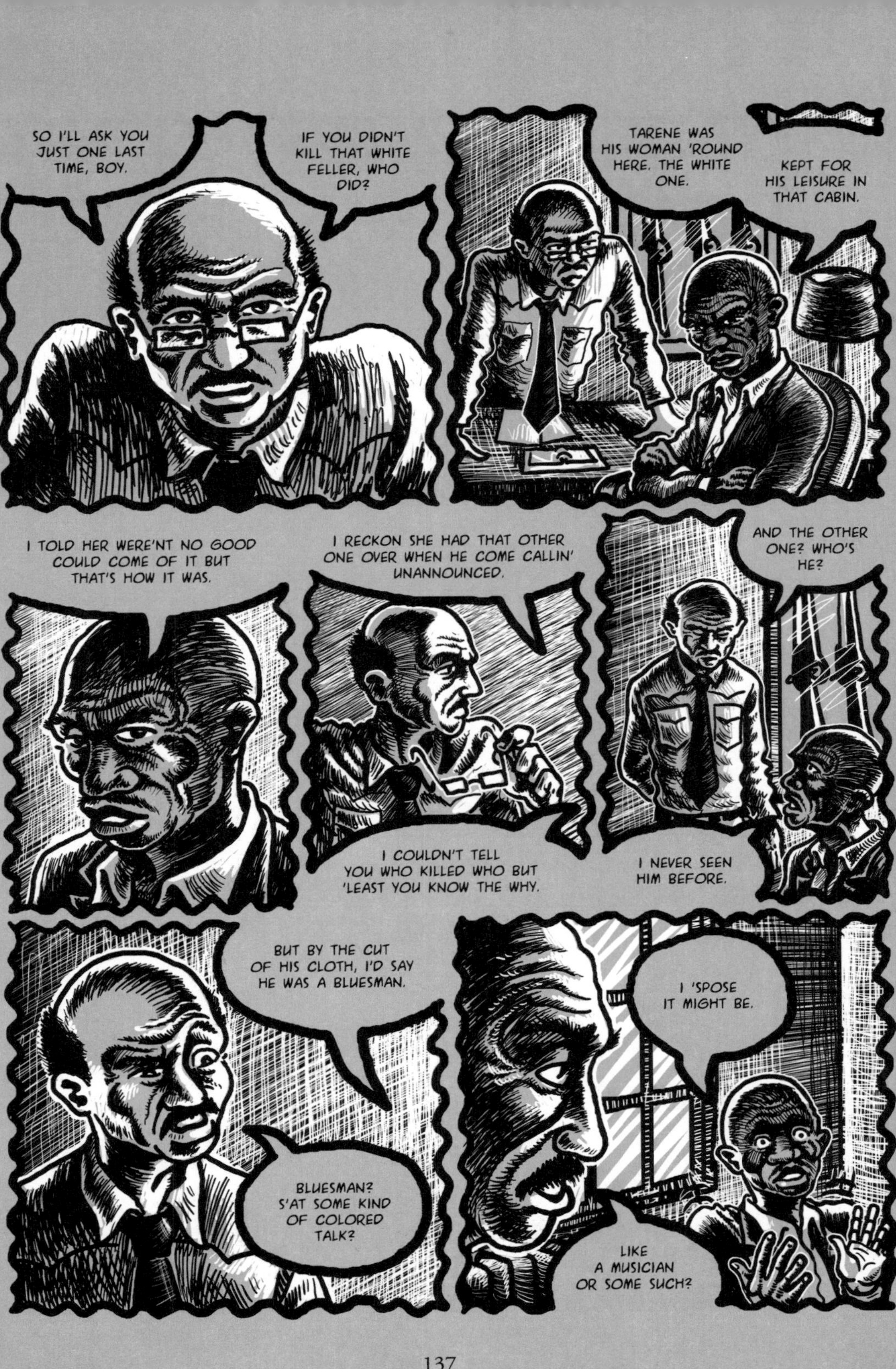
SO I'LL ASK YOU JUST ONE LAST TIME, BOY.
IF YOU DIDN'T KILL THAT WHITE FELLER, WHO DID?
TARENE WAS HIS WOMAN 'ROUND HERE. THE WHITE ONE.
KEPT FOR HIS LEISURE IN THAT CABIN.
I TOLD HER WERE'NT NO GOOD COULD COME OF IT BUT THAT'S HOW IT WAS.
I RECKON SHE HAD THAT OTHER ONE OVER WHEN HE COME CALLIN' UNANNOUNCED.
I COULDN'T TELL YOU WHO KILLED WHO BUT 'LEAST YOU KNOW THE WHY.
AND THE OTHER ONE? WHO'S HE?
I NEVER SEEN HIM BEFORE.
BUT BY THE CUT OF HIS CLOTH, I'D SAY HE WAS A BLUESMAN.
BLUESMAN? S'AT SOME KIND OF COLORED TALK?
I 'SPOSE IT MIGHT BE.
LIKE A MUSICIAN OR SOME SUCH?

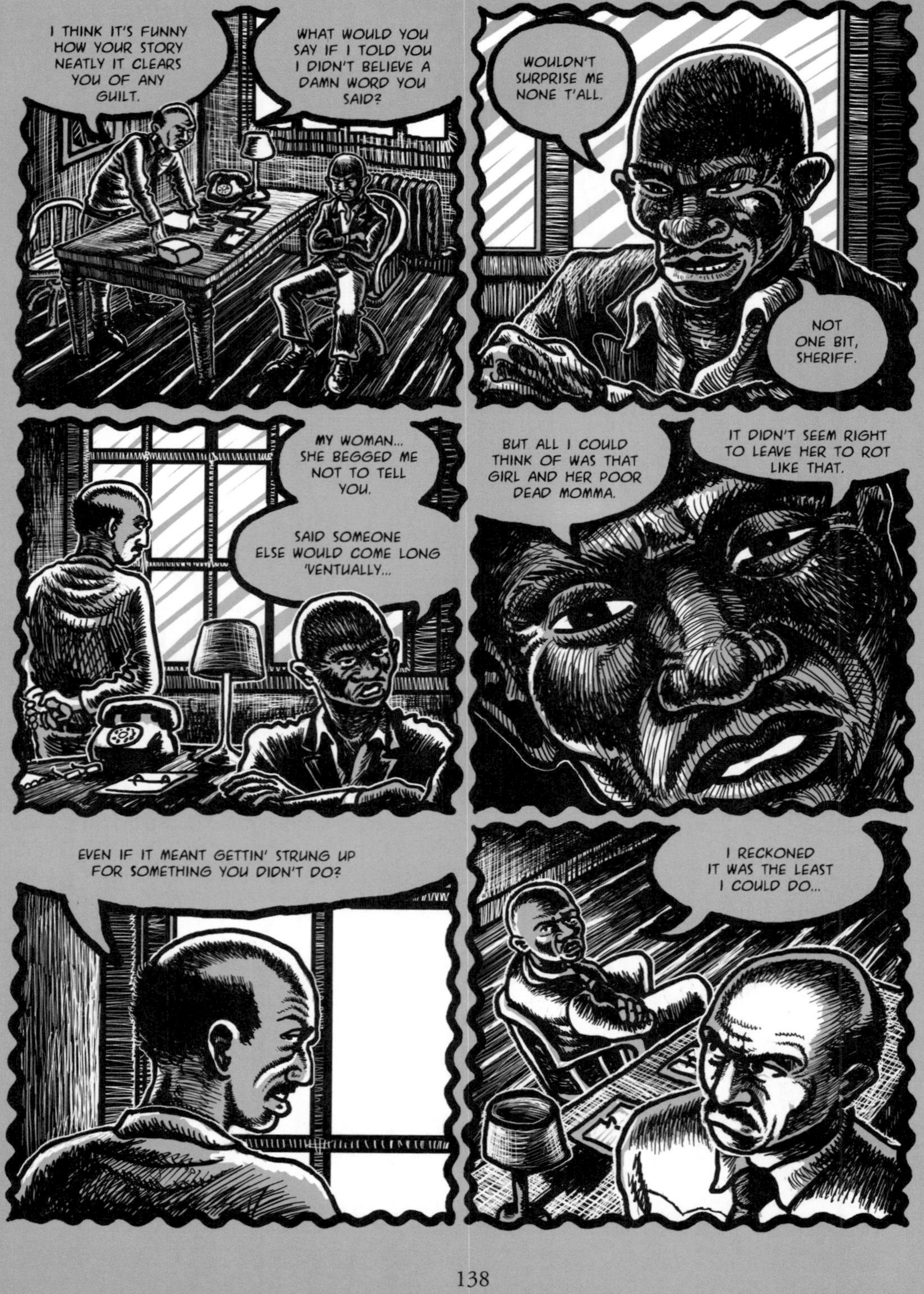
I THINK IT'S FUNNY HOW YOUR STORY NEATLY IT CLEARS YOU OF ANY GUILT.
WHAT WOULD YOU SAY IF I TOLD YOU I DIDN'T BELIEVE A DAMN WORD YOU SAID?
WOULDN'T SURPRISE ME NONE T'ALL.
NOT ONE BIT, SHERIFF.
MY WOMAN... SHE BEGGED ME NOT TO TELL YOU.
SAID SOMEONE ELSE WOULD COME LONG 'VENTUALLY...
BUT ALL I COULD THINK OF WAS THAT GIRL AND HER POOR DEAD MOMMA.
IT DIDN'T SEEM RIGHT TO LEAVE HER TO ROT LIKE THAT.
EVEN IF IT MEANT GETTIN' STRUNG UP FOR SOMETHING YOU DIDN'T DO?
I RECKONED IT WAS THE LEAST I COULD DO...

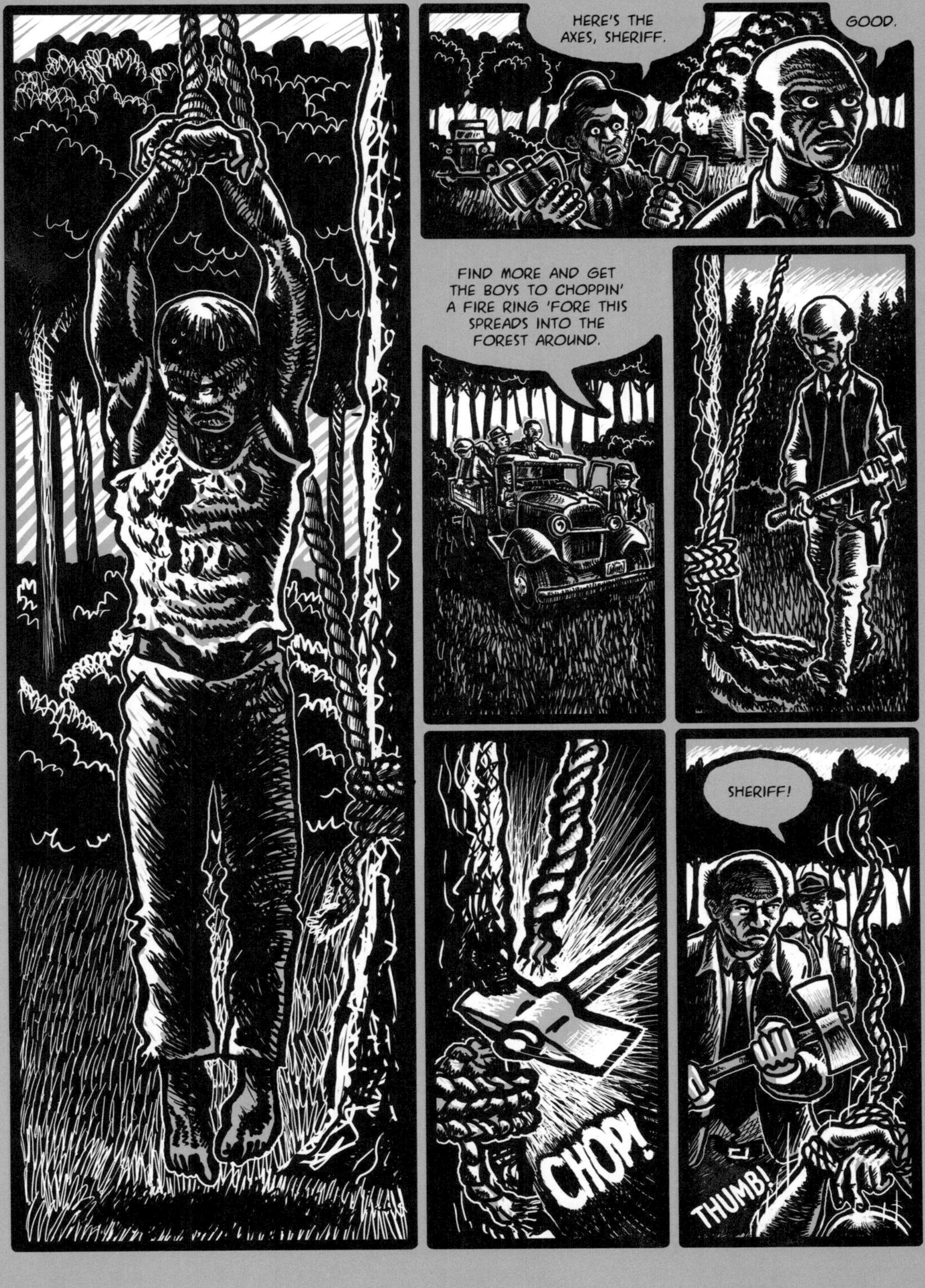
HERE'S THE AXES, SHERIFF.
GOOD.
FIND MORE AND GET THE BOYS TO CHOPPIN' A FIRE RING 'FORE THIS SPREADS INTO THE FOREST AROUND.
CHOP!
SHERIFF!
THUMB!

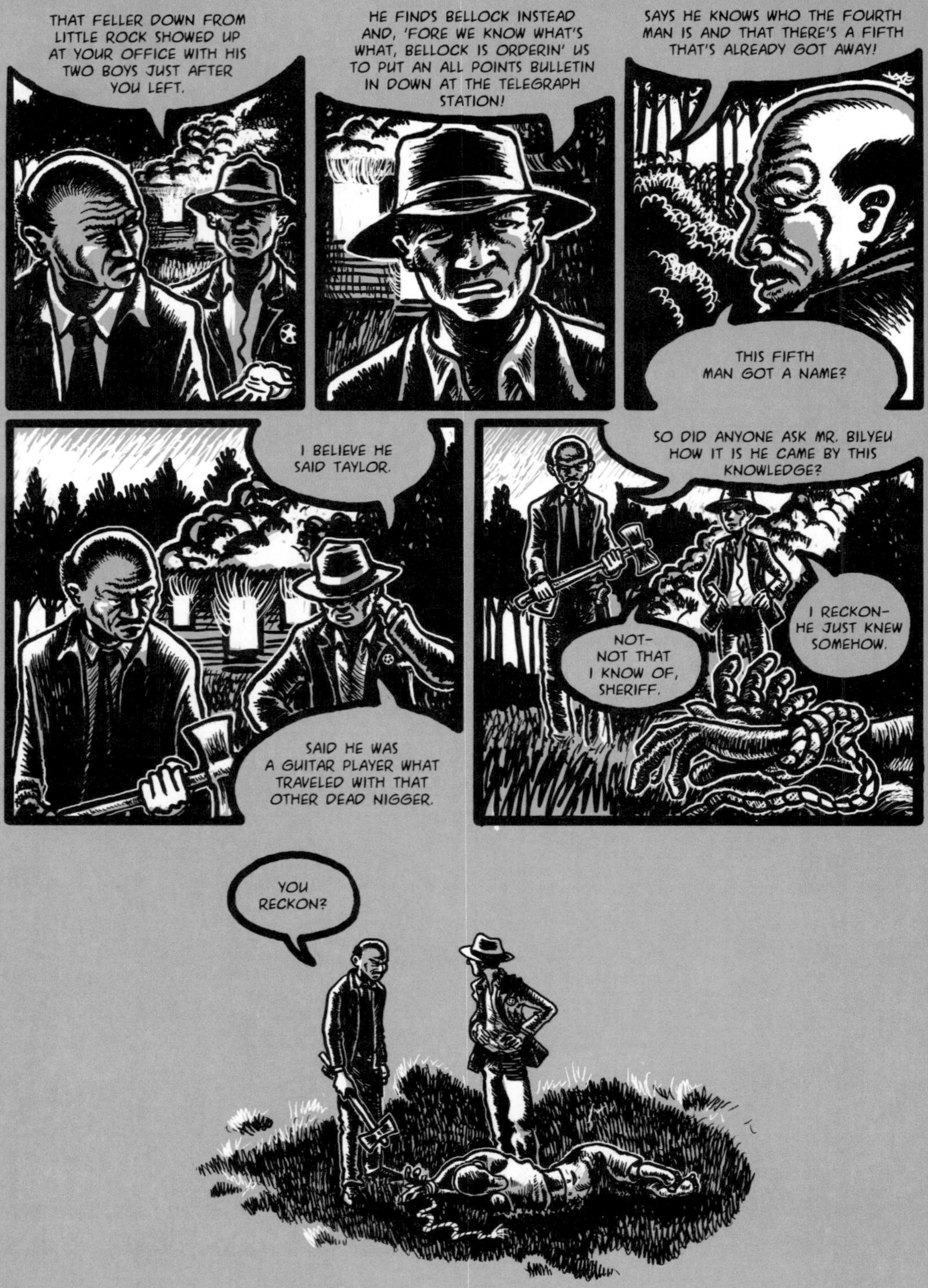
THAT FELLER DOWN FROM LITTLE ROCK SHOWED UP AT YOUR OFFICE WITH HIS TWO BOYS JUST AFTER YOU LEFT.
HE FINDS BELLOCK INSTEAD AND, 'FORE WE KNOW WHAT'S WHAT, BELLOCK IS ORDERIN' US TO PUT AN ALL POINTS BULLETIN IN DOWN AT THE TELEGRAPH STATION!
SAYS HE KNOWS WHO THE FOURTH MAN IS AND THAT THERE'S A FIFTH THAT'S ALREADY GOT AWAY!
THIS FIFTH MAN GOT A NAME?
I BELIEVE HE SAID TAYLOR.
SAID HE WAS A GUITAR PLAYER WHAT TRAVELED WITH THAT OTHER DEAD NIGGER.
SO DID ANYONE ASK MR. BILYEU HOW IT IS HE CAME BY THIS KNOWLEDGE?
NOT- NOT THAT I KNOW OF, SHERIFF.
I RECKON- HE JUST KNEW SOMEHOW.
YOU RECKON?

9

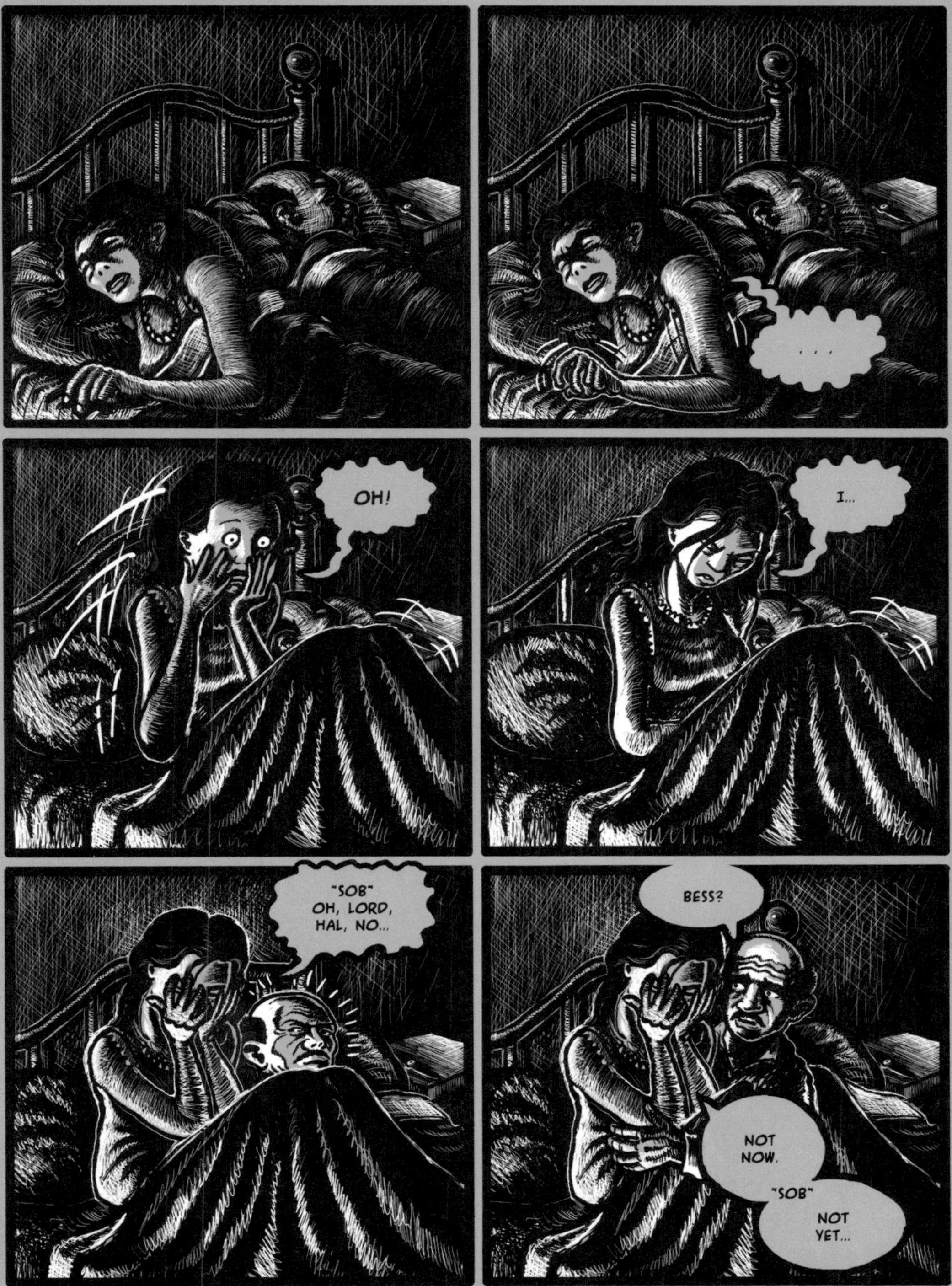
. . .
OH!
I...
"SOB" OH, LORD, HAL, NO...
BESS?
NOT NOW.
"SOB"
NOT YET...

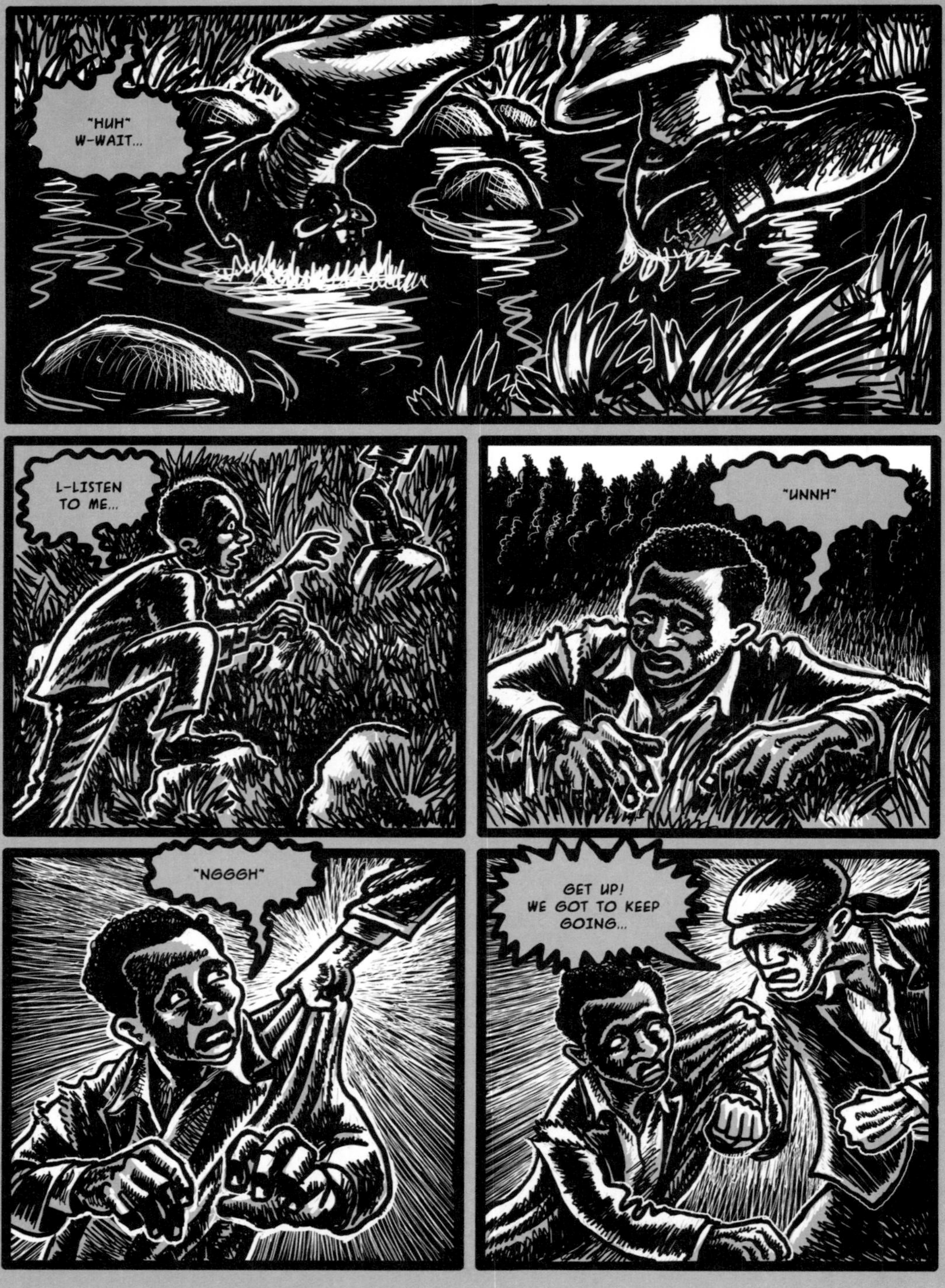
"HUH"
W-WAIT...
L-LISTEN TO ME...
"UNNH"
"NGGGH"
GET UP! WE GOT TO KEEP GOING...

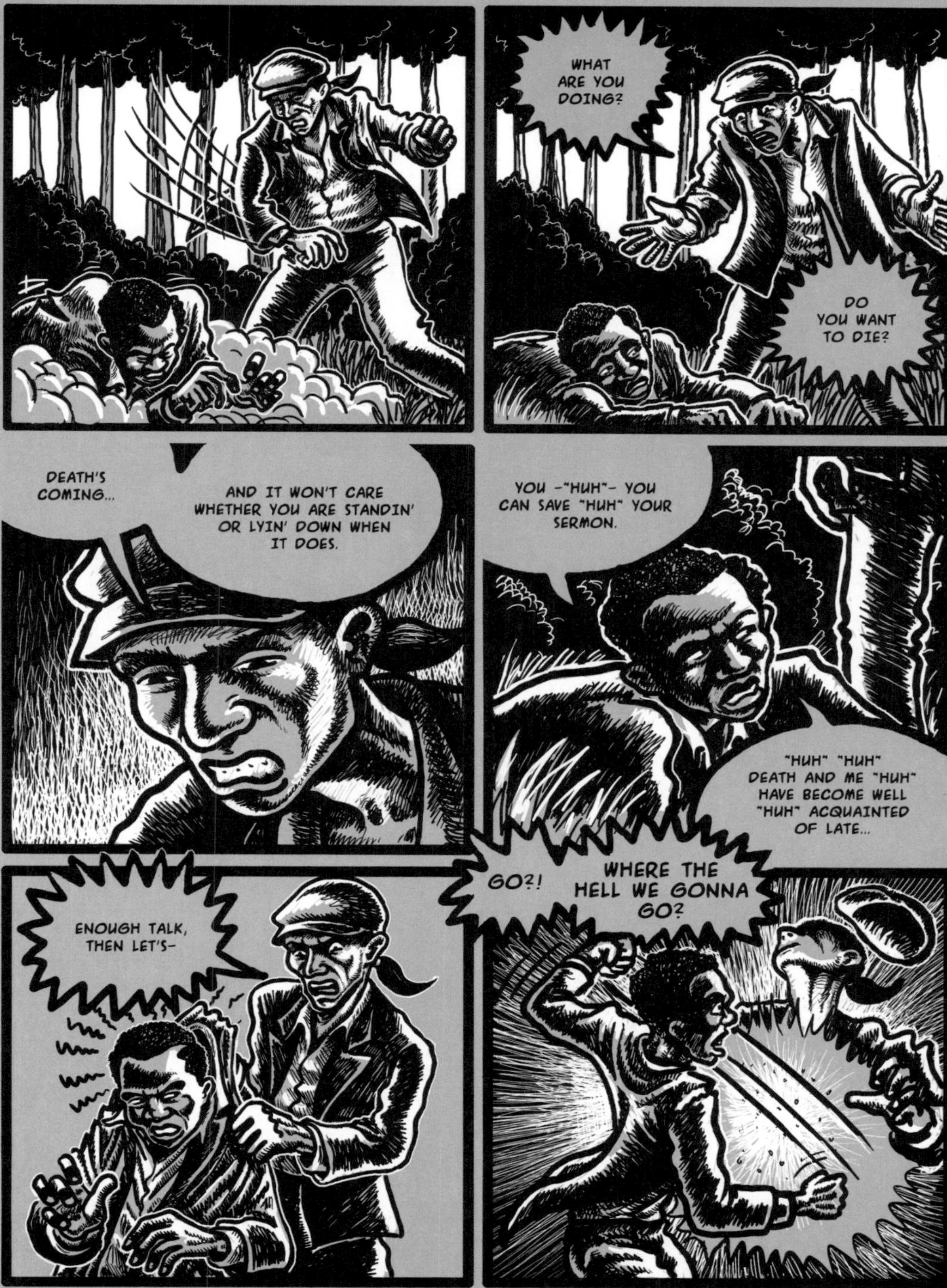
WHAT ARE YOU DOING?
DO YOU WANT TO DIE?
DEATH'S COMING...
AND IT WON'T CARE WHETHER YOU ARE STANDIN' OR LYIN' DOWN WHEN IT DOES.
YOU -"HUH"- YOU CAN SAVE "HUH" YOUR SERMON.
"HUH" "HUH" DEATH AND ME "HUH" HAVE BECOME WELL "HUH" ACQUAINTED OF LATE...
ENOUGH TALK, THEN LET'S-
GO?!
WHERE THE HELL WE GONNA GO?

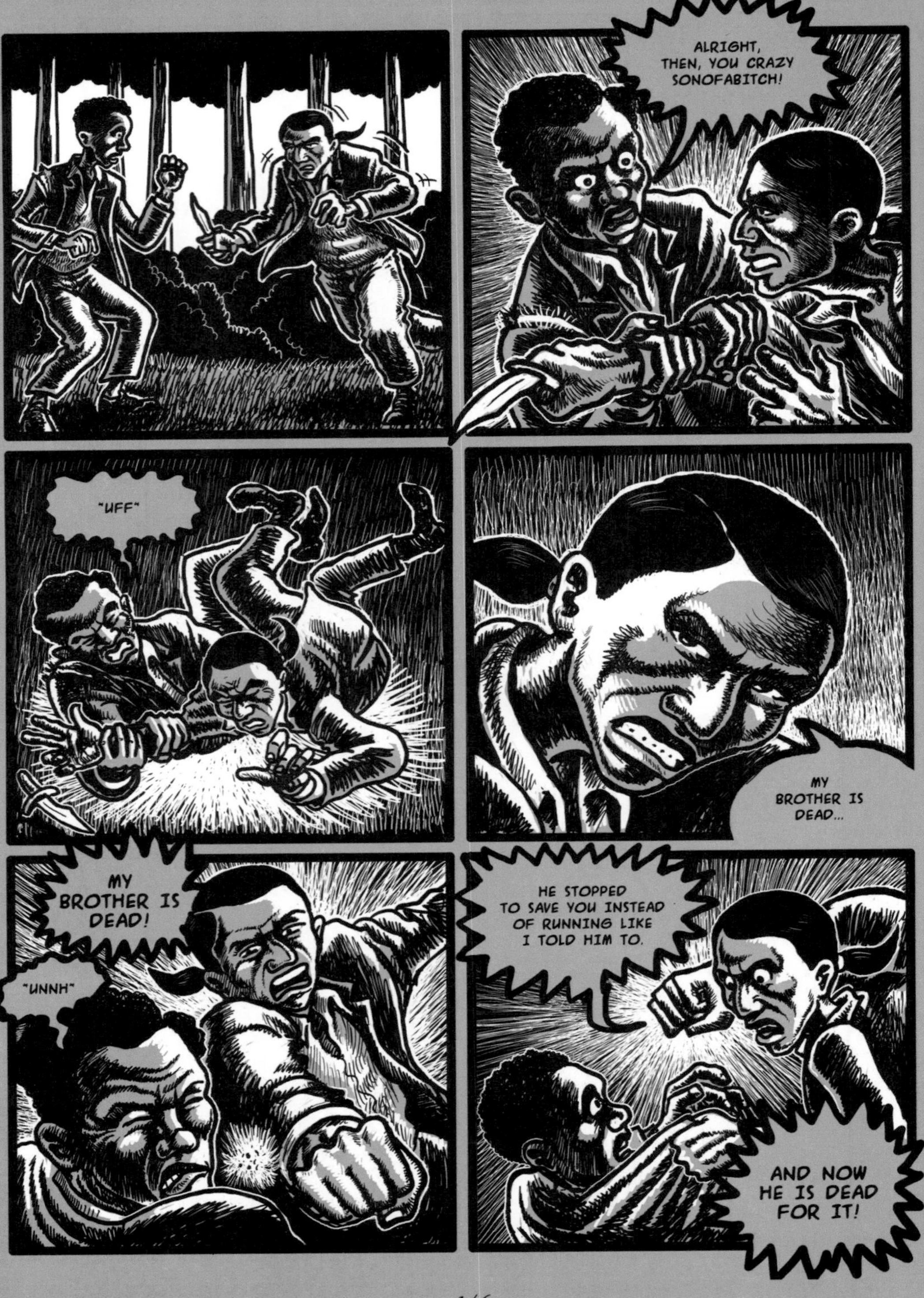
ALRIGHT, THEN, YOU CRAZY SONOFABITCH!
"UFF"
MY BROTHER IS DEAD...
MY BROTHER IS DEAD!
"UNNH"
HE STOPPED TO SAVE YOU INSTEAD OF RUNNING LIKE I TOLD HIM TO.
AND NOW HE IS DEAD FOR IT!

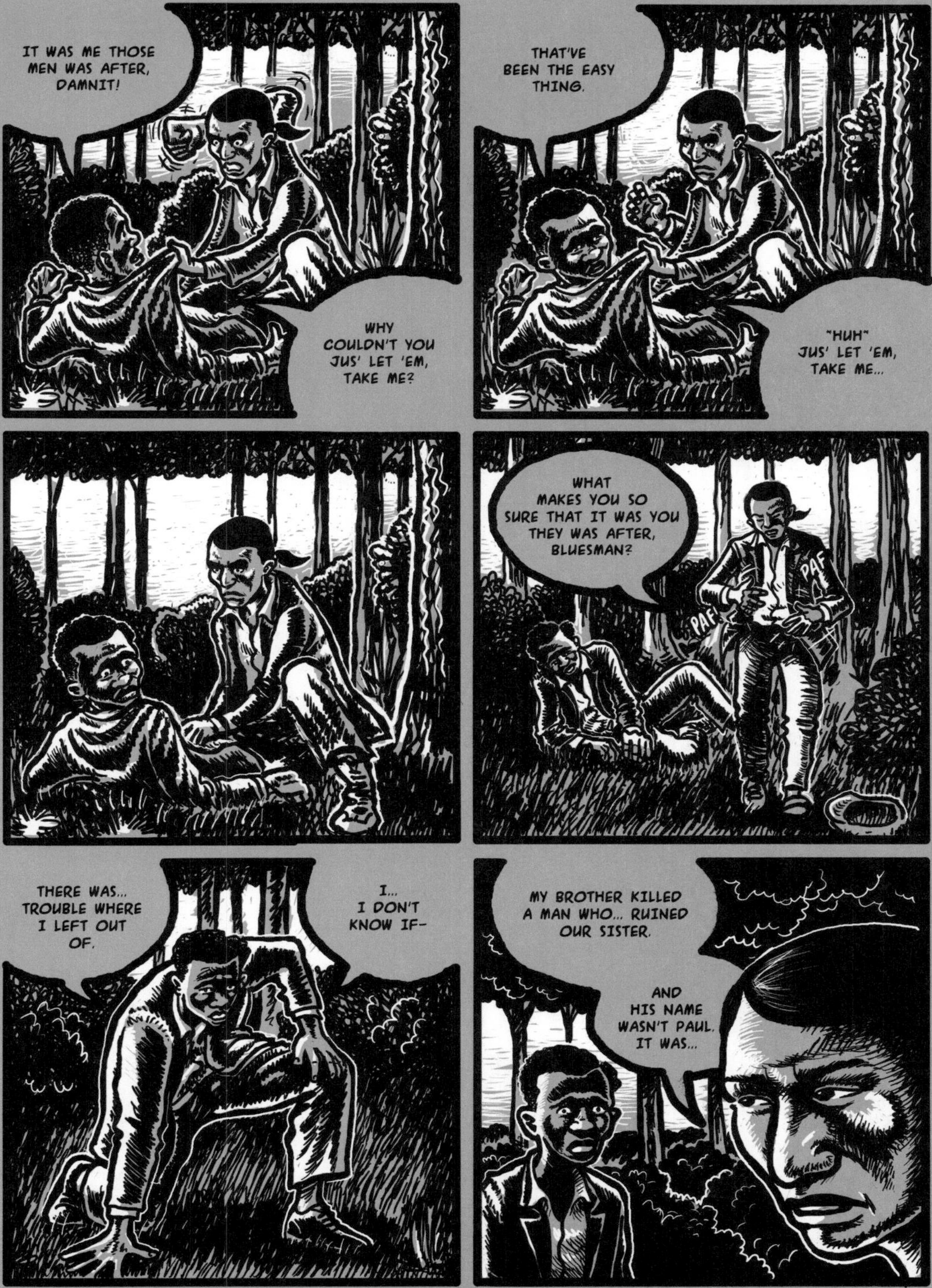
IT WAS ME THOSE MEN WAS AFTER, DAMNIT!
WHY COULDN'T YOU JUS' LET 'EM, TAKE ME?
THAT'VE BEEN THE EASY THING.
"HUH" JUS' LET 'EM, TAKE ME...
WHAT MAKES YOU SO SURE THAT IT WAS YOU THEY WAS AFTER, BLUESMAN?
PAF
PAF
THERE WAS... TROUBLE WHERE I LEFT OUT OF.
I... I DON'T KNOW IF-
MY BROTHER KILLED A MAN WHO... RUINED OUR SISTER.
AND HIS NAME WASN'T PAUL. IT WAS...

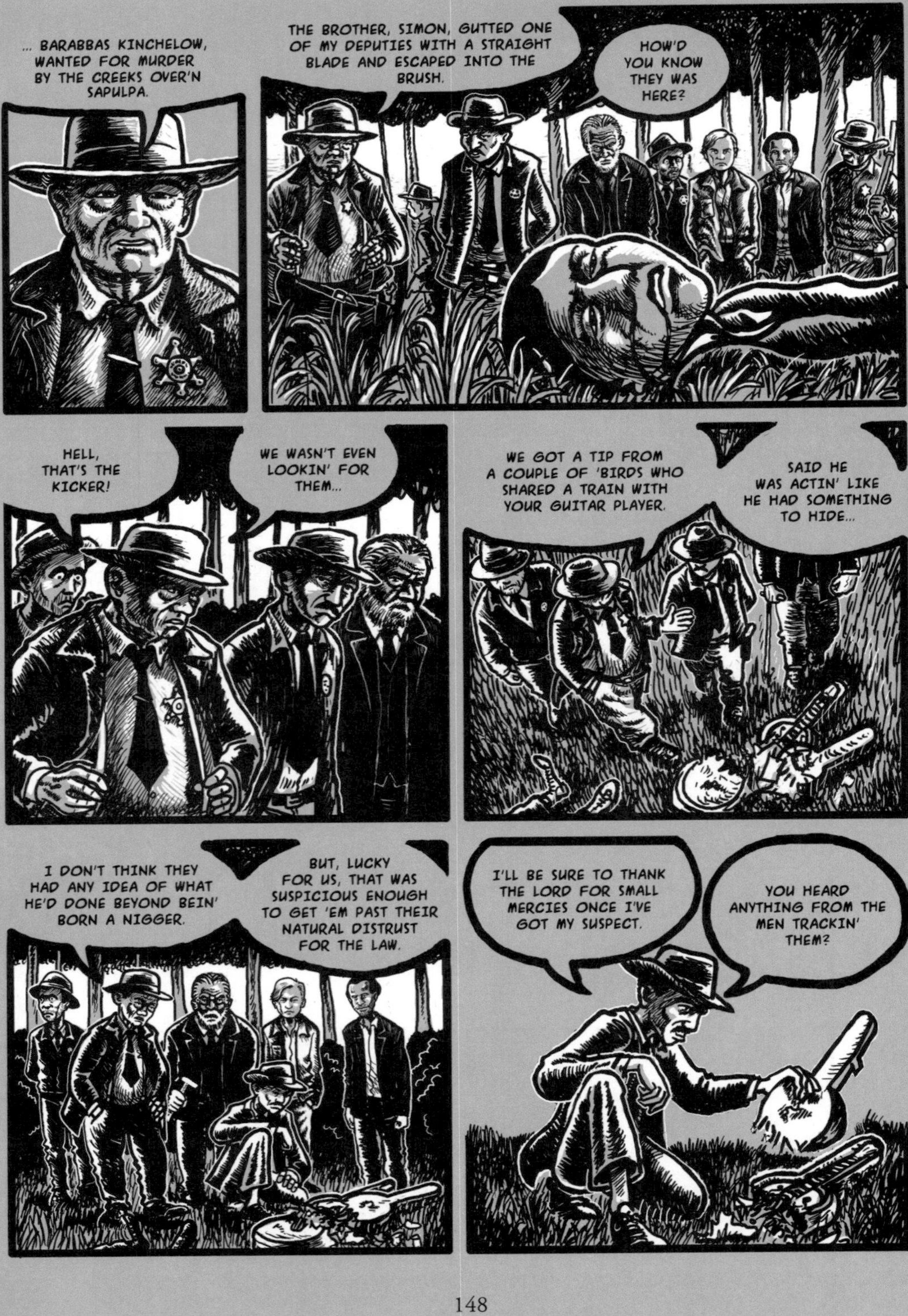
... BARABBAS KINCHELOW, WANTED FOR MURDER BY THE CREEKS OVER'N SAPULPA.
THE BROTHER, SIMON, GUTTED ONE OF MY DEPUTIES WITH A STRAIGHT BLADE AND ESCAPED INTO THE BRUSH.
HOW'D YOU KNOW THEY WAS HERE?
HELL, THAT'S THE KICKER!
WE WASN'T EVEN LOOKIN' FOR THEM...
WE GOT A TIP FROM A COUPLE OF 'BIRDS WHO SHARED A TRAIN WITH YOUR GUITAR PLAYER.
SAID HE WAS ACTIN' LIKE HE HAD SOMETHING TO HIDE...
I DON'T THINK THEY HAD ANY IDEA OF WHAT HE'D DONE BEYOND BEIN' BORN A NIGGER.
BUT, LUCKY FOR US, THAT WAS SUSPICIOUS ENOUGH TO GET 'EM PAST THEIR NATURAL DISTRUST FOR THE LAW.
I'LL BE SURE TO THANK THE LORD FOR SMALL MERCIES ONCE I'VE GOT MY SUSPECT.
YOU HEARD ANYTHING FROM THE MEN TRACKIN' THEM?

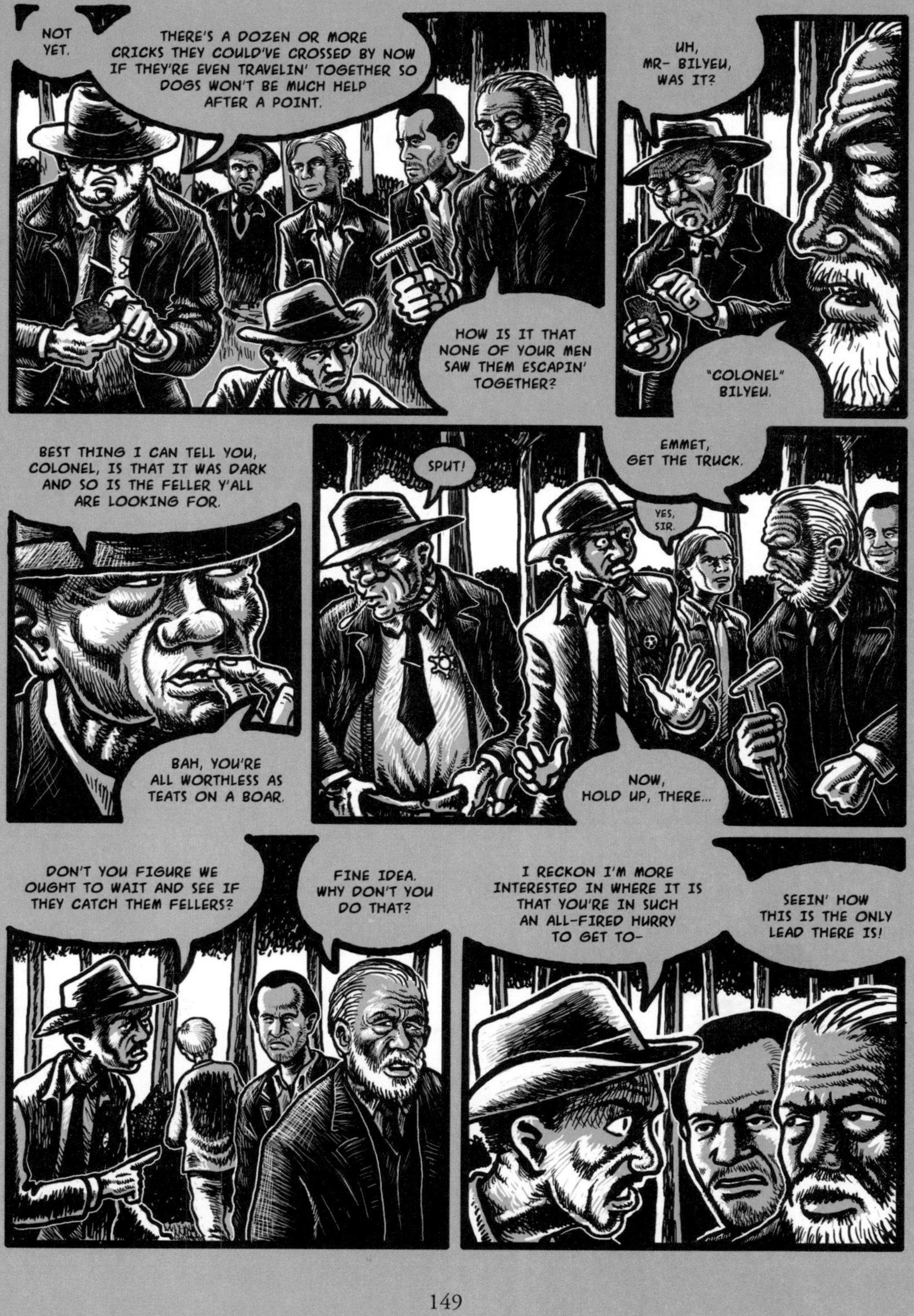
NOT YET.
THERE'S A DOZEN OR MORE CRICKS THEY COULD'VE CROSSED BY NOW IF THEY'RE EVEN TRAVELIN' TOGETHER SO DOGS WON'T BE MUCH HELP AFTER A POINT.
HOW IS IT THAT NONE OF YOUR MEN SAW THEM ESCAPIN' TOGETHER?
UH, MR- BILYEU, WAS IT?
"COLONEL" BILYEU.
BEST THING I CAN TELL YOU, COLONEL, IS THAT IT WAS DARK AND SO IS THE FELLER Y'ALL ARE LOOKING FOR.
BAH, YOU'RE ALL WORTHLESS AS TEATS ON A BOAR.
SPUT!
EMMET, GET THE TRUCK.
YES, SIR.
NOW, HOLD UP, THERE...
DON'T YOU FIGURE WE OUGHT TO WAIT AND SEE IF THEY CATCH THEM FELLERS?
FINE IDEA. WHY DON'T YOU DO THAT?
I RECKON I'M MORE INTERESTED IN WHERE IT IS THAT YOU'RE IN SUCH AN ALL-FIRED HURRY TO GET TO-
SEEIN' HOW THIS IS THE ONLY LEAD THERE IS!

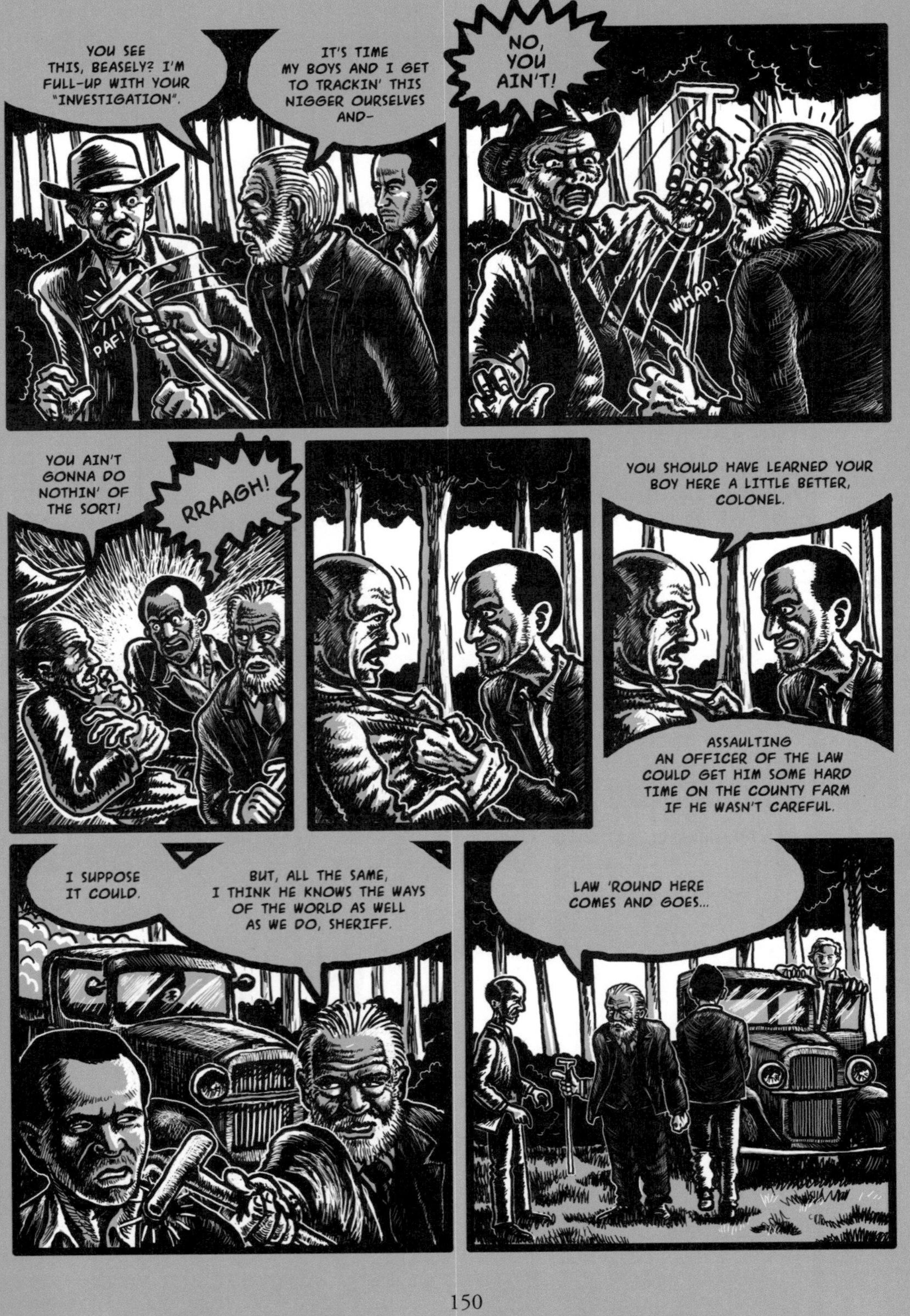
YOU SEE THIS, BEASELY? I'M FULL-UP WITH YOUR "INVESTIGATION".
IT'S TIME MY BOYS AND I GET TO TRACKIN' THIS NIGGER OURSELVES AND–
PAF!
NO, YOU AIN'T!
WHAP!
YOU AIN'T GONNA DO NOTHIN' OF THE SORT!
RRAAGH!
YOU SHOULD HAVE LEARNED YOUR BOY HERE A LITTLE BETTER, COLONEL.
ASSAULTING AN OFFICER OF THE LAW COULD GET HIM SOME HARD TIME ON THE COUNTY FARM IF HE WASN'T CAREFUL.
I SUPPOSE IT COULD.
BUT, ALL THE SAME, I THINK HE KNOWS THE WAYS OF THE WORLD AS WELL AS WE DO, SHERIFF.
LAW 'ROUND HERE COMES AND GOES...

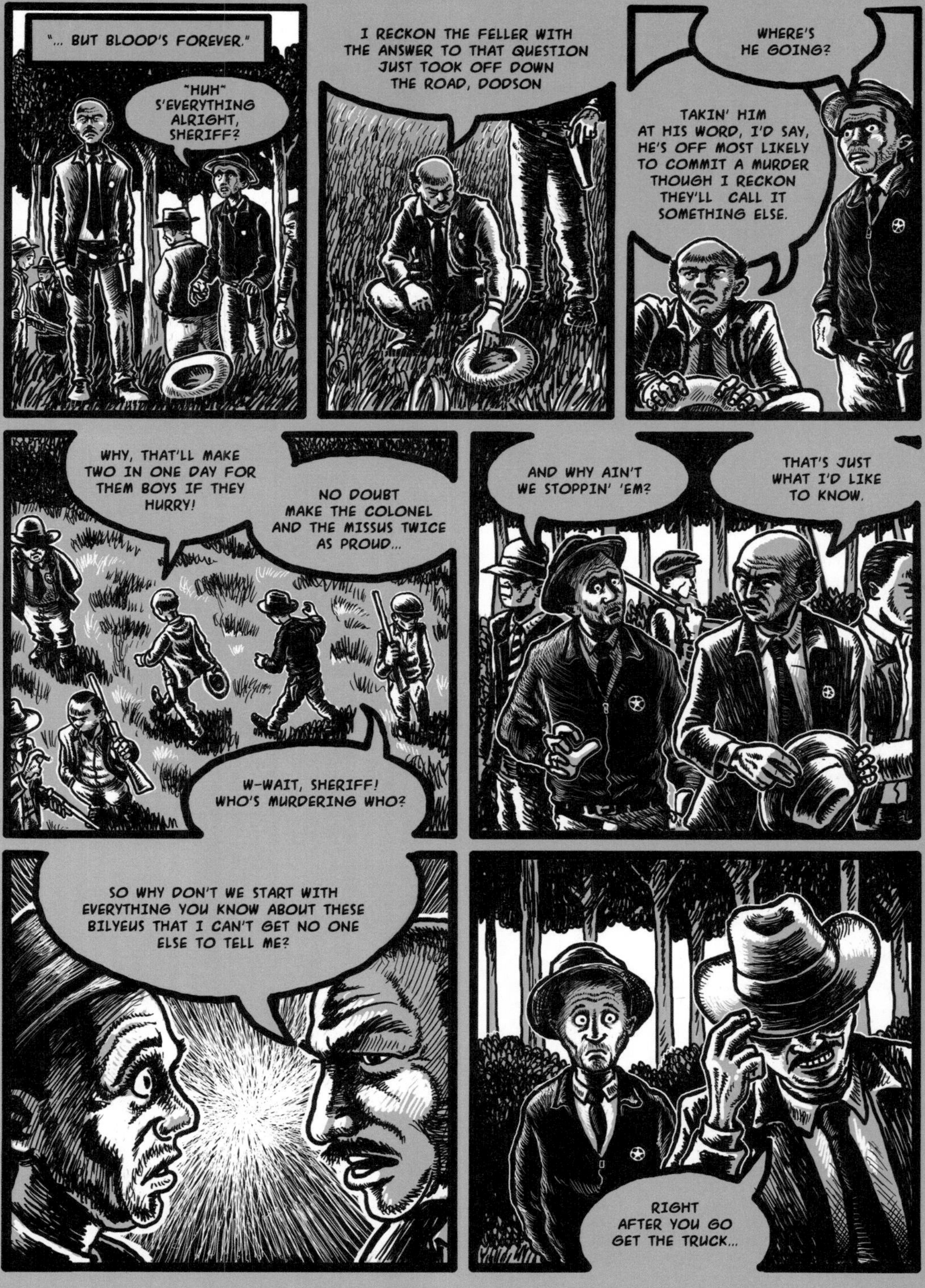
"... BUT BLOOD'S FOREVER."
"HUH" S'EVERYTHING ALRIGHT, SHERIFF?
I RECKON THE FELLER WITH THE ANSWER TO THAT QUESTION JUST TOOK OFF DOWN THE ROAD, DODSON
WHERE'S HE GOING?
TAKIN' HIM AT HIS WORD, I'D SAY, HE'S OFF MOST LIKELY TO COMMIT A MURDER THOUGH I RECKON THEY'LL CALL IT SOMETHING ELSE.
WHY, THAT'LL MAKE TWO IN ONE DAY FOR THEM BOYS IF THEY HURRY!
NO DOUBT MAKE THE COLONEL AND THE MISSUS TWICE AS PROUD...
W-WAIT, SHERIFF! WHO'S MURDERING WHO?
AND WHY AIN'T WE STOPPIN' 'EM?
THAT'S JUST WHAT I'D LIKE TO KNOW.
SO WHY DON'T WE START WITH EVERYTHING YOU KNOW ABOUT THESE BILYEUS THAT I CAN'T GET NO ONE ELSE TO TELL ME?
RIGHT AFTER YOU GO GET THE TRUCK...

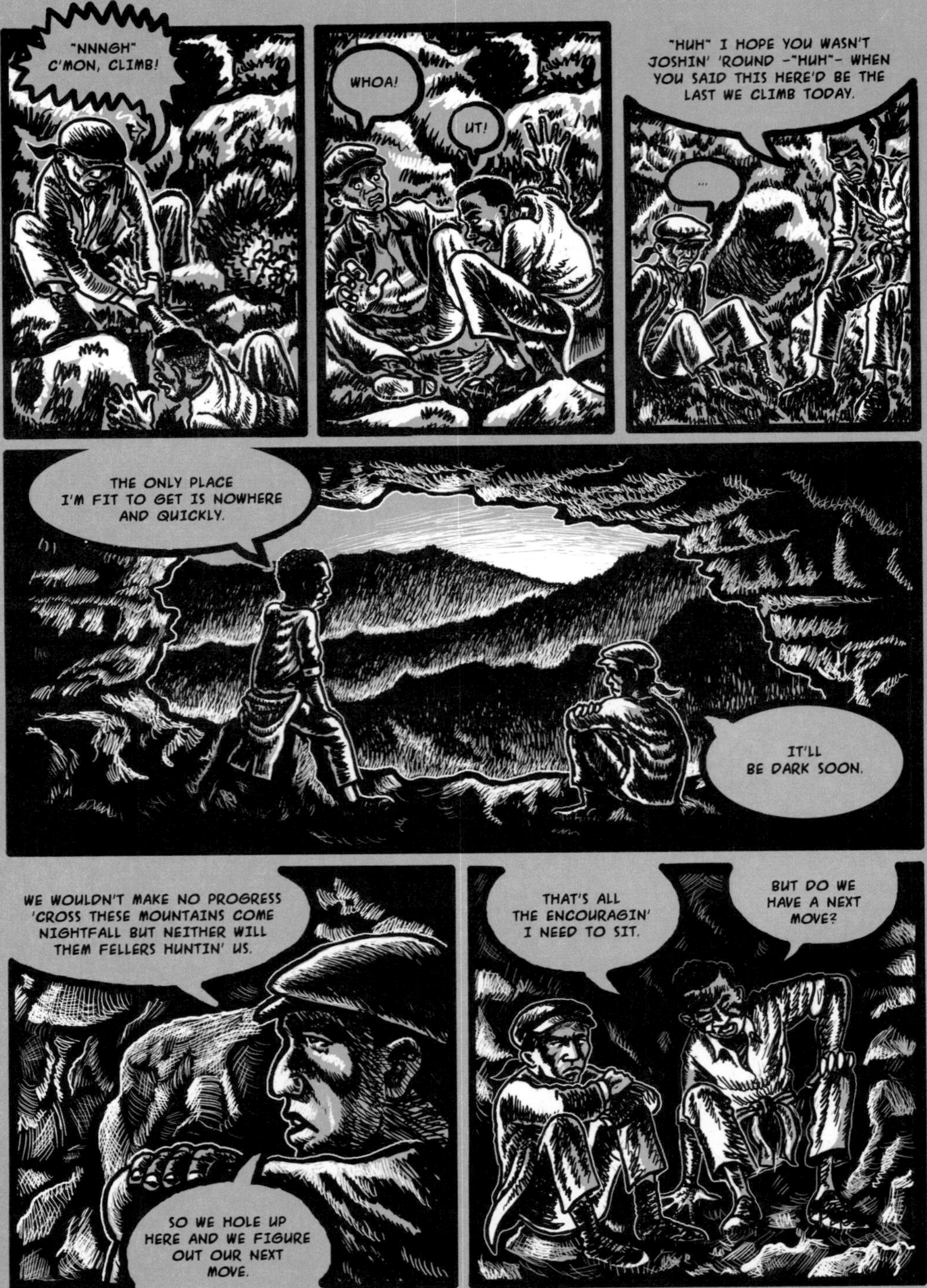
"NNNGH"
C'MON, CLIMB!
WHOA!
UT!
"HUH" I HOPE YOU WASN'T JOSHIN' 'ROUND -"HUH"- WHEN YOU SAID THIS HERE'D BE THE LAST WE CLIMB TODAY.
...
THE ONLY PLACE I'M FIT TO GET IS NOWHERE AND QUICKLY.
IT'LL BE DARK SOON.
WE WOULDN'T MAKE NO PROGRESS 'CROSS THESE MOUNTAINS COME NIGHTFALL BUT NEITHER WILL THEM FELLERS HUNTIN' US.
SO WE HOLE UP HERE AND WE FIGURE OUT OUR NEXT MOVE.
THAT'S ALL THE ENCOURAGIN' I NEED TO SIT.
BUT DO WE HAVE A NEXT MOVE?

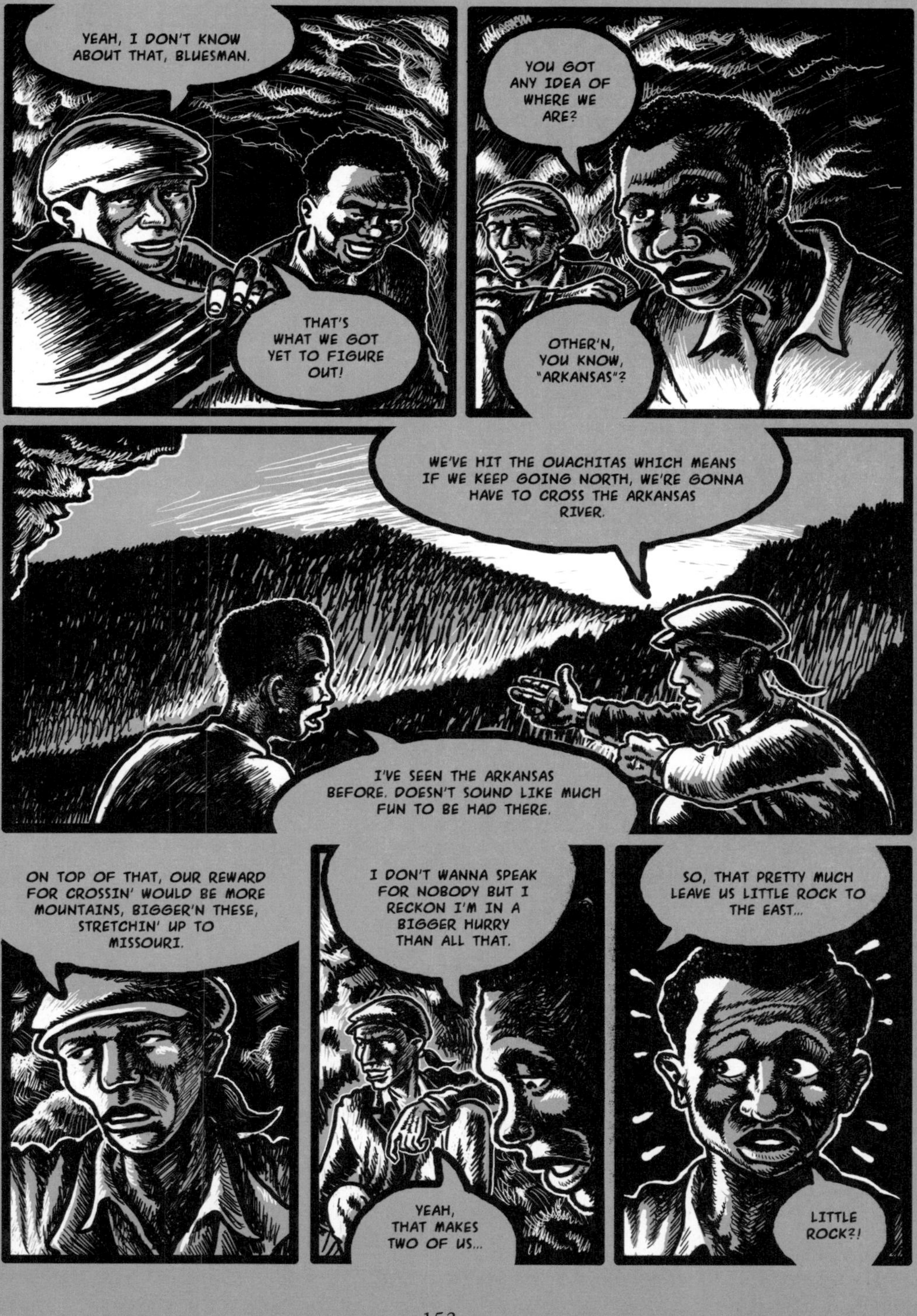
YEAH, I DON'T KNOW ABOUT THAT, BLUESMAN.
THAT'S WHAT WE GOT YET TO FIGURE OUT!
YOU GOT ANY IDEA OF WHERE WE ARE?
OTHER'N, YOU KNOW, "ARKANSAS"?
WE'VE HIT THE OUACHITAS WHICH MEANS IF WE KEEP GOING NORTH, WE'RE GONNA HAVE TO CROSS THE ARKANSAS RIVER.
I'VE SEEN THE ARKANSAS BEFORE. DOESN'T SOUND LIKE MUCH FUN TO BE HAD THERE.
ON TOP OF THAT, OUR REWARD FOR CROSSIN' WOULD BE MORE MOUNTAINS, BIGGER'N THESE, STRETCHIN' UP TO MISSOURI.
I DON'T WANNA SPEAK FOR NOBODY BUT I RECKON I'M IN A BIGGER HURRY THAN ALL THAT.
YEAH, THAT MAKES TWO OF US...
SO, THAT PRETTY MUCH LEAVE US LITTLE ROCK TO THE EAST...
LITTLE ROCK?!

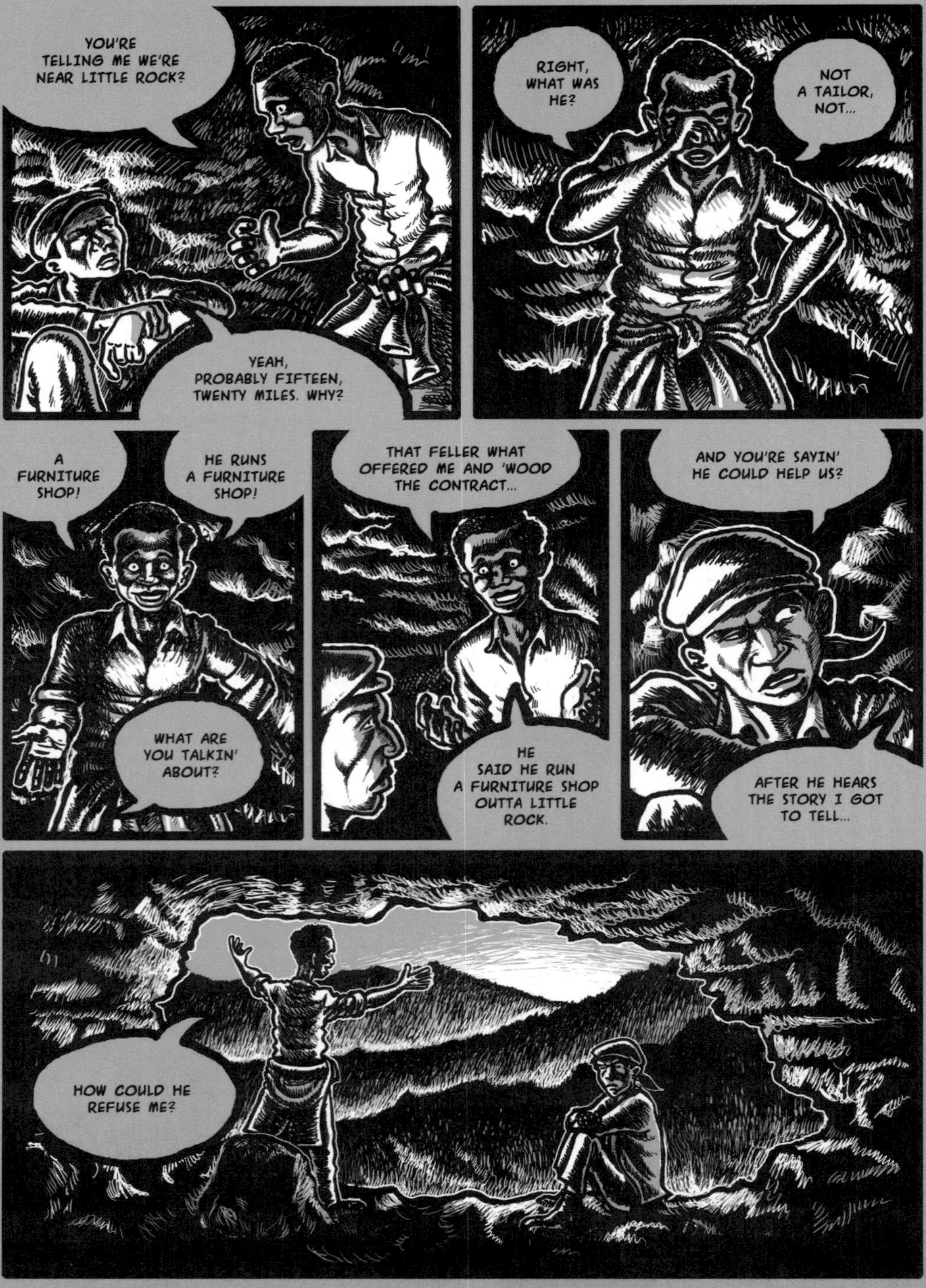
YOU'RE TELLING ME WE'RE NEAR LITTLE ROCK?
YEAH, PROBABLY FIFTEEN, TWENTY MILES. WHY?
RIGHT, WHAT WAS HE?
NOT A TAILOR, NOT...
A FURNITURE SHOP!
HE RUNS A FURNITURE SHOP!
WHAT ARE YOU TALKIN' ABOUT?
THAT FELLER WHAT OFFERED ME AND 'WOOD THE CONTRACT...
HE SAID HE RUN A FURNITURE SHOP OUTTA LITTLE ROCK.
AND YOU'RE SAYIN' HE COULD HELP US?
AFTER HE HEARS THE STORY I GOT TO TELL...
HOW COULD HE REFUSE ME?

10

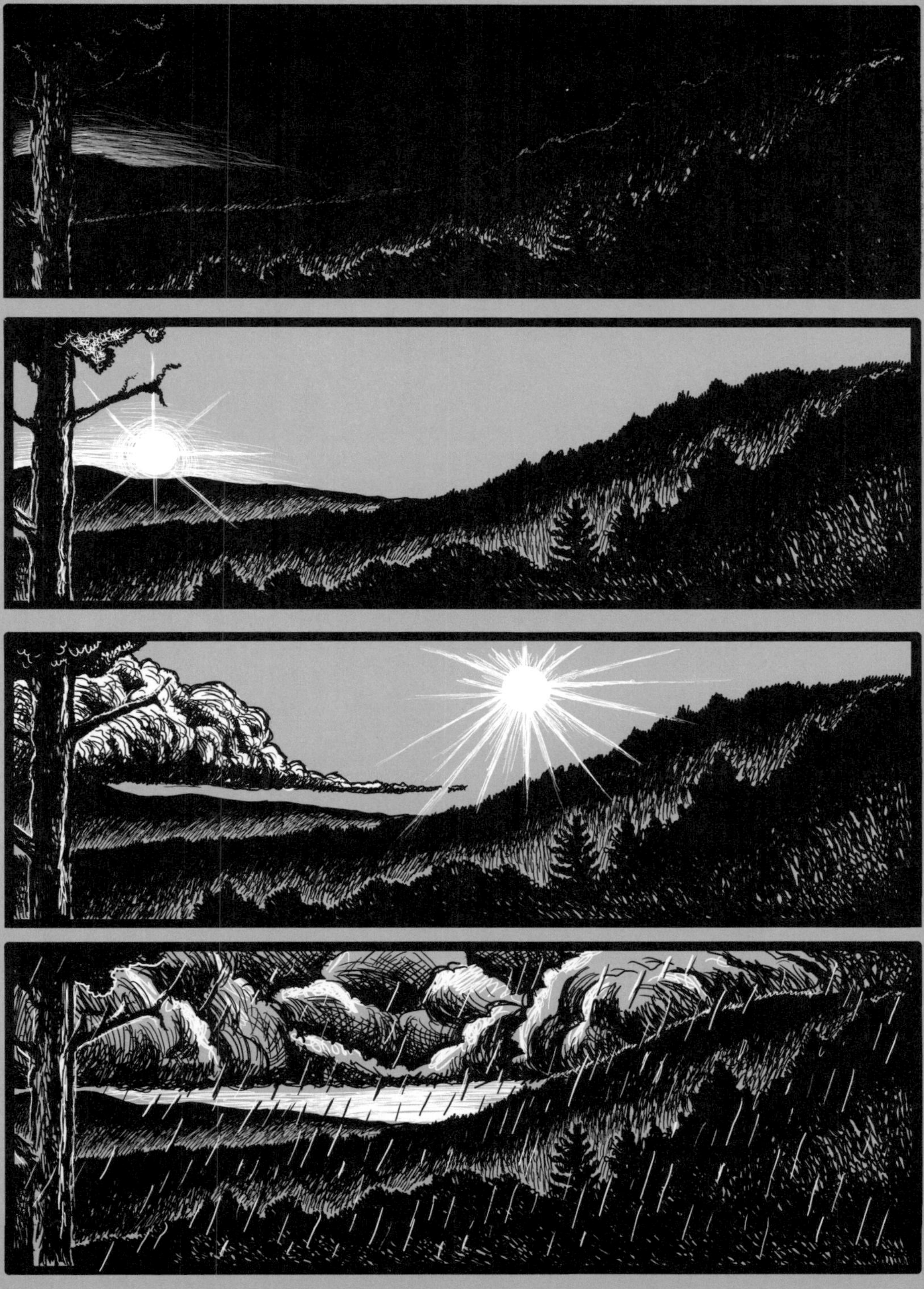

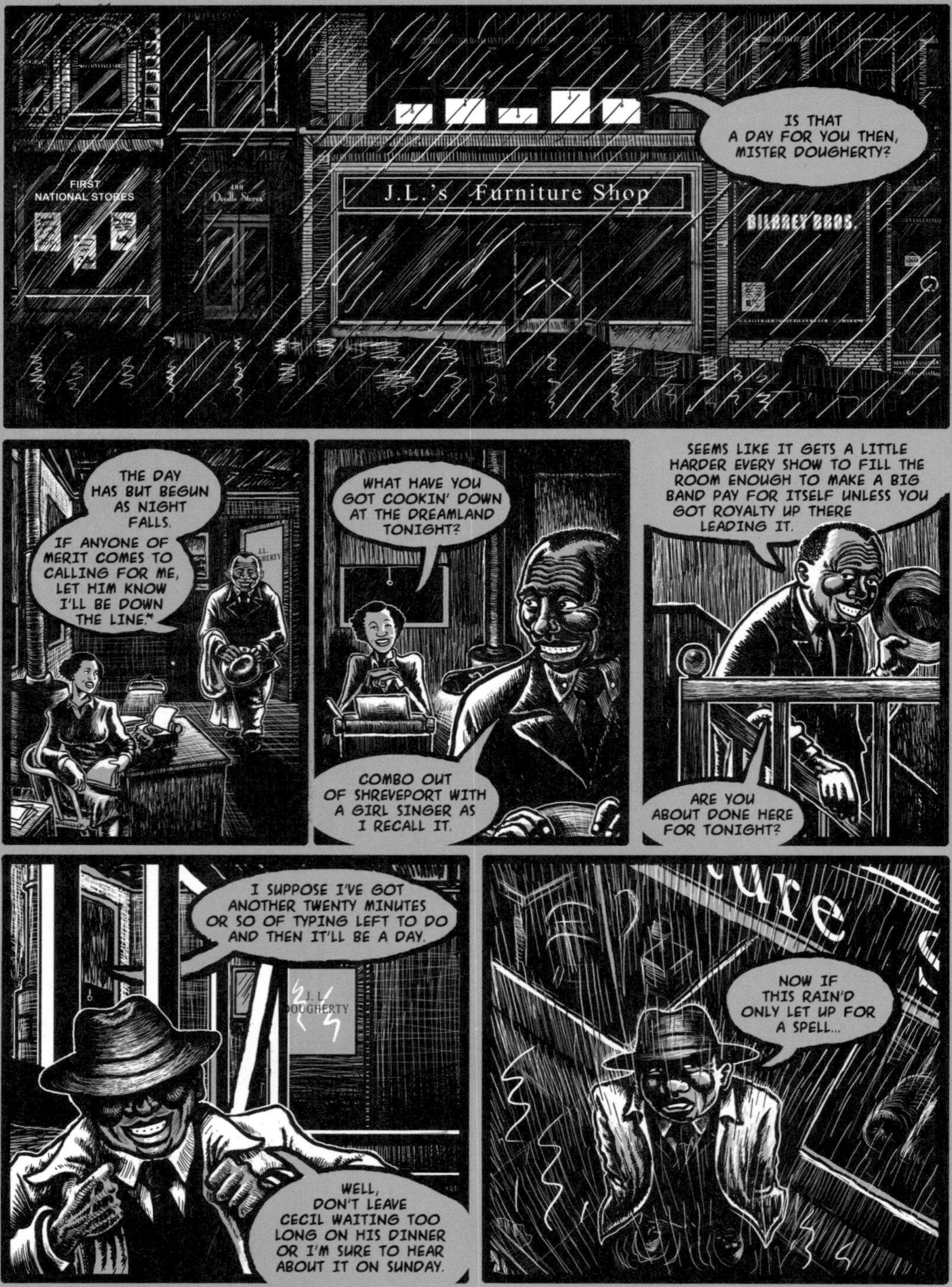
FIRST NATIONAL STORES
J.L.'s Furniture Shop
BILBREY BROS.
IS THAT A DAY FOR YOU THEN, MISTER DOUGHERTY?
THE DAY HAS BUT BEGUN AS NIGHT FALLS.
IF ANYONE OF MERIT COMES TO CALLING FOR ME, LET HIM KNOW I'LL BE DOWN THE LINE.*
WHAT HAVE YOU GOT COOKIN' DOWN AT THE DREAMLAND TONIGHT?
COMBO OUT OF SHREVEPORT WITH A GIRL SINGER AS I RECALL IT.
SEEMS LIKE IT GETS A LITTLE HARDER EVERY SHOW TO FILL THE ROOM ENOUGH TO MAKE A BIG BAND PAY FOR ITSELF UNLESS YOU GOT ROYALTY UP THERE LEADING IT.
ARE YOU ABOUT DONE HERE FOR TONIGHT?
I SUPPOSE I'VE GOT ANOTHER TWENTY MINUTES OR SO OF TYPING LEFT TO DO AND THEN IT'LL BE A DAY.
J. L. DOUGHERTY
WELL, DON'T LEAVE CECIL WAITING TOO LONG ON HIS DINNER OR I'M SURE TO HEAR ABOUT IT ON SUNDAY.
NOW IF THIS RAIN'D ONLY LET UP FOR A SPELL...

* "DOWN THE LINE" WAS A COLLOQUIAL EXPRESSION SPECIFIC TO LITTLE ROCK IN THIS PERIOD. "THE LINE" WAS THE MUSIC DISTRICT ON NINTH STREET.

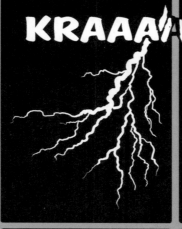

KRAAAAAASSH!

OH!

NOW I'M GOIN' TO BE WET AND LATE FIXIN' DINNER. GLORIOUS...

OOH... WHY DIDN'T I BRING AN UMBRELLA TODAY?

LORD!

EEEEEEE—

NO! DON'T TOUCH M—MMF!

HUSH, NOW! AIN'T NO ONE GETTIN' HURT HERE!

JUS' TELL US WHERE WE CAN FIND J.L. DOUGHERTY...

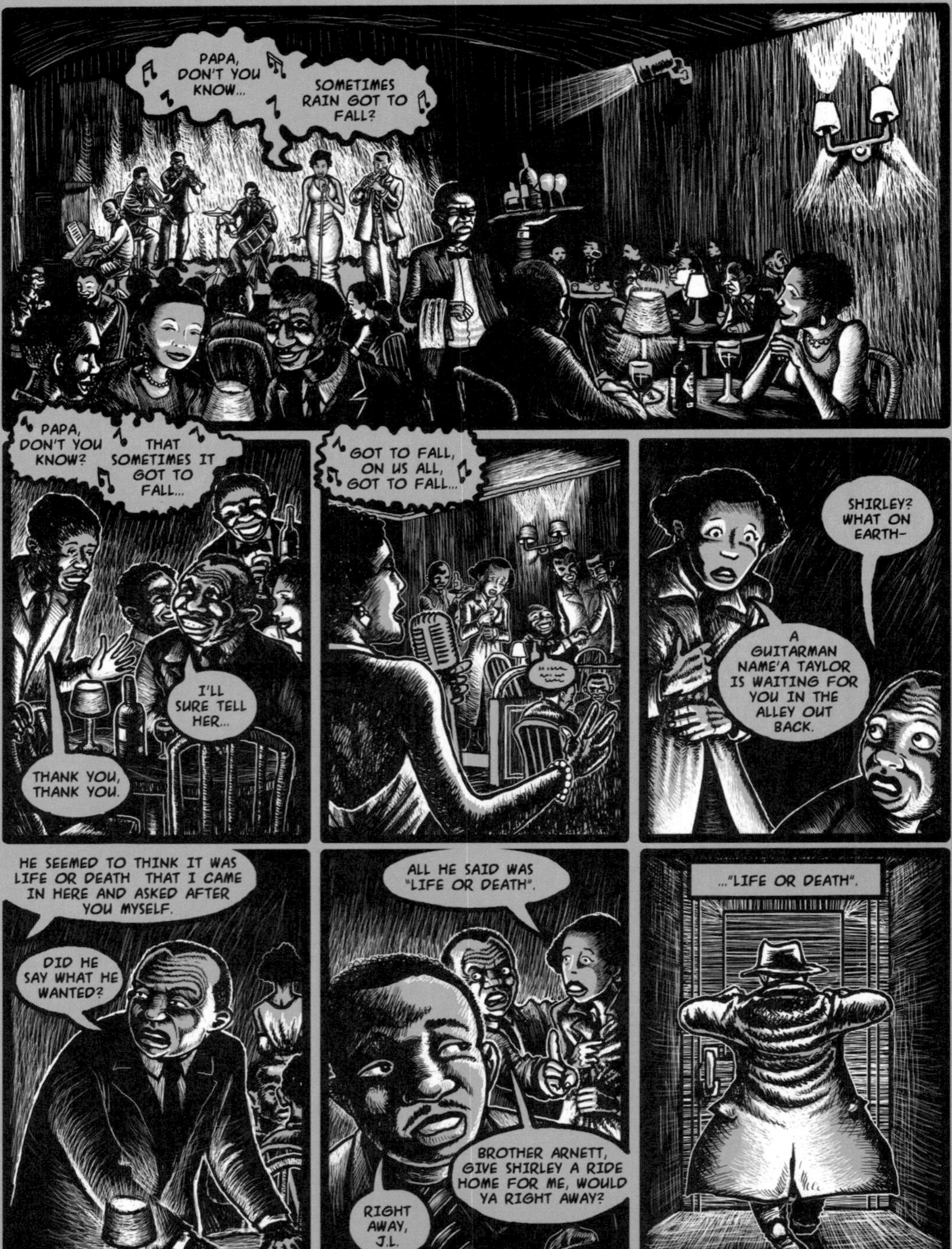
PAPA, DON'T YOU KNOW...
SOMETIMES RAIN GOT TO FALL?
PAPA, DON'T YOU KNOW?
THAT SOMETIMES IT GOT TO FALL...
I'LL SURE TELL HER...
THANK YOU, THANK YOU.
GOT TO FALL, ON US ALL, GOT TO FALL...
SHIRLEY? WHAT ON EARTH-
A GUITARMAN NAME'A TAYLOR IS WAITING FOR YOU IN THE ALLEY OUT BACK.
HE SEEMED TO THINK IT WAS LIFE OR DEATH THAT I CAME IN HERE AND ASKED AFTER YOU MYSELF.
DID HE SAY WHAT HE WANTED?
ALL HE SAID WAS "LIFE OR DEATH".
BROTHER ARNETT, GIVE SHIRLEY A RIDE HOME FOR ME, WOULD YA RIGHT AWAY?
RIGHT AWAY, J.L.
..."LIFE OR DEATH".

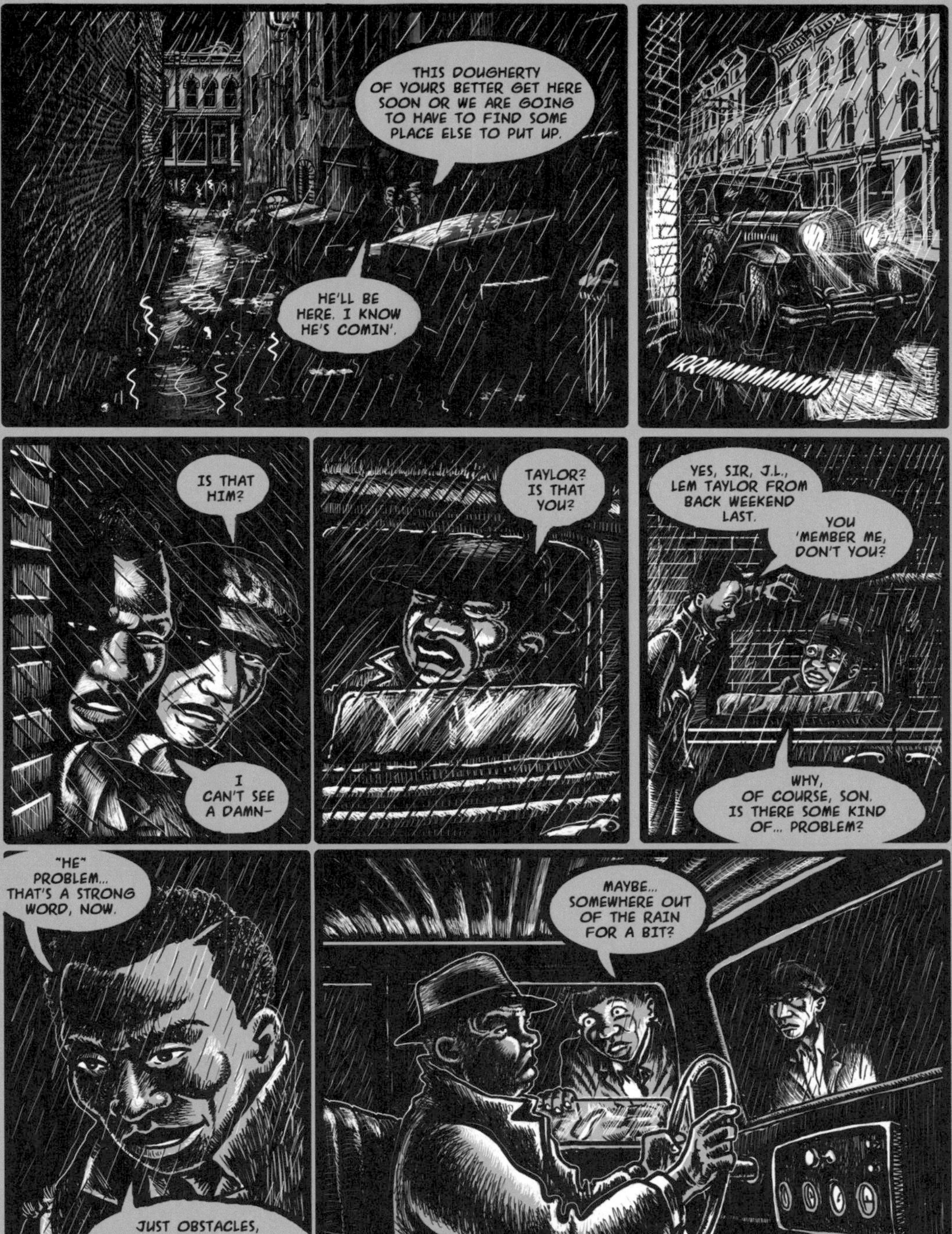
THIS DOUGHERTY OF YOURS BETTER GET HERE SOON OR WE ARE GOING TO HAVE TO FIND SOME PLACE ELSE TO PUT UP.
HE'LL BE HERE. I KNOW HE'S COMIN'.
VRRMMMMMMMM
IS THAT HIM?
I CAN'T SEE A DAMN-
TAYLOR? IS THAT YOU?
YES, SIR, J.L., LEM TAYLOR FROM BACK WEEKEND LAST.
YOU 'MEMBER ME, DON'T YOU?
WHY, OF COURSE, SON. IS THERE SOME KIND OF... PROBLEM?
"HE" PROBLEM... THAT'S A STRONG WORD, NOW.
JUST OBSTACLES, REALLY THAT I NEED TO TALK YOU ABOUT-
MAYBE... SOMEWHERE OUT OF THE RAIN FOR A BIT?

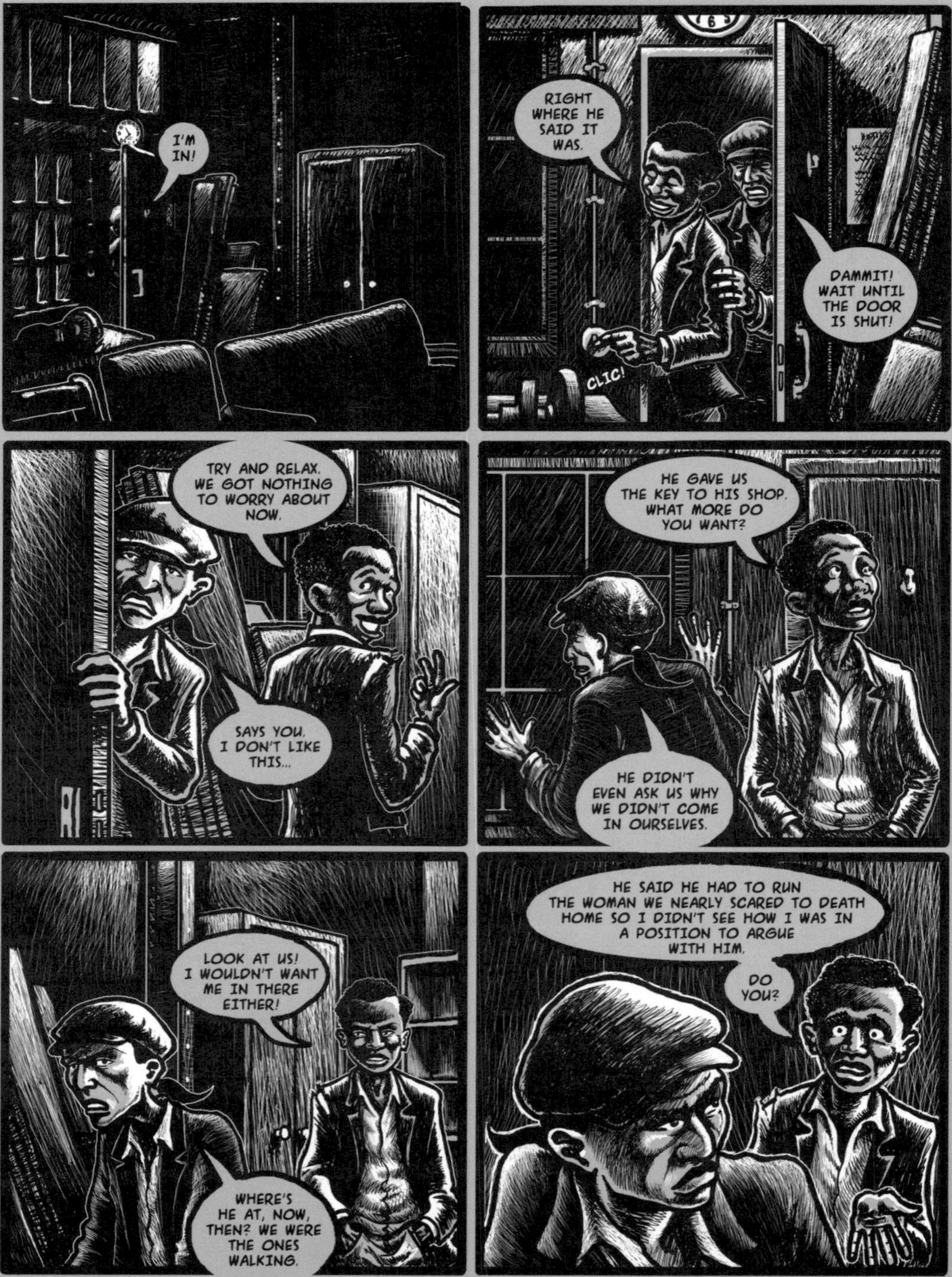
I'M IN!
RIGHT WHERE HE SAID IT WAS.
CLIC!
DAMMIT! WAIT UNTIL THE DOOR IS SHUT!
TRY AND RELAX. WE GOT NOTHING TO WORRY ABOUT NOW.
SAYS YOU. I DON'T LIKE THIS...
HE GAVE US THE KEY TO HIS SHOP. WHAT MORE DO YOU WANT?
HE DIDN'T EVEN ASK US WHY WE DIDN'T COME IN OURSELVES.
LOOK AT US! I WOULDN'T WANT ME IN THERE EITHER!
WHERE'S HE AT, NOW, THEN? WE WERE THE ONES WALKING.
HE SAID HE HAD TO RUN THE WOMAN WE NEARLY SCARED TO DEATH HOME SO I DIDN'T SEE HOW I WAS IN A POSITION TO ARGUE WITH HIM.
DO YOU?

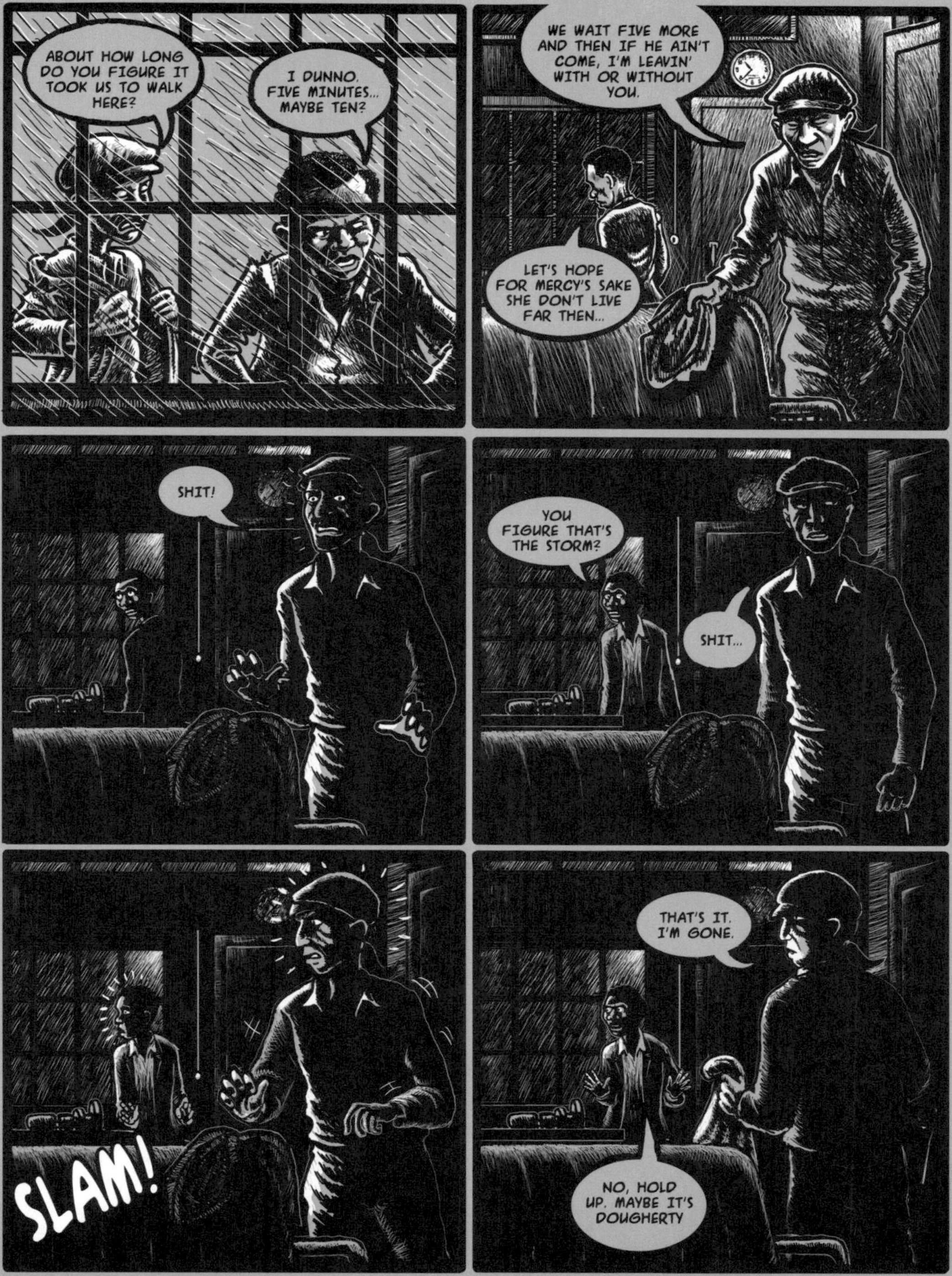
ABOUT HOW LONG DO YOU FIGURE IT TOOK US TO WALK HERE?
I DUNNO. FIVE MINUTES... MAYBE TEN?
WE WAIT FIVE MORE AND THEN IF HE AIN'T COME, I'M LEAVIN' WITH OR WITHOUT YOU.
LET'S HOPE FOR MERCY'S SAKE SHE DON'T LIVE FAR THEN...
SHIT!
YOU FIGURE THAT'S THE STORM?
SHIT...
SLAM!
THAT'S IT. I'M GONE.
NO, HOLD UP. MAYBE IT'S DOUGHERTY

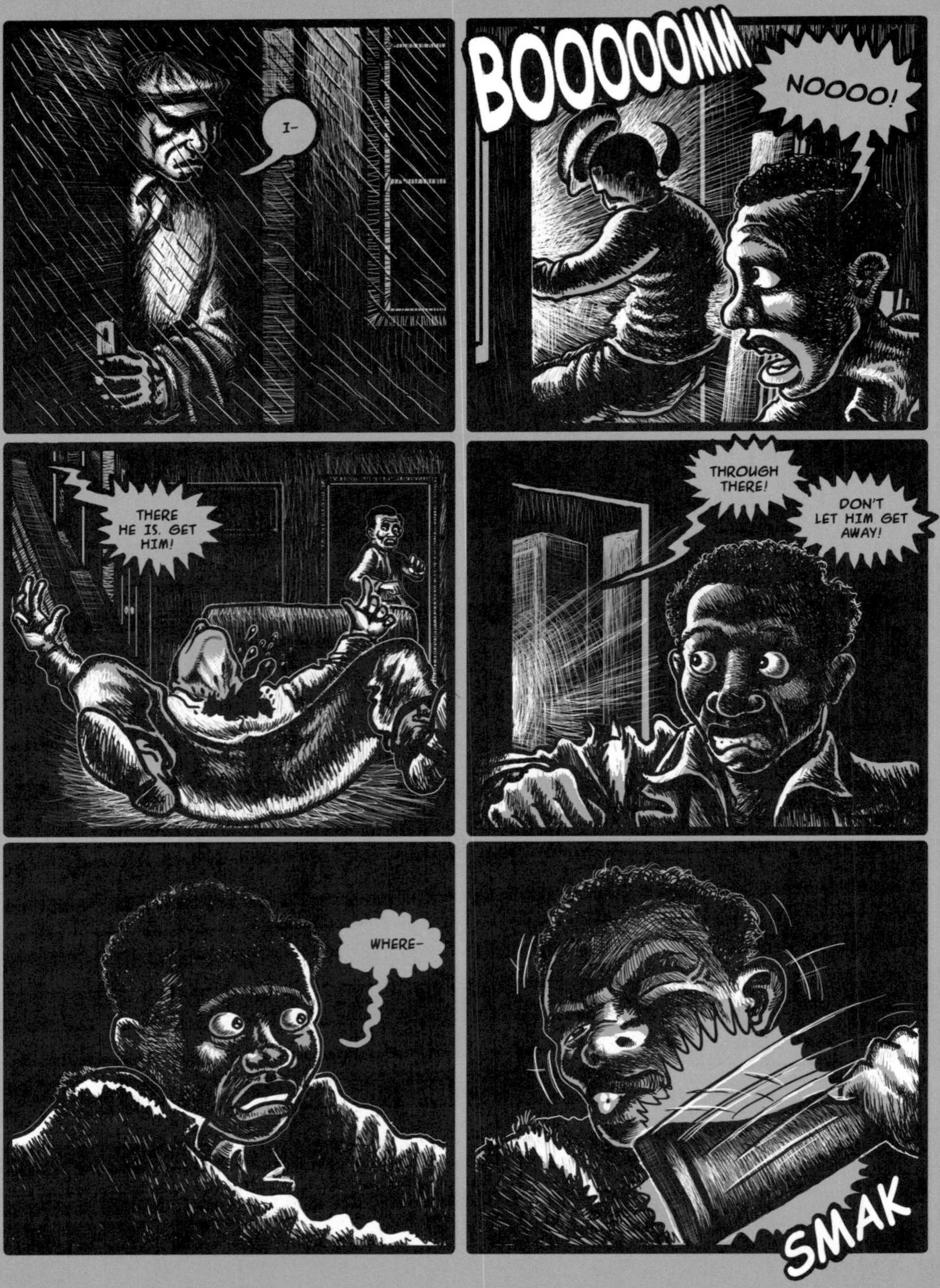
I-
BOOOOOMM
NOOOO!
THERE HE IS. GET HIM!
THROUGH THERE!
DON'T LET HIM GET AWAY!
WHERE-
SMAK

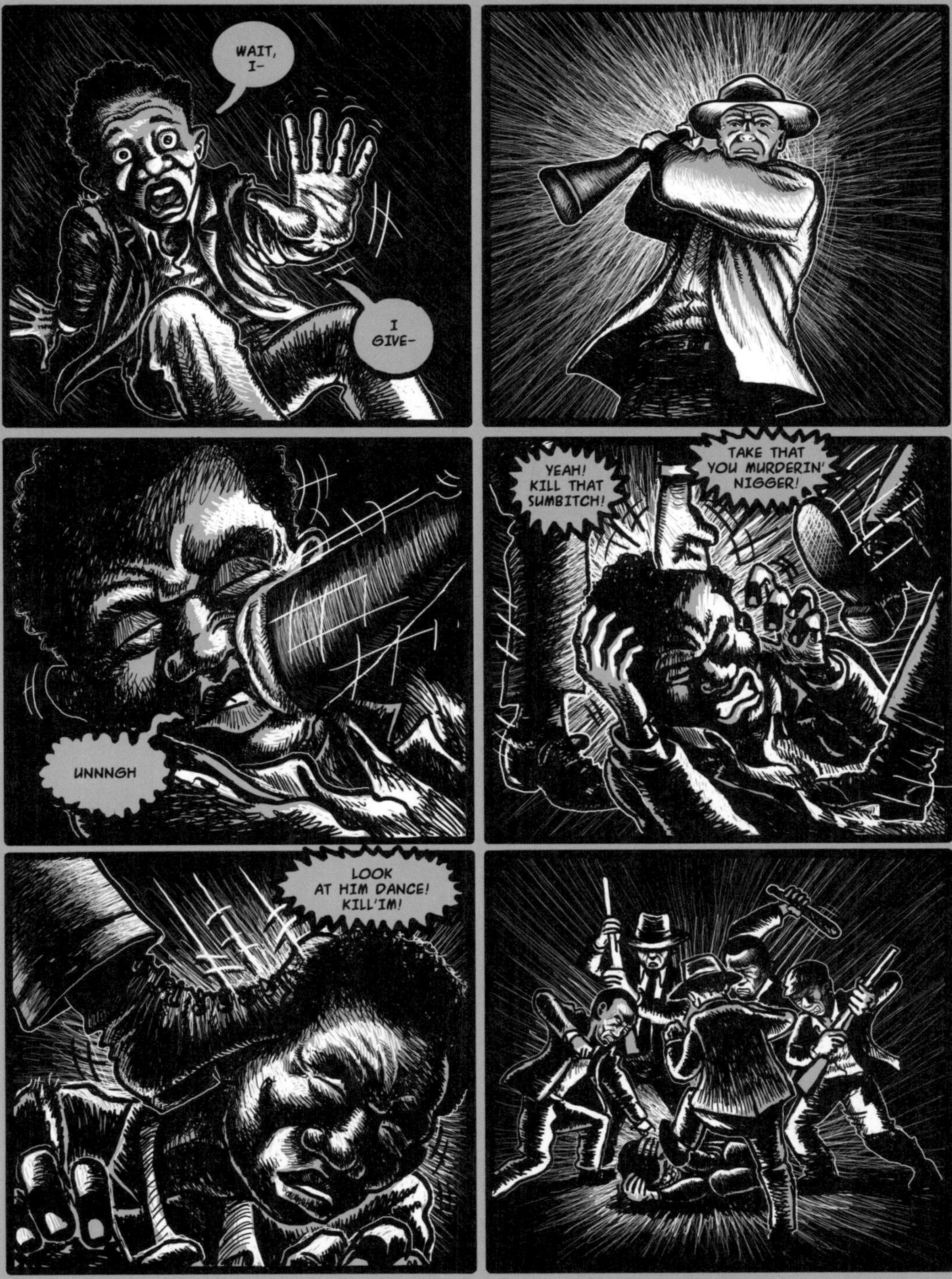
WAIT, I-
I GIVE-
UNNNGH
YEAH! KILL THAT SUMBITCH!
TAKE THAT YOU MURDERIN' NIGGER!
LOOK AT HIM DANCE! KILL'IM!

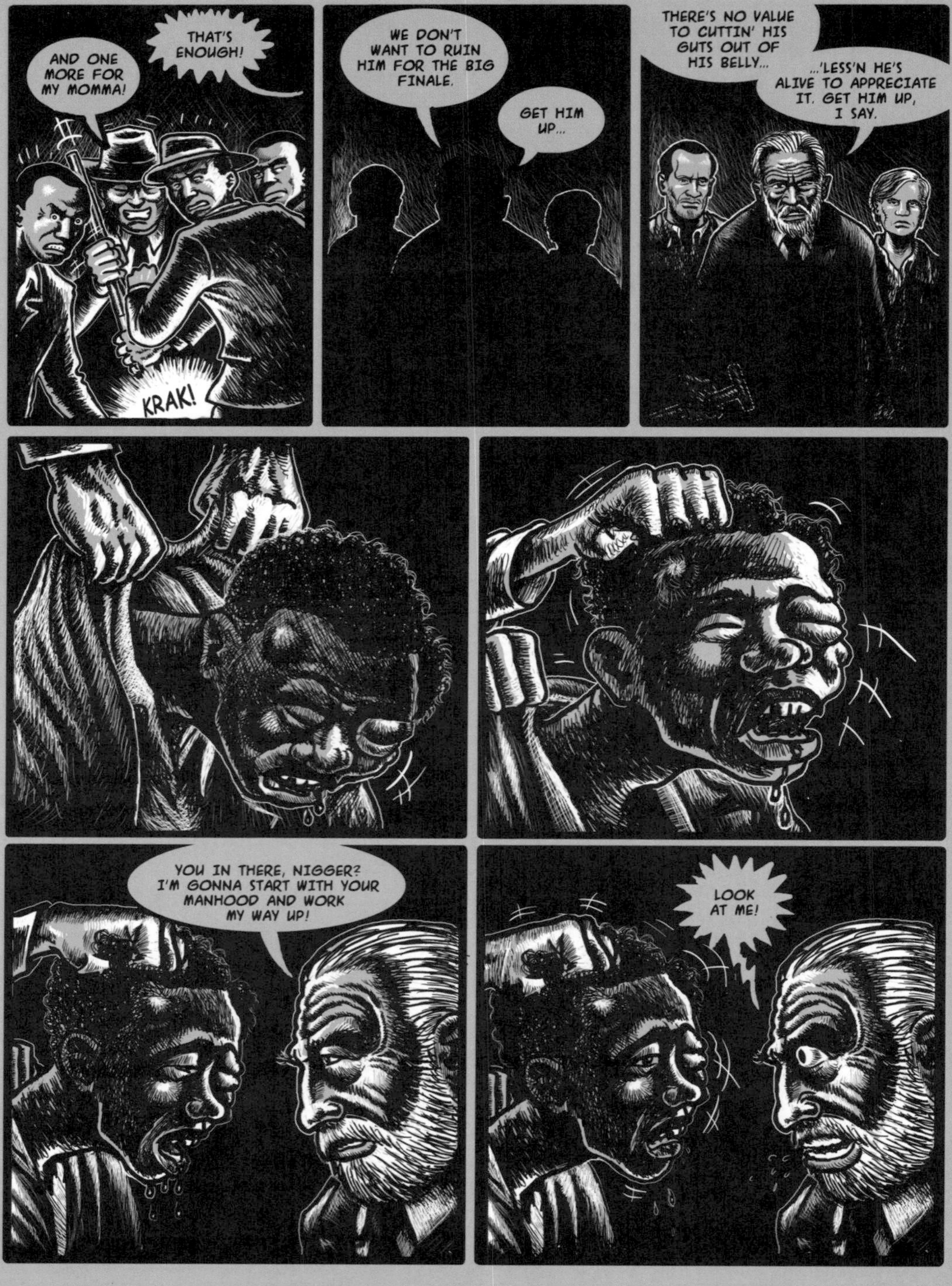

AND ONE MORE FOR MY MOMMA!
THAT'S ENOUGH!
KRAK!
WE DON'T WANT TO RUIN HIM FOR THE BIG FINALE.
GET HIM UP...
THERE'S NO VALUE TO CUTTIN' HIS GUTS OUT OF HIS BELLY...
...'LESS'N HE'S ALIVE TO APPRECIATE IT. GET HIM UP, I SAY.
YOU IN THERE, NIGGER? I'M GONNA START WITH YOUR MANHOOD AND WORK MY WAY UP!
LOOK AT ME!

THAT WAS MY BOY YOU KILLED BACK THERE IN HOPE.

YOU, YOUR ACCOMPLICE, AND YOUR WHORES!

YOU HOLD HIM, JUNIOR.

YES, PA.

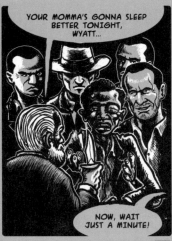

YOUR MOMMA'S GONNA SLEEP BETTER TONIGHT, WYATT...

NOW, WAIT JUST A MINUTE!

YOU CAN'T... KILL THAT CRIMINAL HERE!

I DON'T THINK I CARE FOR YOUR TONE, BOY.

AFTER ALL, WE CAUGHT THESE KILLERS IN YOUR SHOP FOR YOU!

YOU'RE ON NINTH STREET! LITTLE AFRICA! YOU ALREADY GOT ONE DEAD BODY TO MOVE AND AIN'T NOTHING STAY SECRET HERE FOR LONG...

TAKE HIM OUT IN THE COUNTRY AND DO WHATEVER YOU GOT TO DO, FINE.

YOU KILL HIM HERE AND THERE'LL BE A RIOT!

WE *COULD* TORTURE HIM A LOT LONGER THAT WAY...

CLIC!

SPECIAL SALE!! 20% off

ACTUALLY...

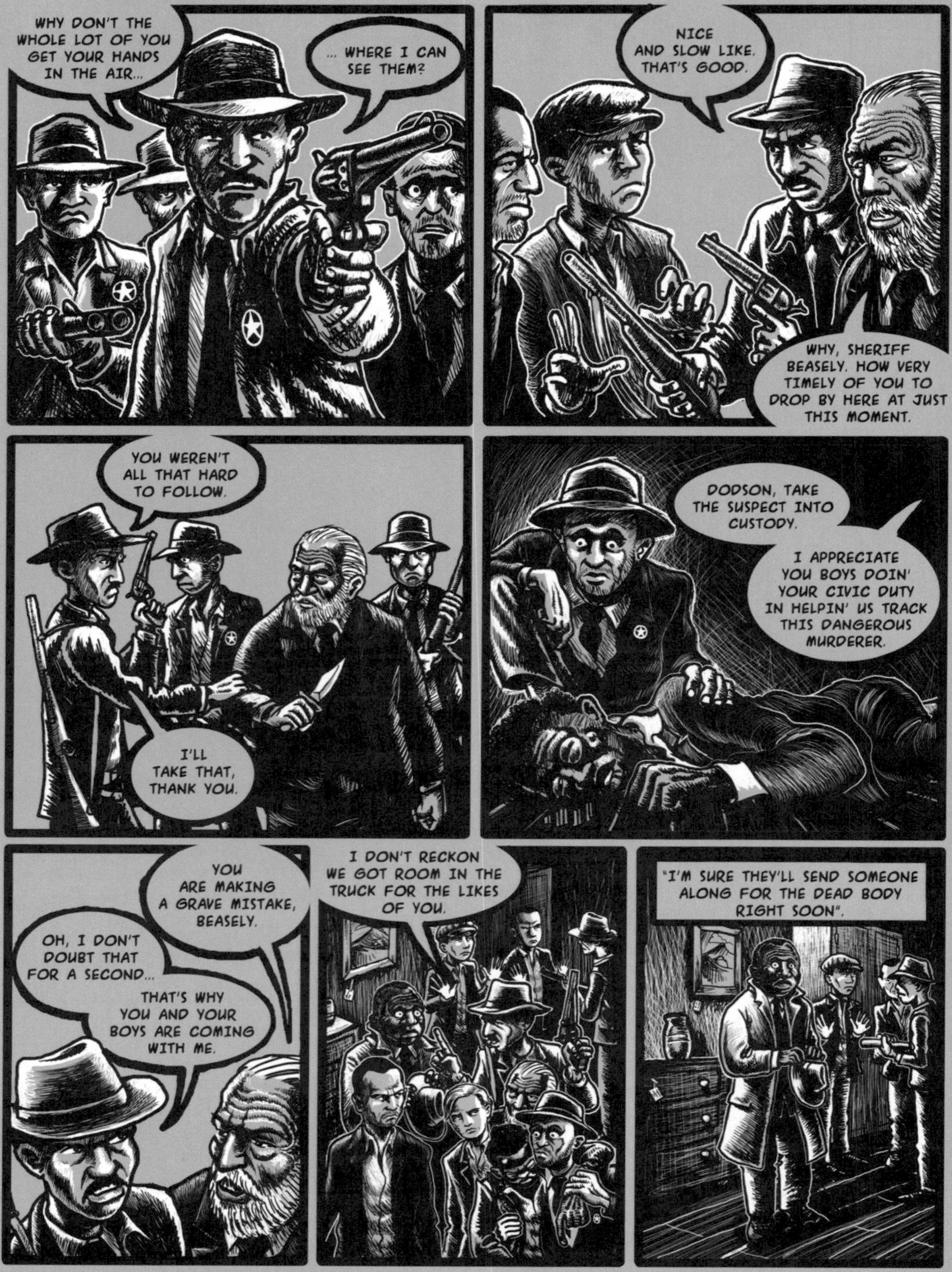
WHY DON'T THE WHOLE LOT OF YOU GET YOUR HANDS IN THE AIR...
... WHERE I CAN SEE THEM?
NICE AND SLOW LIKE. THAT'S GOOD.
WHY, SHERIFF BEASELY. HOW VERY TIMELY OF YOU TO DROP BY HERE AT JUST THIS MOMENT.
YOU WEREN'T ALL THAT HARD TO FOLLOW.
I'LL TAKE THAT, THANK YOU.
DODSON, TAKE THE SUSPECT INTO CUSTODY.
I APPRECIATE YOU BOYS DOIN' YOUR CIVIC DUTY IN HELPIN' US TRACK THIS DANGEROUS MURDERER.
YOU ARE MAKING A GRAVE MISTAKE, BEASELY.
OH, I DON'T DOUBT THAT FOR A SECOND...
THAT'S WHY YOU AND YOUR BOYS ARE COMING WITH ME.
I DON'T RECKON WE GOT ROOM IN THE TRUCK FOR THE LIKES OF YOU.
"I'M SURE THEY'LL SEND SOMEONE ALONG FOR THE DEAD BODY RIGHT SOON".

11

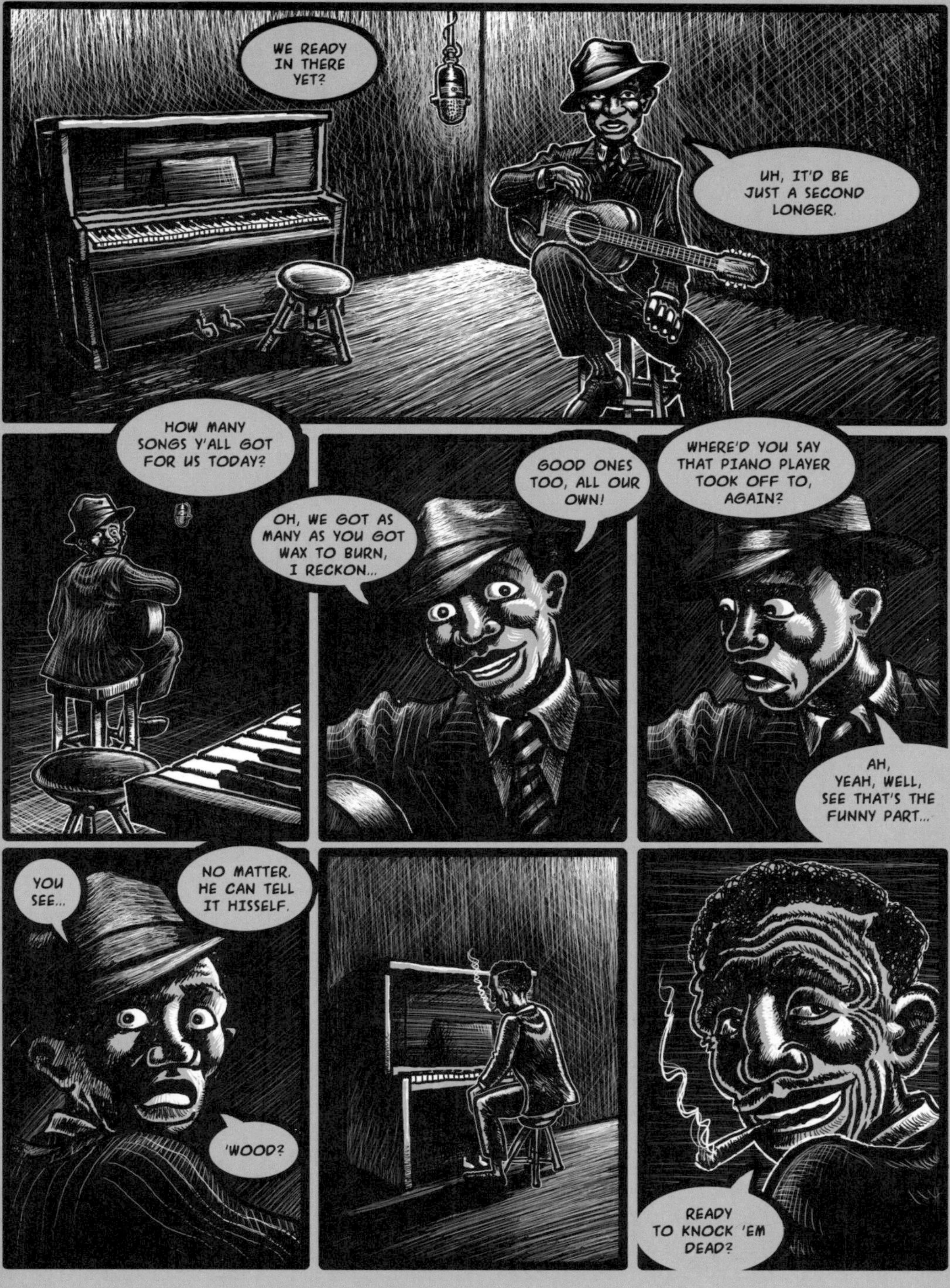
WE READY IN THERE YET?
UH, IT'D BE JUST A SECOND LONGER.
HOW MANY SONGS Y'ALL GOT FOR US TODAY?
OH, WE GOT AS MANY AS YOU GOT WAX TO BURN, I RECKON...
GOOD ONES TOO, ALL OUR OWN!
WHERE'D YOU SAY THAT PIANO PLAYER TOOK OFF TO, AGAIN?
AH, YEAH, WELL, SEE THAT'S THE FUNNY PART...
YOU SEE...
NO MATTER. HE CAN TELL IT HISSELF.
'WOOD?
READY TO KNOCK 'EM DEAD?

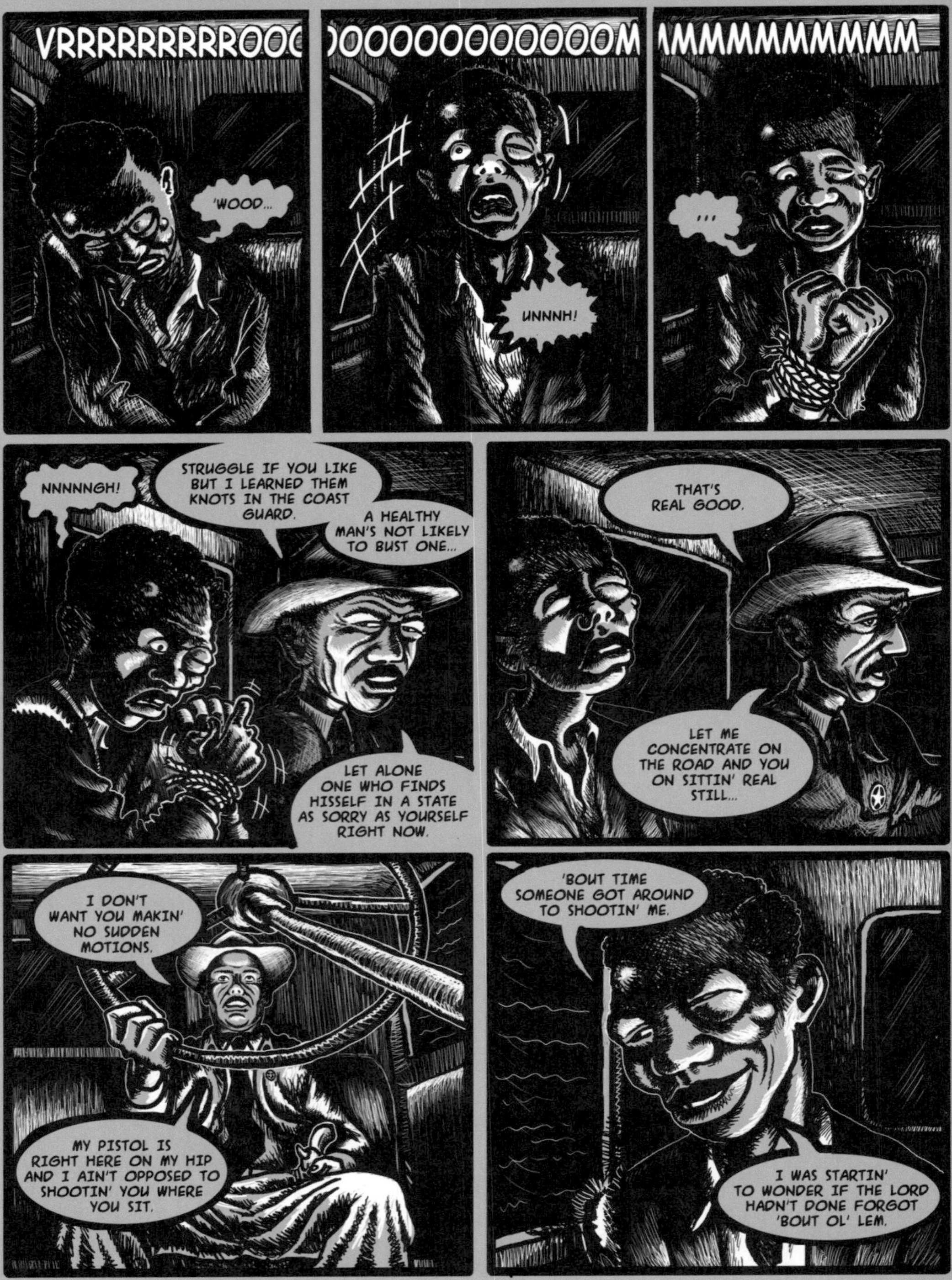
VRRRRRRRRROOOOOOOOOOOOOOOOMMMMMMMMMMM
'WOOD...
UNNNH!
...
NNNNNGH!
STRUGGLE IF YOU LIKE BUT I LEARNED THEM KNOTS IN THE COAST GUARD.
A HEALTHY MAN'S NOT LIKELY TO BUST ONE...
LET ALONE ONE WHO FINDS HISSELF IN A STATE AS SORRY AS YOURSELF RIGHT NOW.
THAT'S REAL GOOD.
LET ME CONCENTRATE ON THE ROAD AND YOU ON SITTIN' REAL STILL...
I DON'T WANT YOU MAKIN' NO SUDDEN MOTIONS.
MY PISTOL IS RIGHT HERE ON MY HIP AND I AIN'T OPPOSED TO SHOOTIN' YOU WHERE YOU SIT.
'BOUT TIME SOMEONE GOT AROUND TO SHOOTIN' ME.
I WAS STARTIN' TO WONDER IF THE LORD HADN'T DONE FORGOT 'BOUT OL' LEM.

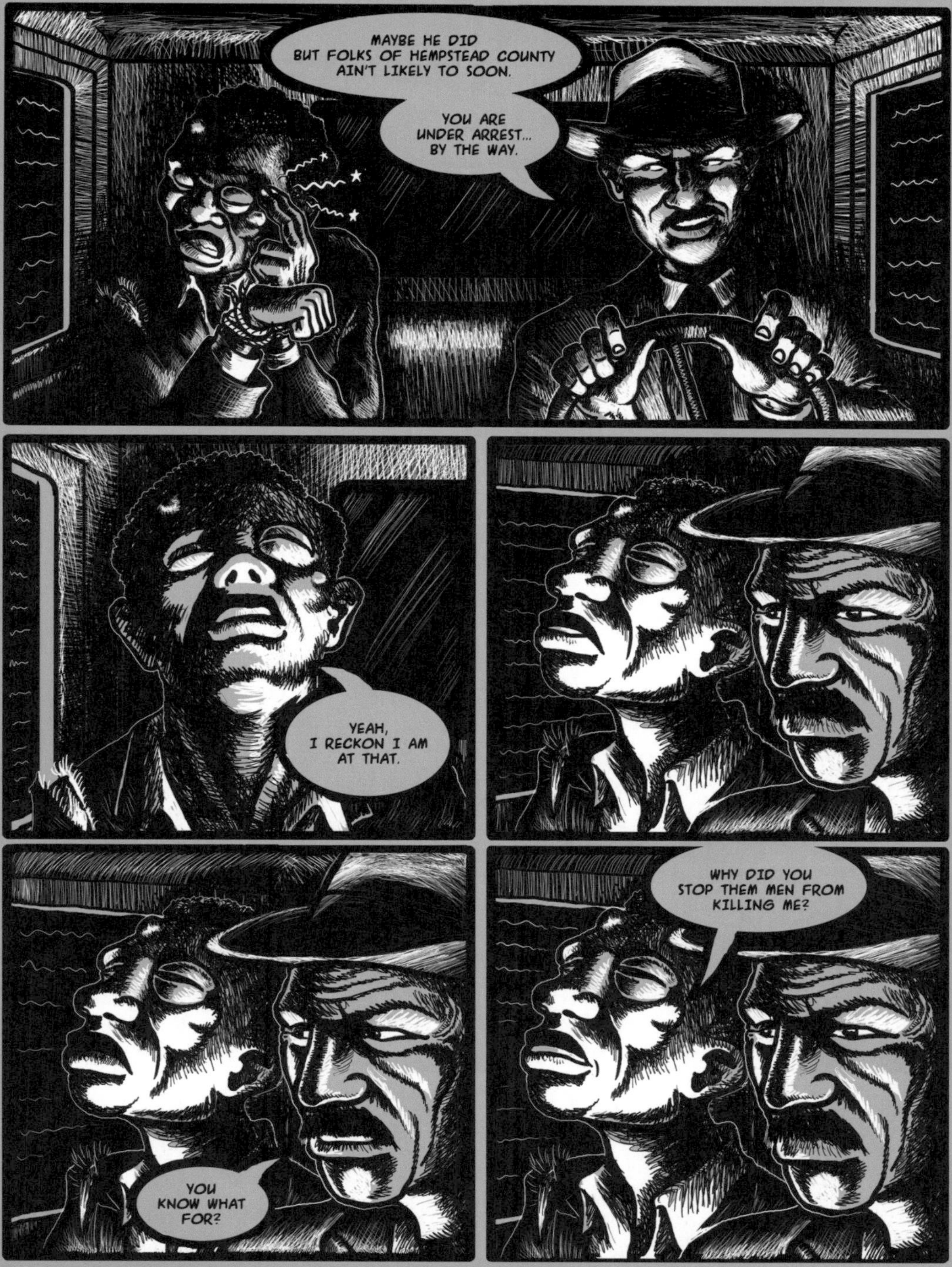
MAYBE HE DID
BUT FOLKS OF HEMPSTEAD COUNTY
AIN'T LIKELY TO SOON.
YOU ARE
UNDER ARREST...
BY THE WAY.
YEAH,
I RECKON I AM
AT THAT.
YOU
KNOW WHAT
FOR?
WHY DID YOU
STOP THEM MEN FROM
KILLING ME?

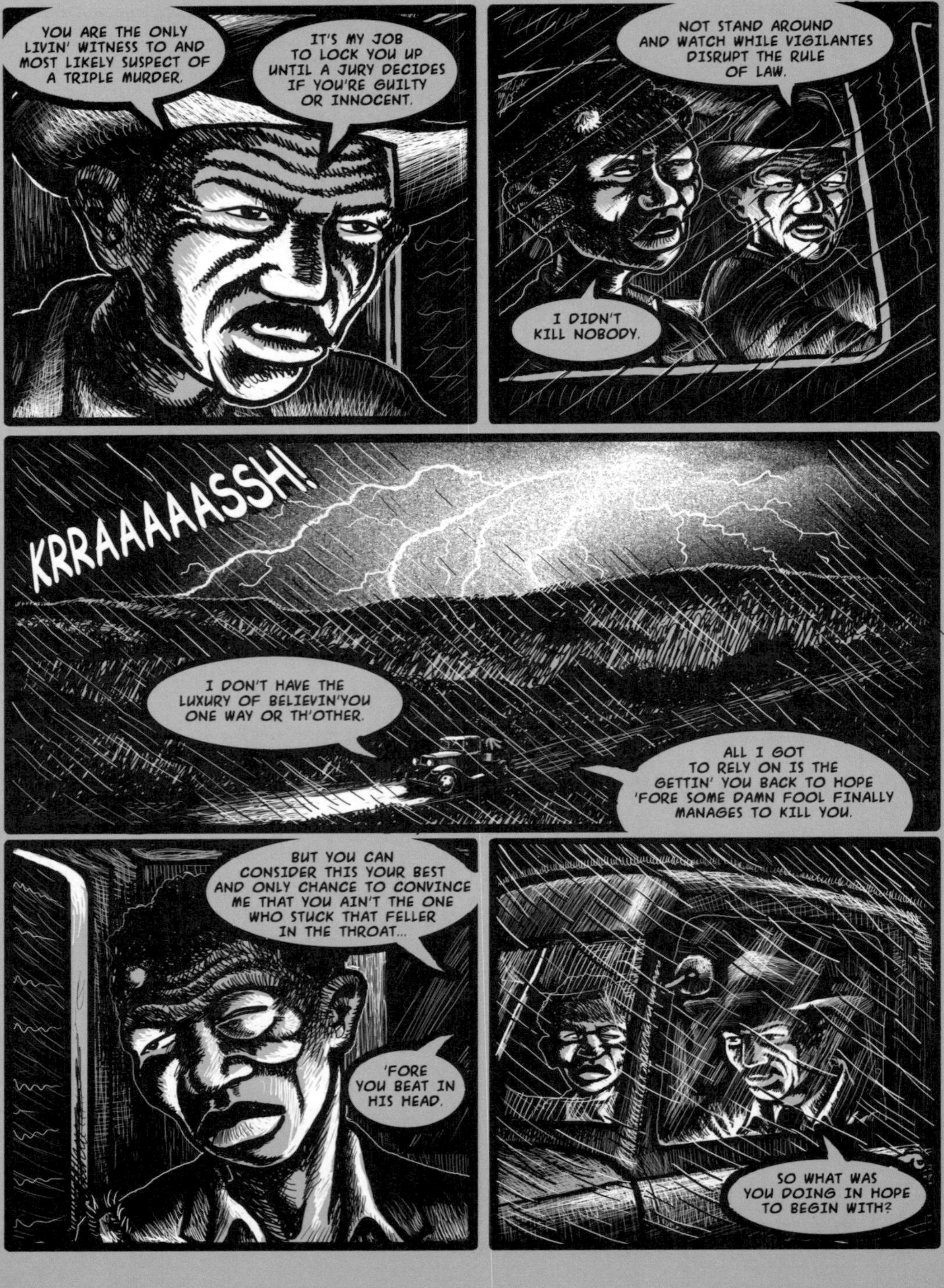
YOU ARE THE ONLY LIVIN' WITNESS TO AND MOST LIKELY SUSPECT OF A TRIPLE MURDER.
IT'S MY JOB TO LOCK YOU UP UNTIL A JURY DECIDES IF YOU'RE GUILTY OR INNOCENT.
NOT STAND AROUND AND WATCH WHILE VIGILANTES DISRUPT THE RULE OF LAW.
I DIDN'T KILL NOBODY.
KRRAAAAASSH!
I DON'T HAVE THE LUXURY OF BELIEVIN'YOU ONE WAY OR TH'OTHER.
ALL I GOT TO RELY ON IS THE GETTIN' YOU BACK TO HOPE 'FORE SOME DAMN FOOL FINALLY MANAGES TO KILL YOU.
BUT YOU CAN CONSIDER THIS YOUR BEST AND ONLY CHANCE TO CONVINCE ME THAT YOU AIN'T THE ONE WHO STUCK THAT FELLER IN THE THROAT...
'FORE YOU BEAT IN HIS HEAD.
SO WHAT WAS YOU DOING IN HOPE TO BEGIN WITH?

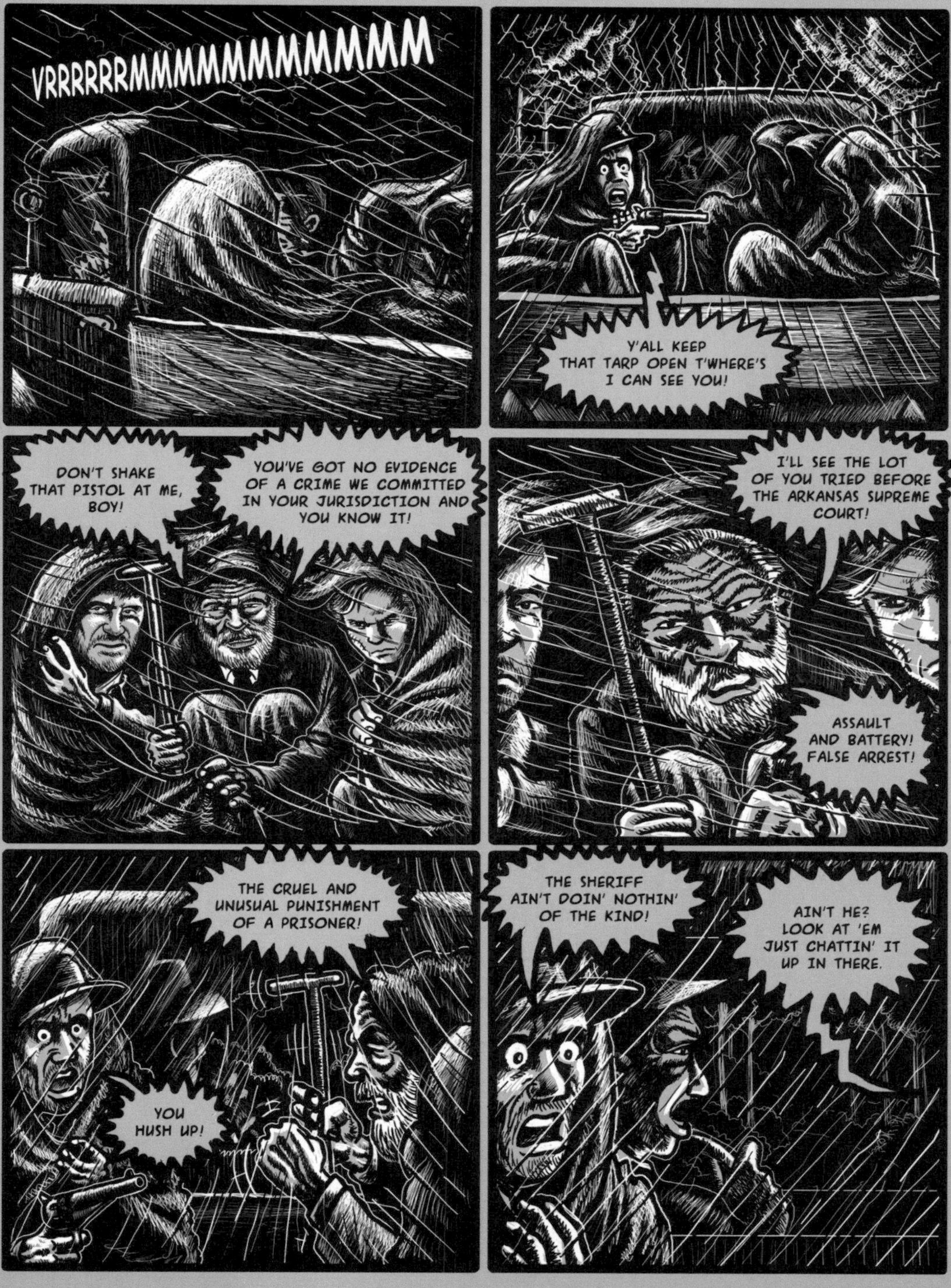
VRRRRRMMMMMMMMMMMM
Y'ALL KEEP THAT TARP OPEN T'WHERE'S I CAN SEE YOU!
DON'T SHAKE THAT PISTOL AT ME, BOY!
YOU'VE GOT NO EVIDENCE OF A CRIME WE COMMITTED IN YOUR JURISDICTION AND YOU KNOW IT!
I'LL SEE THE LOT OF YOU TRIED BEFORE THE ARKANSAS SUPREME COURT!
ASSAULT AND BATTERY! FALSE ARREST!
THE CRUEL AND UNUSUAL PUNISHMENT OF A PRISONER!
YOU HUSH UP!
THE SHERIFF AIN'T DOIN' NOTHIN' OF THE KIND!
AIN'T HE? LOOK AT 'EM JUST CHATTIN' IT UP IN THERE.

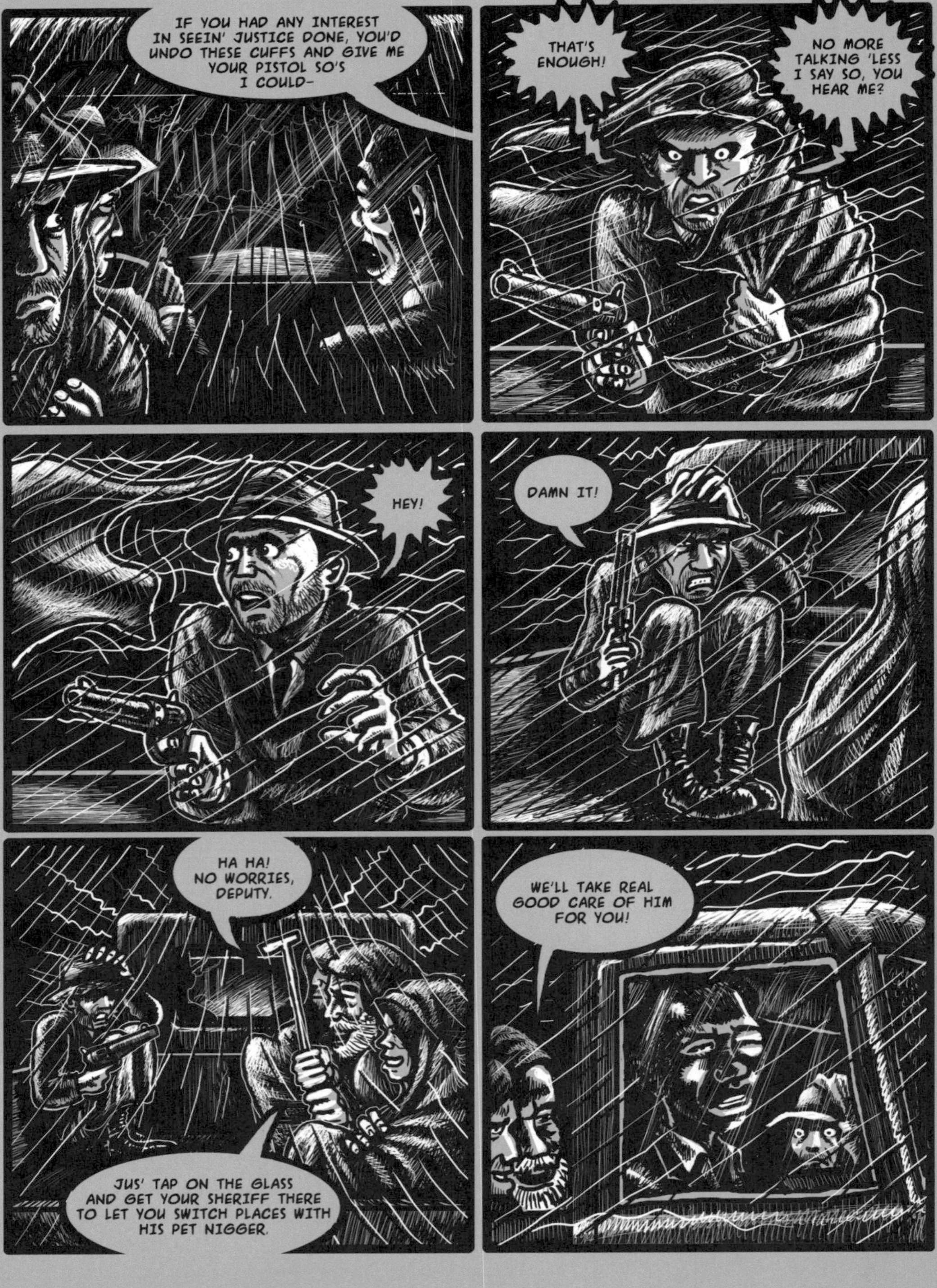
IF YOU HAD ANY INTEREST IN SEEIN' JUSTICE DONE, YOU'D UNDO THESE CUFFS AND GIVE ME YOUR PISTOL SO'S I COULD-
THAT'S ENOUGH!
NO MORE TALKING 'LESS I SAY SO, YOU HEAR ME?
HEY!
DAMN IT!
HA HA! NO WORRIES, DEPUTY.
JUS' TAP ON THE GLASS AND GET YOUR SHERIFF THERE TO LET YOU SWITCH PLACES WITH HIS PET NIGGER.
WE'LL TAKE REAL GOOD CARE OF HIM FOR YOU!

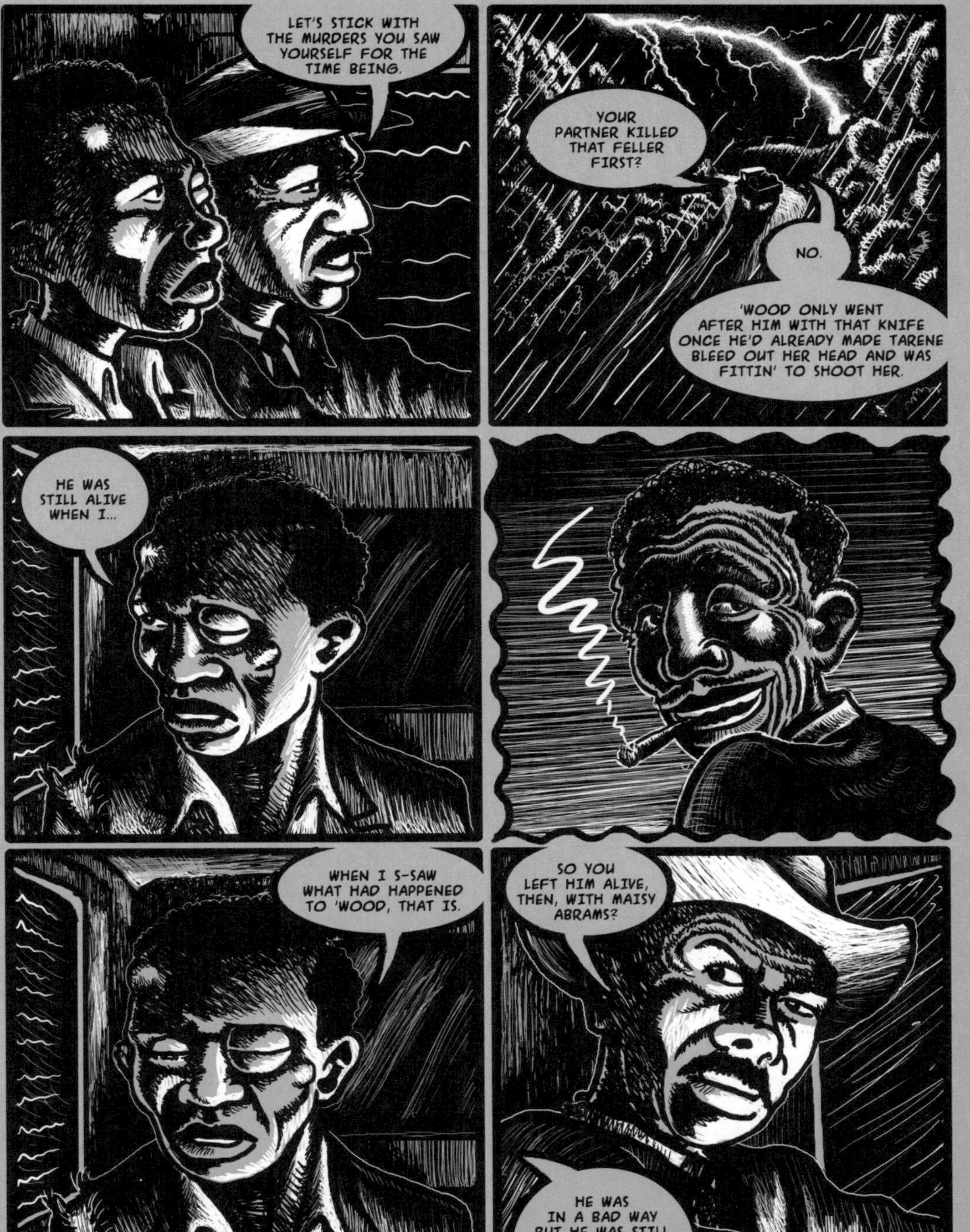

LET'S STICK WITH THE MURDERS YOU SAW YOURSELF FOR THE TIME BEING.
YOUR PARTNER KILLED THAT FELLER FIRST?
NO.
'WOOD ONLY WENT AFTER HIM WITH THAT KNIFE ONCE HE'D ALREADY MADE TARENE BLEED OUT HER HEAD AND WAS FITTIN' TO SHOOT HER.
HE WAS STILL ALIVE WHEN I...
WHEN I S-SAW WHAT HAD HAPPENED TO 'WOOD, THAT IS.
SO YOU LEFT HIM ALIVE, THEN, WITH MAISY ABRAMS?
HE WAS IN A BAD WAY BUT HE WAS STILL ALIVE.

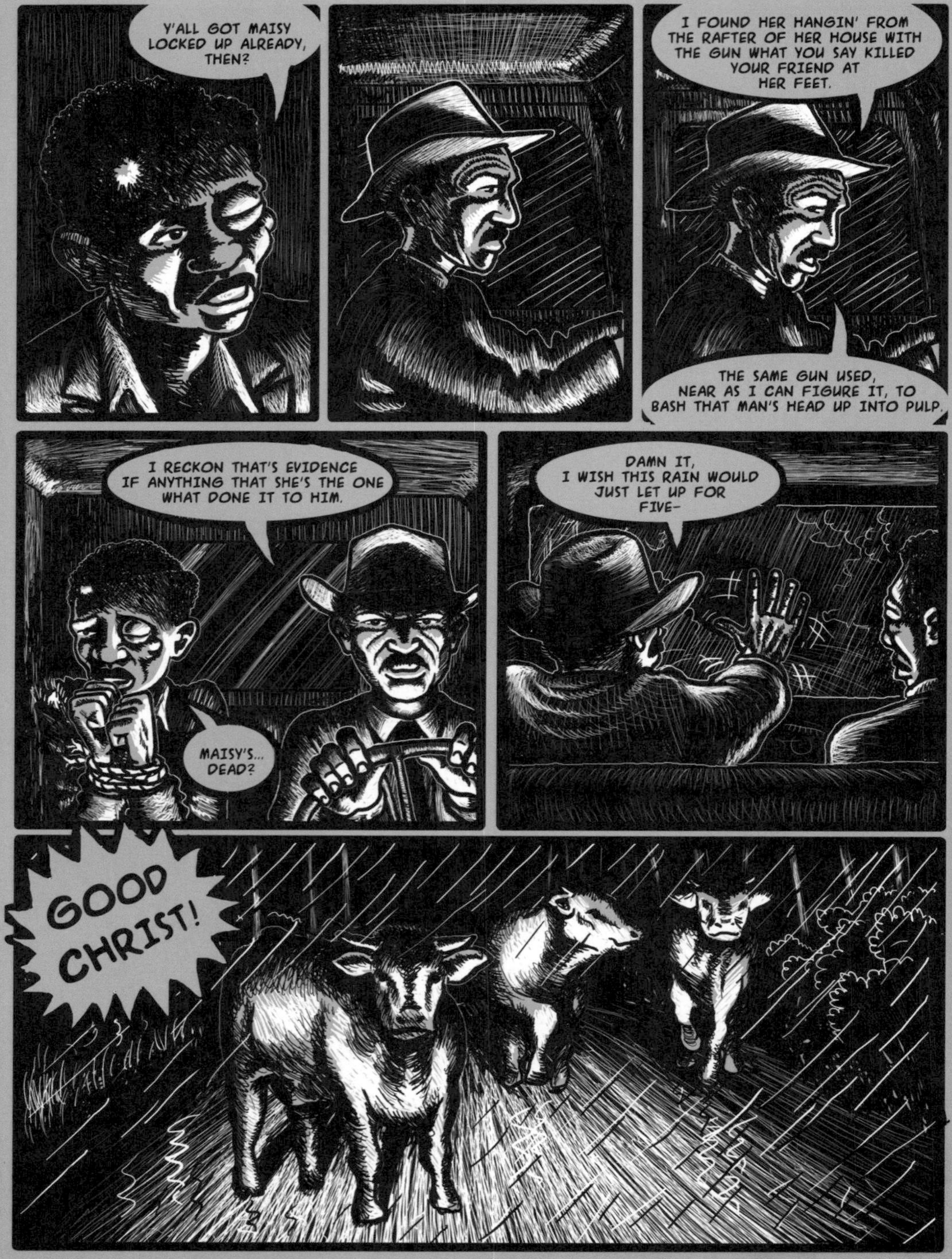

Y'ALL GOT MAISY LOCKED UP ALREADY, THEN?
I FOUND HER HANGIN' FROM THE RAFTER OF HER HOUSE WITH THE GUN WHAT YOU SAY KILLED YOUR FRIEND AT HER FEET.
THE SAME GUN USED, NEAR AS I CAN FIGURE IT, TO BASH THAT MAN'S HEAD UP INTO PULP.
I RECKON THAT'S EVIDENCE IF ANYTHING THAT SHE'S THE ONE WHAT DONE IT TO HIM.
MAISY'S... DEAD?
DAMN IT, I WISH THIS RAIN WOULD JUST LET UP FOR FIVE-
GOOD CHRIST!

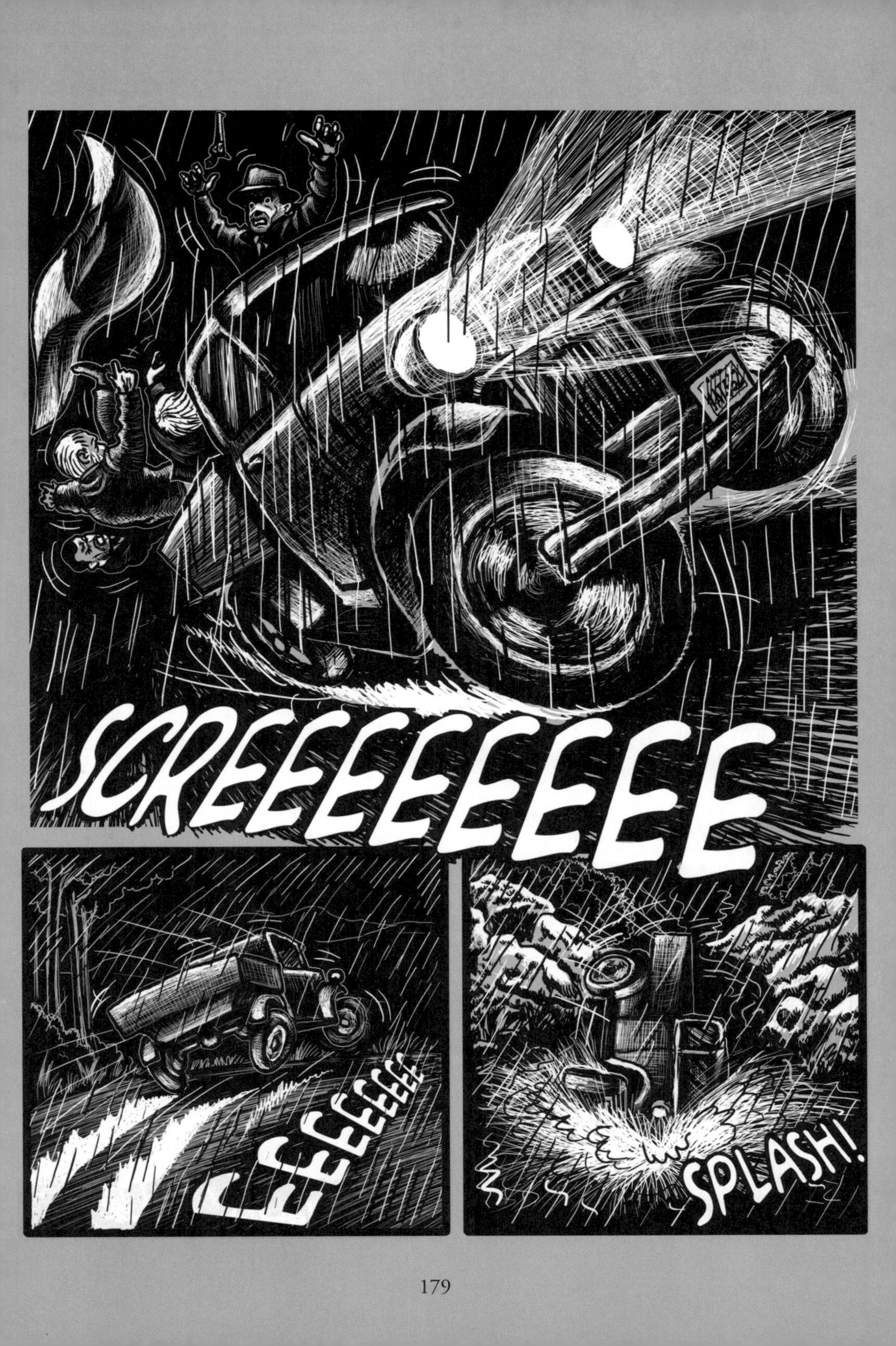
SCREEEEEEEE
EEEEEEEEE
SPLASH!

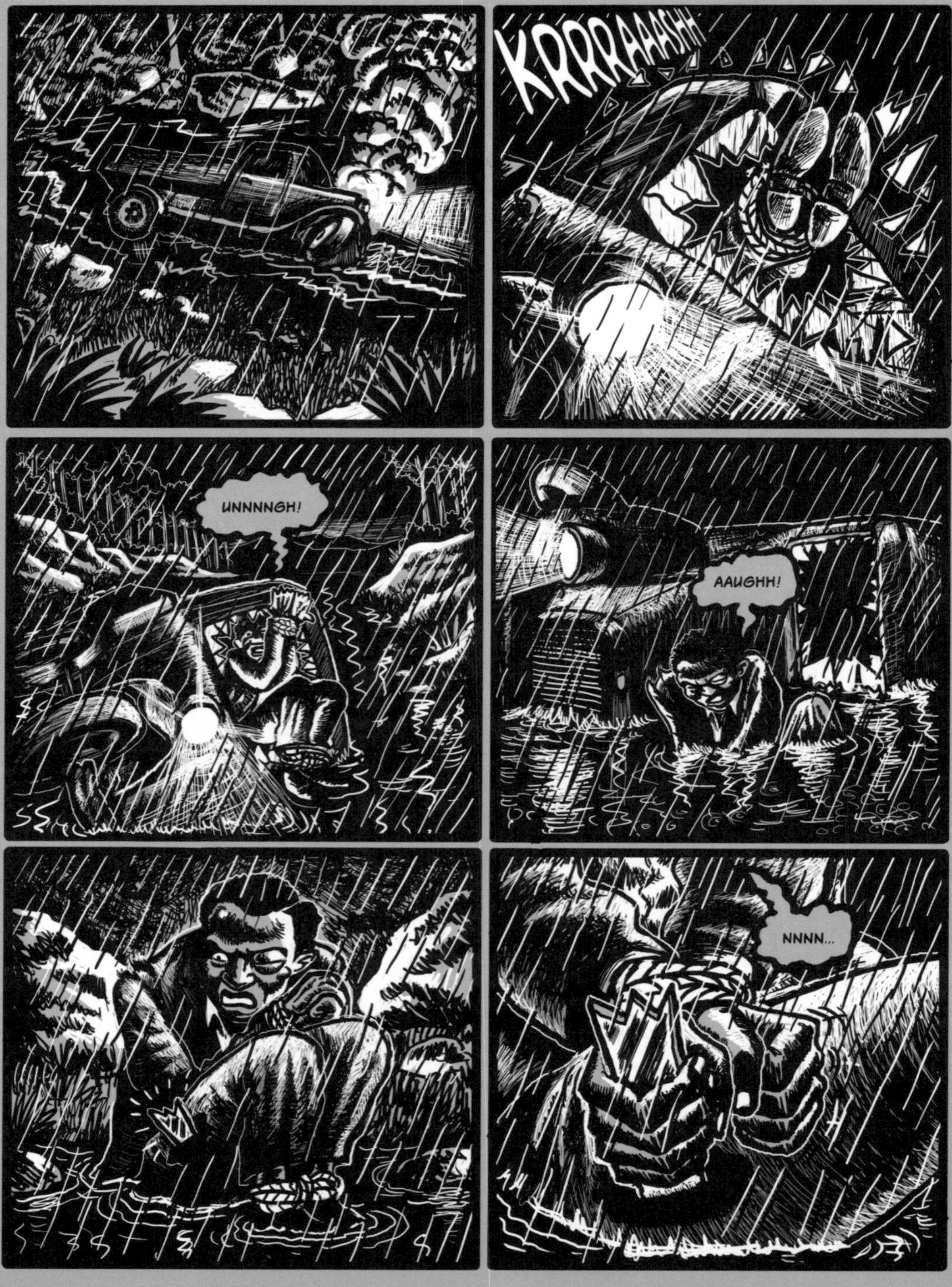
KRRRAAASHH
UNNNNGH!
AAUGHH!
NNNN...

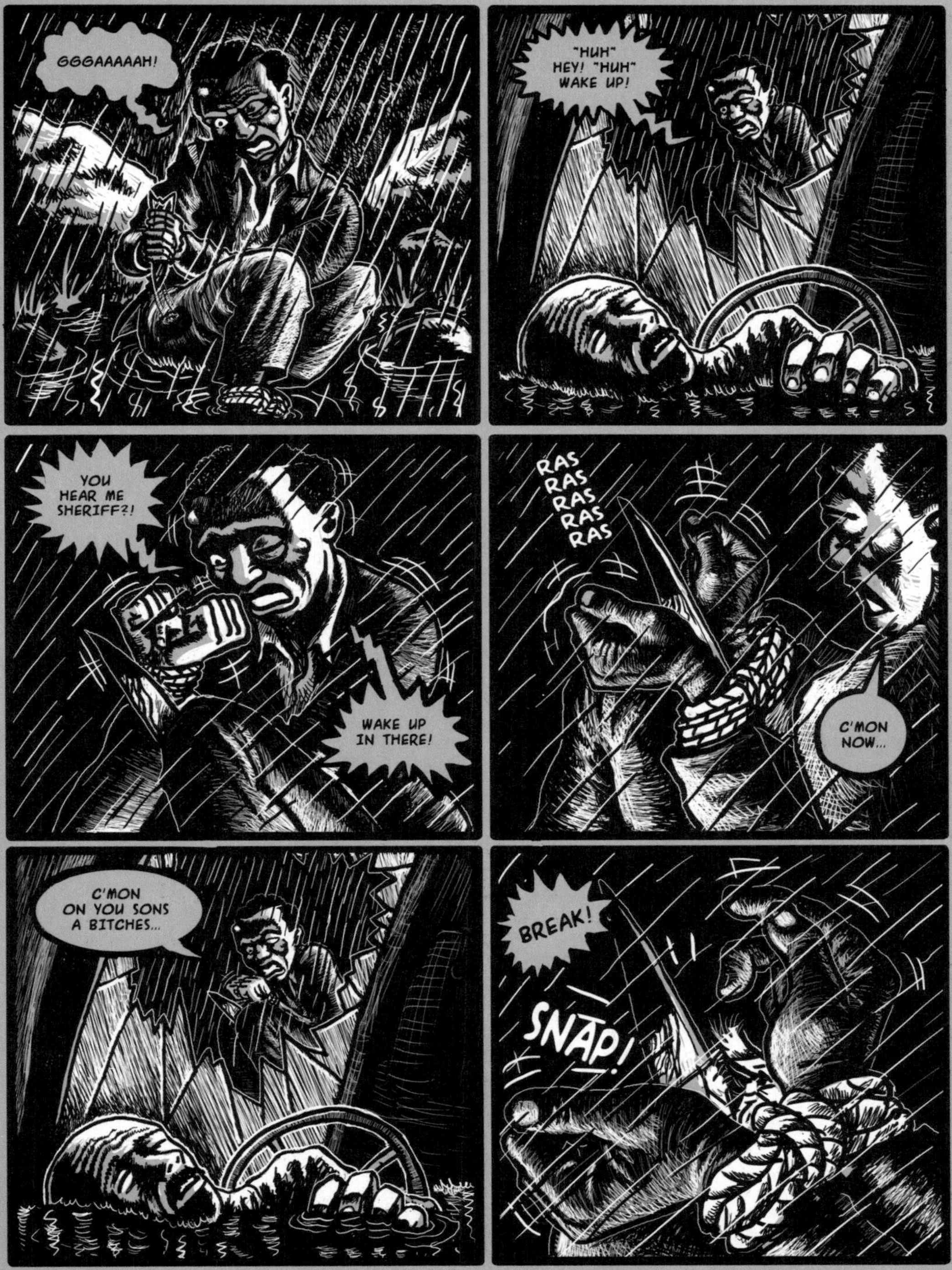
GGGAAAAAAH!
"HUH"
HEY! "HUH"
WAKE UP!
YOU
HEAR ME
SHERIFF?!
WAKE UP
IN THERE!
RAS
RAS
RAS
RAS
RAS
C'MON
NOW...
C'MON
ON YOU SONS
A BITCHES...
BREAK!
SNAP!

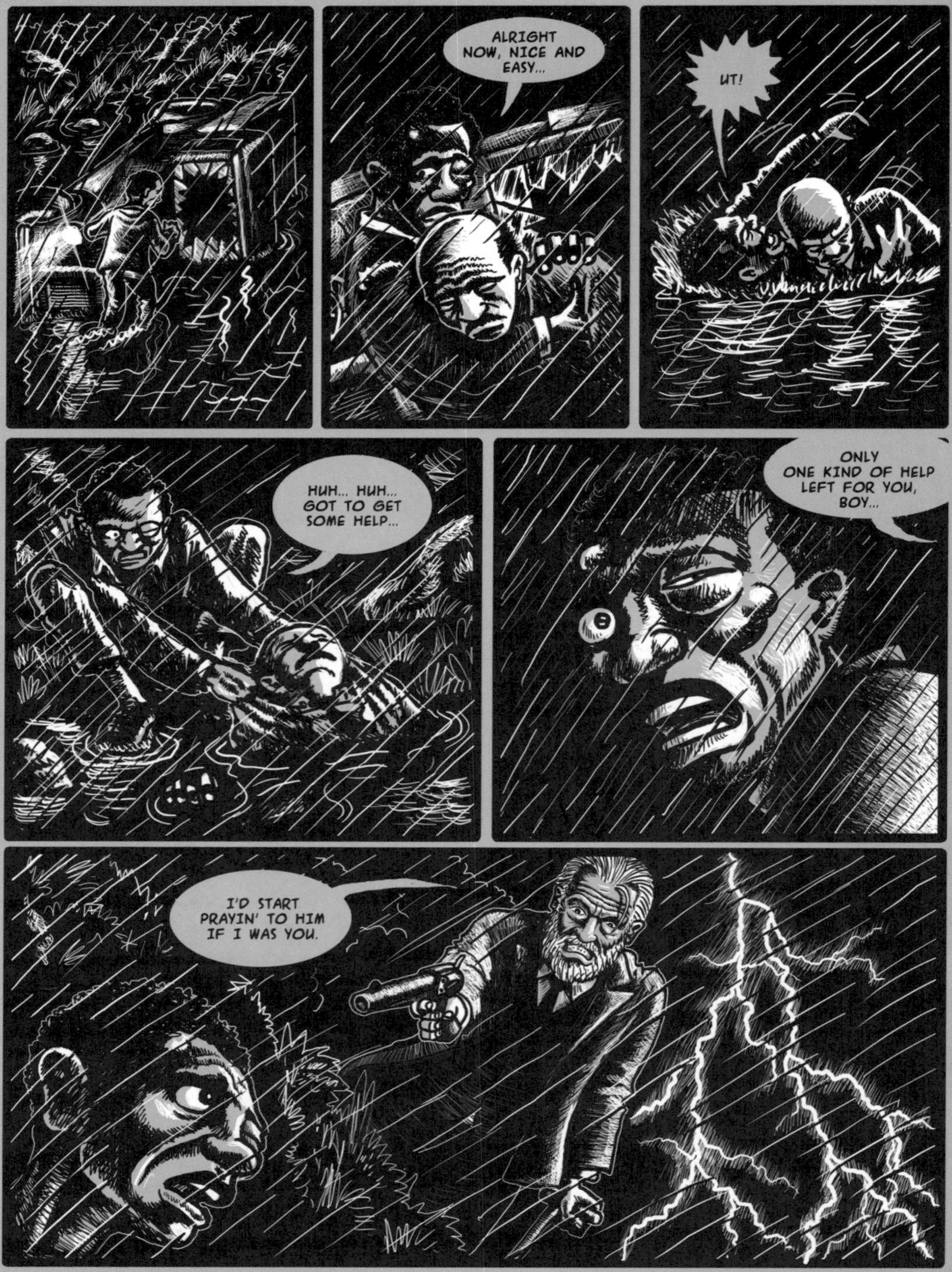
ALRIGHT NOW, NICE AND EASY...
UT!
HUH... HUH... GOT TO GET SOME HELP...
ONLY ONE KIND OF HELP LEFT FOR YOU, BOY...
I'D START PRAYIN' TO HIM IF I WAS YOU.

12

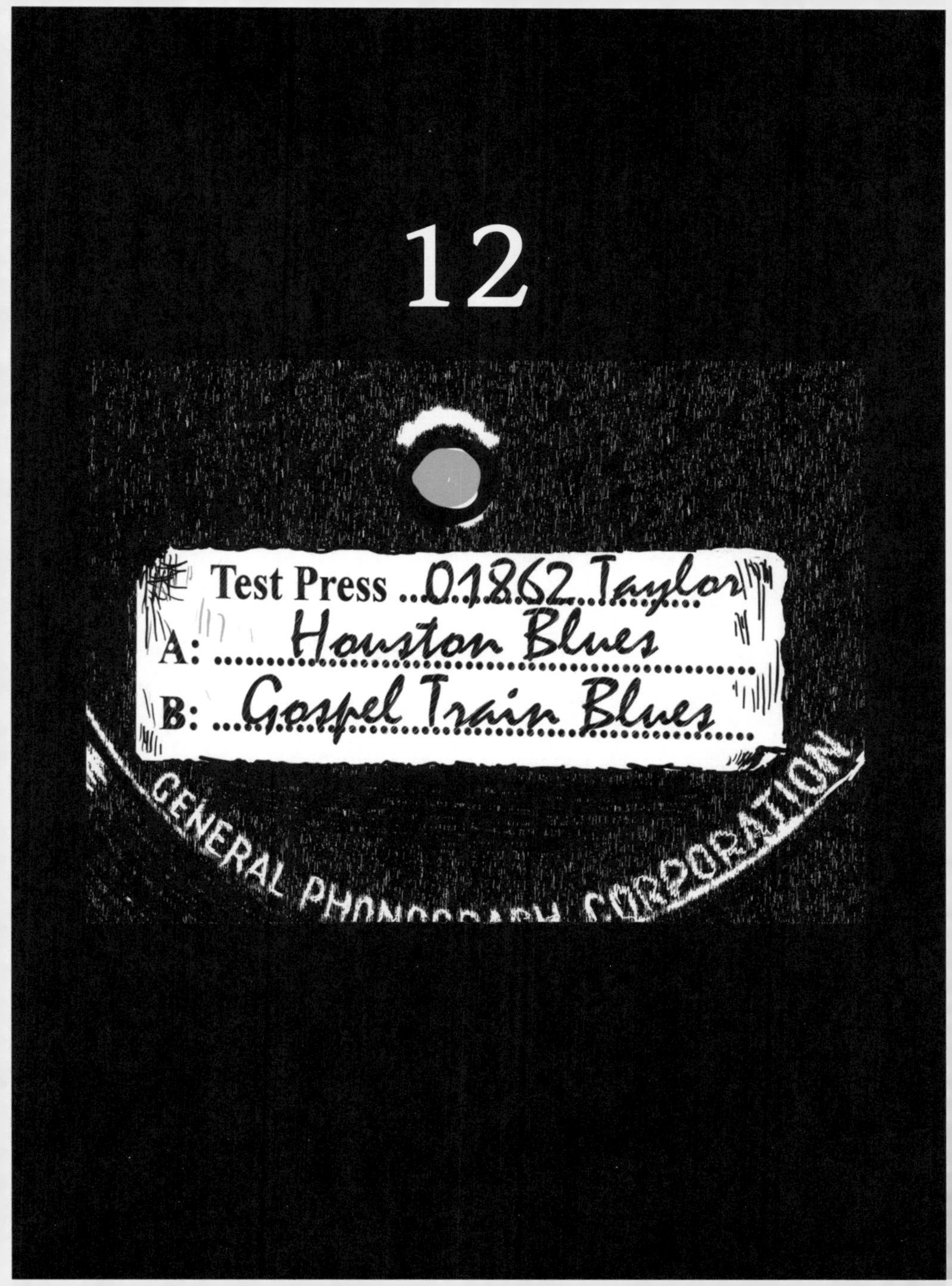
Test Press 01862 Taylor
A: Houston Blues
B: Gospel Train Blues
GENERAL PHONOGRAPH CORPORATION

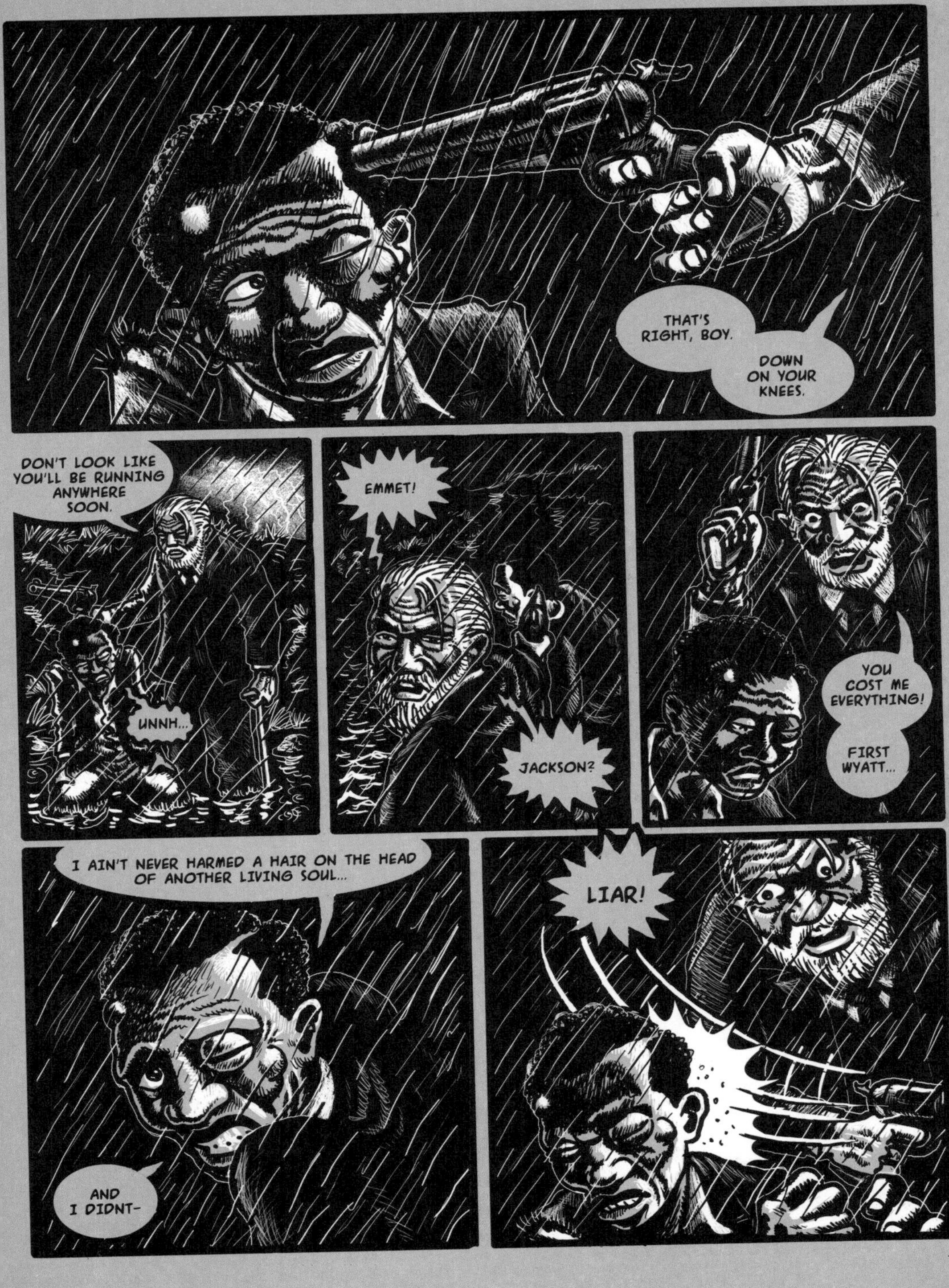
THAT'S RIGHT, BOY.
DOWN ON YOUR KNEES.
DON'T LOOK LIKE YOU'LL BE RUNNING ANYWHERE SOON.
UNNH...
EMMET!
JACKSON?
YOU COST ME EVERYTHING!
FIRST WYATT...
I AIN'T NEVER HARMED A HAIR ON THE HEAD OF ANOTHER LIVING SOUL...
AND I DIDNT-
LIAR!

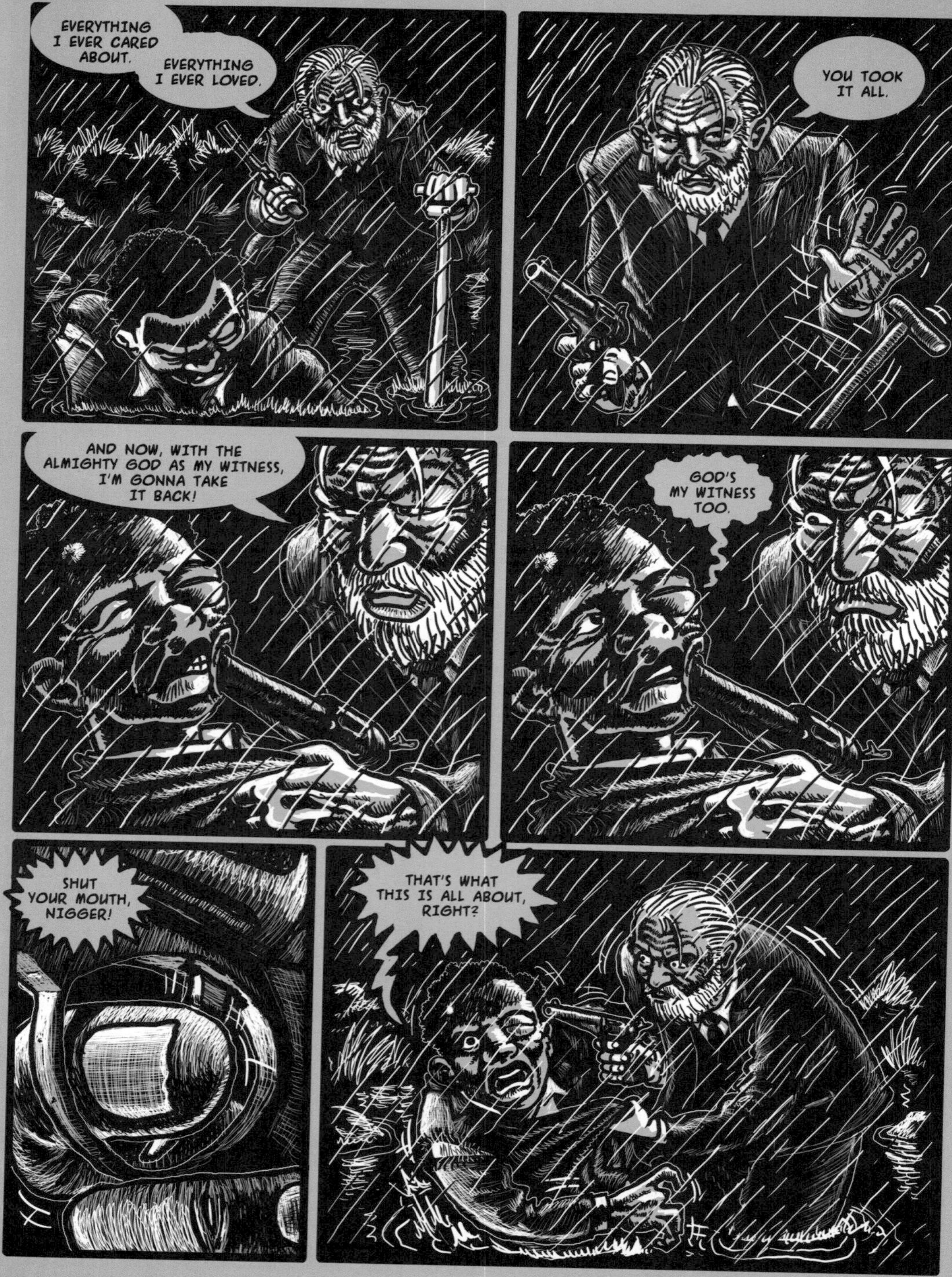
EVERYTHING I EVER CARED ABOUT.
EVERYTHING I EVER LOVED.
YOU TOOK IT ALL.
AND NOW, WITH THE ALMIGHTY GOD AS MY WITNESS, I'M GONNA TAKE IT BACK!
GOD'S MY WITNESS TOO.
SHUT YOUR MOUTH, NIGGER!
THAT'S WHAT THIS IS ALL ABOUT, RIGHT?

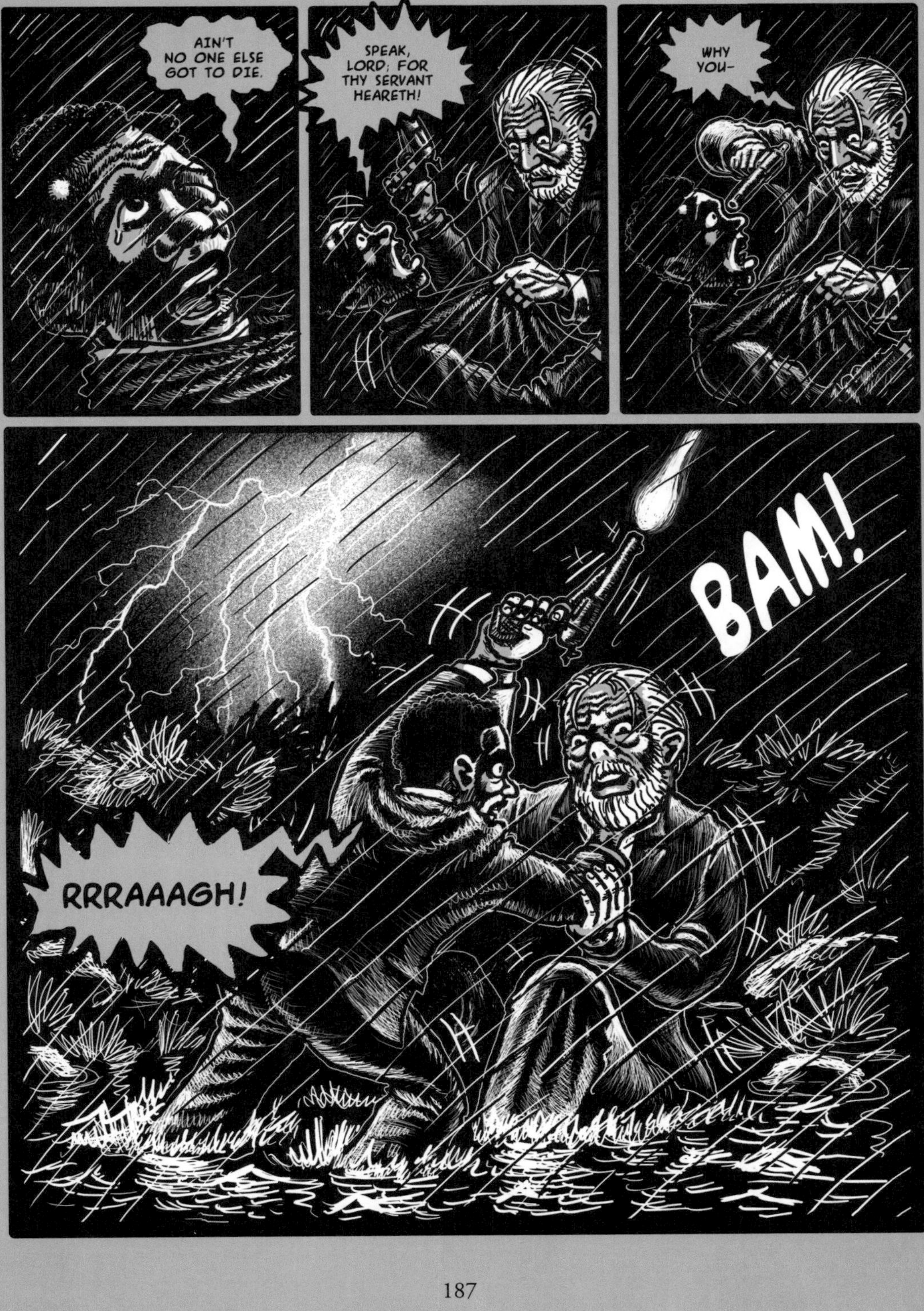
AIN'T NO ONE ELSE GOT TO DIE.
SPEAK, LORD; FOR THY SERVANT HEARETH!
WHY YOU-
BAM!
RRRAAAGH!

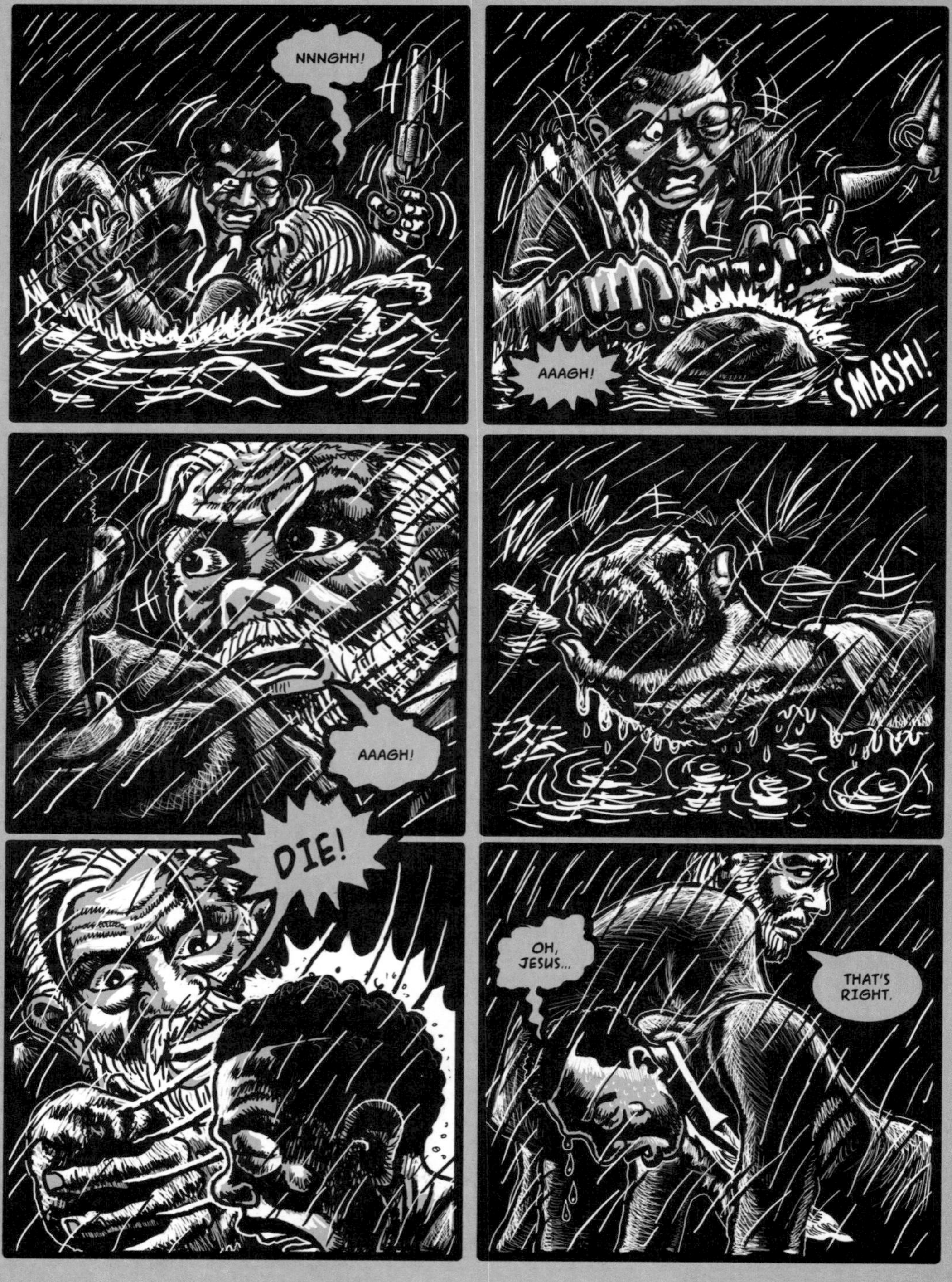
NNNGHH!
AAAGH!
SMASH!
AAAGH!
DIE!
OH, JESUS...
THAT'S RIGHT.

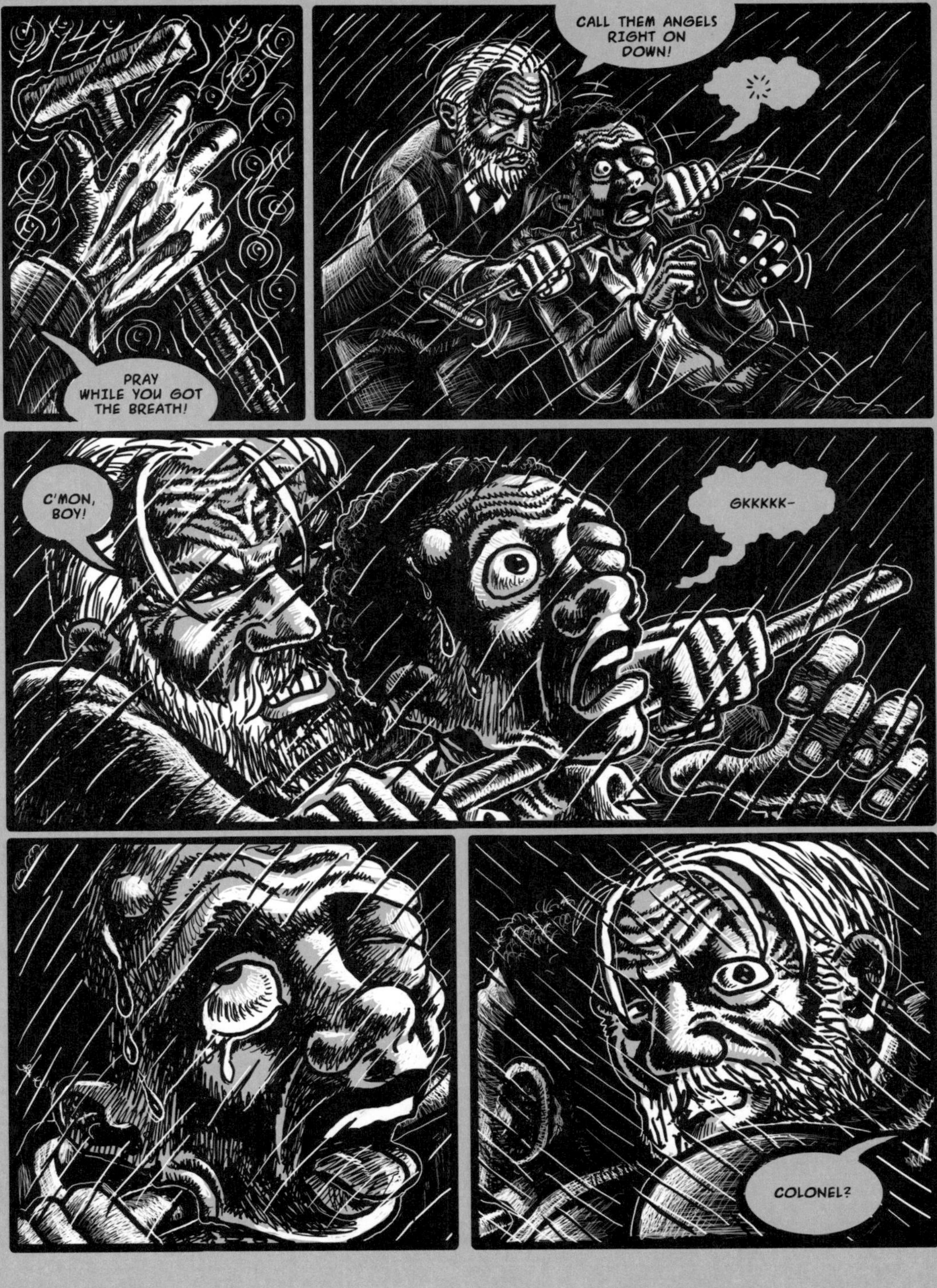
PRAY WHILE YOU GOT THE BREATH!
CALL THEM ANGELS RIGHT ON DOWN!
C'MON, BOY!
GKKKKK-
COLONEL?

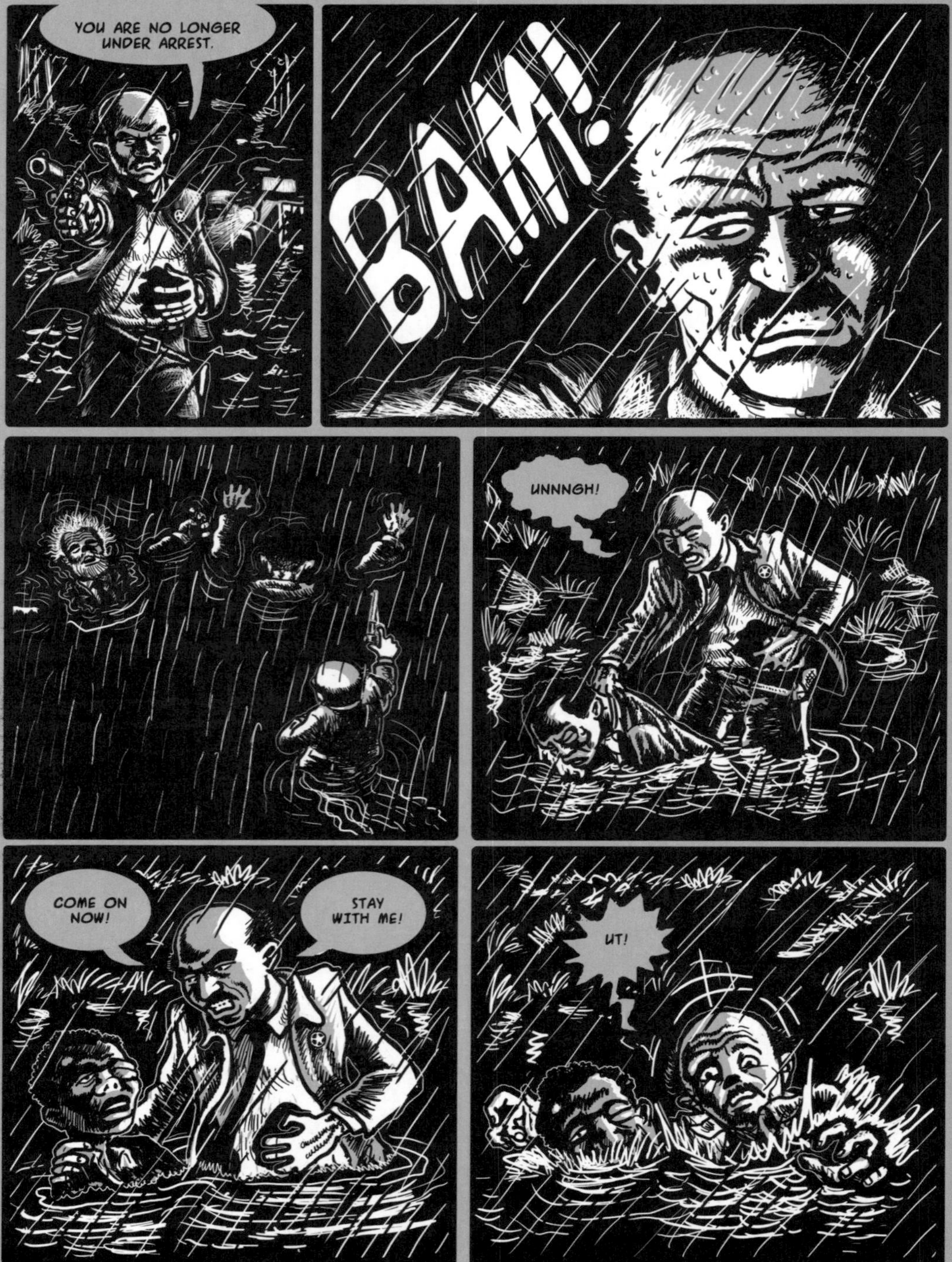
YOU ARE NO LONGER UNDER ARREST.
BAM!!
UNNNGH!
COME ON NOW!
STAY WITH ME!
UT!

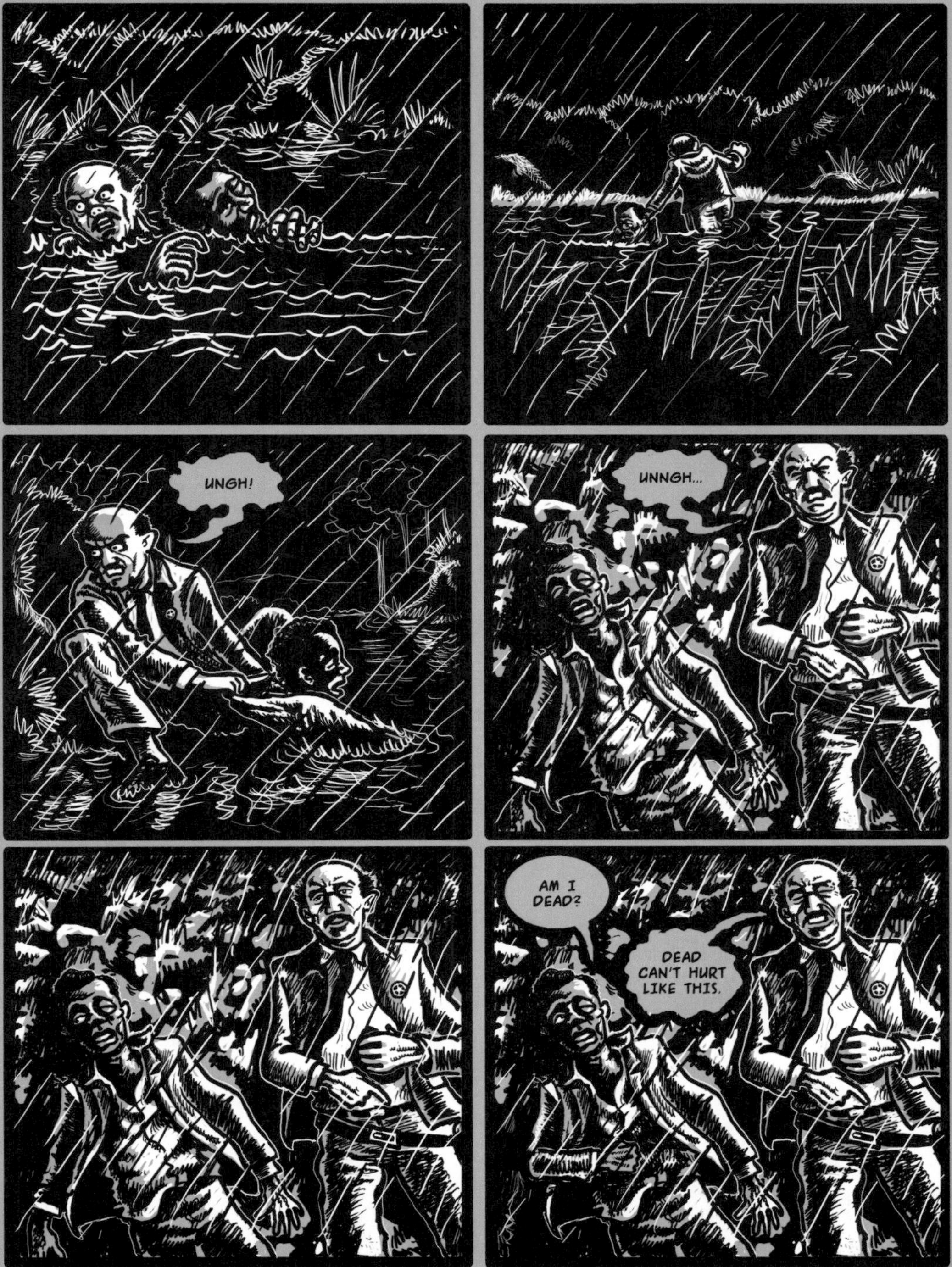
UNGH!
UNNGH...
AM I DEAD?
DEAD CAN'T HURT LIKE THIS.

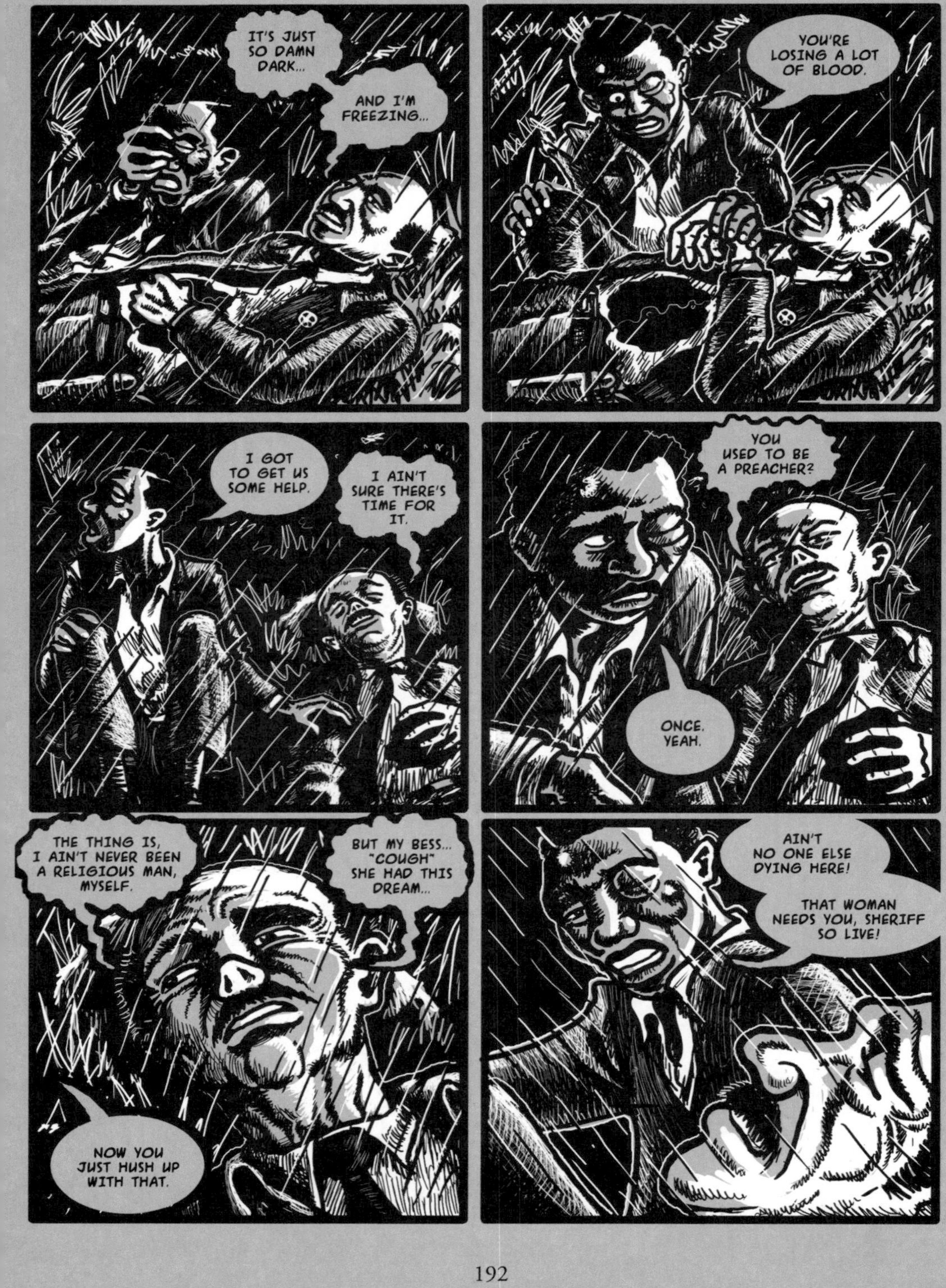
IT'S JUST SO DAMN DARK...
AND I'M FREEZING...
YOU'RE LOSING A LOT OF BLOOD.
I GOT TO GET US SOME HELP.
I AIN'T SURE THERE'S TIME FOR IT.
YOU USED TO BE A PREACHER?
ONCE. YEAH.
THE THING IS, I AIN'T NEVER BEEN A RELIGIOUS MAN, MYSELF.
BUT MY BESS... "COUGH" SHE HAD THIS DREAM...
NOW YOU JUST HUSH UP WITH THAT.
AIN'T NO ONE ELSE DYING HERE!
THAT WOMAN NEEDS YOU, SHERIFF SO LIVE!

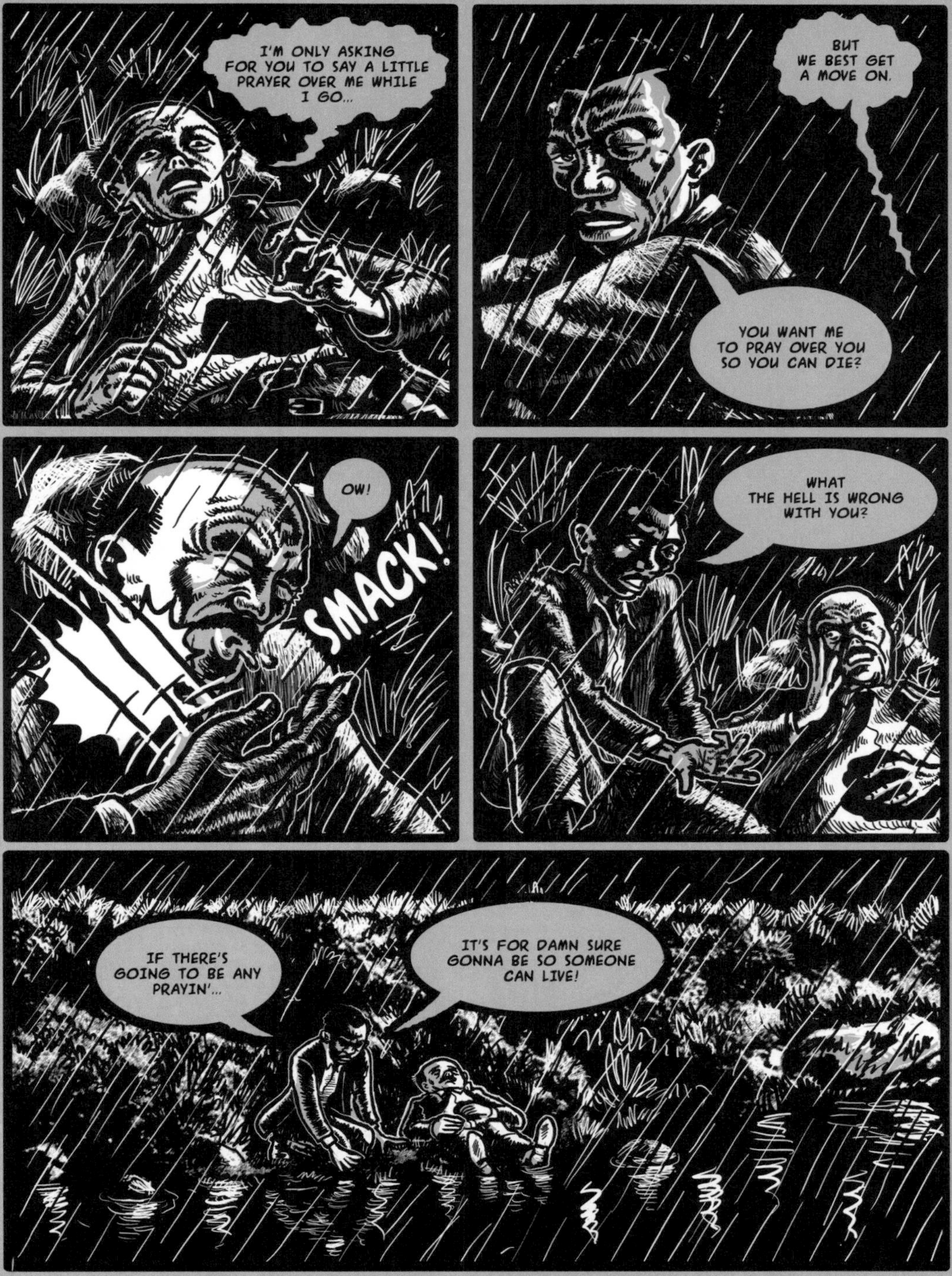
I'M ONLY ASKING FOR YOU TO SAY A LITTLE PRAYER OVER ME WHILE I GO...
BUT WE BEST GET A MOVE ON.
YOU WANT ME TO PRAY OVER YOU SO YOU CAN DIE?
OW!
SMACK!
WHAT THE HELL IS WRONG WITH YOU?
IF THERE'S GOING TO BE ANY PRAYIN'...
IT'S FOR DAMN SURE GONNA BE SO SOMEONE CAN LIVE!

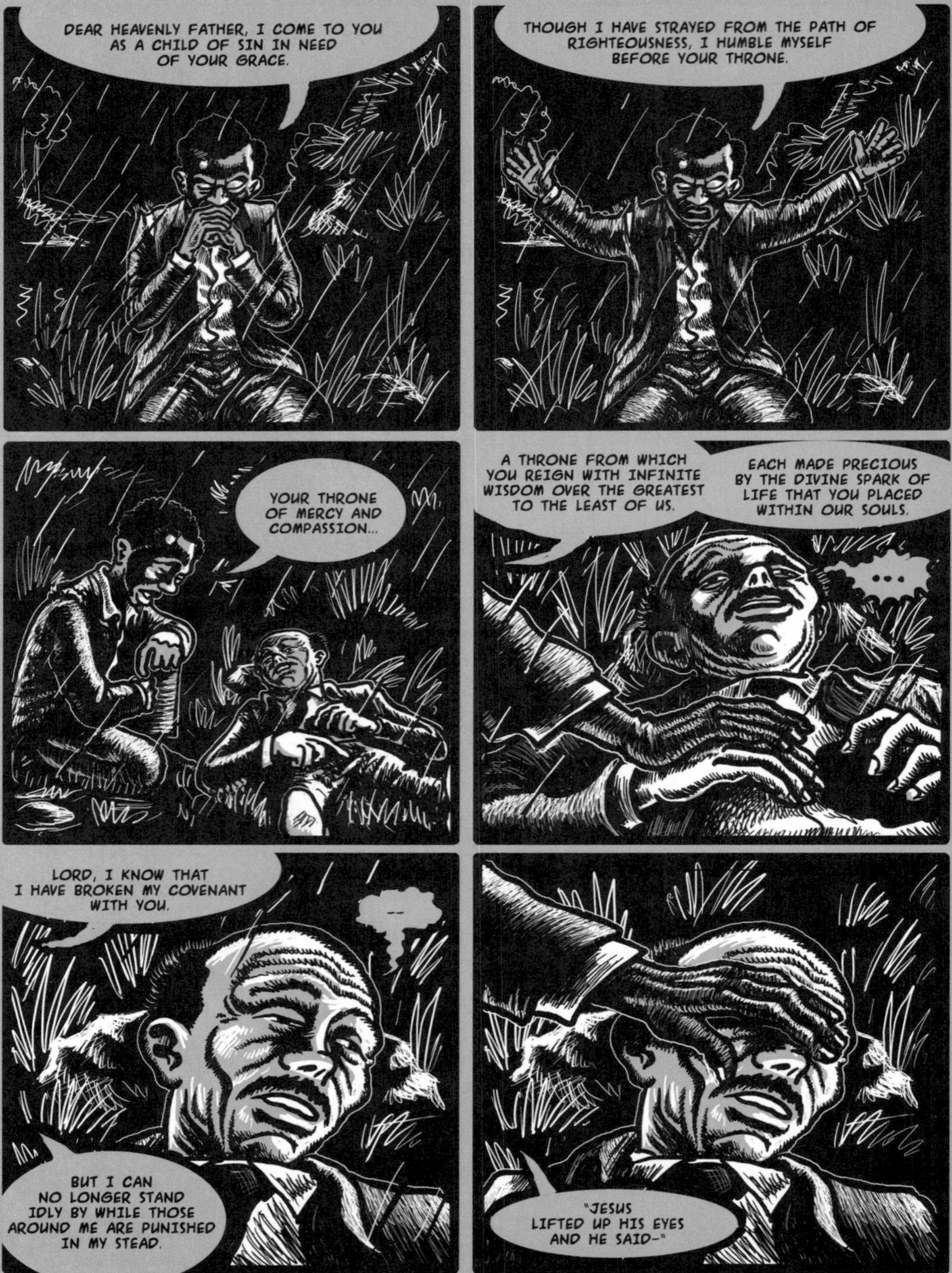
DEAR HEAVENLY FATHER, I COME TO YOU AS A CHILD OF SIN IN NEED OF YOUR GRACE.
THOUGH I HAVE STRAYED FROM THE PATH OF RIGHTEOUSNESS, I HUMBLE MYSELF BEFORE YOUR THRONE.
YOUR THRONE OF MERCY AND COMPASSION...
A THRONE FROM WHICH YOU REIGN WITH INFINITE WISDOM OVER THE GREATEST TO THE LEAST OF US.
EACH MADE PRECIOUS BY THE DIVINE SPARK OF LIFE THAT YOU PLACED WITHIN OUR SOULS.
...
LORD, I KNOW THAT I HAVE BROKEN MY COVENANT WITH YOU.
--
BUT I CAN NO LONGER STAND IDLY BY WHILE THOSE AROUND ME ARE PUNISHED IN MY STEAD.
"JESUS LIFTED UP HIS EYES AND HE SAID-"

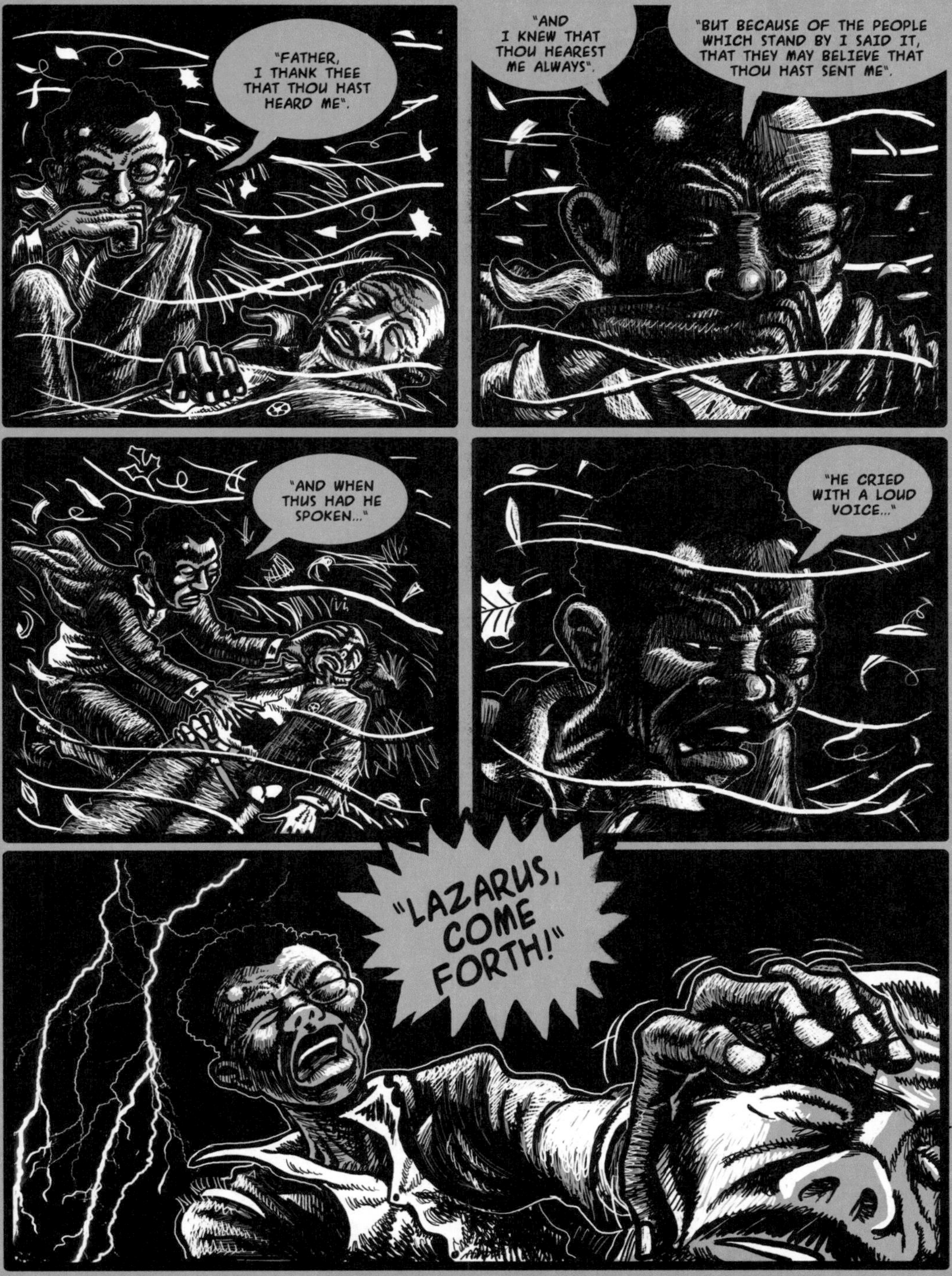
"FATHER, I THANK THEE THAT THOU HAST HEARD ME".
"AND I KNEW THAT THOU HEAREST ME ALWAYS".
"BUT BECAUSE OF THE PEOPLE WHICH STAND BY I SAID IT, THAT THEY MAY BELIEVE THAT THOU HAST SENT ME".
"AND WHEN THUS HAD HE SPOKEN..."
"HE CRIED WITH A LOUD VOICE..."
"LAZARUS, COME FORTH!"

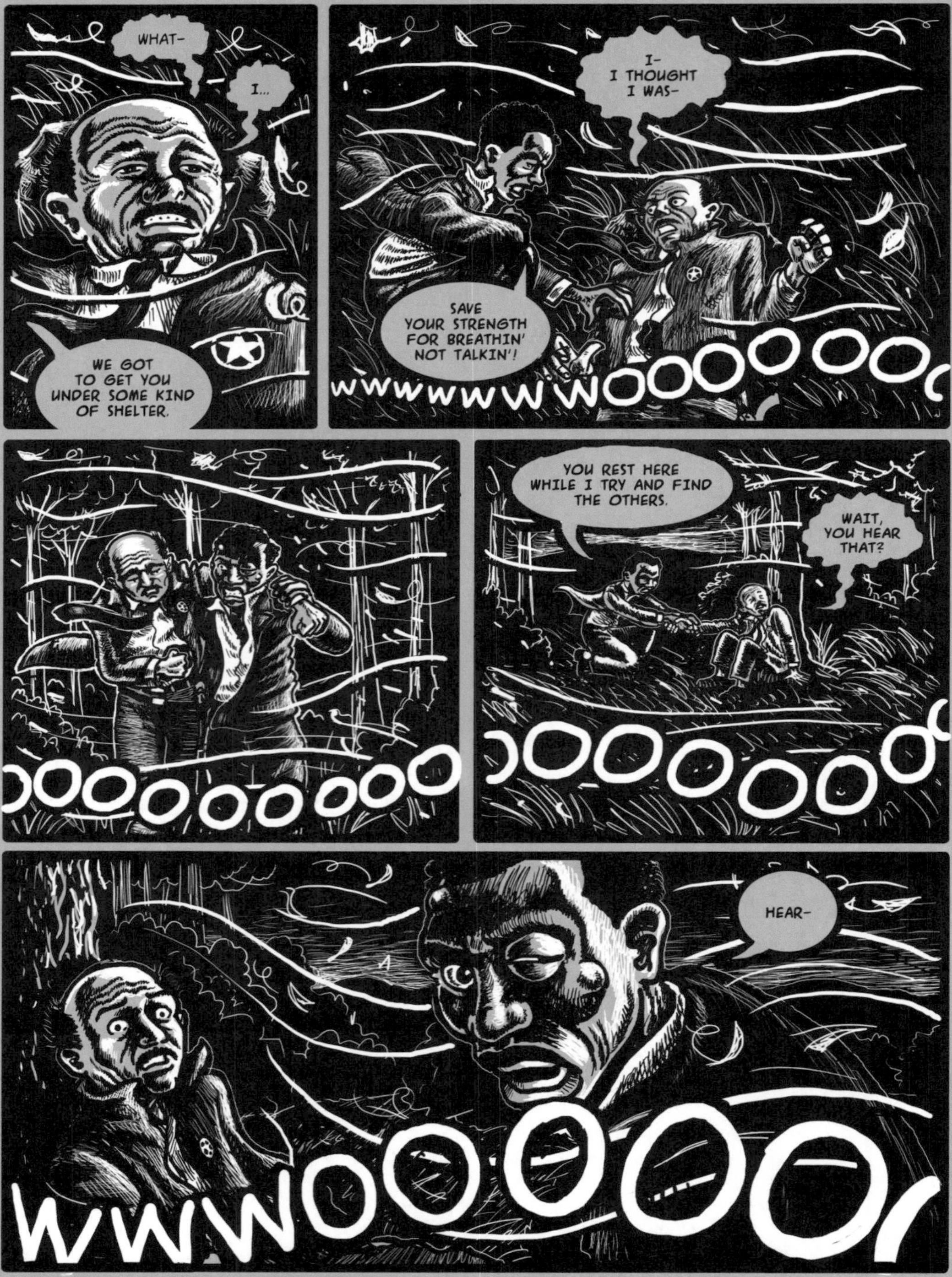
WHAT-
I...
WE GOT TO GET YOU UNDER SOME KIND OF SHELTER.
I- I THOUGHT I WAS-
SAVE YOUR STRENGTH FOR BREATHIN' NOT TALKIN'!
WWWWWWWWOOOOOOOOO
OOOOOOOOOOO
YOU REST HERE WHILE I TRY AND FIND THE OTHERS.
WAIT, YOU HEAR THAT?
OOOOOOOOOO
HEAR-
WWWOOOOO

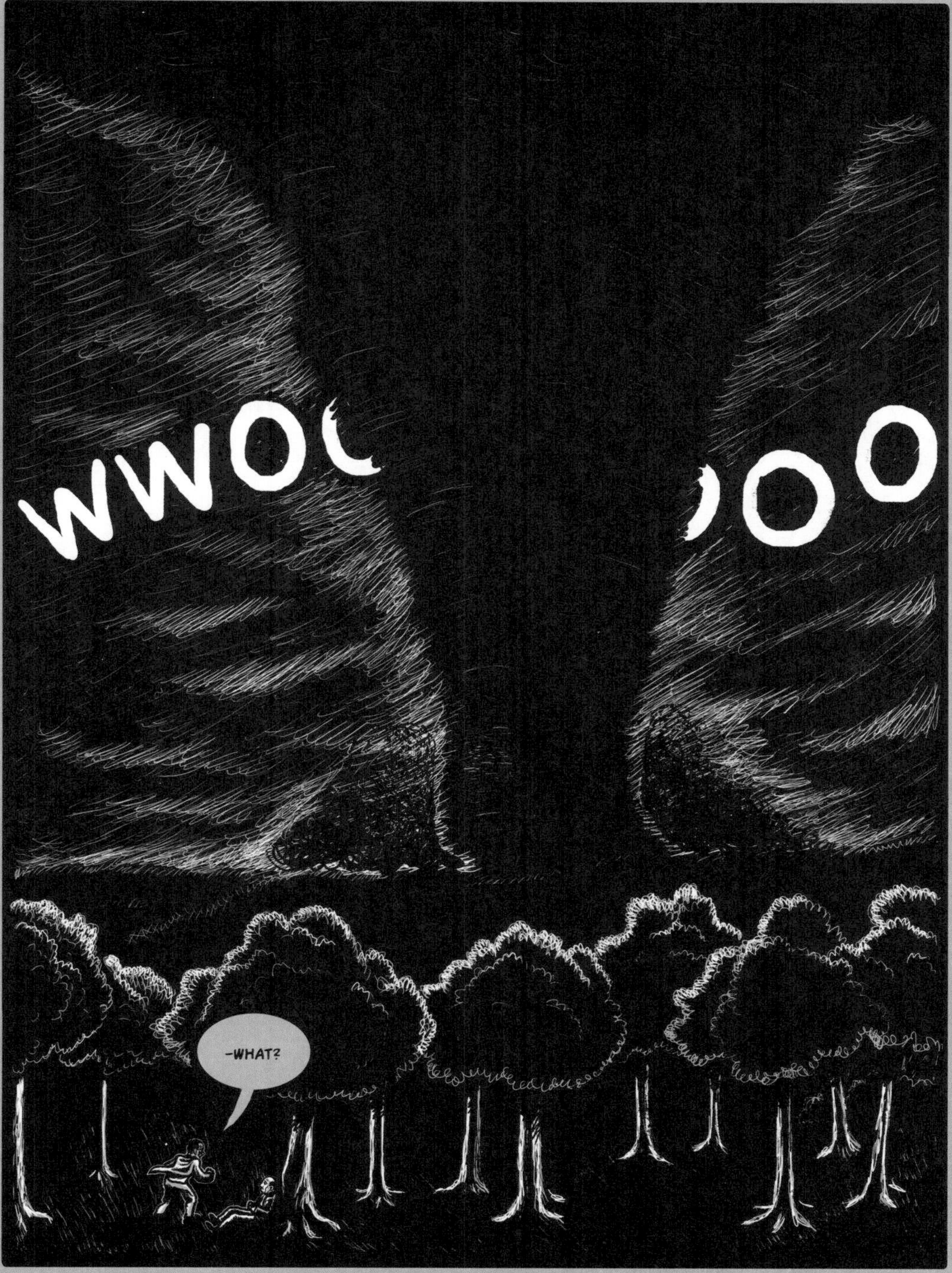
WWOO OOO
-WHAT?

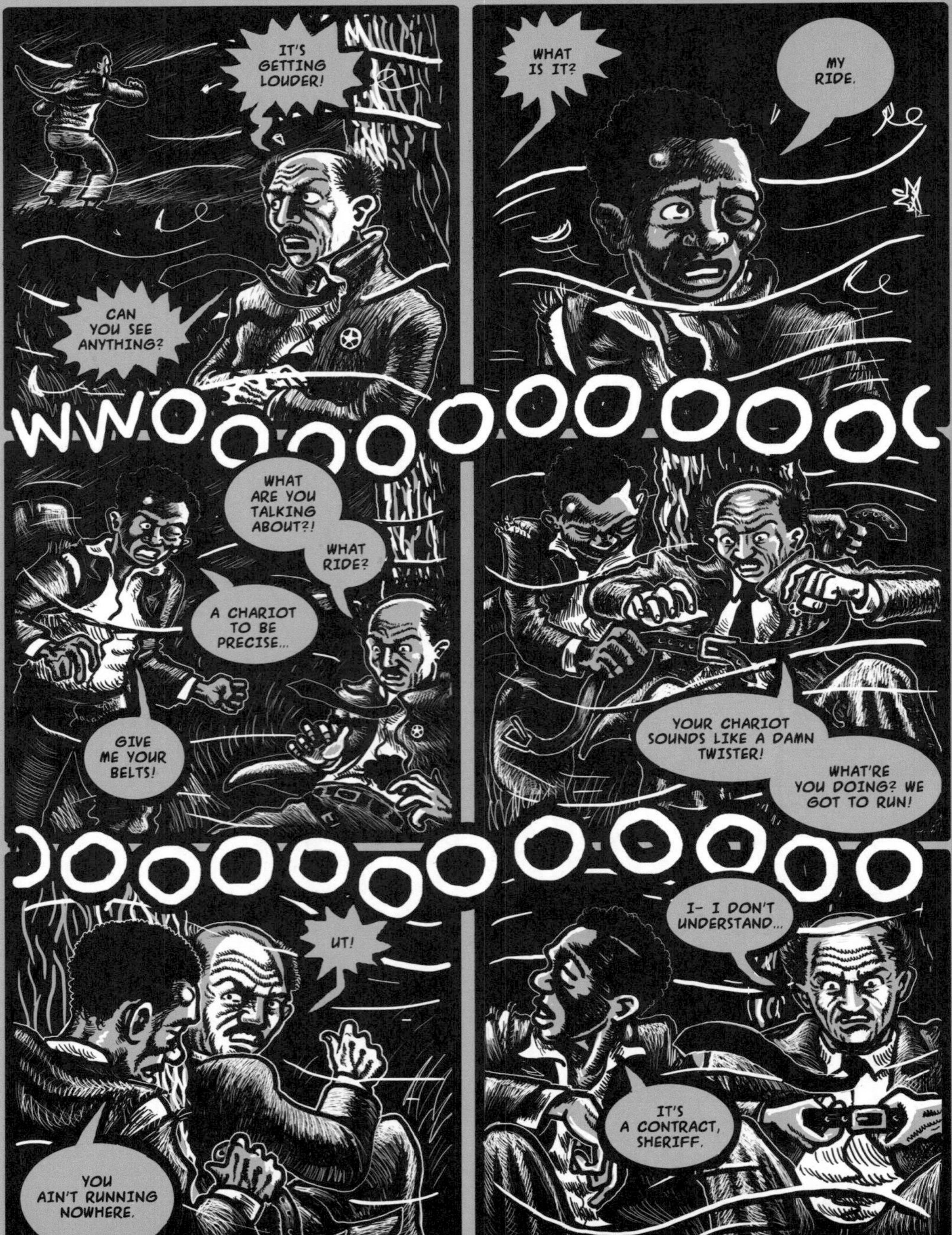
IT'S GETTING LOUDER!
CAN YOU SEE ANYTHING?
WHAT IS IT?
MY RIDE.
WWOOOOOOOOOOOO
WHAT ARE YOU TALKING ABOUT?!
WHAT RIDE?
A CHARIOT TO BE PRECISE...
GIVE ME YOUR BELTS!
YOUR CHARIOT SOUNDS LIKE A DAMN TWISTER!
WHAT'RE YOU DOING? WE GOT TO RUN!
OOOOOOOOOOOOOOOO
UT!
YOU AIN'T RUNNING NOWHERE.
I- I DON'T UNDERSTAND...
IT'S A CONTRACT, SHERIFF.

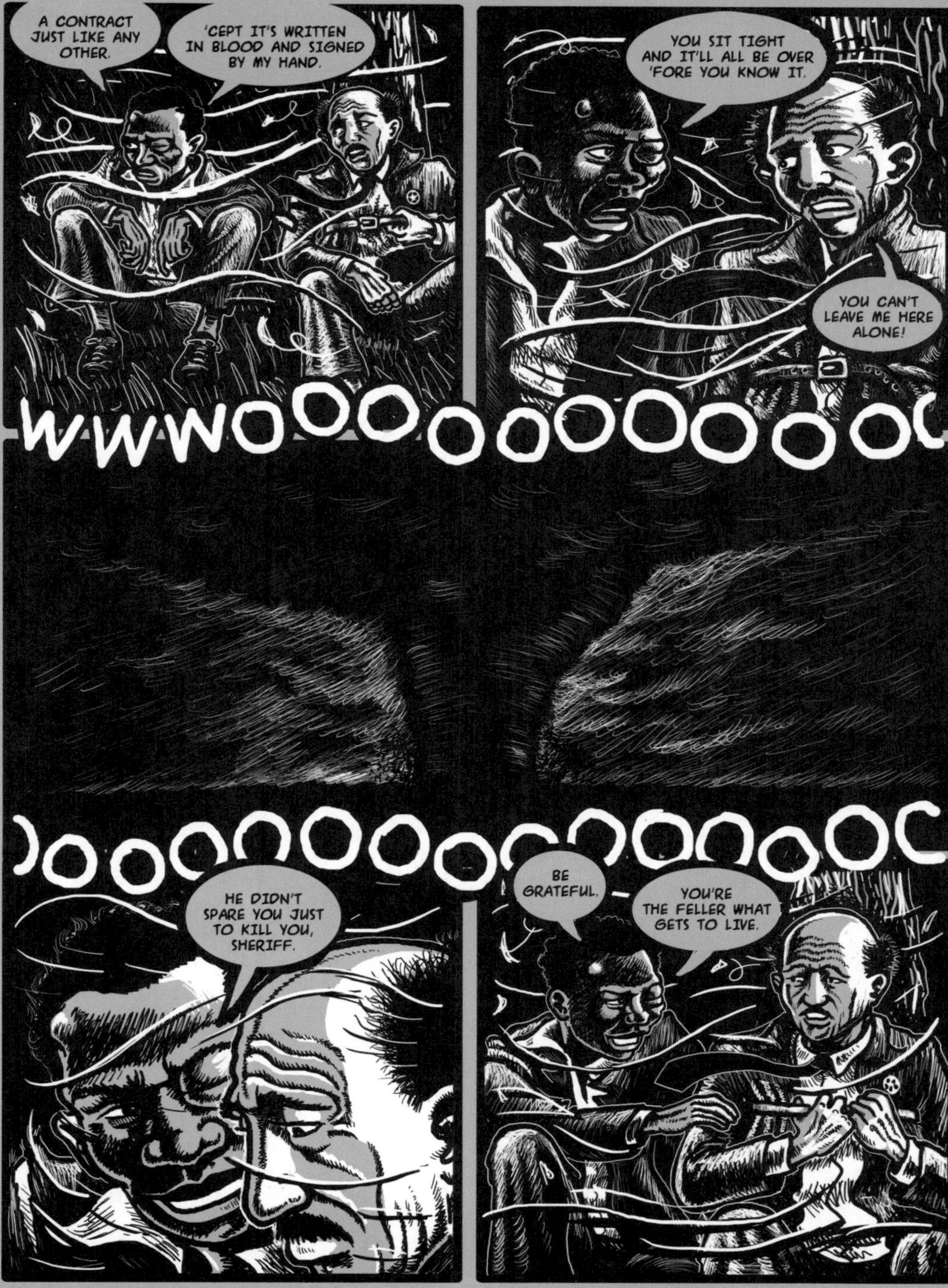
A CONTRACT JUST LIKE ANY OTHER.
'CEPT IT'S WRITTEN IN BLOOD AND SIGNED BY MY HAND.
YOU SIT TIGHT AND IT'LL ALL BE OVER 'FORE YOU KNOW IT.
YOU CAN'T LEAVE ME HERE ALONE!
WWWOOOOOOOOOOOOOOOOOOOOOOOOOOOO
HE DIDN'T SPARE YOU JUST TO KILL YOU, SHERIFF.
BE GRATEFUL.
YOU'RE THE FELLER WHAT GETS TO LIVE.

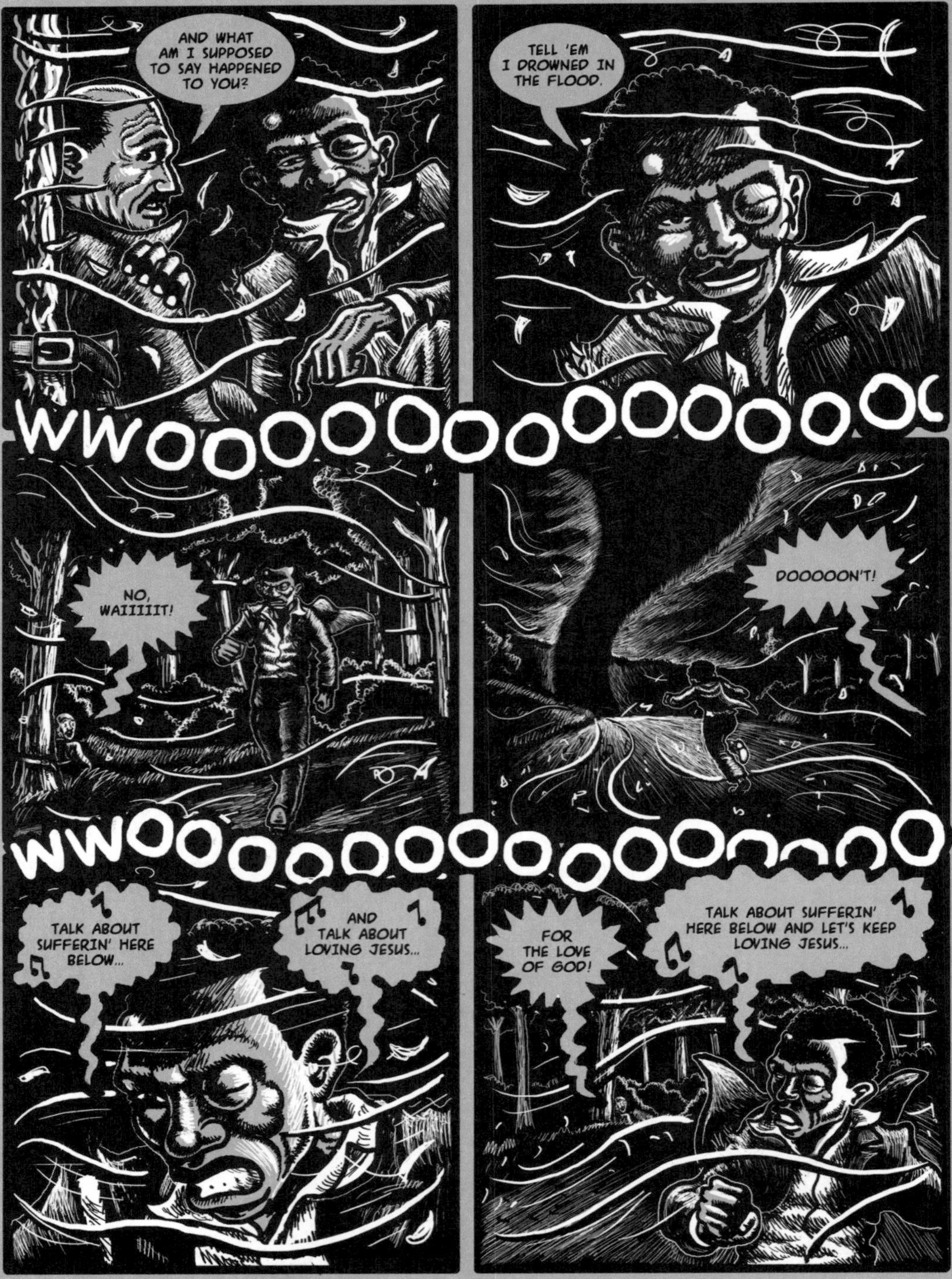
AND WHAT AM I SUPPOSED TO SAY HAPPENED TO YOU?
TELL 'EM I DROWNED IN THE FLOOD.
WWOOOOOOOOOOOOOOOOO
NO, WAIIIIIT!
DOOOOON'T!
WWOOOOOOOOOOOOOOOOOO
TALK ABOUT SUFFERIN' HERE BELOW...
AND TALK ABOUT LOVING JESUS...
FOR THE LOVE OF GOD!
TALK ABOUT SUFFERIN' HERE BELOW AND LET'S KEEP LOVING JESUS...

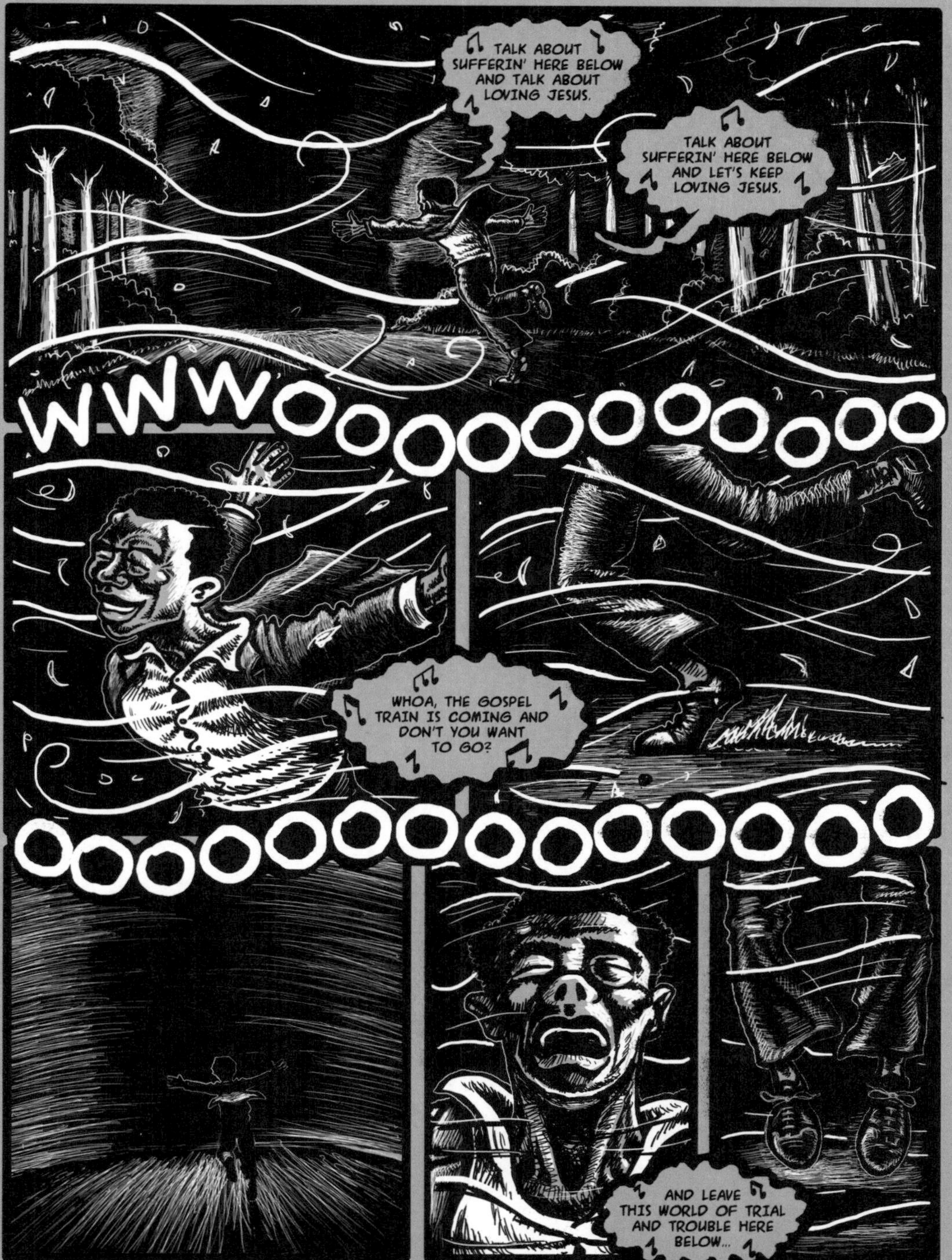
TALK ABOUT SUFFERIN' HERE BELOW AND TALK ABOUT LOVING JESUS.
TALK ABOUT SUFFERIN' HERE BELOW AND LET'S KEEP LOVING JESUS.
WWWOOOOOOOOOOOOOO
WHOA, THE GOSPEL TRAIN IS COMING AND DON'T YOU WANT TO GO?
OOOOOOOOOOOOOOOO
AND LEAVE THIS WORLD OF TRIAL AND TROUBLE HERE BELOW...

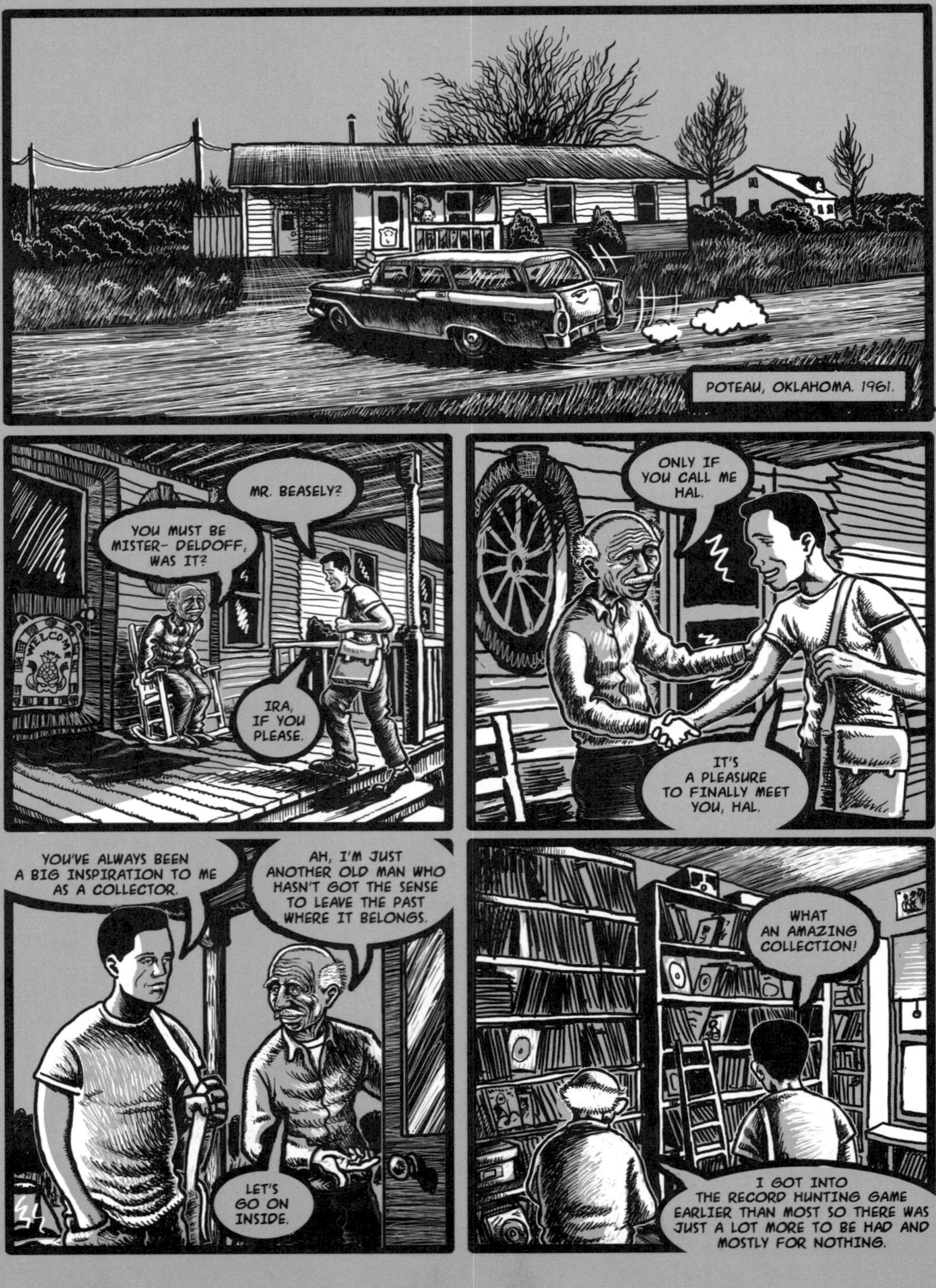

POTEAU, OKLAHOMA. 1961.
MR. BEASELY?
YOU MUST BE MISTER- DELDOFF, WAS IT?
IRA, IF YOU PLEASE.
ONLY IF YOU CALL ME HAL.
IT'S A PLEASURE TO FINALLY MEET YOU, HAL.
YOU'VE ALWAYS BEEN A BIG INSPIRATION TO ME AS A COLLECTOR.
AH, I'M JUST ANOTHER OLD MAN WHO HASN'T GOT THE SENSE TO LEAVE THE PAST WHERE IT BELONGS.
LET'S GO ON INSIDE.
WHAT AN AMAZING COLLECTION!
I GOT INTO THE RECORD HUNTING GAME EARLIER THAN MOST SO THERE WAS JUST A LOT MORE TO BE HAD AND MOSTLY FOR NOTHING.

THERE'S A COLD ONE FOR YOU.

MUCH OBLIGED.

I GOT TO ADMIT THAT YOU'VE KEPT ME WONDERIN' JUST WHAT THIS VISIT IS ALL ABOUT.

NOT THAT I MIND THE COMPANY.

WELL, THIS WASN'T SOMETHING I FIGURE YOU'D WANT TO DISCUSS OVER THE PHONE, REALLY.

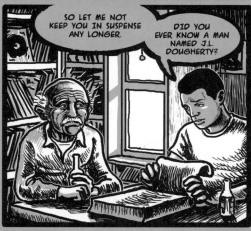

SO LET ME NOT KEEP YOU IN SUSPENSE ANY LONGER.

DID YOU EVER KNOW A MAN NAMED J.L. DOUGHERTY?

I RECKON I REMEMBER A MAN BY THAT NAME.

WHY?

WELL...

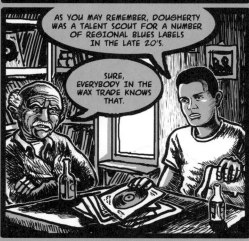

AS YOU MAY REMEMBER, DOUGHERTY WAS A TALENT SCOUT FOR A NUMBER OF REGIONAL BLUES LABELS IN THE LATE 20'S.

SURE, EVERYBODY IN THE WAX TRADE KNOWS THAT.

OK, BUT WHAT NOBODY KNOWS WAS THAT HE ALSO MAINTAINED AN ARCHIVE OF EVERY RECORDING BY EVERY ARTIST THAT HE HAD SCOUTED.

LIKE IT WAS PART OF HIS DEAL WITH THE COMPANIES HE WORKED FOR.

HOW DO YOU KNOW THAT?

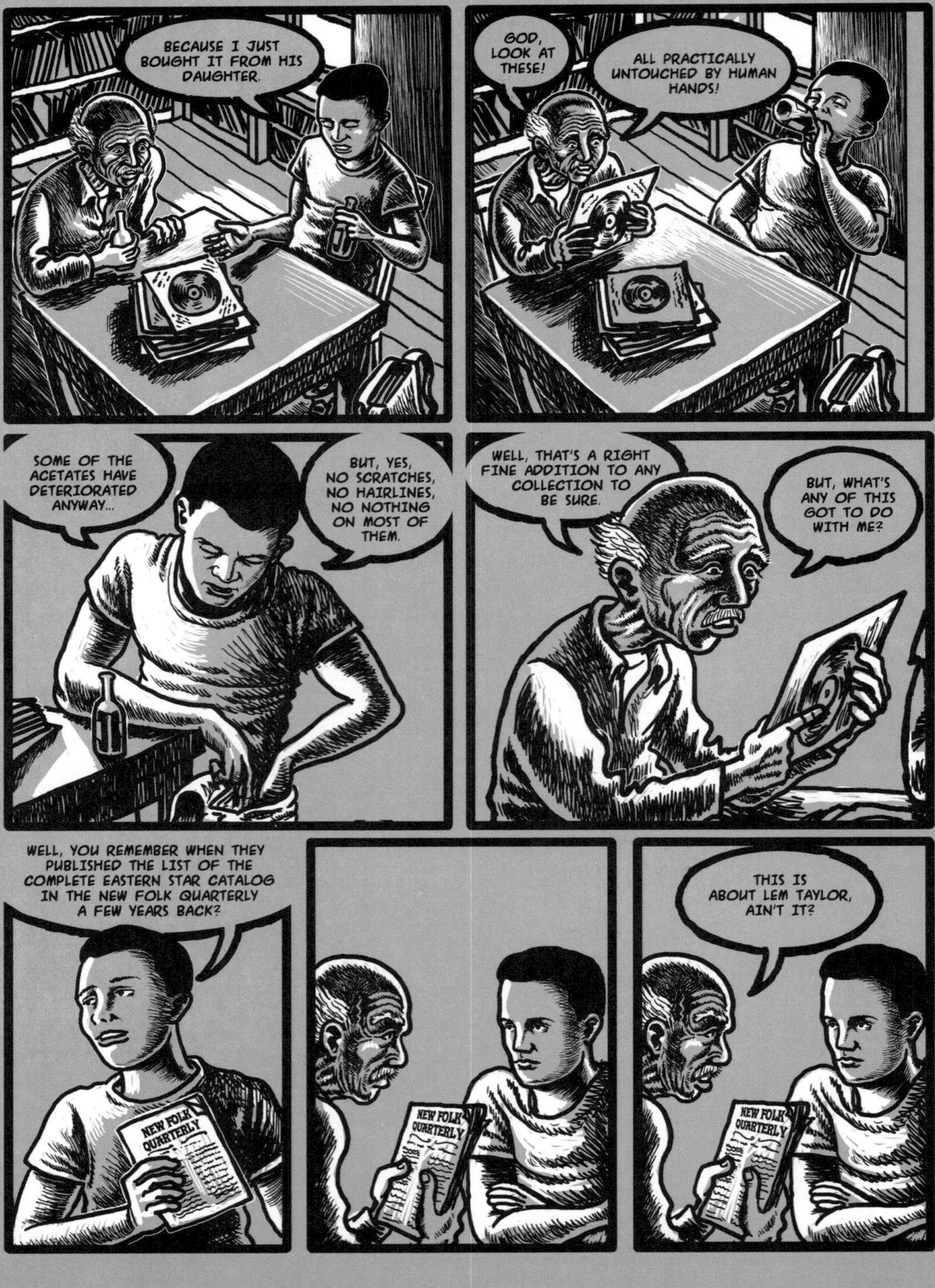
BECAUSE I JUST BOUGHT IT FROM HIS DAUGHTER.
GOD, LOOK AT THESE!
ALL PRACTICALLY UNTOUCHED BY HUMAN HANDS!
SOME OF THE ACETATES HAVE DETERIORATED ANYWAY...
BUT, YES, NO SCRATCHES, NO HAIRLINES, NO NOTHING ON MOST OF THEM.
WELL, THAT'S A RIGHT FINE ADDITION TO ANY COLLECTION TO BE SURE.
BUT, WHAT'S ANY OF THIS GOT TO DO WITH ME?
WELL, YOU REMEMBER WHEN THEY PUBLISHED THE LIST OF THE COMPLETE EASTERN STAR CATALOG IN THE NEW FOLK QUARTERLY A FEW YEARS BACK?
NEW FOLK QUARTERLY
NEW FOLK QUARTERLY
NEW FOLK QUARTERLY
THIS IS ABOUT LEM TAYLOR, AIN'T IT?

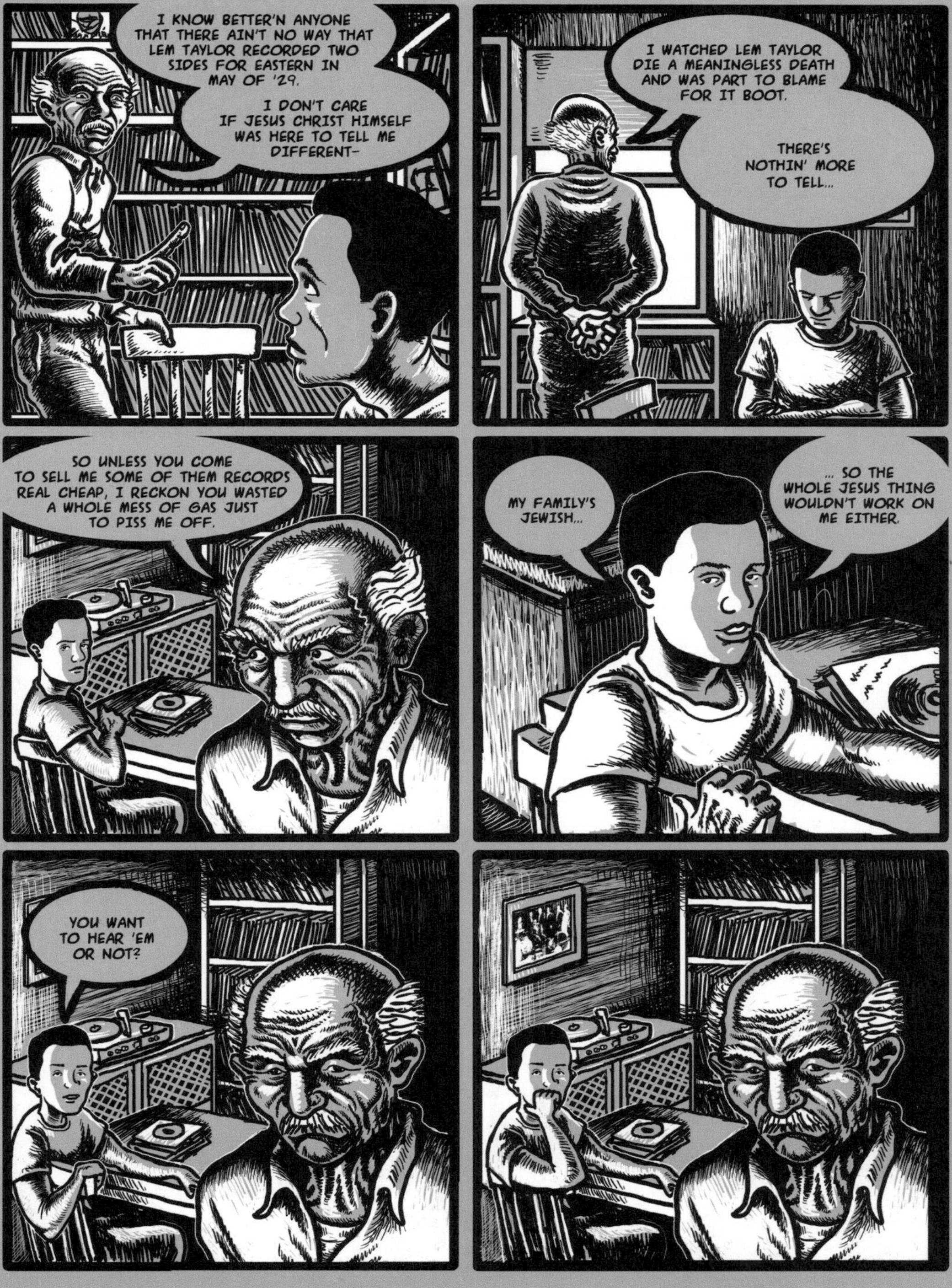
I KNOW BETTER'N ANYONE THAT THERE AIN'T NO WAY THAT LEM TAYLOR RECORDED TWO SIDES FOR EASTERN IN MAY OF '29.
I DON'T CARE IF JESUS CHRIST HIMSELF WAS HERE TO TELL ME DIFFERENT–
I WATCHED LEM TAYLOR DIE A MEANINGLESS DEATH AND WAS PART TO BLAME FOR IT BOOT.
THERE'S NOTHIN' MORE TO TELL...
SO UNLESS YOU COME TO SELL ME SOME OF THEM RECORDS REAL CHEAP, I RECKON YOU WASTED A WHOLE MESS OF GAS JUST TO PISS ME OFF.
MY FAMILY'S JEWISH...
... SO THE WHOLE JESUS THING WOULDN'T WORK ON ME EITHER.
YOU WANT TO HEAR 'EM OR NOT?

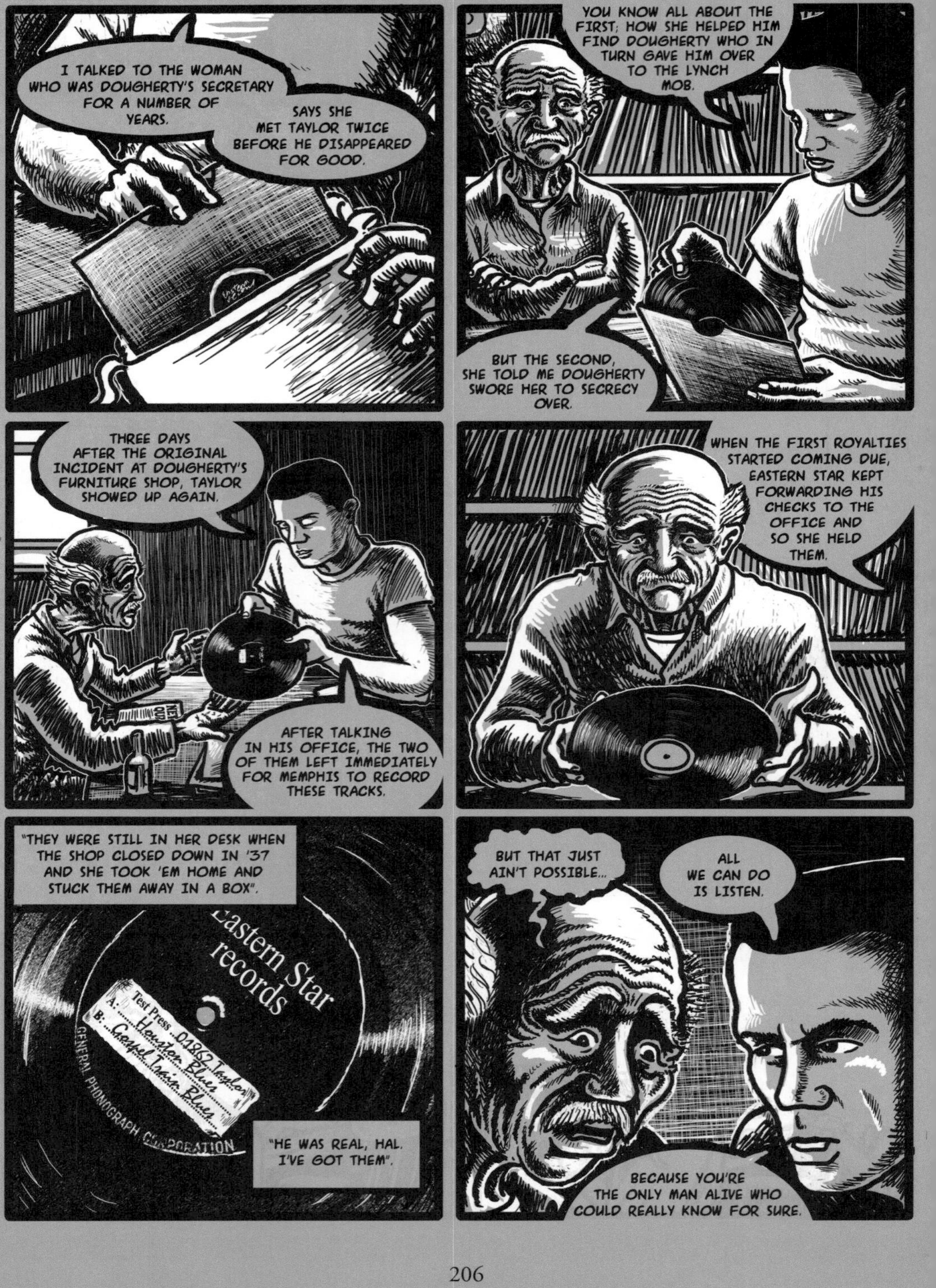
I TALKED TO THE WOMAN WHO WAS DOUGHERTY'S SECRETARY FOR A NUMBER OF YEARS.
SAYS SHE MET TAYLOR TWICE BEFORE HE DISAPPEARED FOR GOOD.
YOU KNOW ALL ABOUT THE FIRST; HOW SHE HELPED HIM FIND DOUGHERTY WHO IN TURN GAVE HIM OVER TO THE LYNCH MOB.
BUT THE SECOND, SHE TOLD ME DOUGHERTY SWORE HER TO SECRECY OVER.
THREE DAYS AFTER THE ORIGINAL INCIDENT AT DOUGHERTY'S FURNITURE SHOP, TAYLOR SHOWED UP AGAIN.
AFTER TALKING IN HIS OFFICE, THE TWO OF THEM LEFT IMMEDIATELY FOR MEMPHIS TO RECORD THESE TRACKS.
WHEN THE FIRST ROYALTIES STARTED COMING DUE, EASTERN STAR KEPT FORWARDING HIS CHECKS TO THE OFFICE AND SO SHE HELD THEM.
"THEY WERE STILL IN HER DESK WHEN THE SHOP CLOSED DOWN IN '37 AND SHE TOOK 'EM HOME AND STUCK THEM AWAY IN A BOX".
Eastern Star records
Test Press ...01862 Taylor
A: ...Houston Blues
B: ...Gospel Train Blues
GENERAL PHONOGRAPH CORPORATION
"HE WAS REAL, HAL. I'VE GOT THEM".
BUT THAT JUST AIN'T POSSIBLE...
ALL WE CAN DO IS LISTEN.
BECAUSE YOU'RE THE ONLY MAN ALIVE WHO COULD REALLY KNOW FOR SURE.

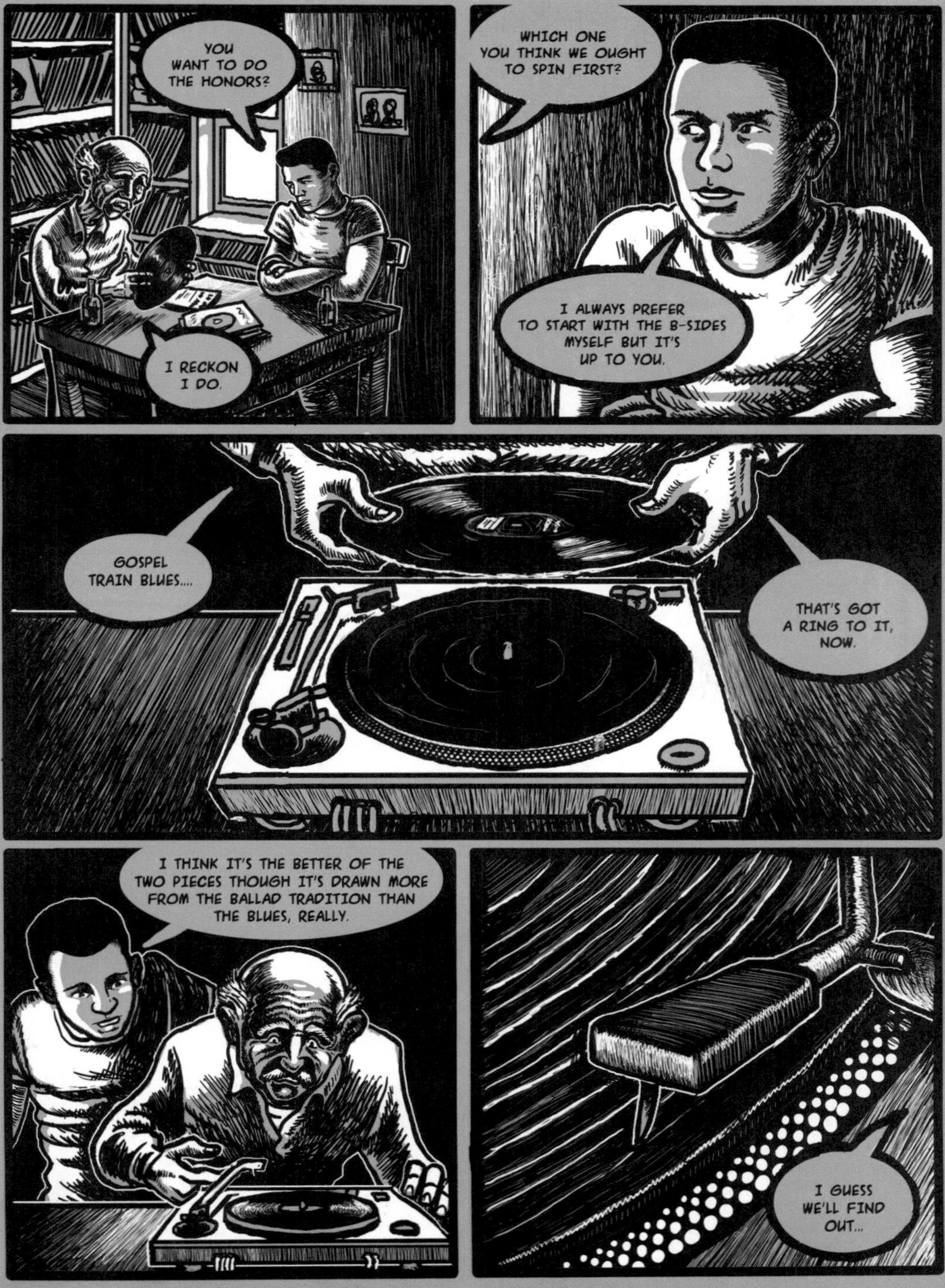
YOU WANT TO DO THE HONORS?
I RECKON I DO.
WHICH ONE YOU THINK WE OUGHT TO SPIN FIRST?
I ALWAYS PREFER TO START WITH THE B-SIDES MYSELF BUT IT'S UP TO YOU.
GOSPEL TRAIN BLUES....
THAT'S GOT A RING TO IT, NOW.
I THINK IT'S THE BETTER OF THE TWO PIECES THOUGH IT'S DRAWN MORE FROM THE BALLAD TRADITION THAN THE BLUES, REALLY.
I GUESS WE'LL FIND OUT...

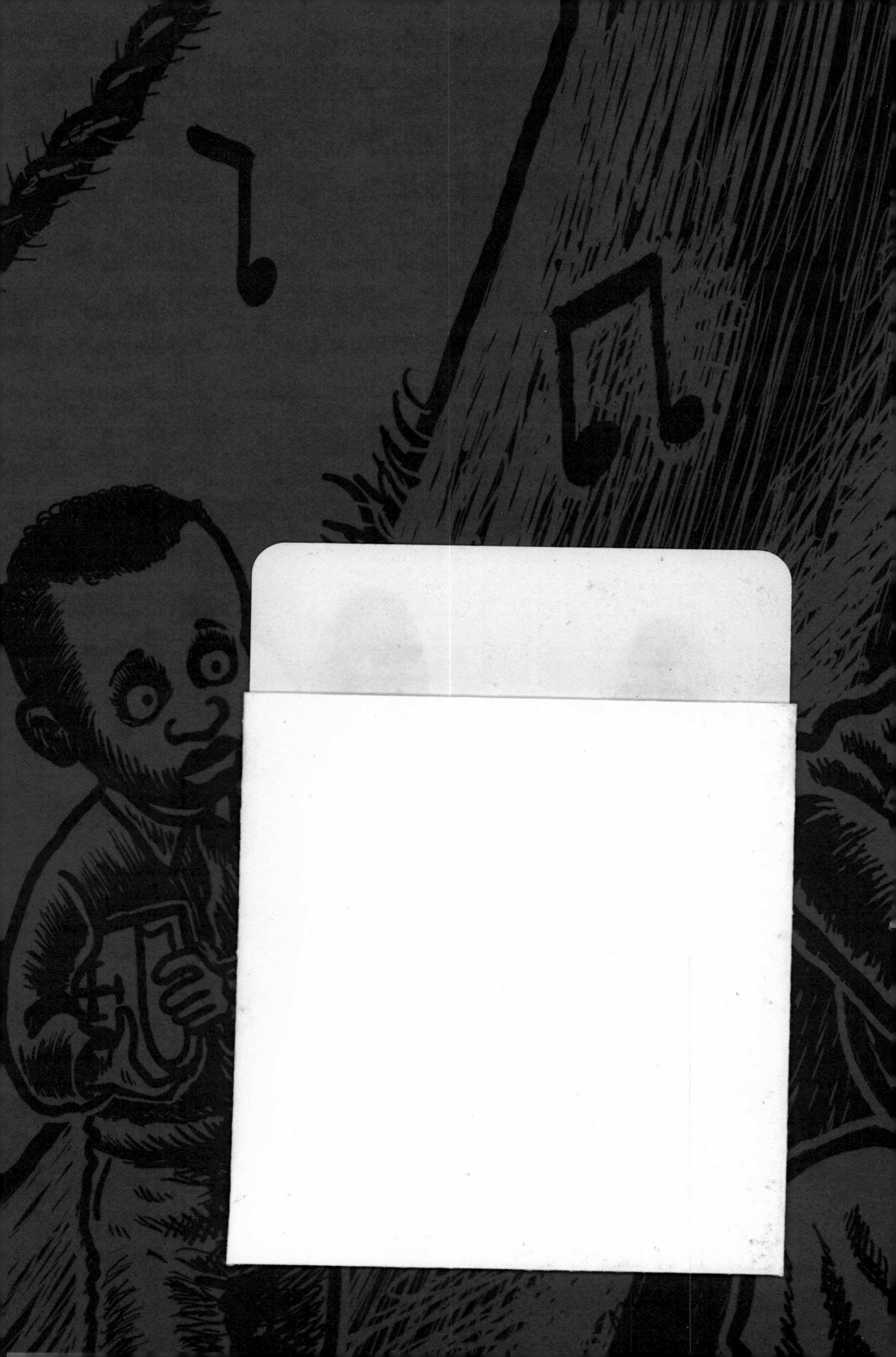